This book
belongs to:

....

Bumble & Snug and the Angry Pirates

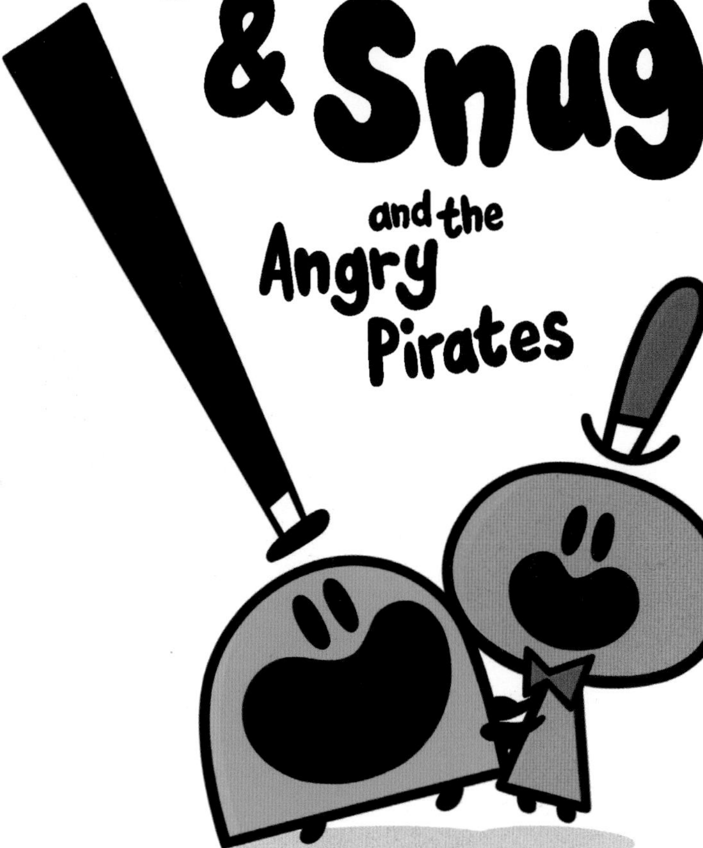

Mark Bradley

Silver Dolphin

Silver Dolphin Books

An imprint of Printers Row Publishing Group
A division of Readerlink Distribution Services, LLC
9717 Pacific Heights Blvd, San Diego, CA 92121
www.silverdolphinbooks.com

Printers Row Publishing Group is a division of Readerlink Distribution Services, LLC.
Silver Dolphin Books is a registered trademark of Readerlink Distribution Services, LLC.

All notations of errors or omissions should be addressed to Silver Dolphin Books,
Editorial Department, at the above address. All other correspondence (author inquiries,
permissions) concerning the content of this book should be addressed to:
Hodder Children's Books
An Imprint of Hachette Children's Group
Part of Hodder & Stoughton
Carmelite House
50 Victoria Embankment
London, EC4Y 0DZ

Paperback ISBN: 978-1-6672-0025-5
Hardcover ISBN: 978-1-6672-0024-8
Manufactured, printed, and assembled in Dongguan, China.
First printing, January 2022. TP/01/22
26 25 24 23 22 1 2 3 4 5

For the most fantastic and fantabulous Sarah, Oliver, and Totoro!

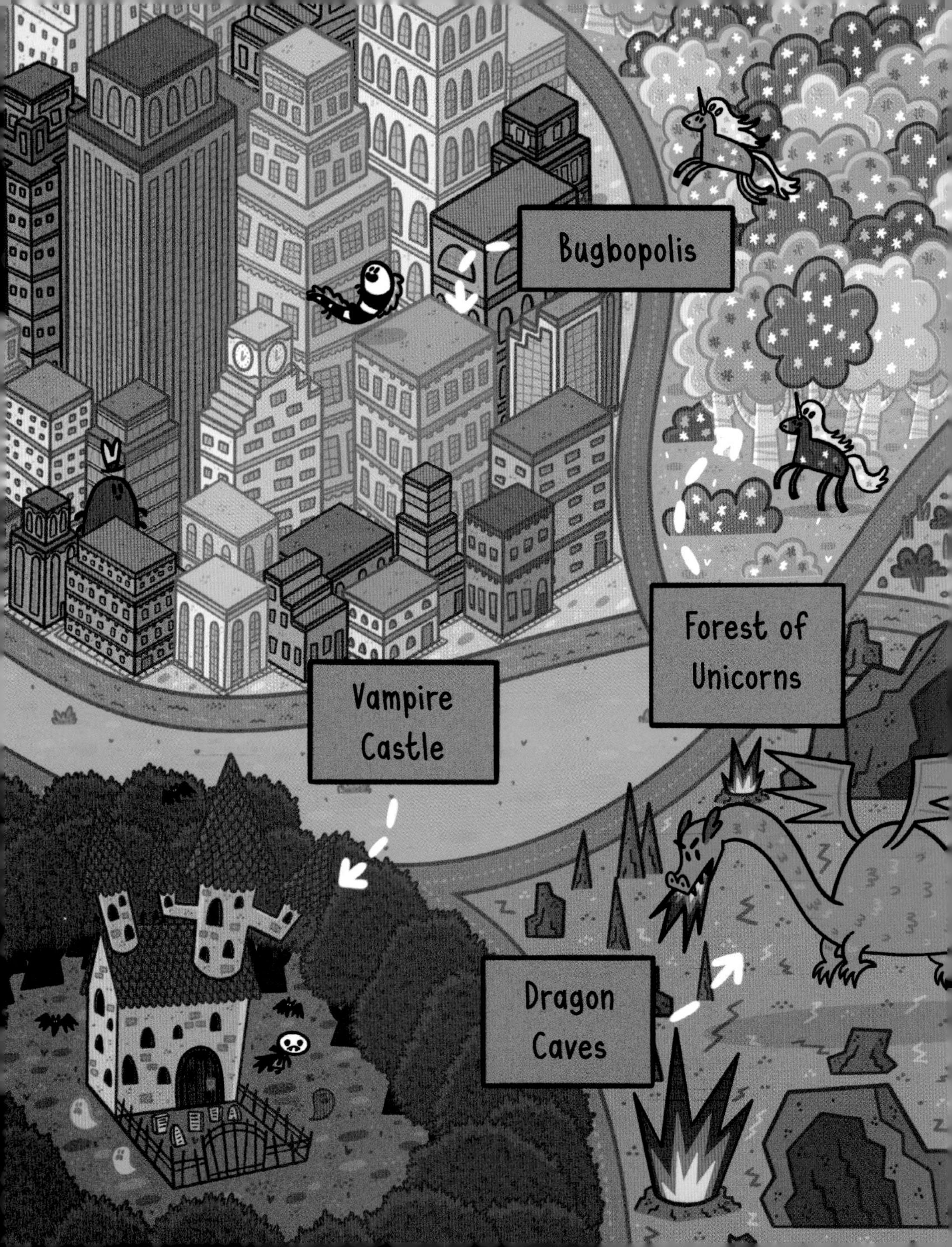
Bugbopolis
Forest of Unicorns
Vampire Castle
Dragon Caves

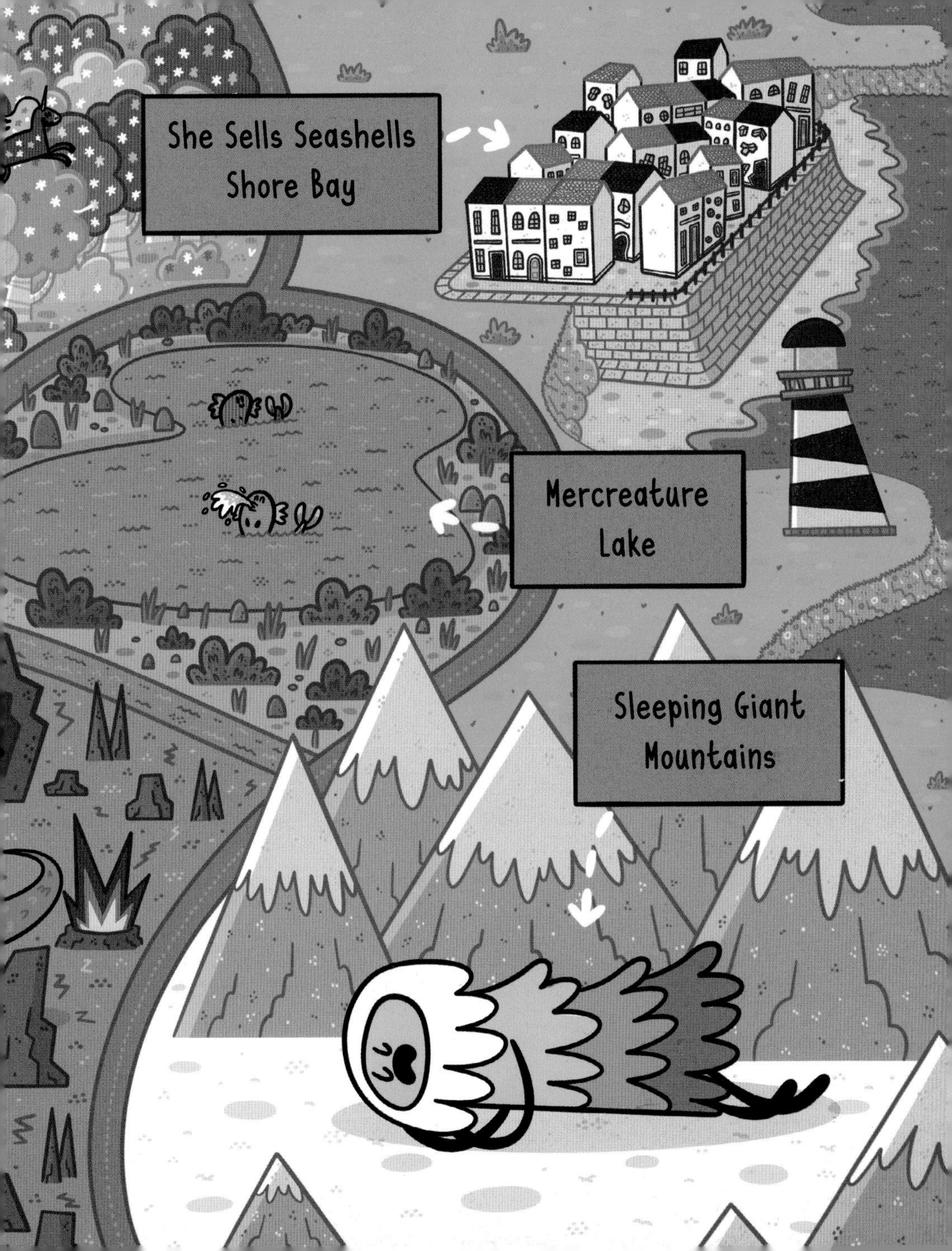
She Sells Seashells Shore Bay
Mercreature Lake
Sleeping Giant Mountains

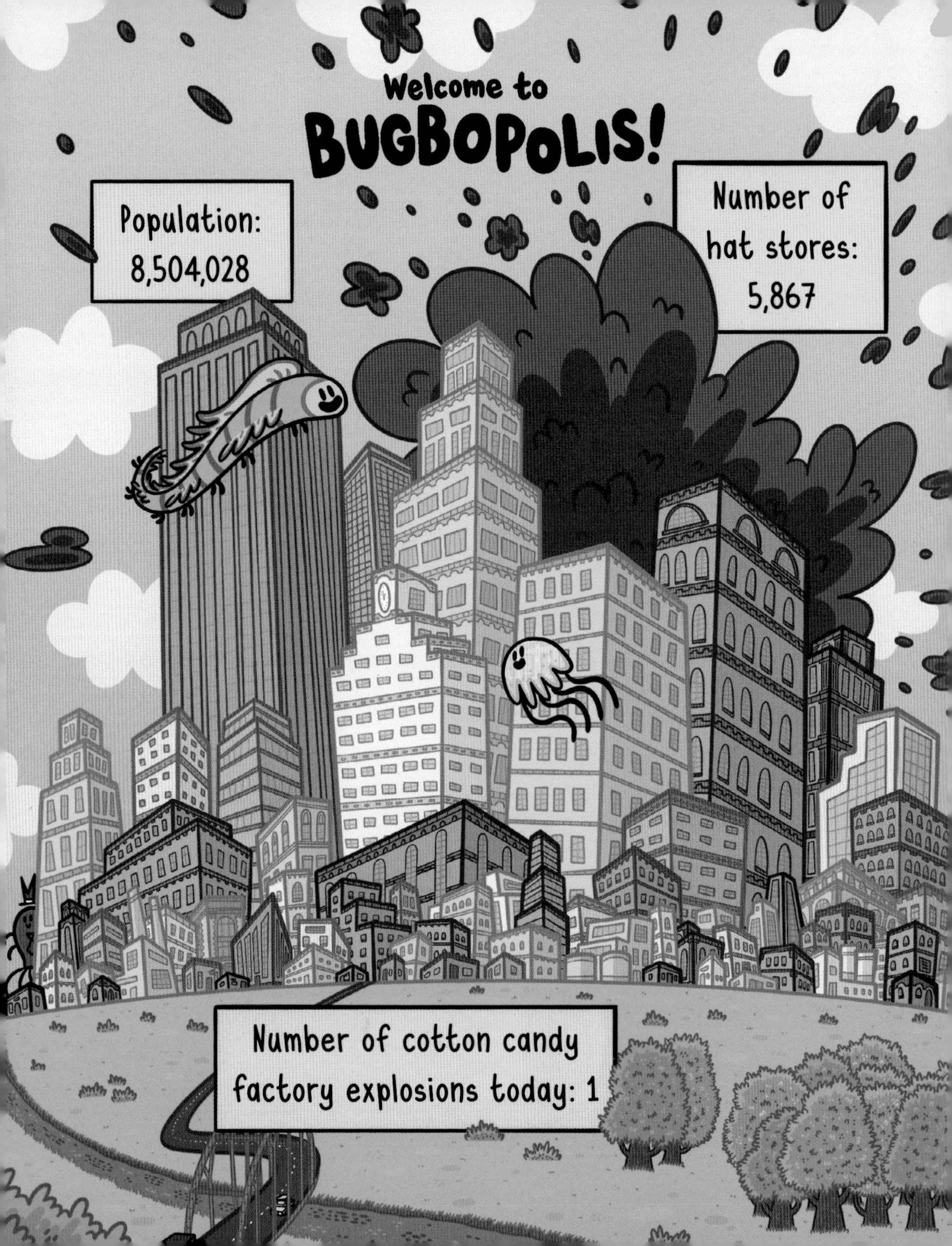
Welcome to
BUGBOPOLIS!
Population: 8,504,028
Number of hat stores: 5,867
Number of cotton candy factory explosions today: 1

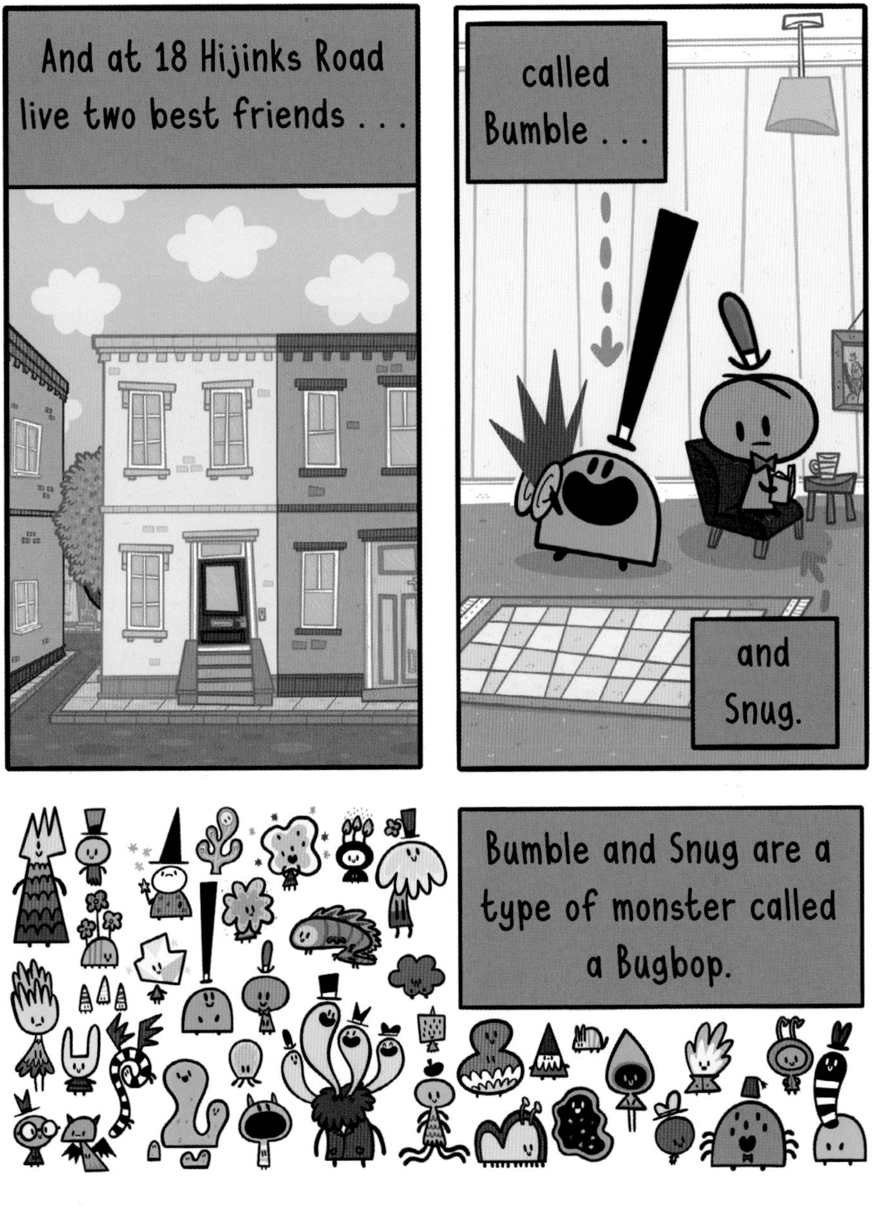
And at 18 Hijinks Road live two best friends . . .
called Bumble . . .
and Snug.
Bumble and Snug are a type of monster called a Bugbop.

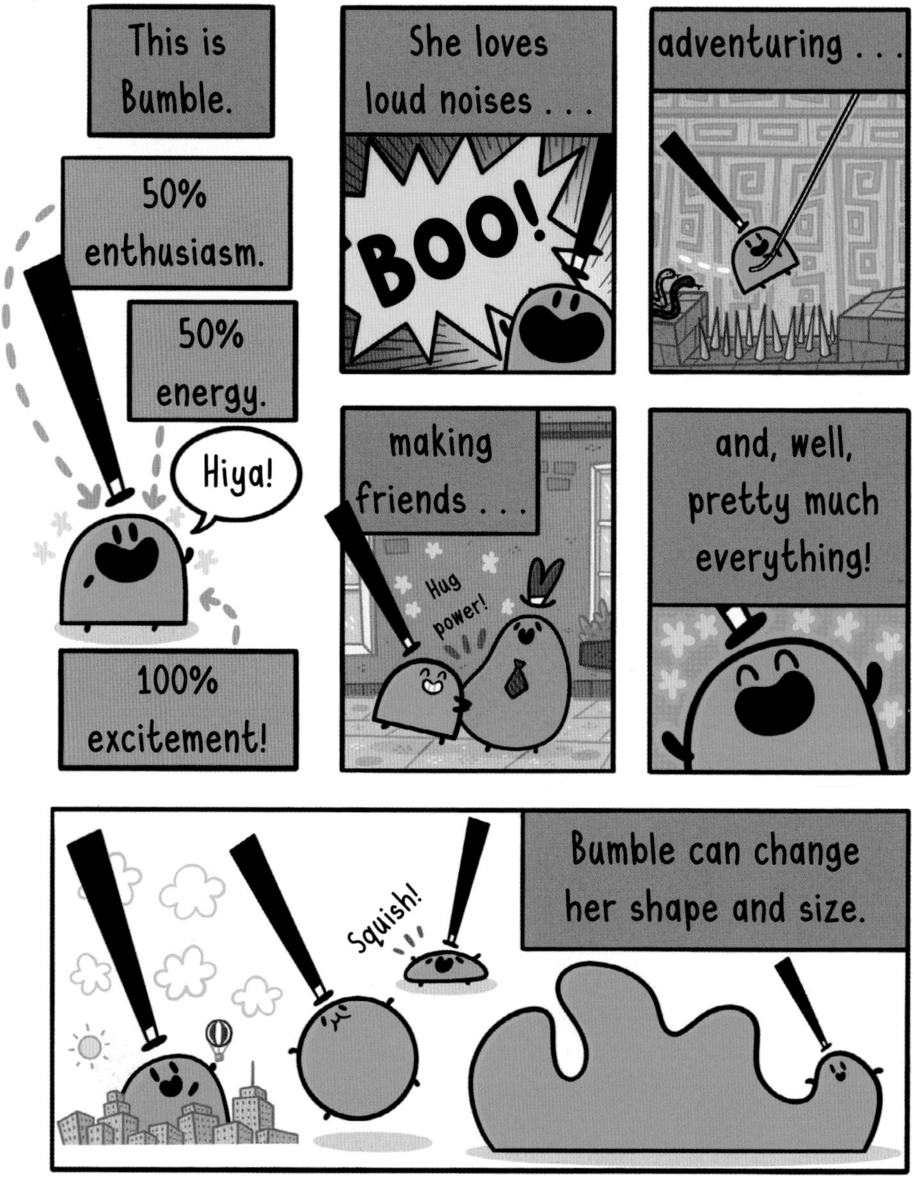
This is Bumble.
50% enthusiasm.
50% energy.
Hiya!
100% excitement!
She loves loud noises . . .
BOO!
adventuring . . .
making friends . . .
Hug power!
and, well, pretty much everything!
Bumble can change her shape and size.
Squish!

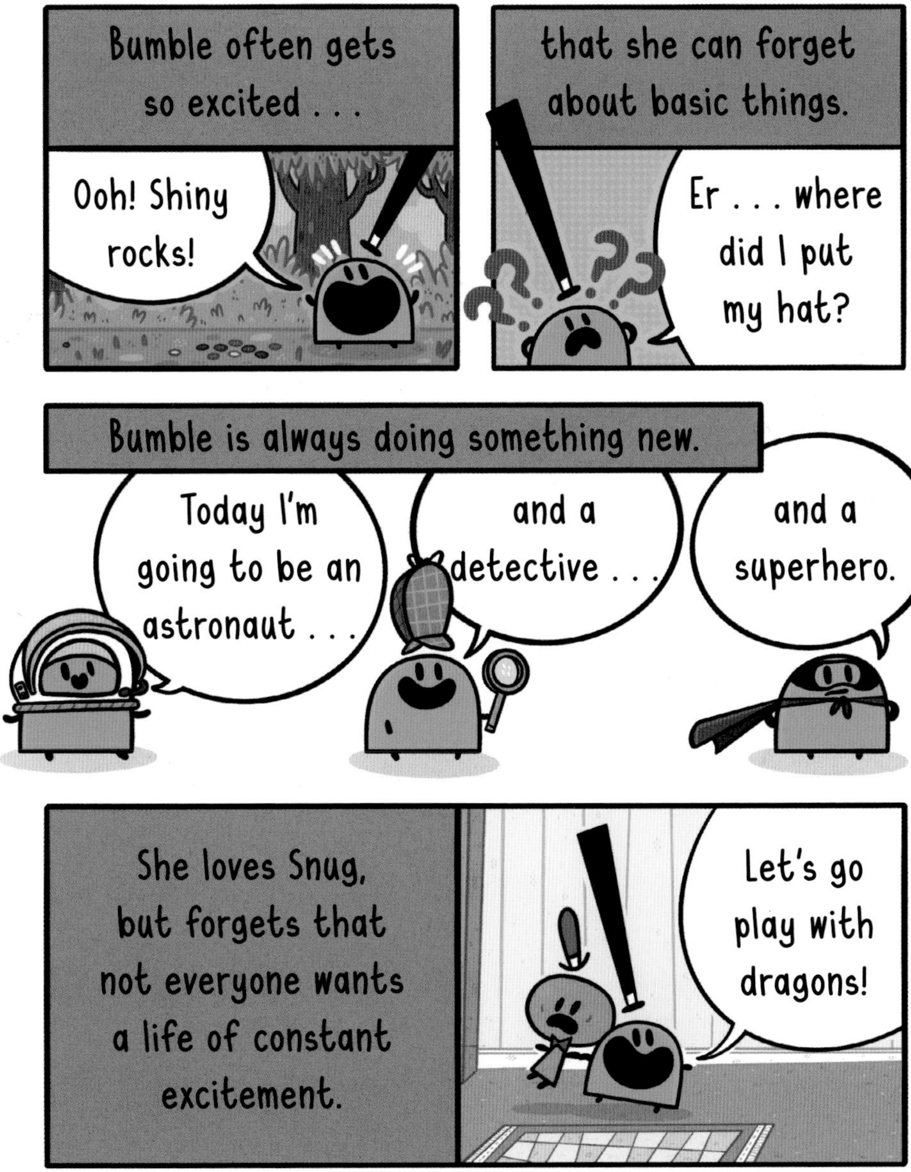
Bumble often gets so excited . . .
Ooh! Shiny rocks!
that she can forget about basic things.
Er . . . where did I put my hat?
Bumble is always doing something new.
Today I'm going to be an astronaut . . .
and a detective . . .
and a superhero.
She loves Snug, but forgets that not everyone wants a life of constant excitement.
Let's go play with dragons!

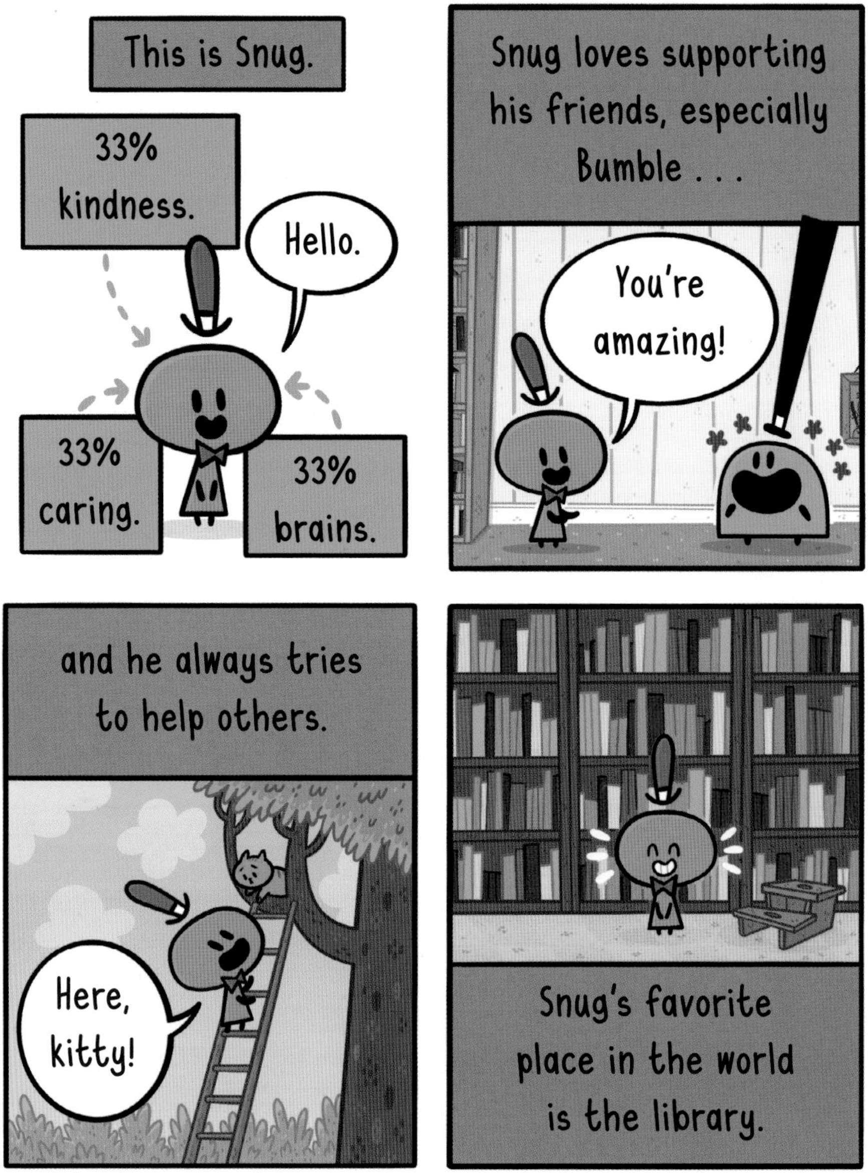
This is Snug.
33% kindness.
Hello.
33% caring.
33% brains.
Snug loves supporting his friends, especially Bumble . . .
You're amazing!
and he always tries to help others.
Here, kitty!
Snug's favorite place in the world is the library.

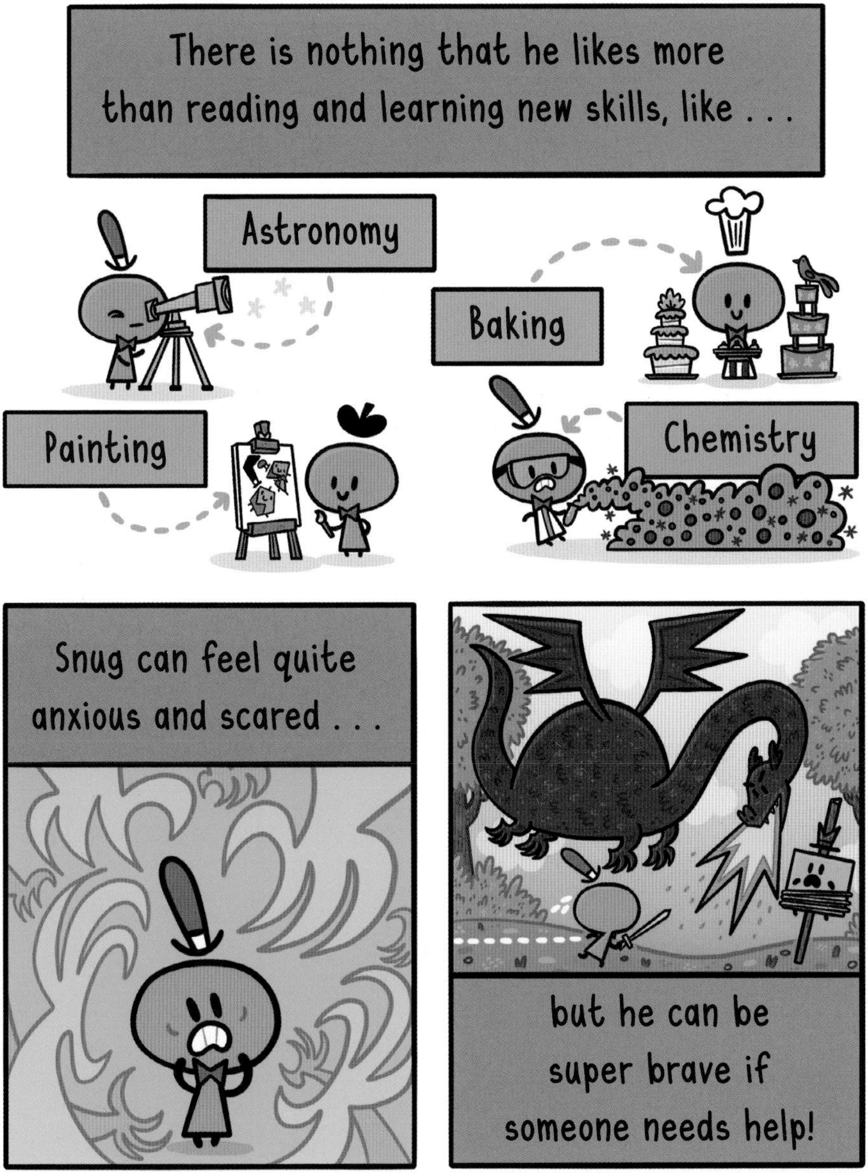
There is nothing that he likes more than reading and learning new skills, like . . .
Astronomy
Baking
Painting
Chemistry
Snug can feel quite anxious and scared . . .
but he can be super brave if someone needs help!

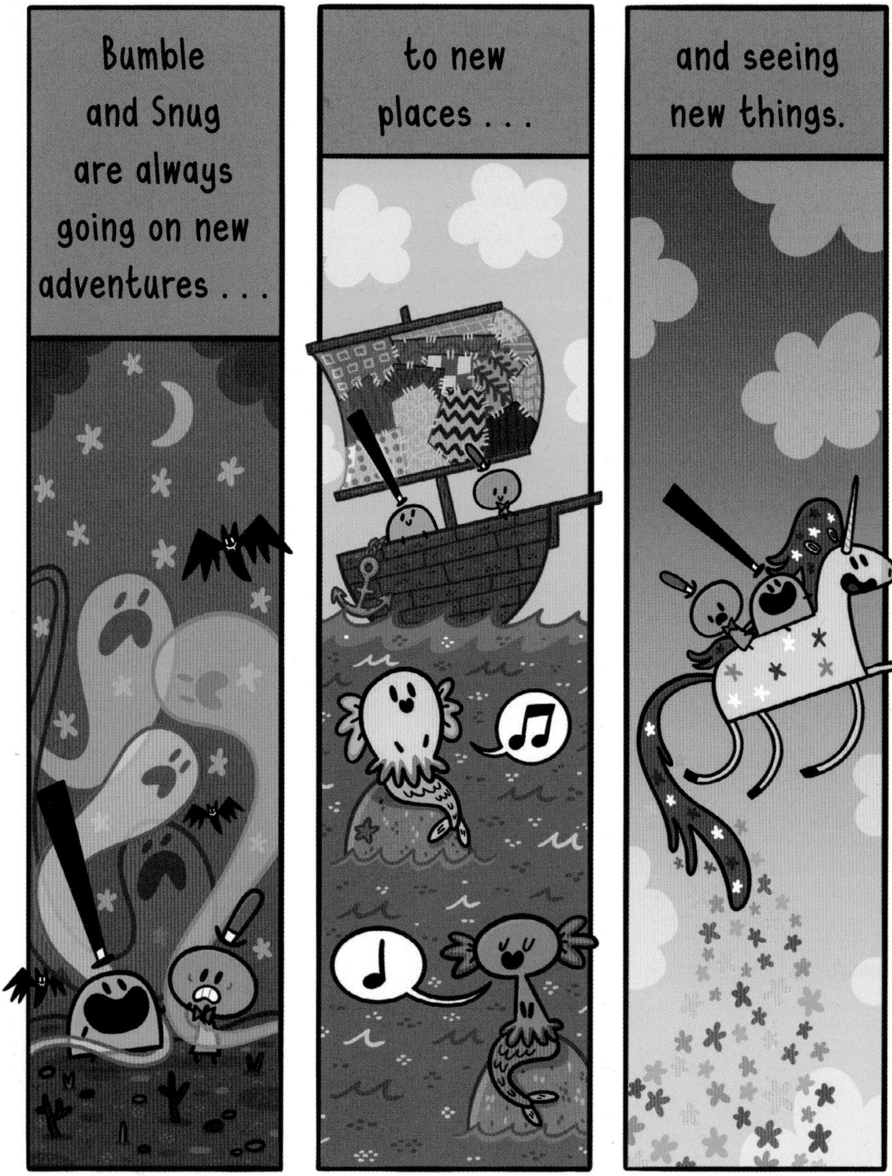
Bumble and Snug are always going on new adventures . . .
to new places . . .
and seeing new things.

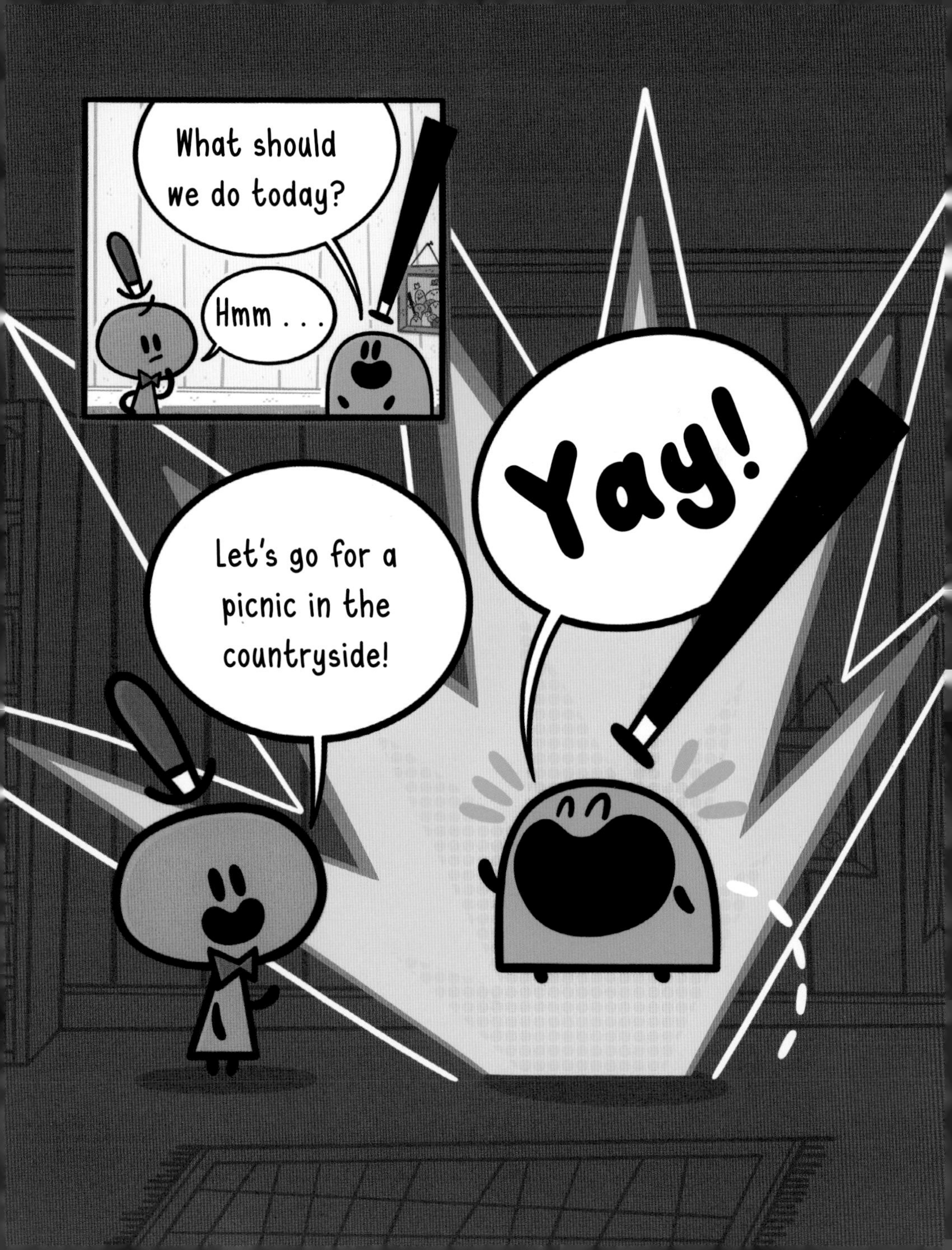
What should we do today?
Hmm . . .
Let's go for a picnic in the countryside!
Yay!

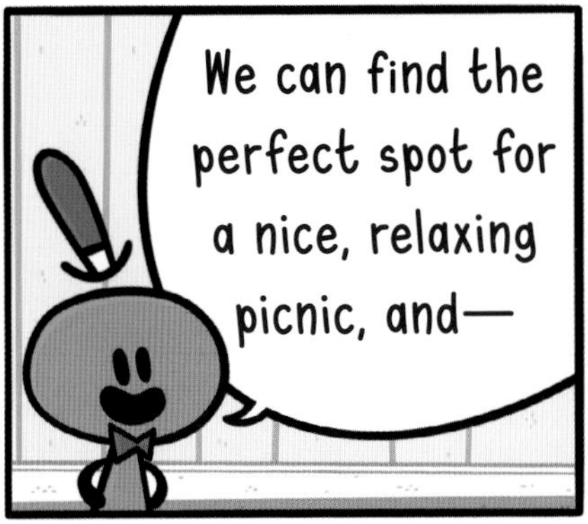
We can find the perfect spot for a nice, relaxing picnic, and—

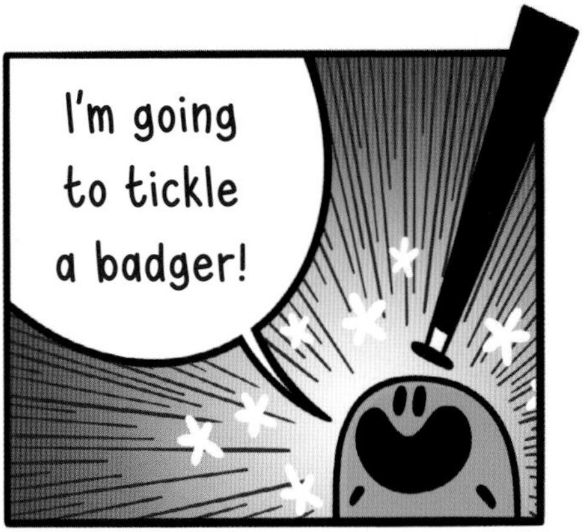
I'm going to tickle a badger!

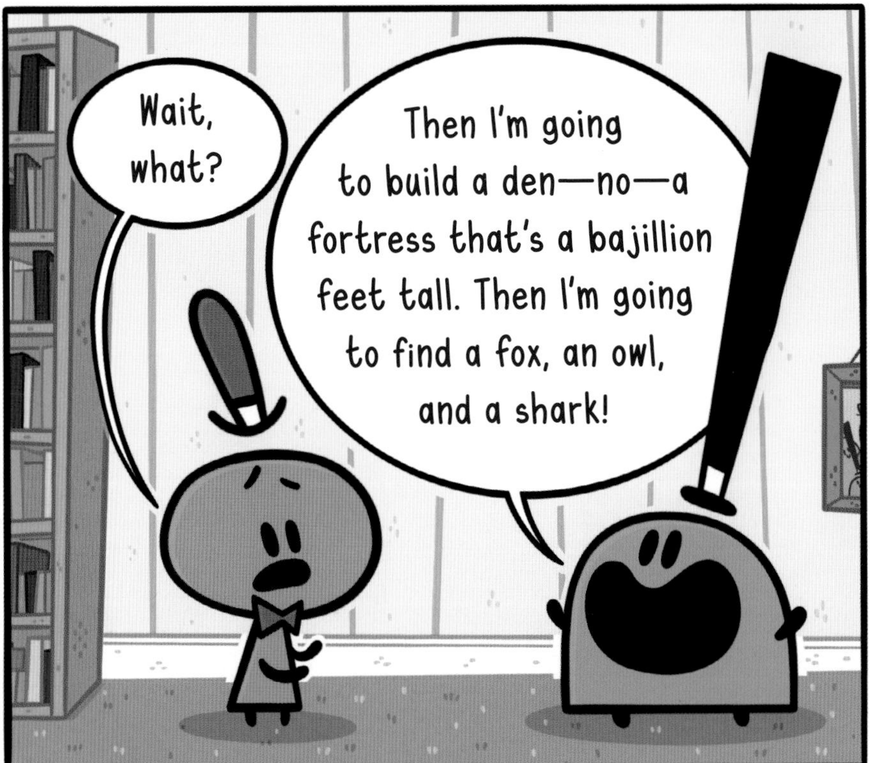
Wait, what?
Then I'm going to build a den—no—a fortress that's a bajillion feet tall. Then I'm going to find a fox, an owl, and a shark!

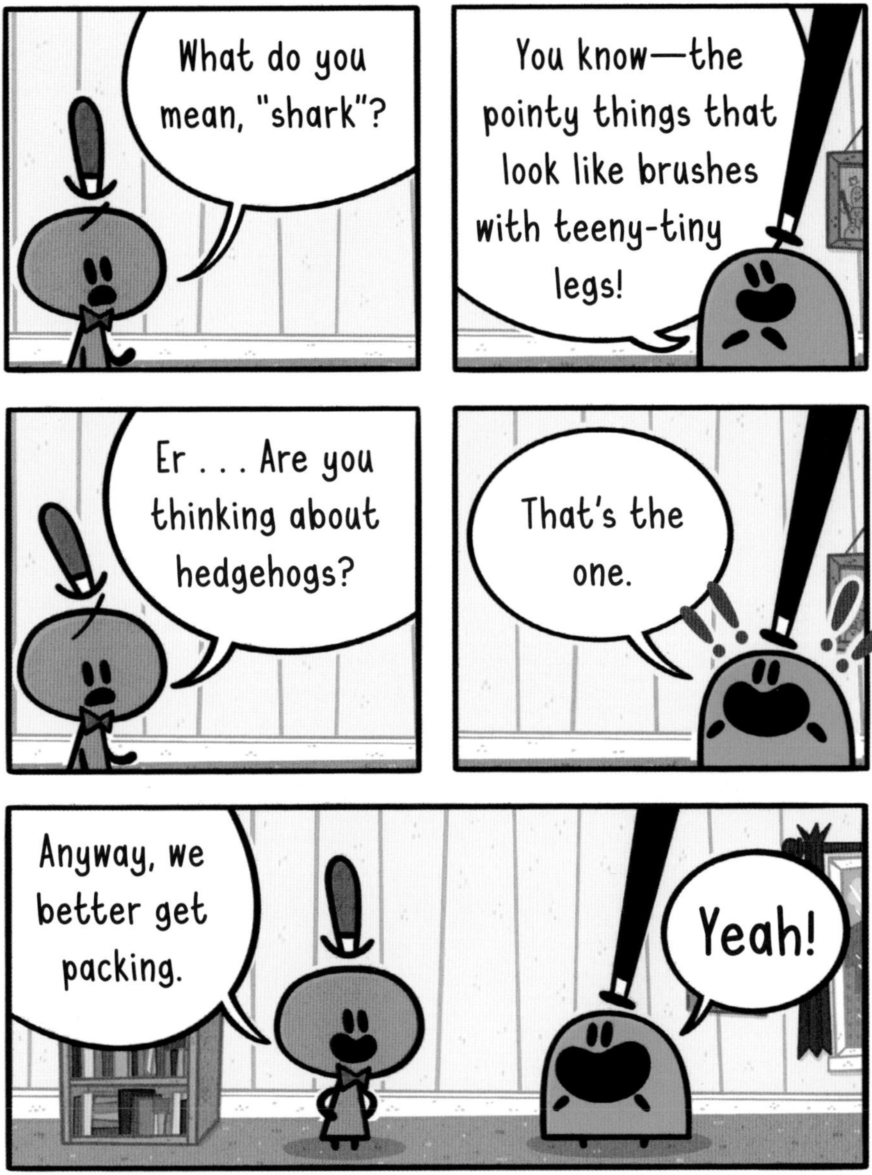
What do you mean, "shark"?
You know—the pointy things that look like brushes with teeny-tiny legs!
Er . . . Are you thinking about hedgehogs?
That's the one.
Anyway, we better get packing.
Yeah!

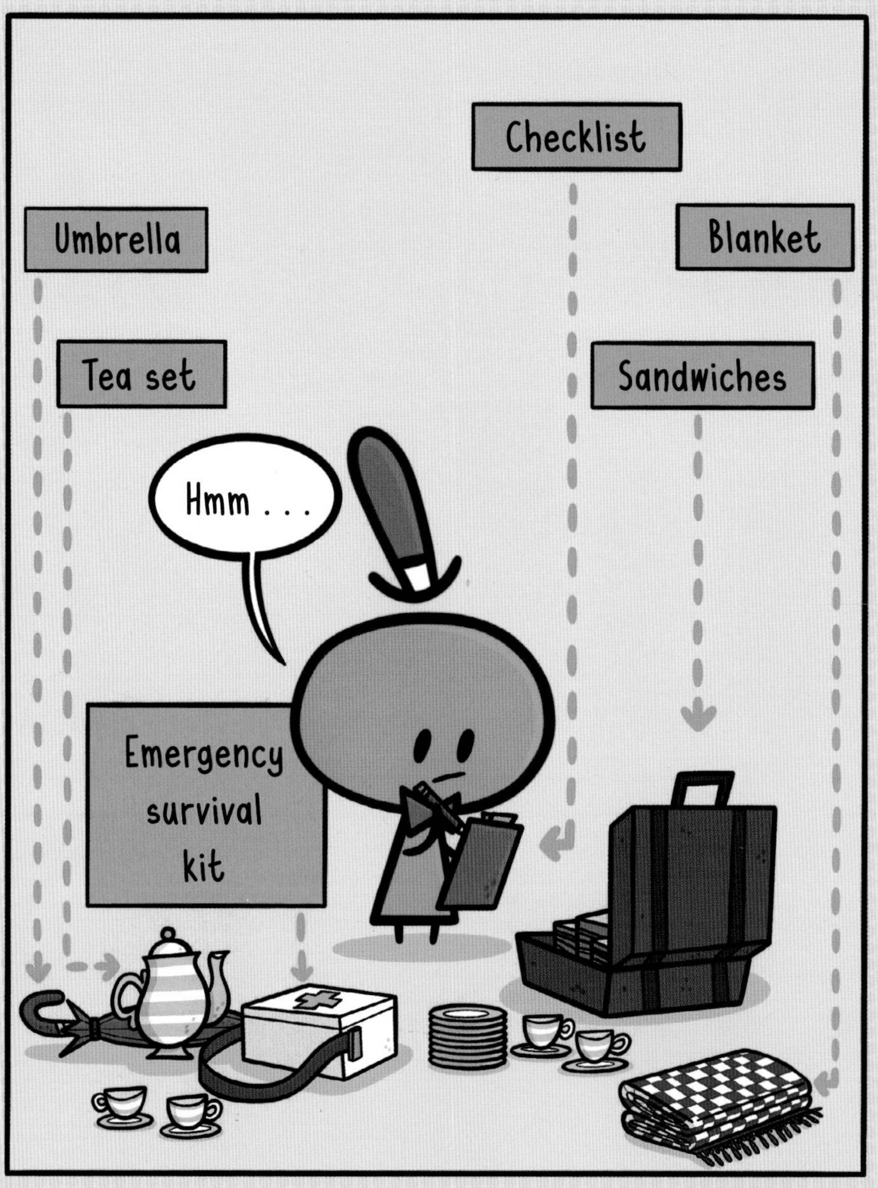
Checklist
Umbrella
Blanket
Tea set
Sandwiches
Hmm . . .
Emergency survival kit

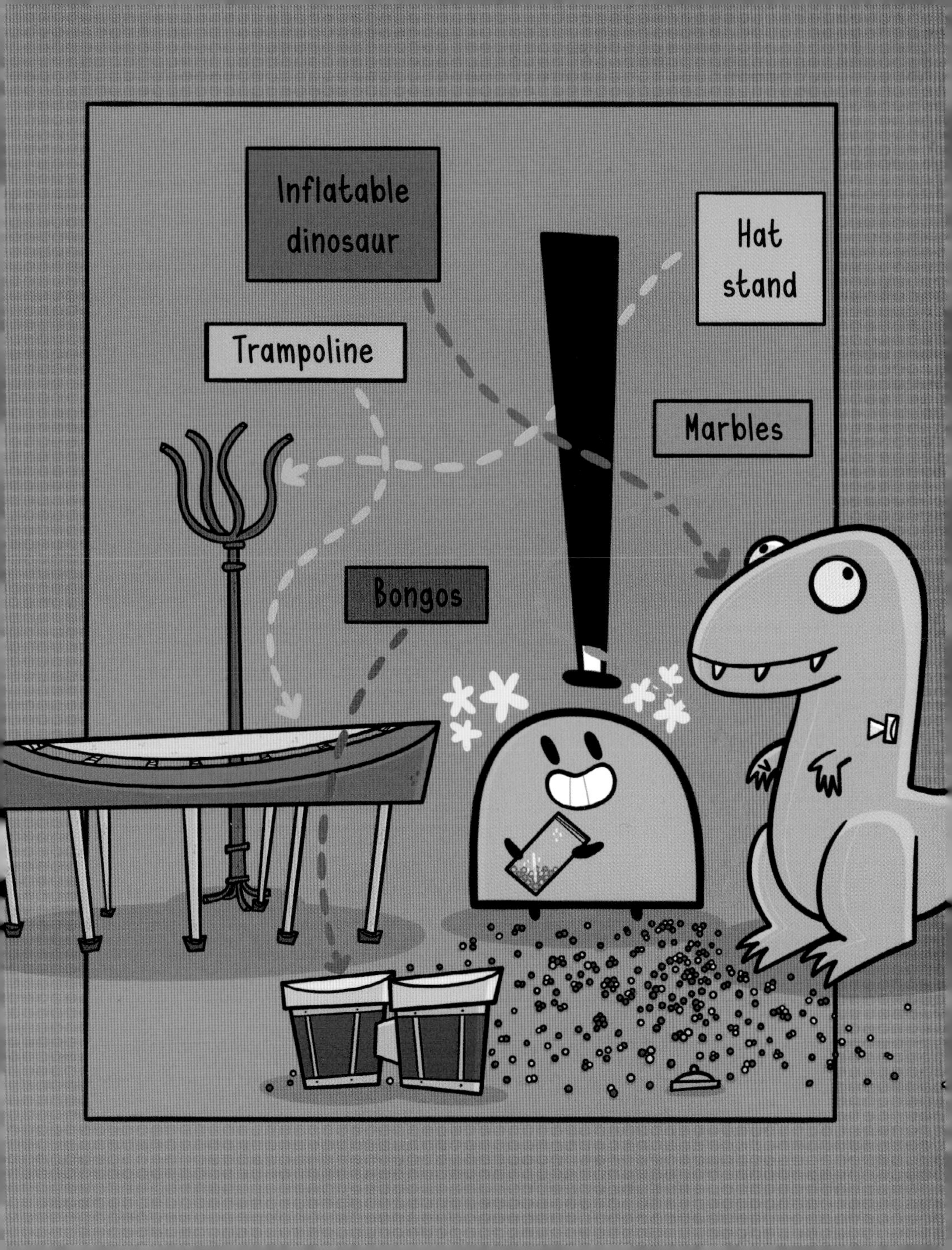
Inflatable dinosaur
Hat stand
Trampoline
Marbles
Bongos

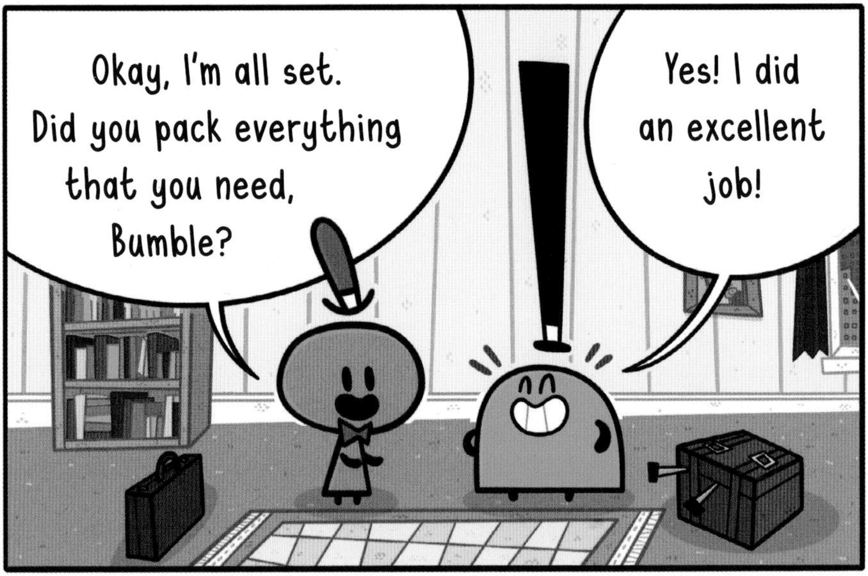
Okay, I'm all set. Did you pack everything that you need, Bumble?
Yes! I did an excellent job!

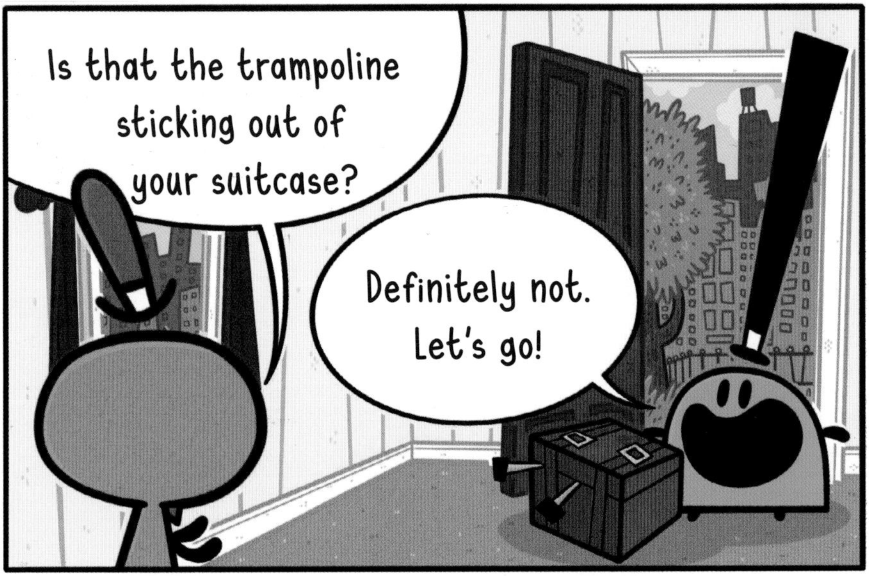
Is that the trampoline sticking out of your suitcase?
Definitely not. Let's go!

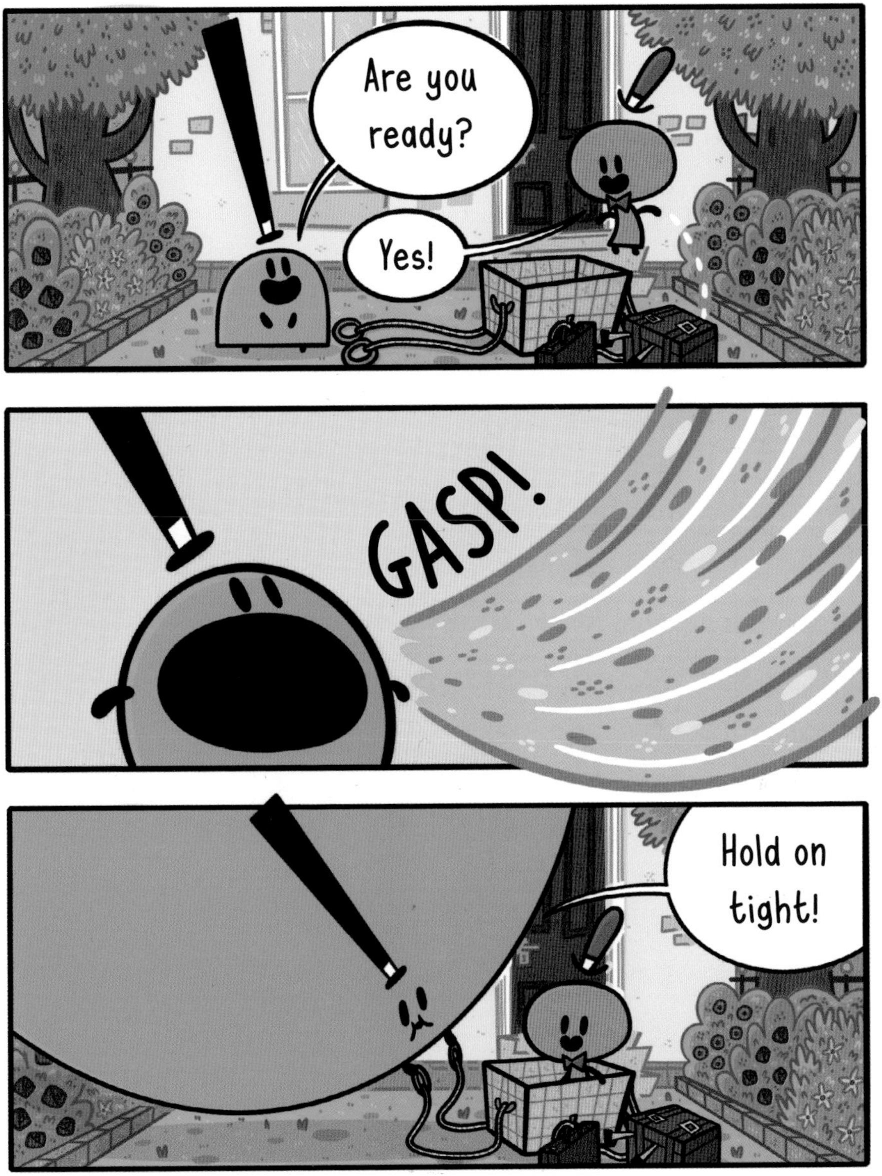
Are you ready?
Yes!
GASP!
Hold on tight!

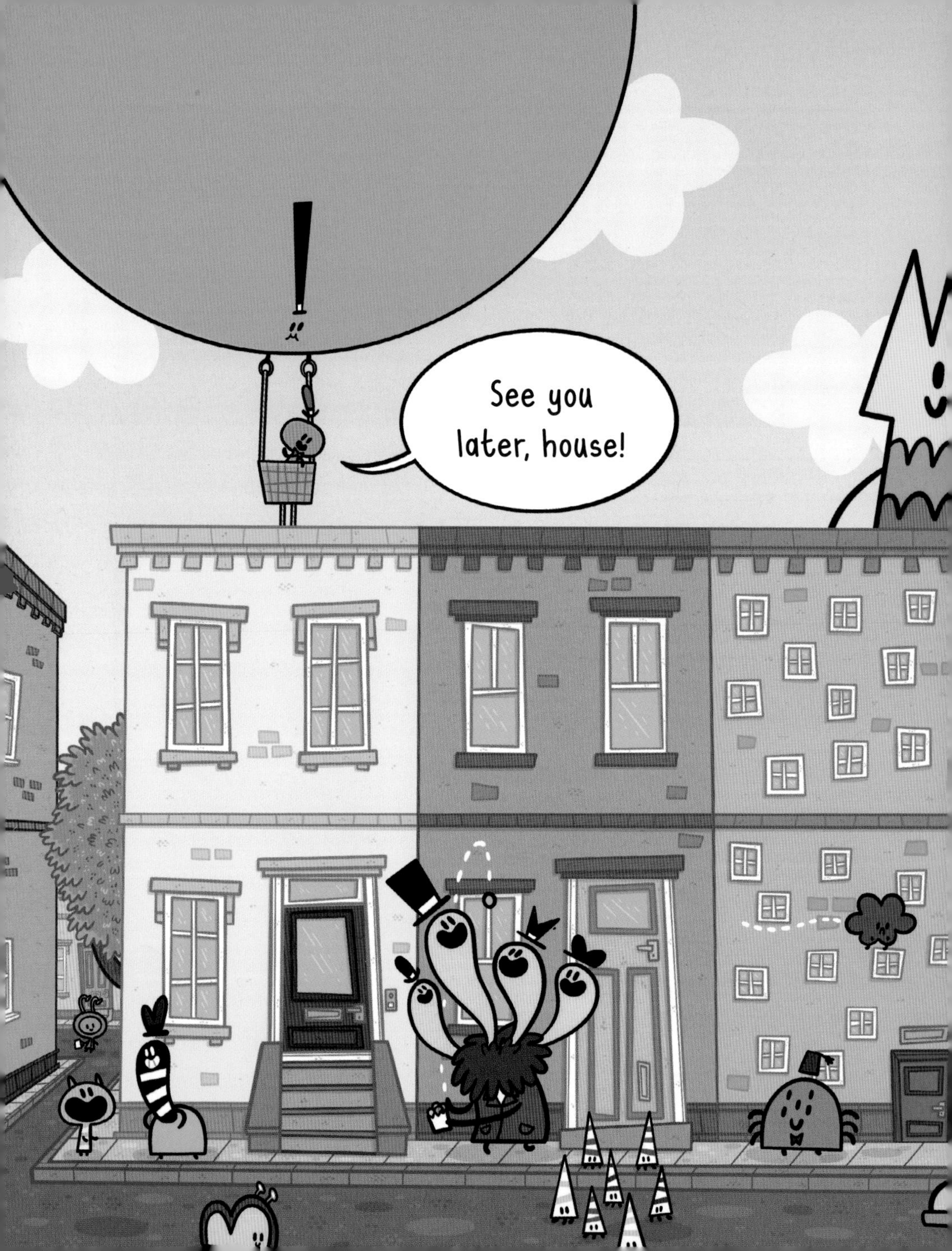
See you later, house!

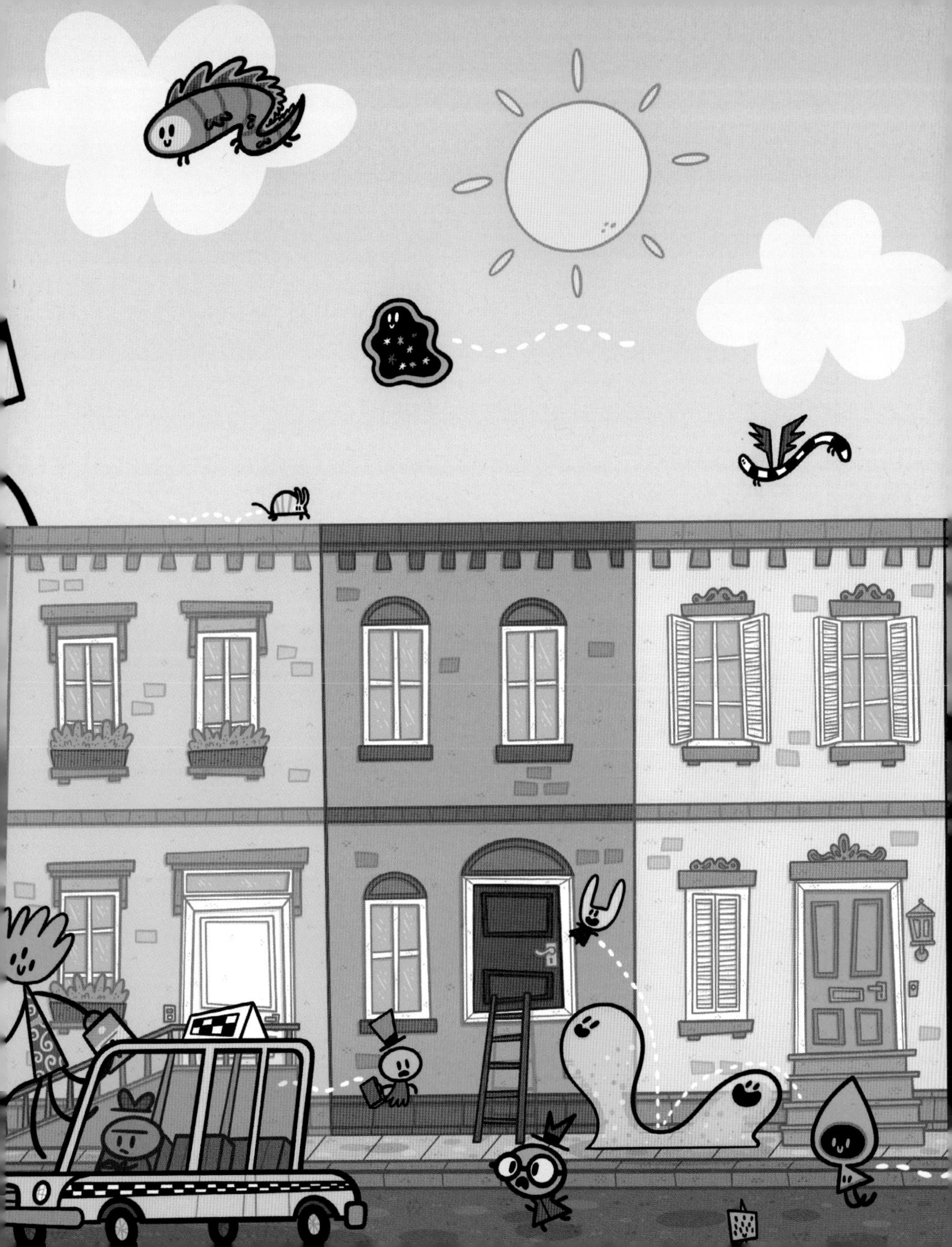

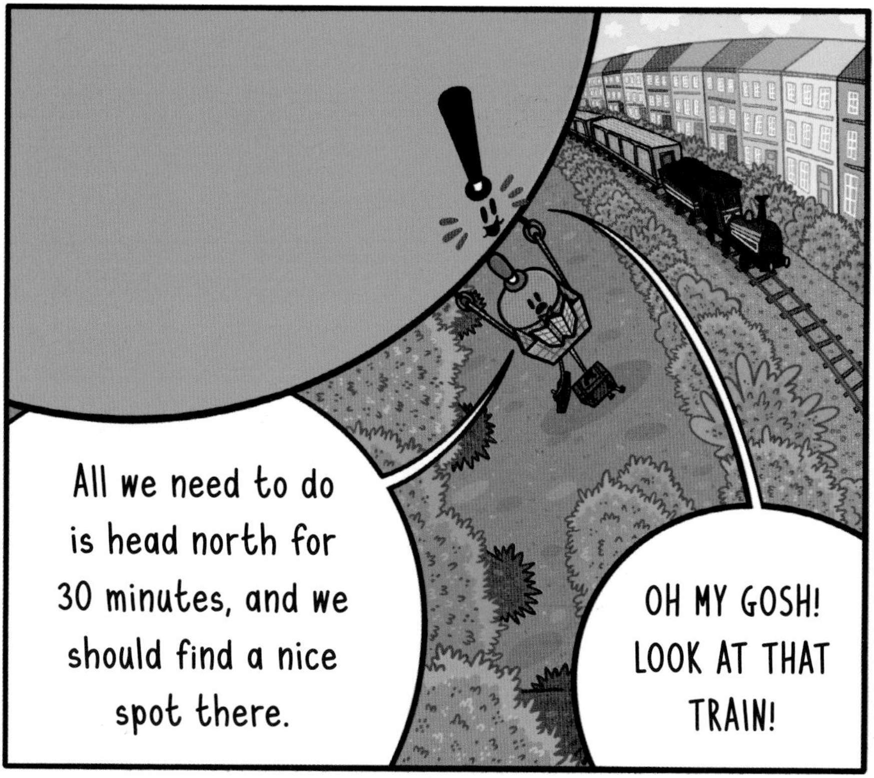
All we need to do is head north for 30 minutes, and we should find a nice spot there.
OH MY GOSH! LOOK AT THAT TRAIN!

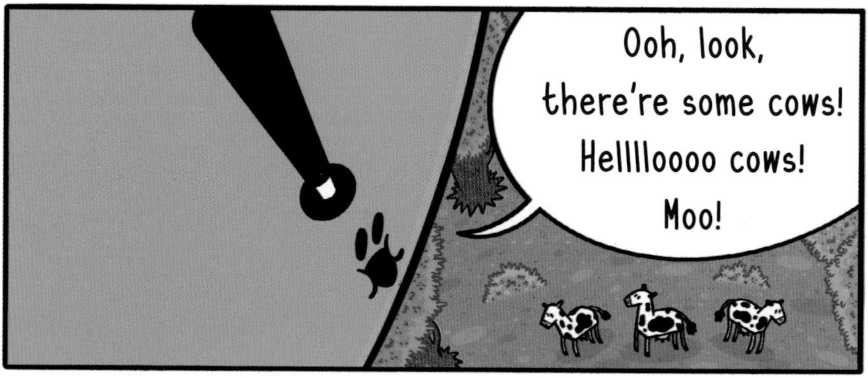
Ooh, look, there're some cows! Helllloooo cows! Moo!

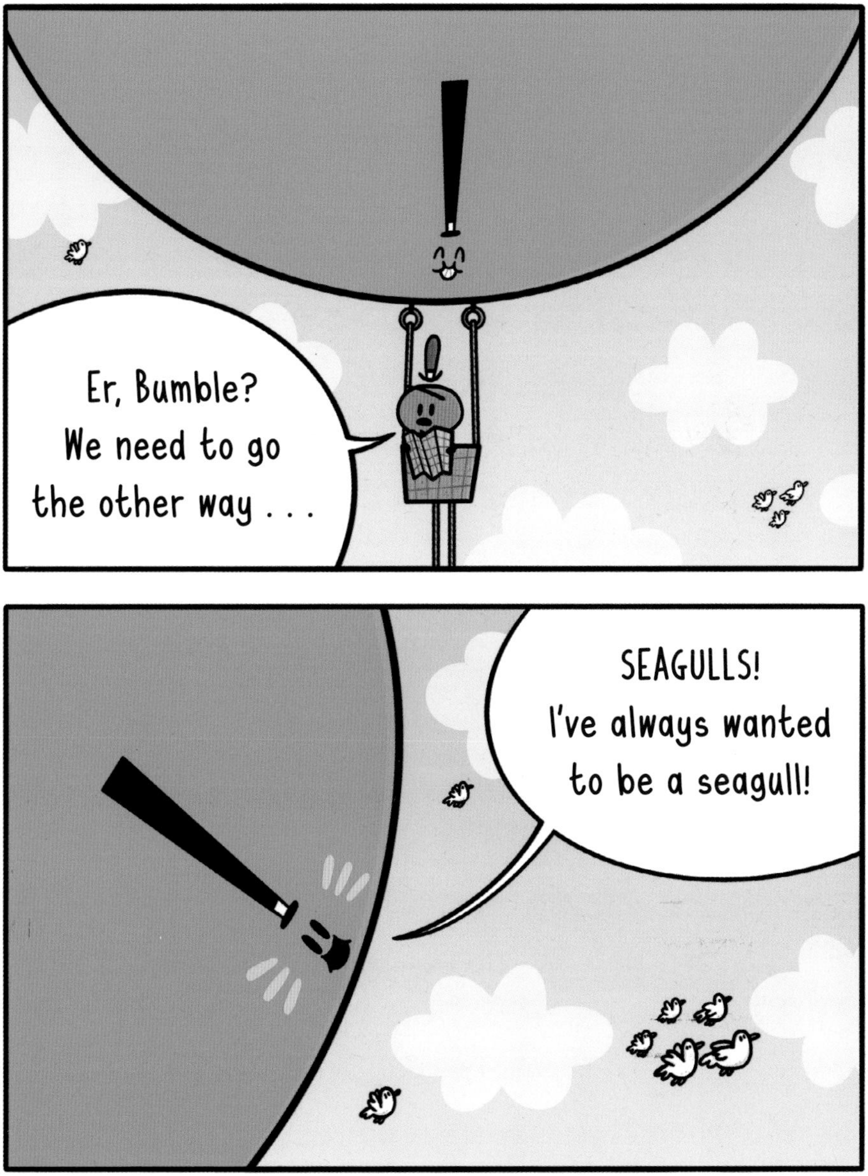
Er, Bumble? We need to go the other way . . .
SEAGULLS! I've always wanted to be a seagull!

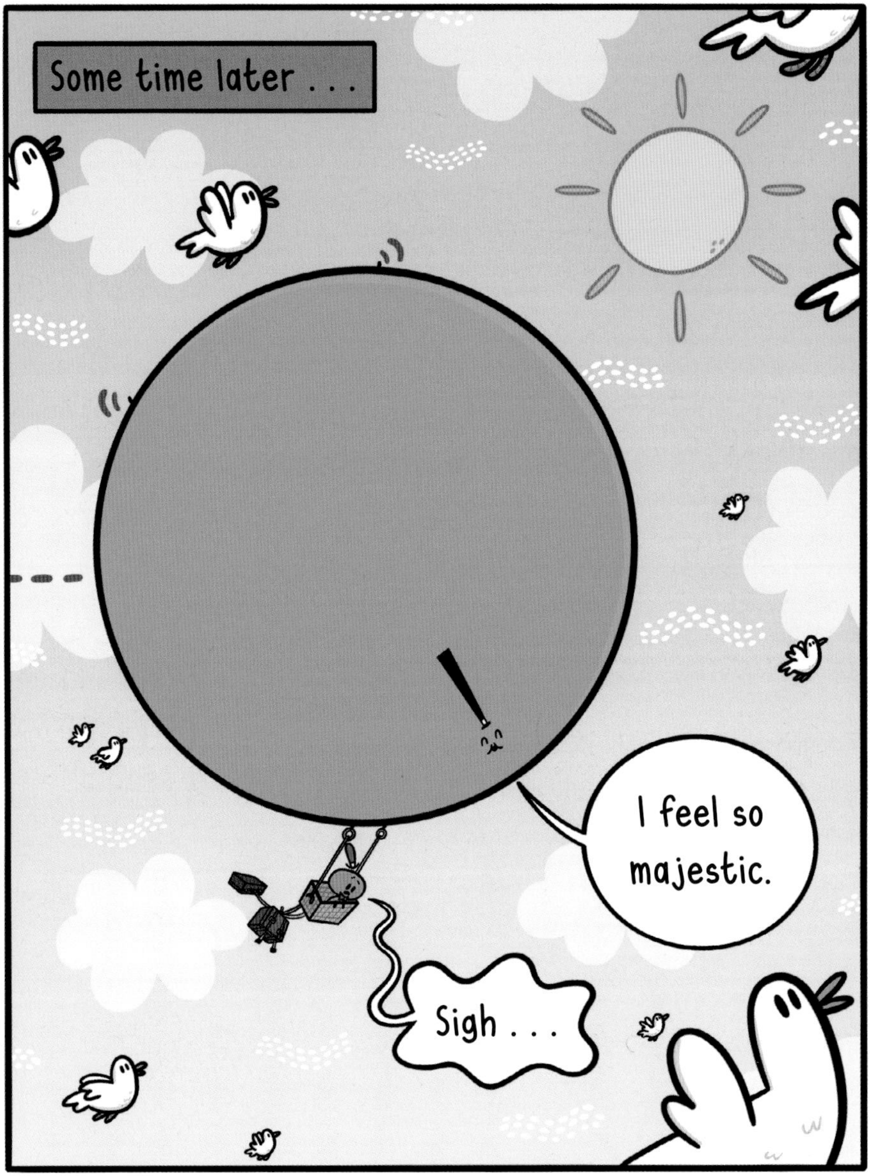
Some time later . . .
I feel so majestic.
Sigh . . .

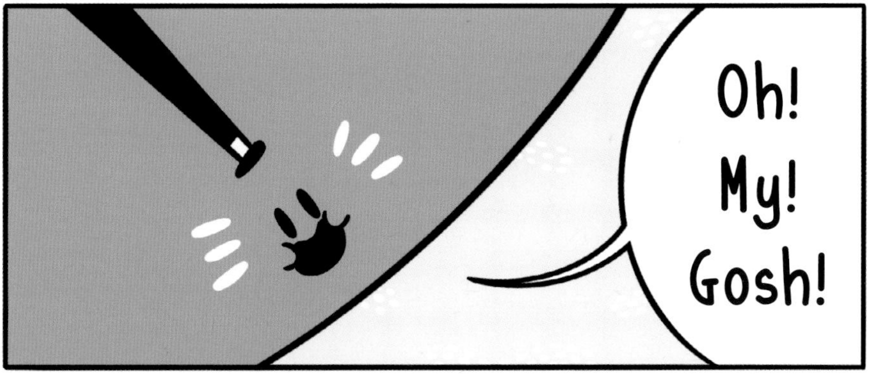
Oh! My! Gosh!

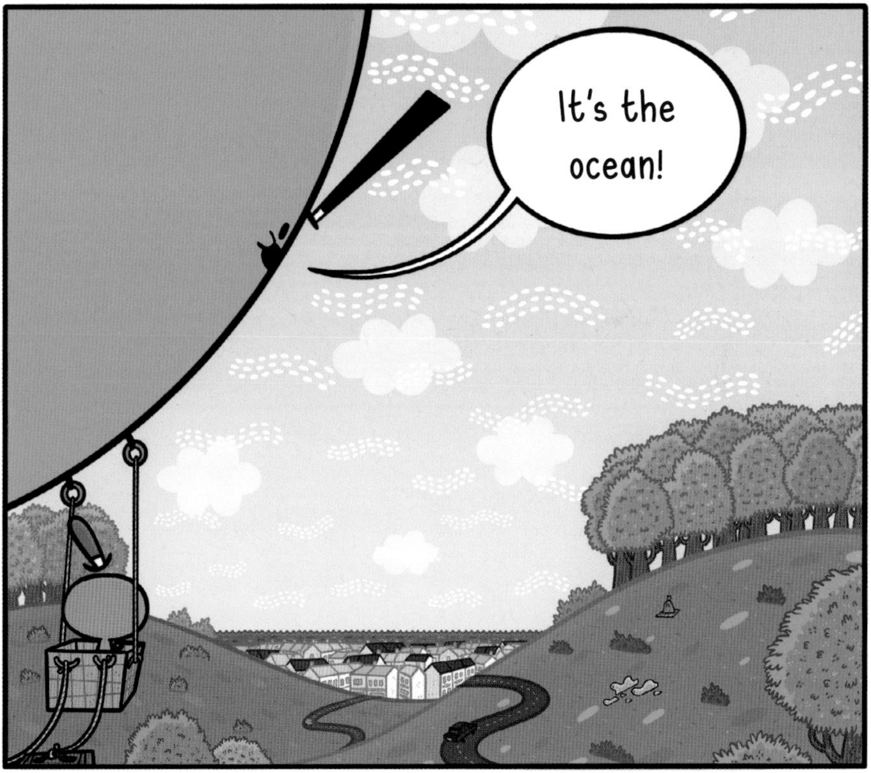
It's the ocean!

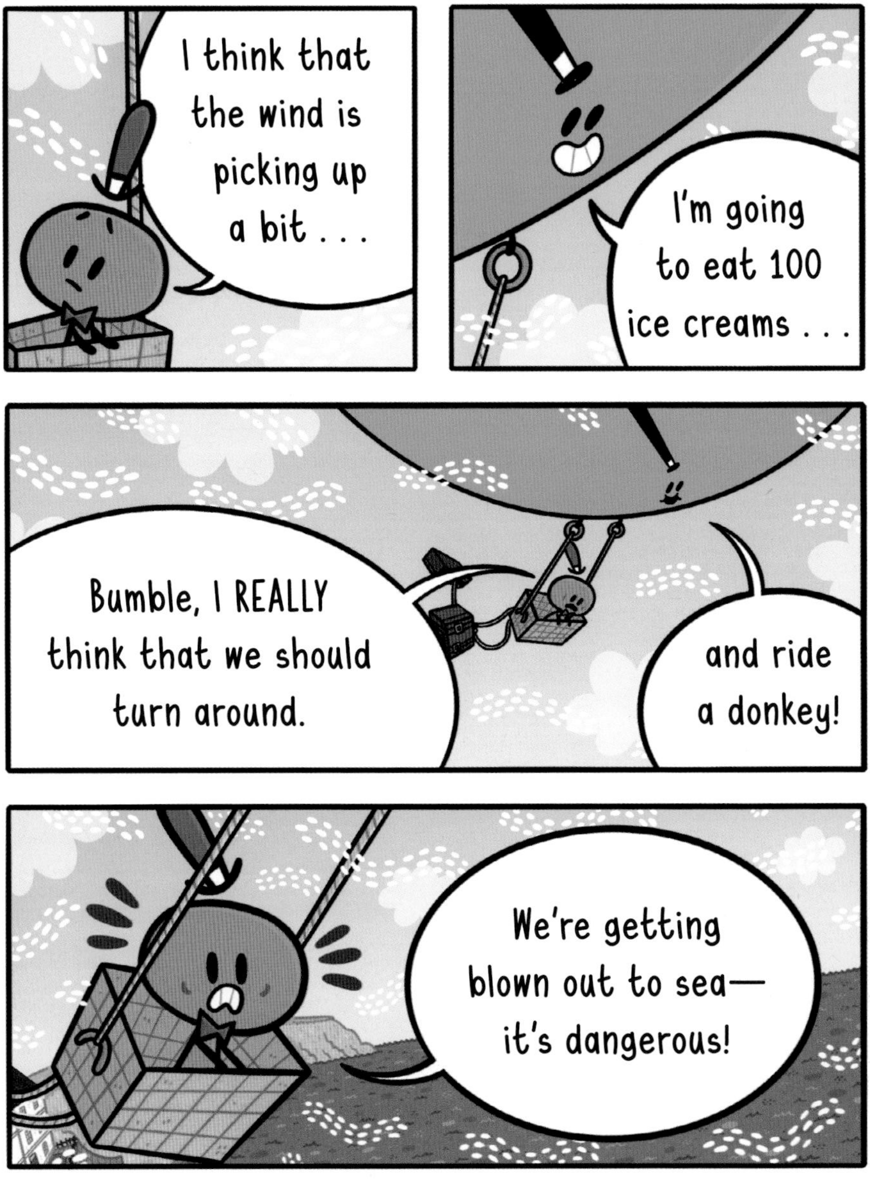
I think that the wind is picking up a bit . . .
I'm going to eat 100 ice creams . . .
Bumble, I REALLY think that we should turn around.
and ride a donkey!
We're getting blown out to sea— it's dangerous!

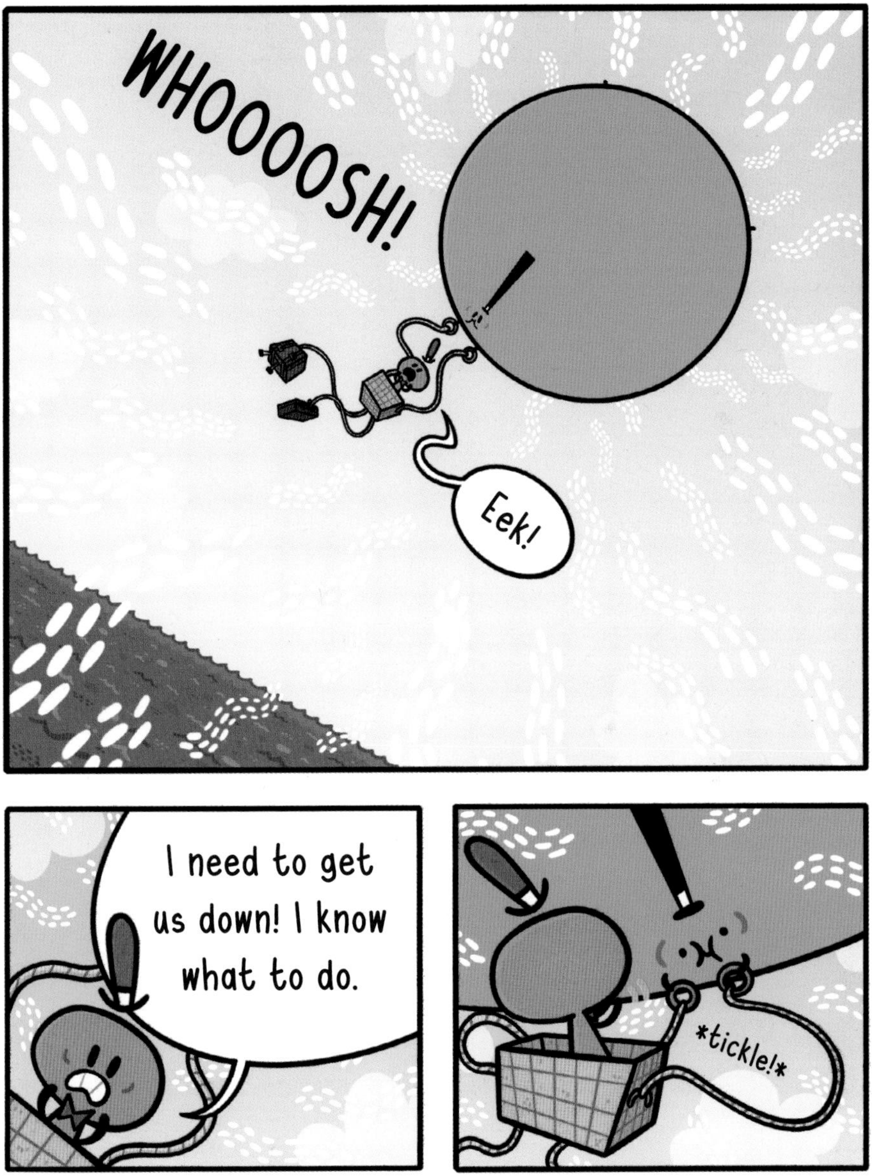
WHOOOOOSH!
Eek!
I need to get us down! I know what to do.
tickle!

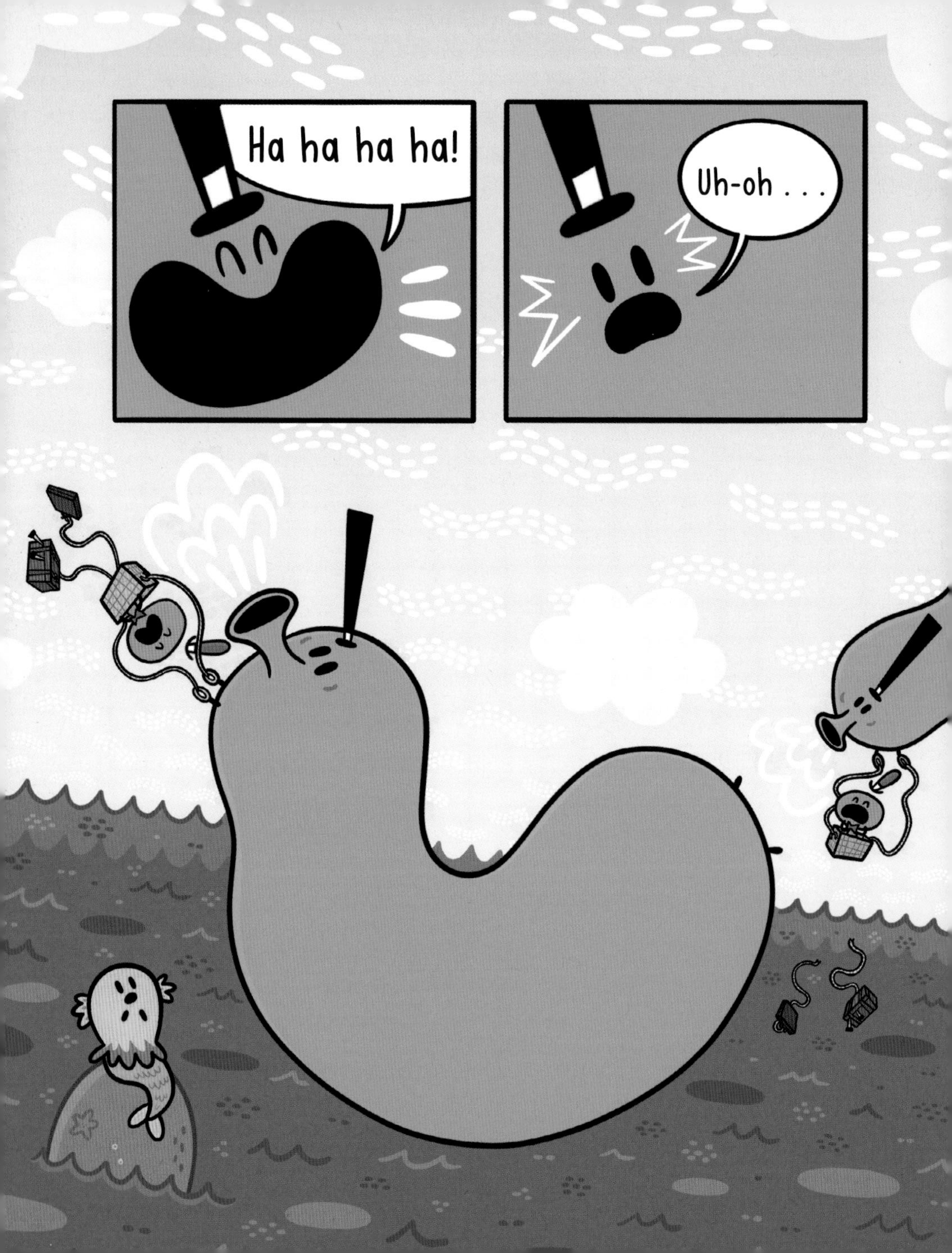
Ha ha ha ha!
Uh-oh . . .

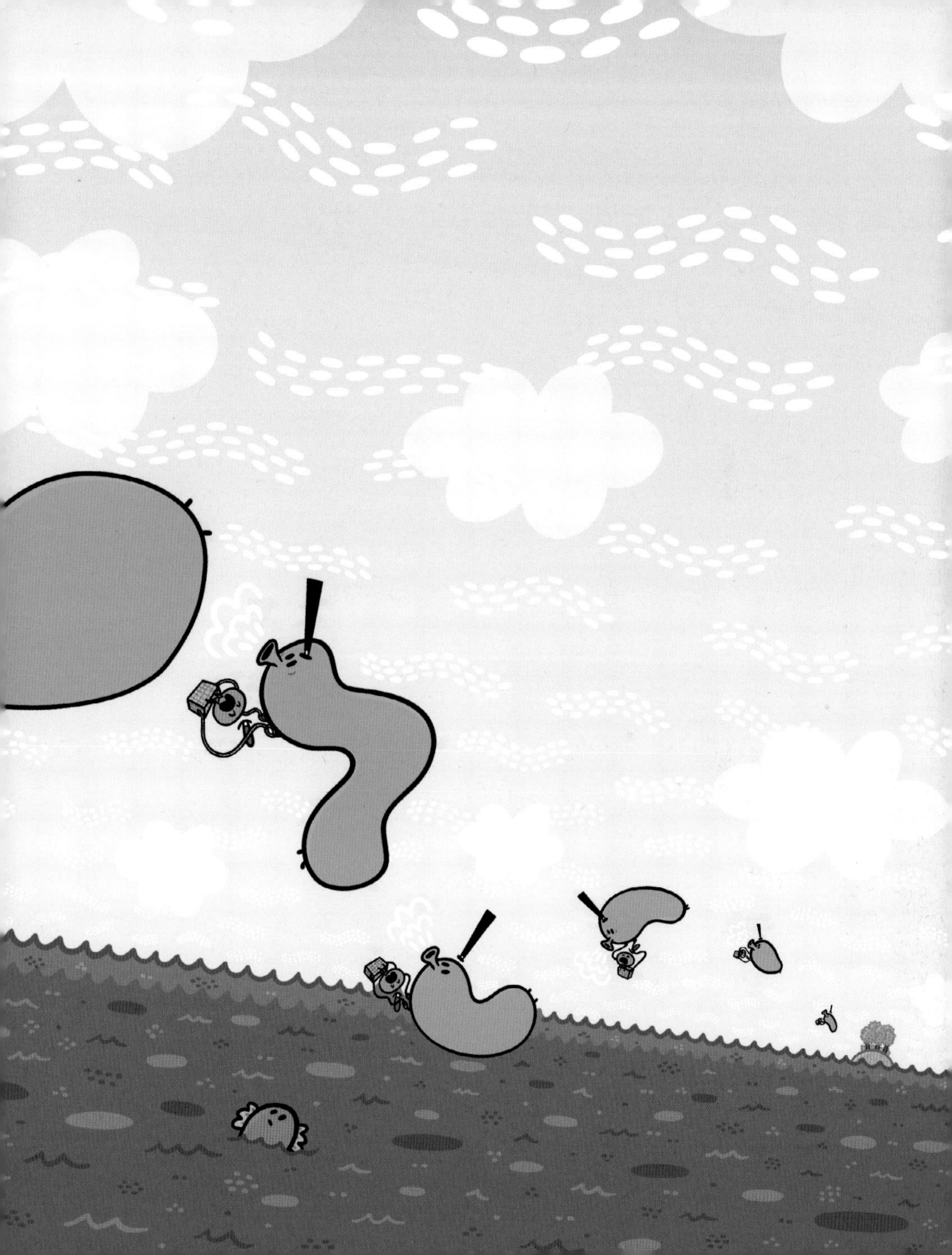

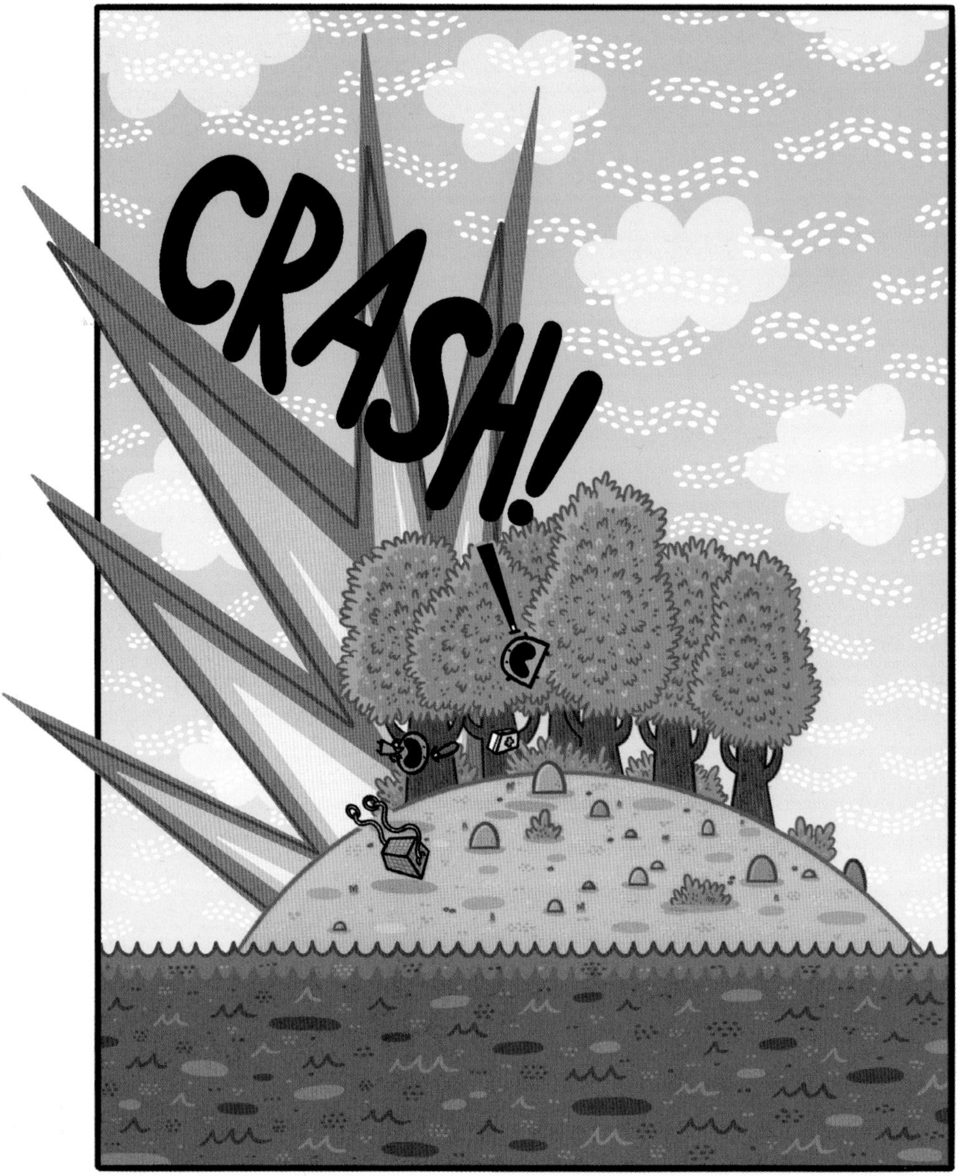
CRASH!

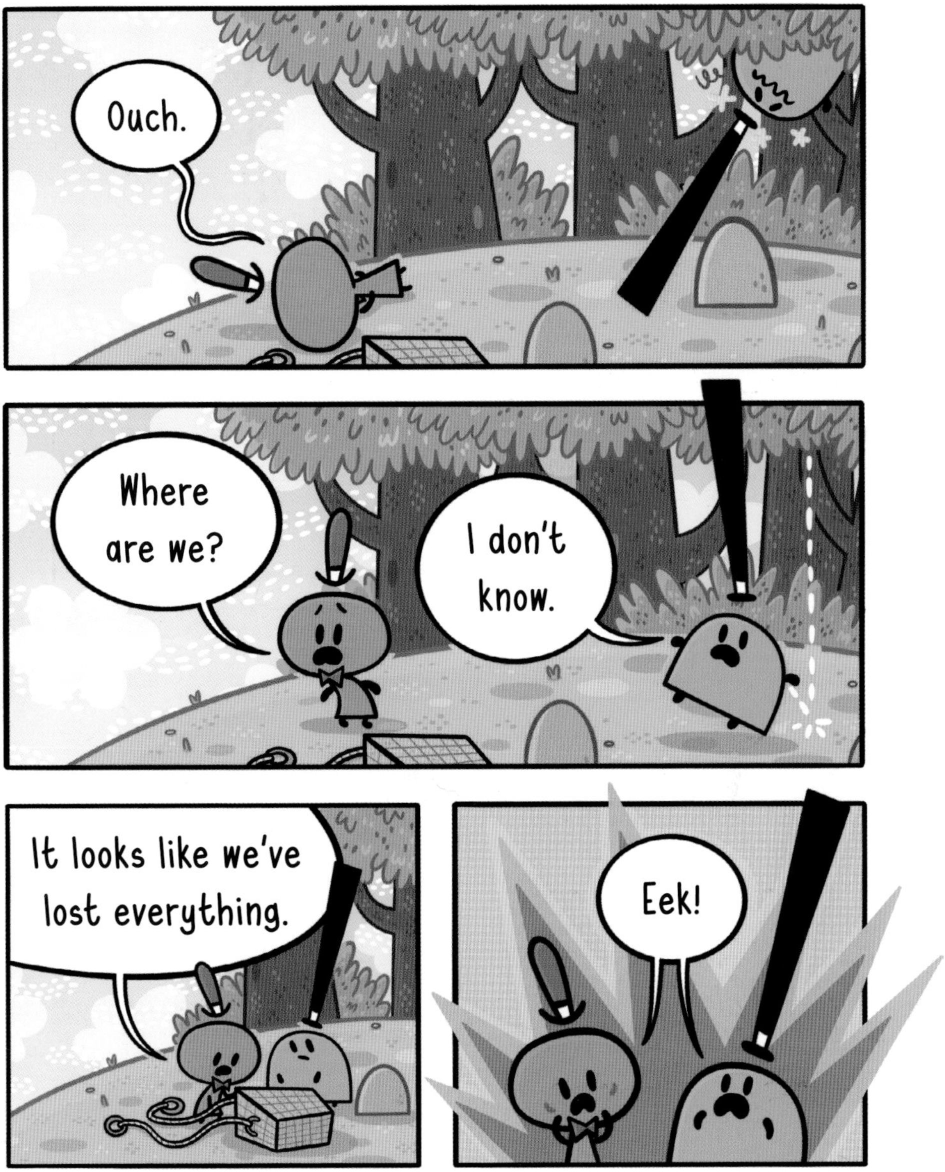

Ouch.
Where are we?
I don't know.
It looks like we've lost everything.
Eek!

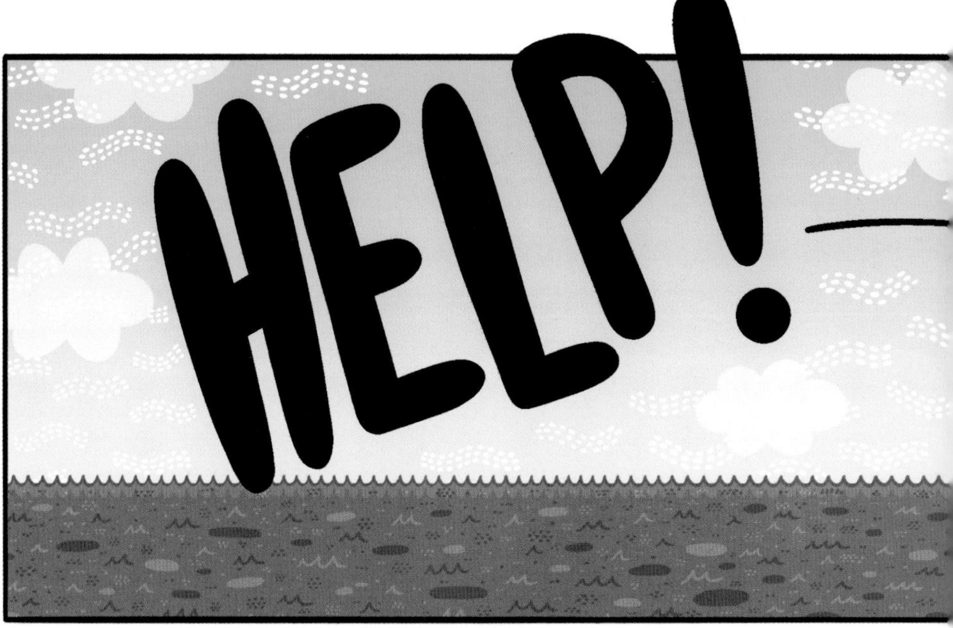
HELP!

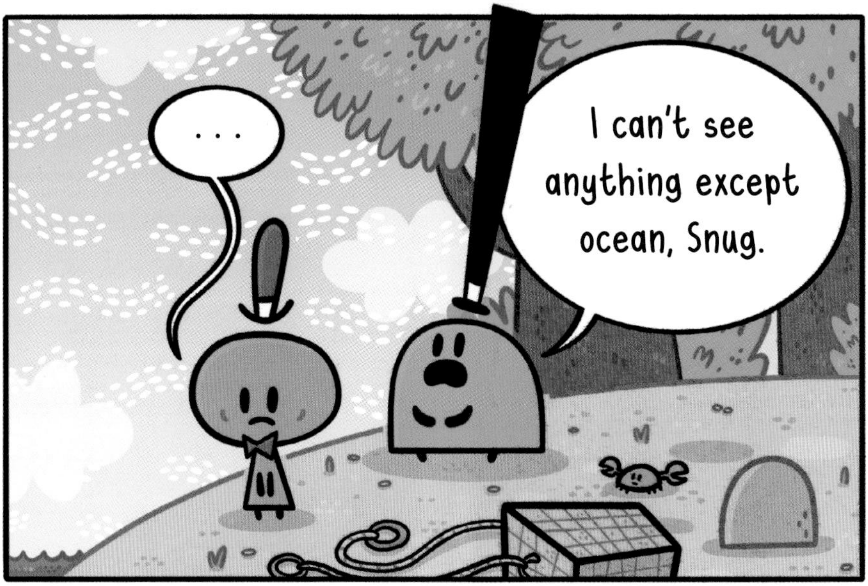
. . .
I can't see anything except ocean, Snug.

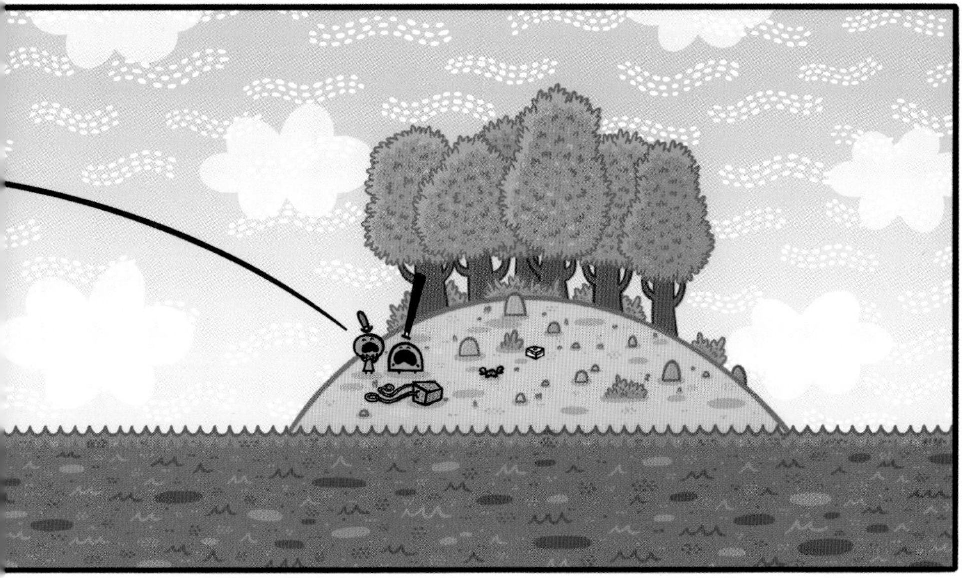

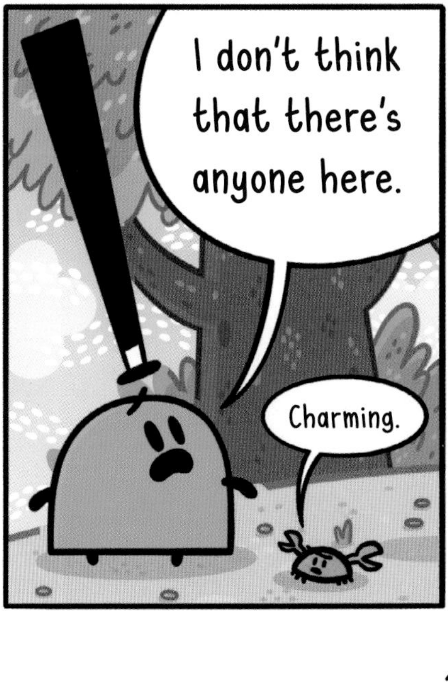
I don't think that there's anyone here.
Charming.

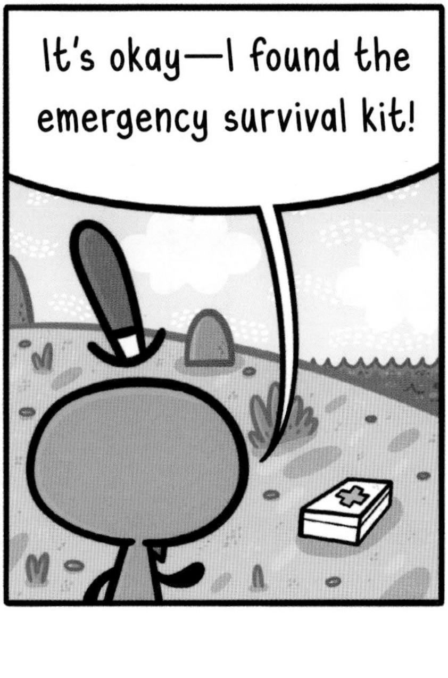
It's okay—I found the emergency survival kit!

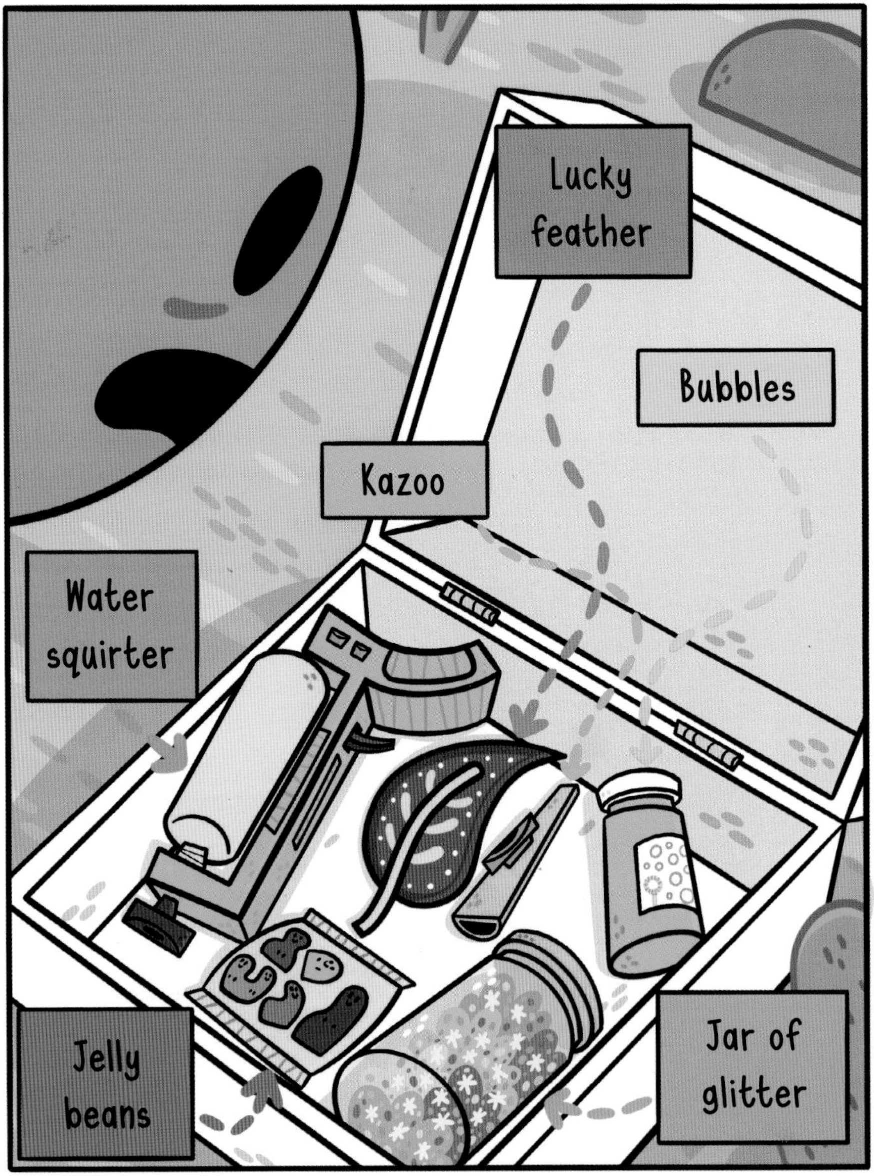
Lucky feather
Bubbles
Kazoo
Water squirter
Jelly beans
Jar of glitter

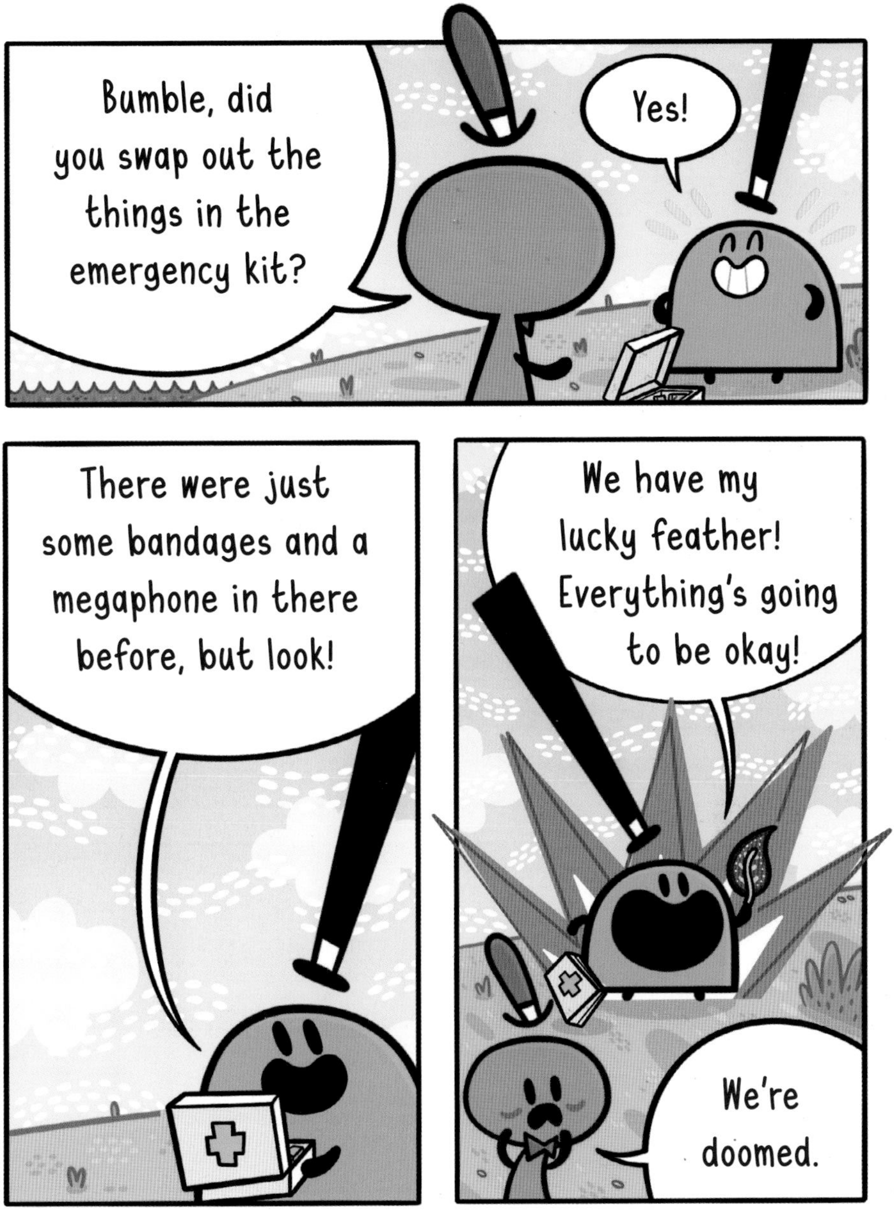
Bumble, did you swap out the things in the emergency kit?
Yes!
There were just some bandages and a megaphone in there before, but look!
We have my lucky feather! Everything's going to be okay!
We're doomed.

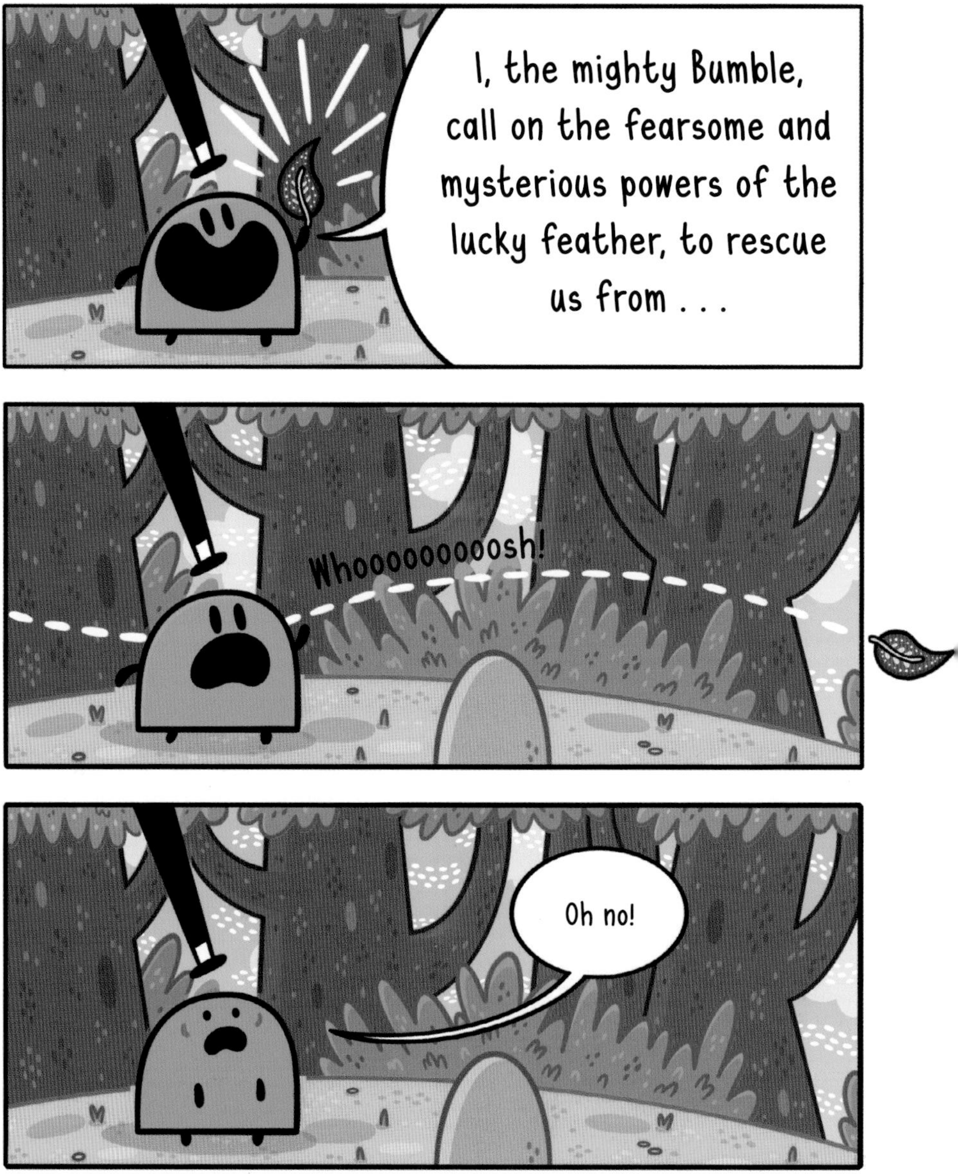
I, the mighty Bumble, call on the fearsome and mysterious powers of the lucky feather, to rescue us from . . .
Whoooooooooosh!
Oh no!

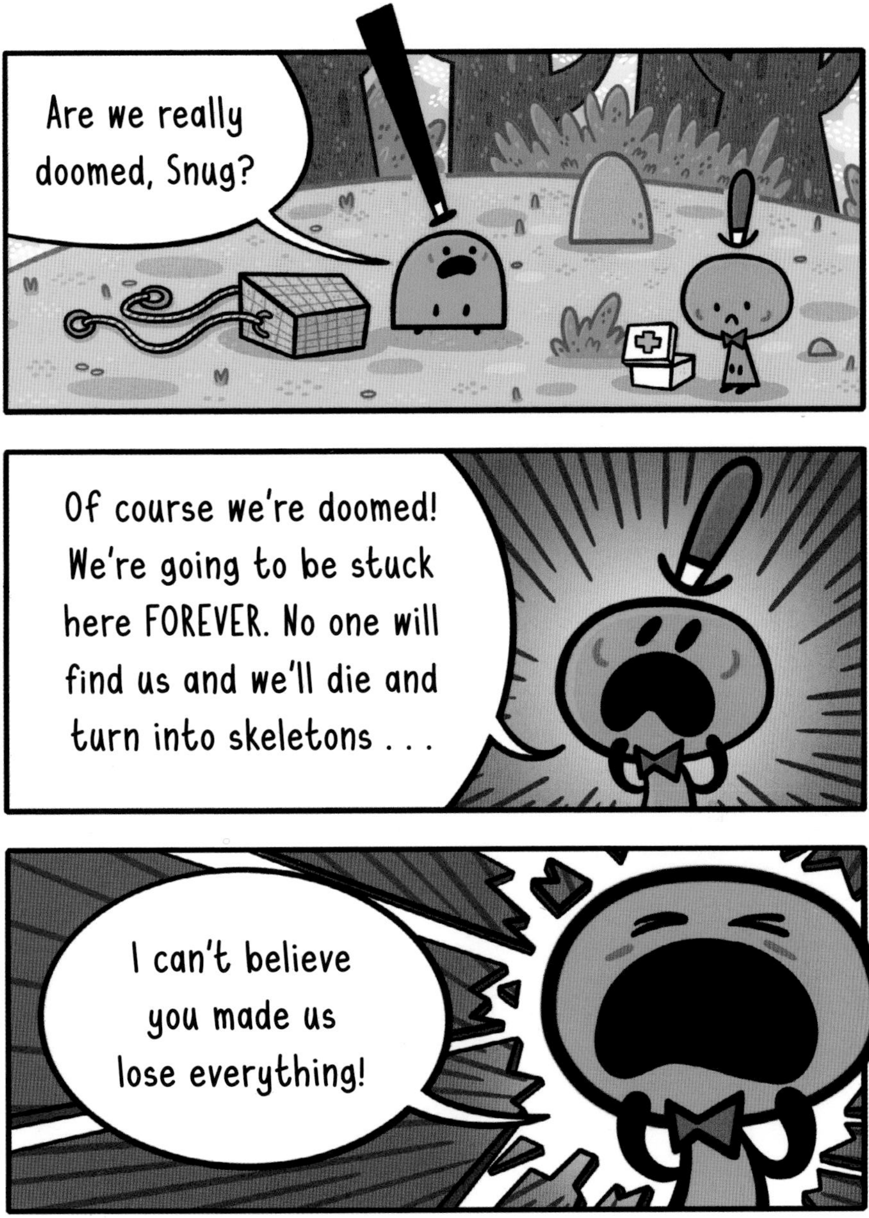
Are we really doomed, Snug?
Of course we're doomed! We're going to be stuck here FOREVER. No one will find us and we'll die and turn into skeletons . . .
I can't believe you made us lose everything!

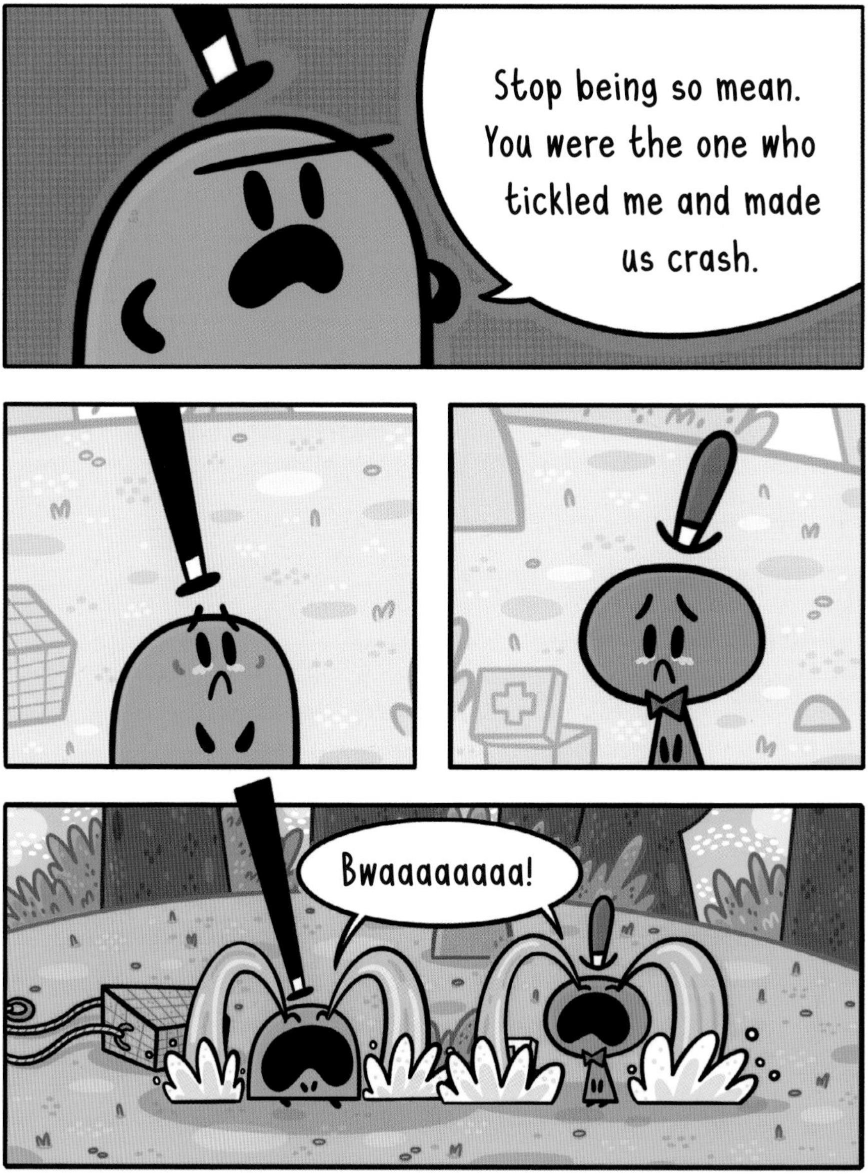
Stop being so mean. You were the one who tickled me and made us crash.
Bwaaaaaaaa!

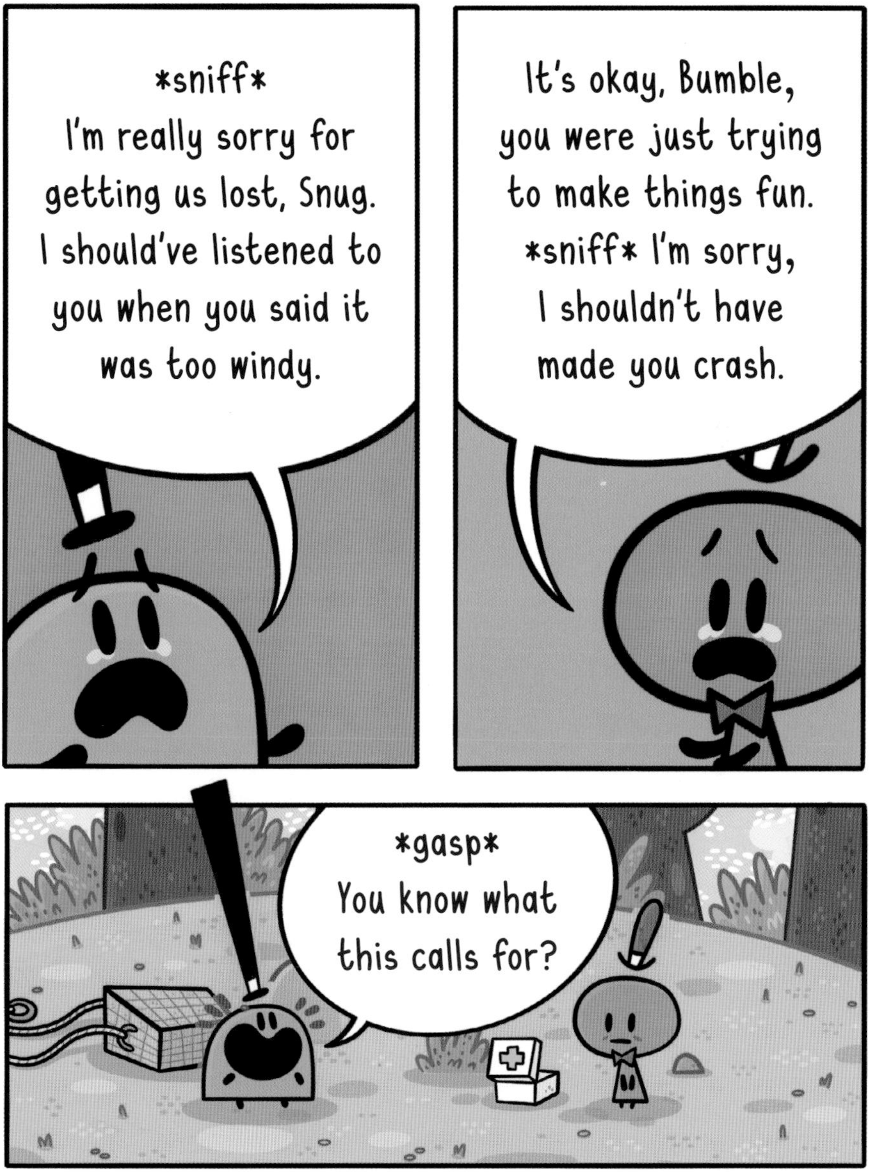
sniff
I'm really sorry for getting us lost, Snug. I should've listened to you when you said it was too windy.
It's okay, Bumble, you were just trying to make things fun. *sniff* I'm sorry, I shouldn't have made you crash.
gasp
You know what this calls for?

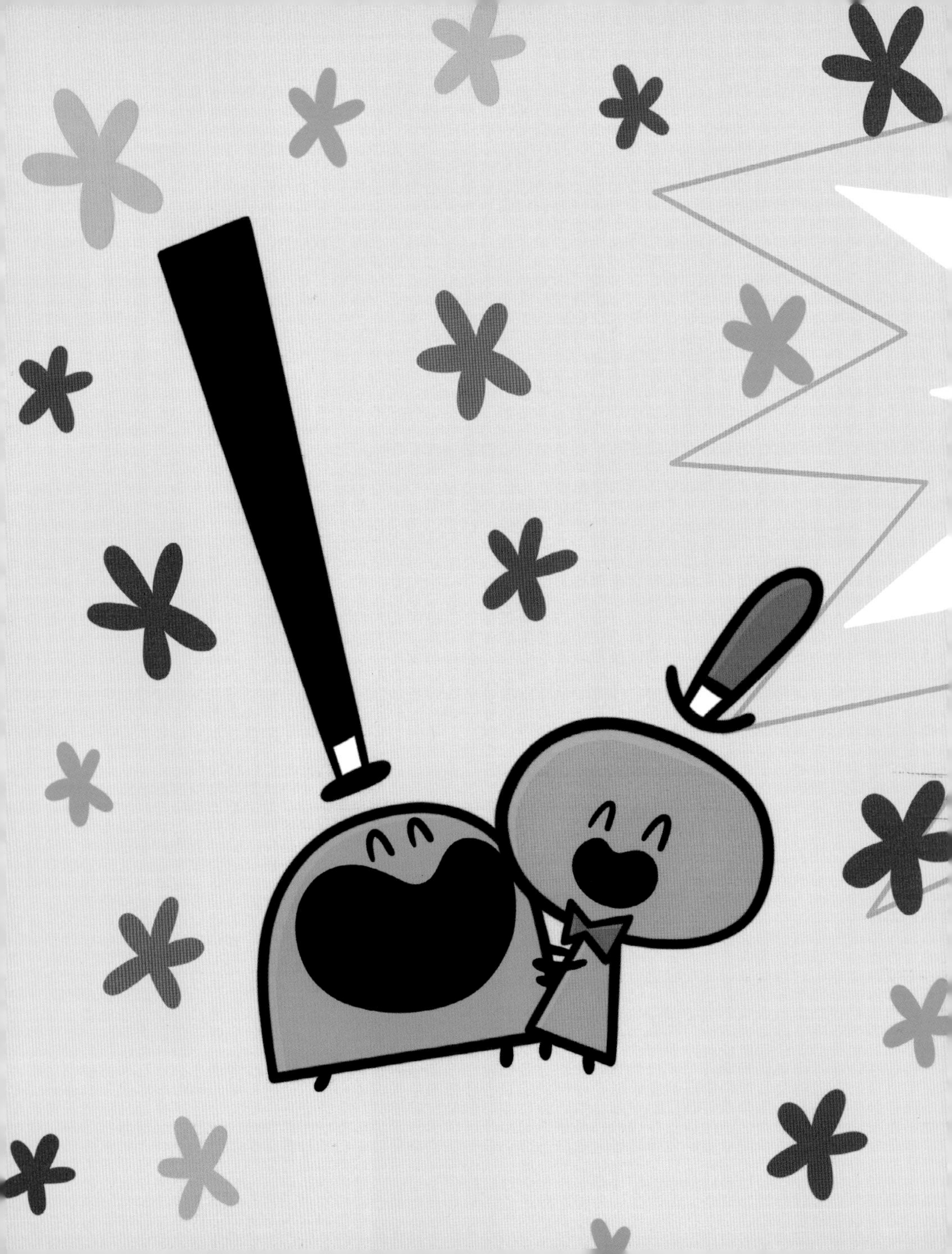

BEST FRIENDS MEGA-HUG!

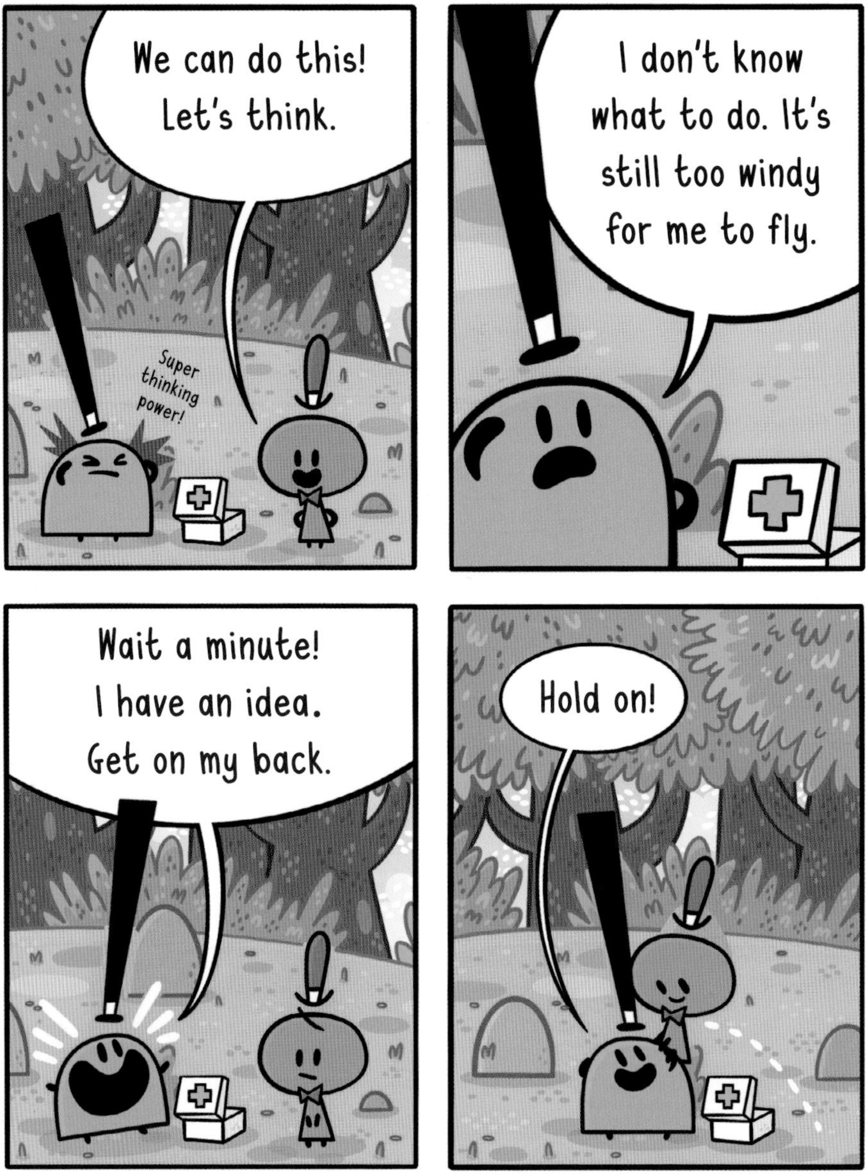
We can do this! Let's think.
Super thinking power!
I don't know what to do. It's still too windy for me to fly.
Wait a minute! I have an idea. Get on my back.
Hold on!

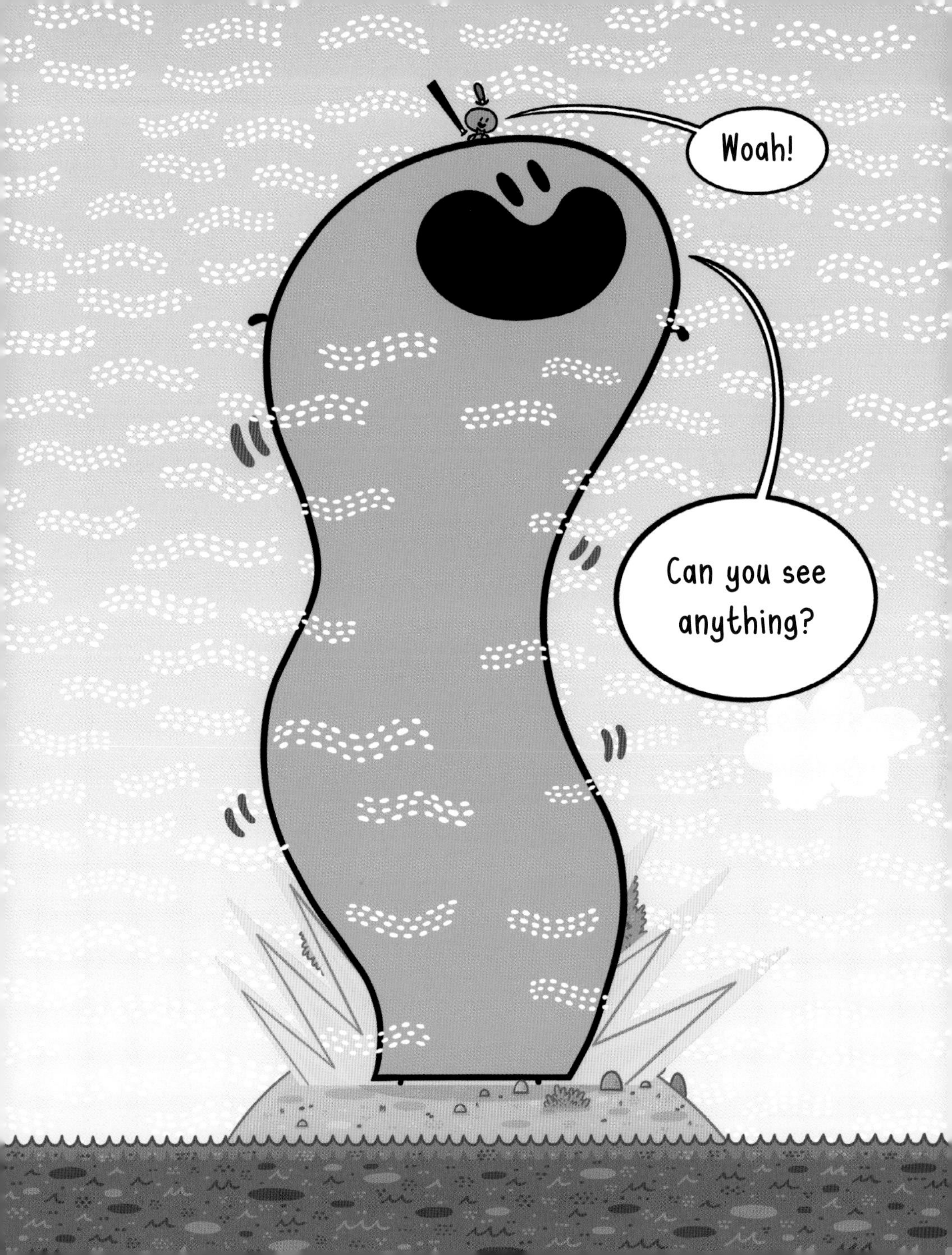
Woah!
Can you see anything?

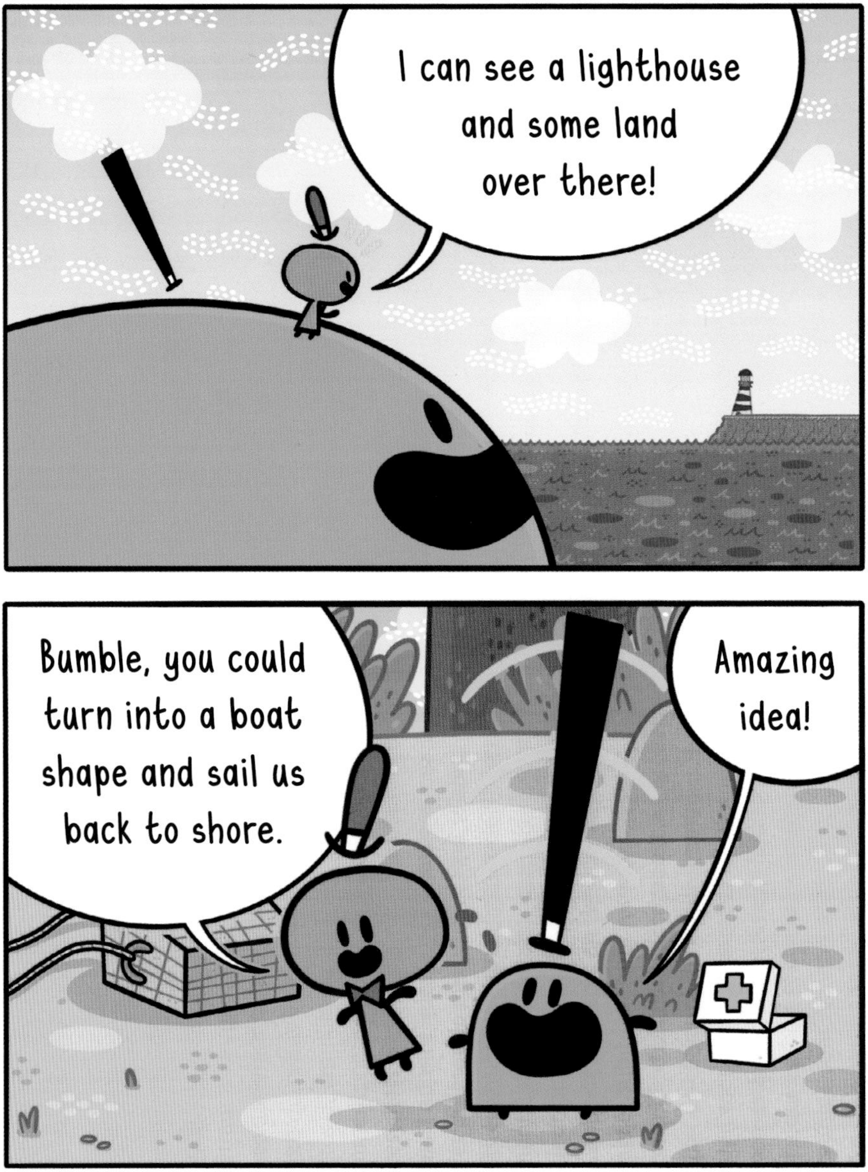
I can see a lighthouse and some land over there!
Bumble, you could turn into a boat shape and sail us back to shore.
Amazing idea!

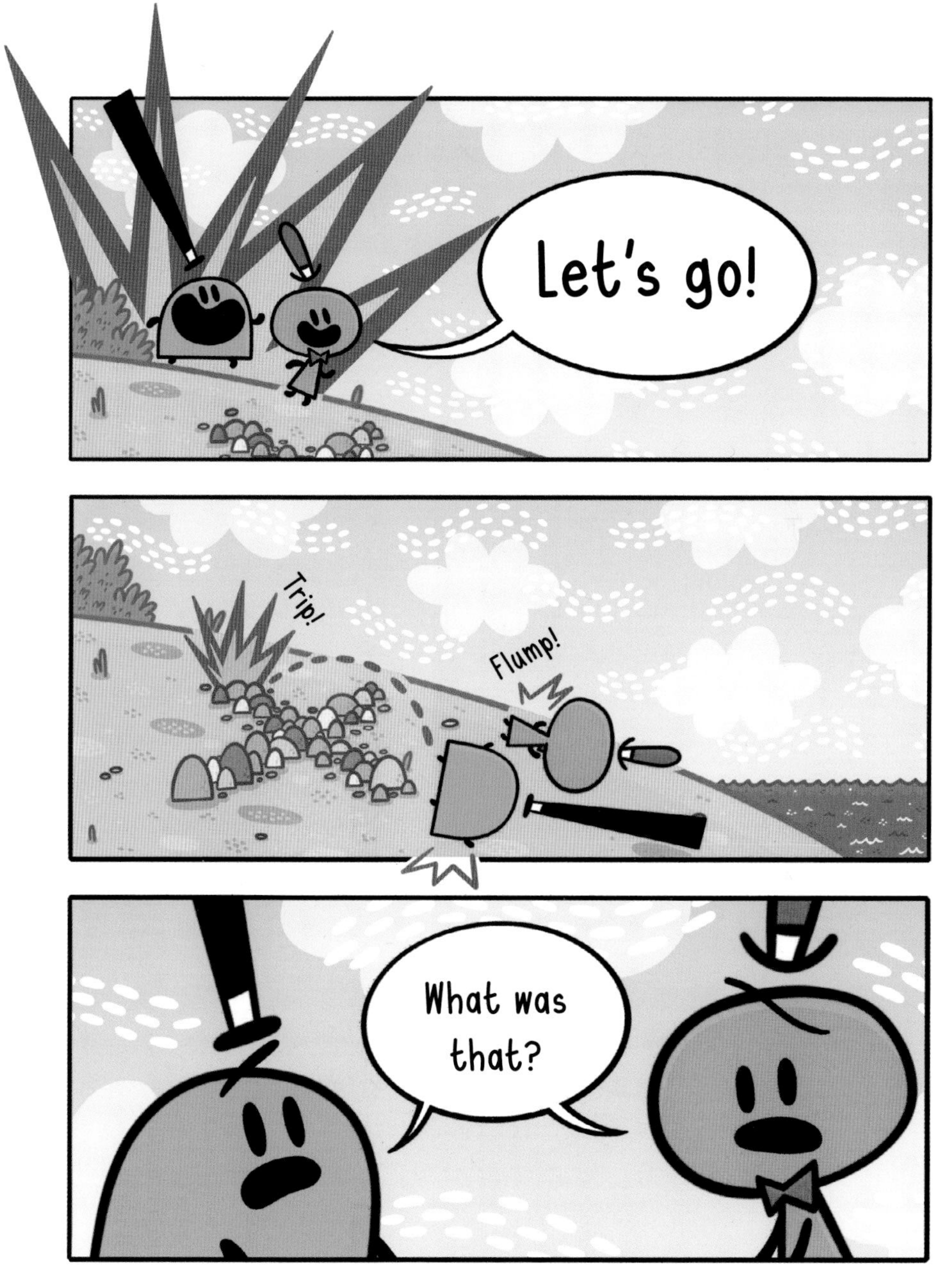
Let's go!
Trip!
Flump!
What was that?

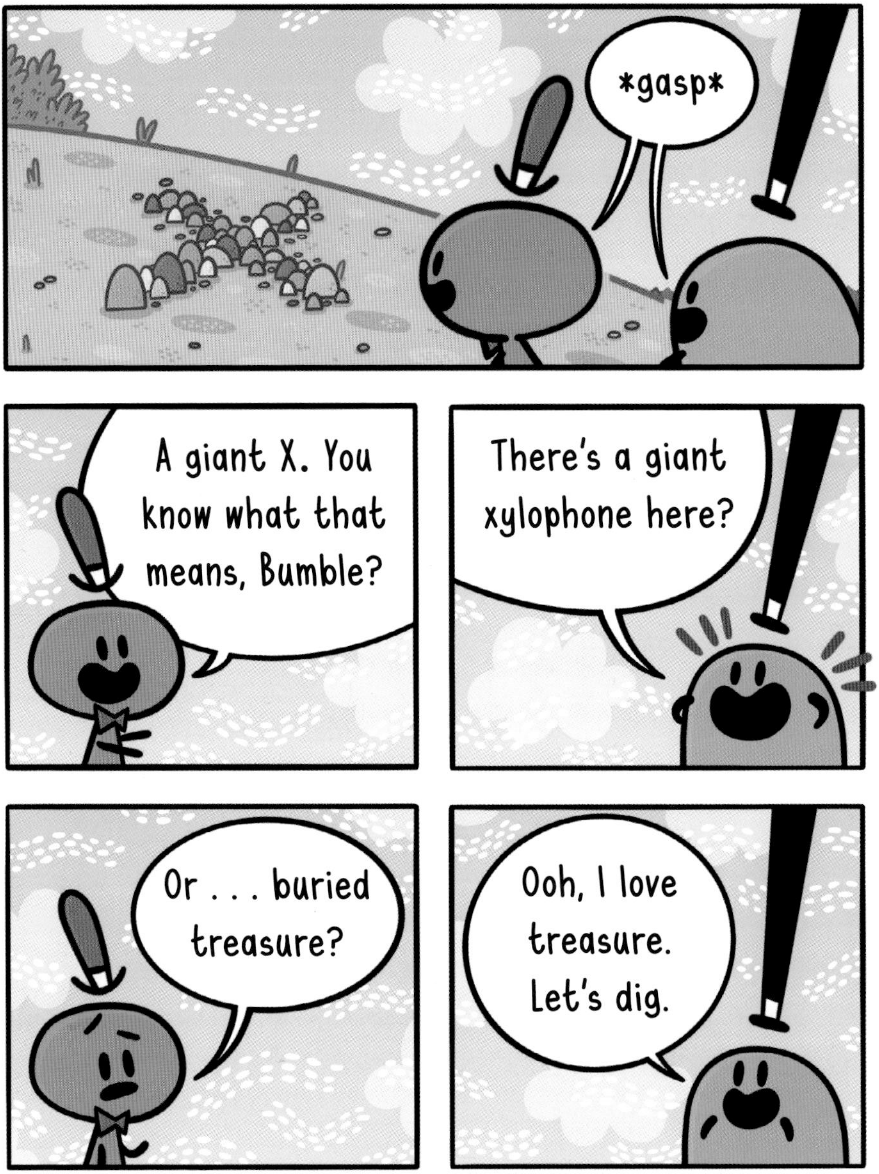
gasp
A giant X. You know what that means, Bumble?
There's a giant xylophone here?
Or . . . buried treasure?
Ooh, I love treasure. Let's dig.

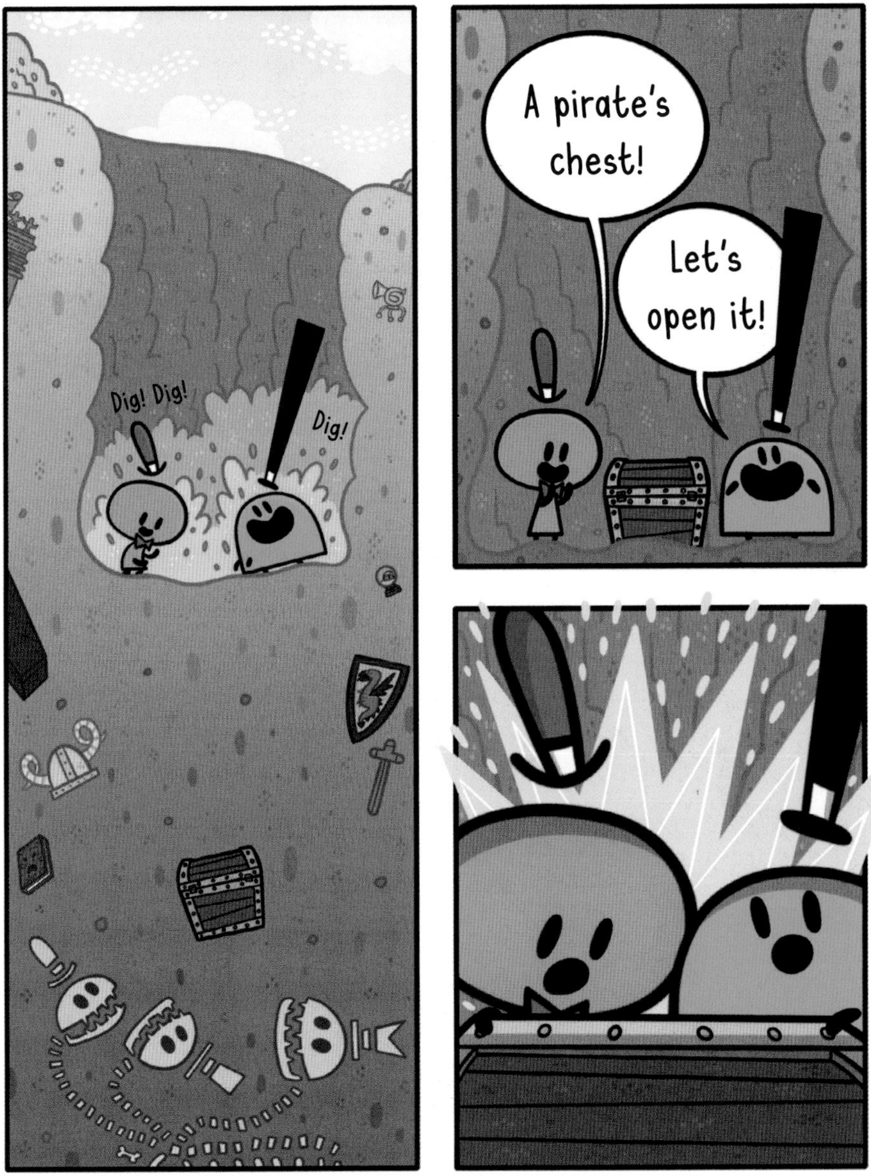
Dig! Dig!
Dig!
A pirate's chest!
Let's open it!

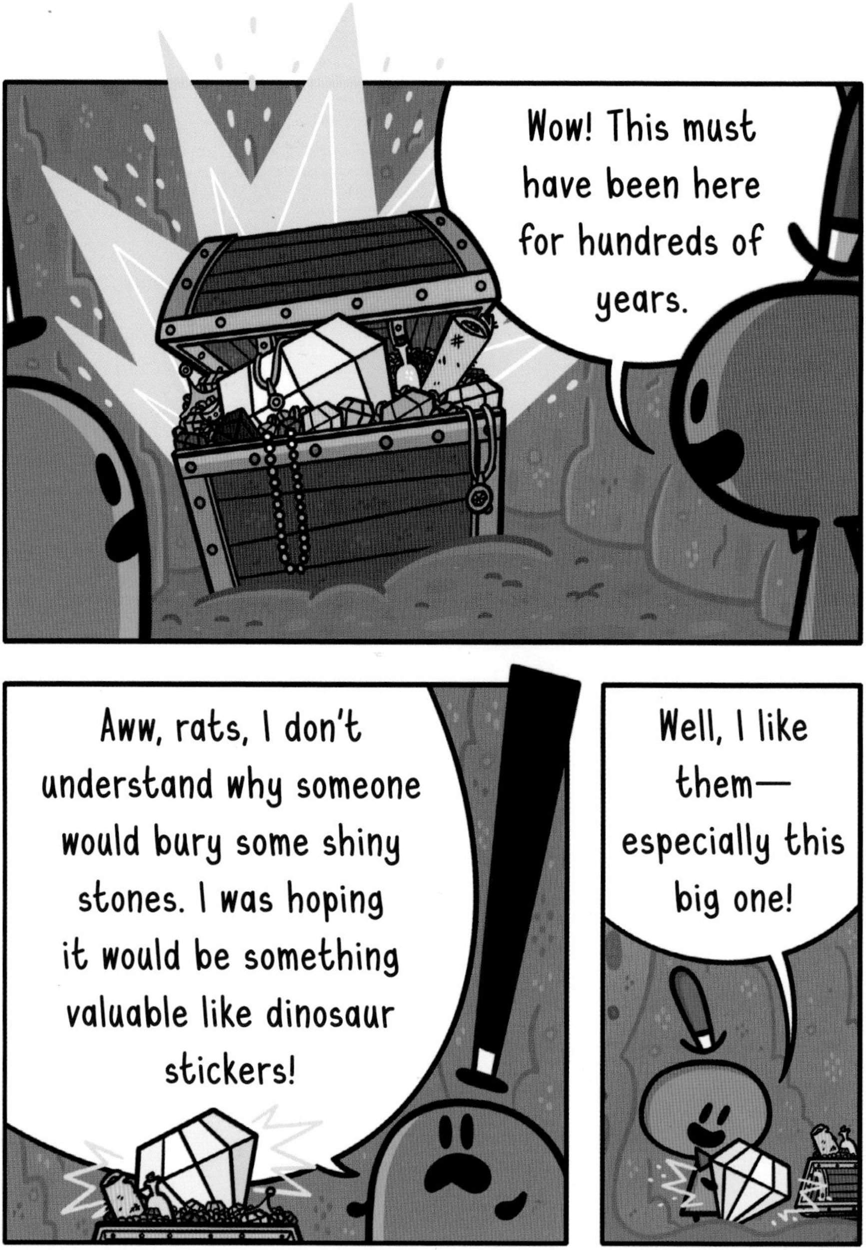
Wow! This must have been here for hundreds of years.
Aww, rats, I don't understand why someone would bury some shiny stones. I was hoping it would be something valuable like dinosaur stickers!
Well, I like them—especially this big one!

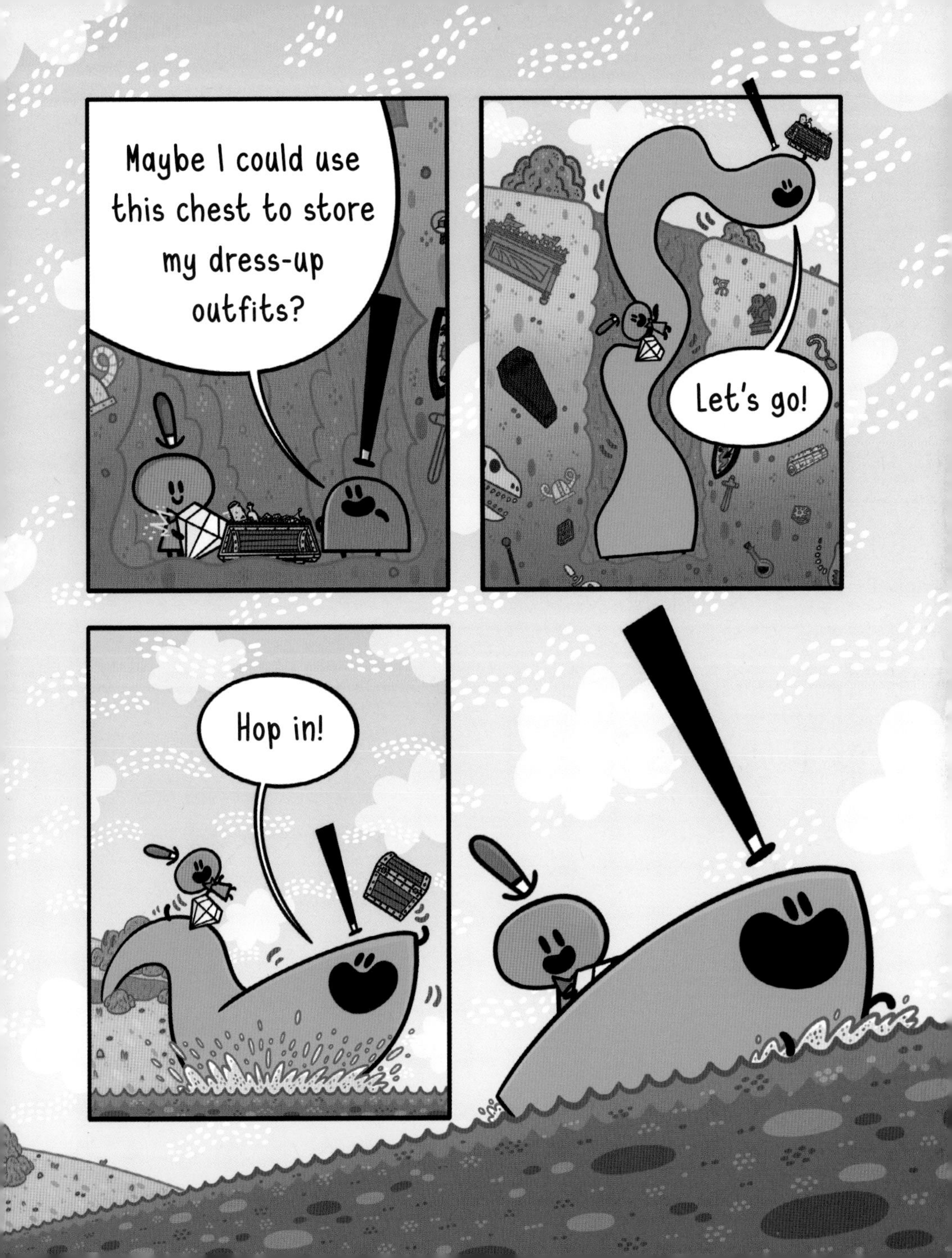
Maybe I could use this chest to store my dress-up outfits?
Let's go!
Hop in!

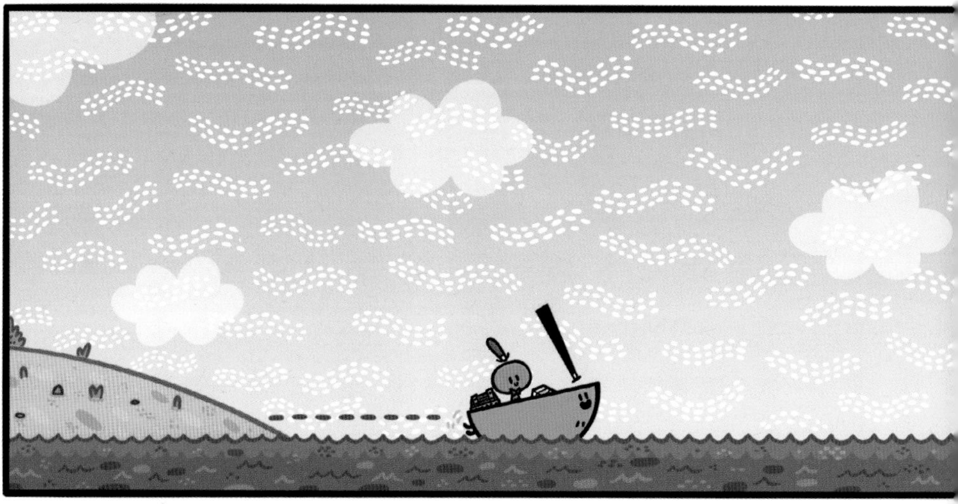

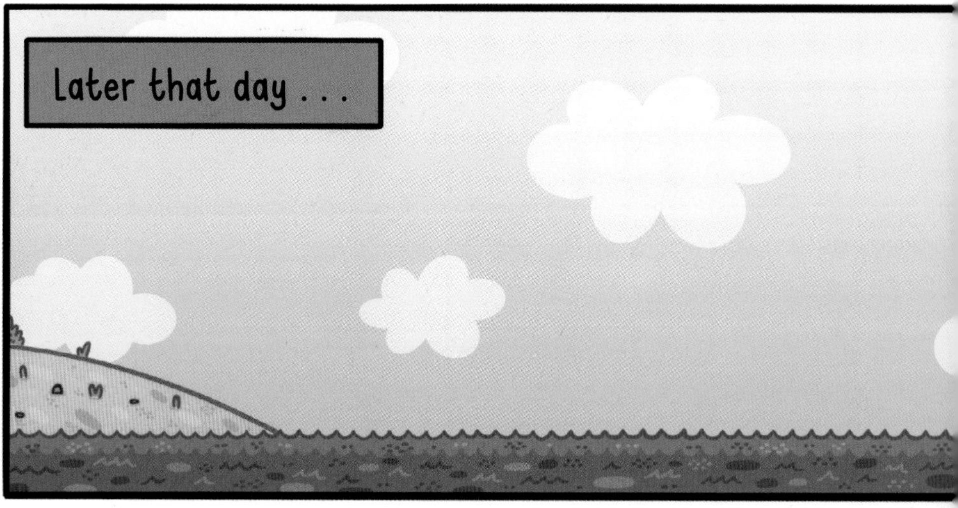
Later that day . . .

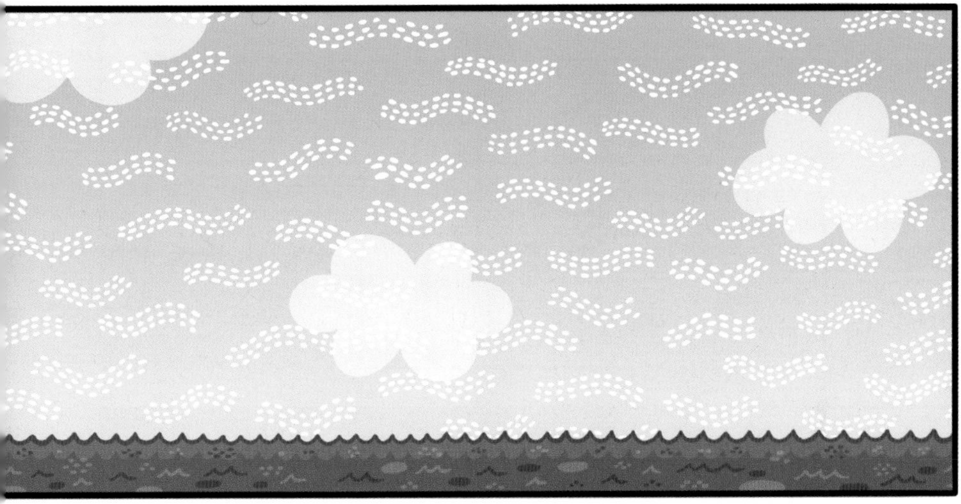

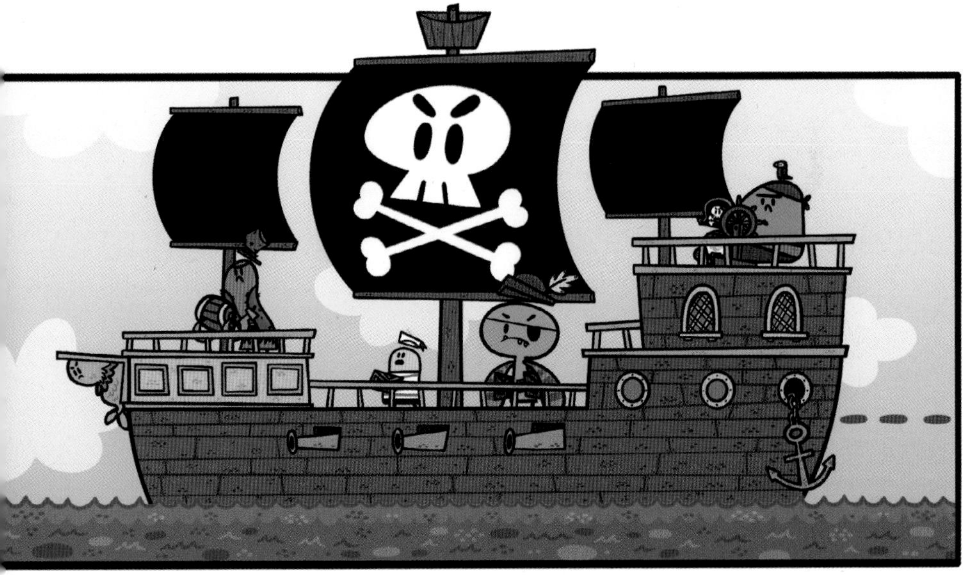

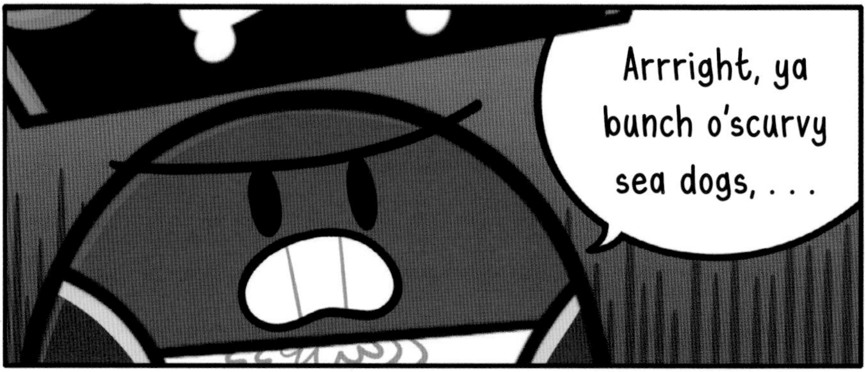
Arrright, ya bunch o'scurvy sea dogs, . . .

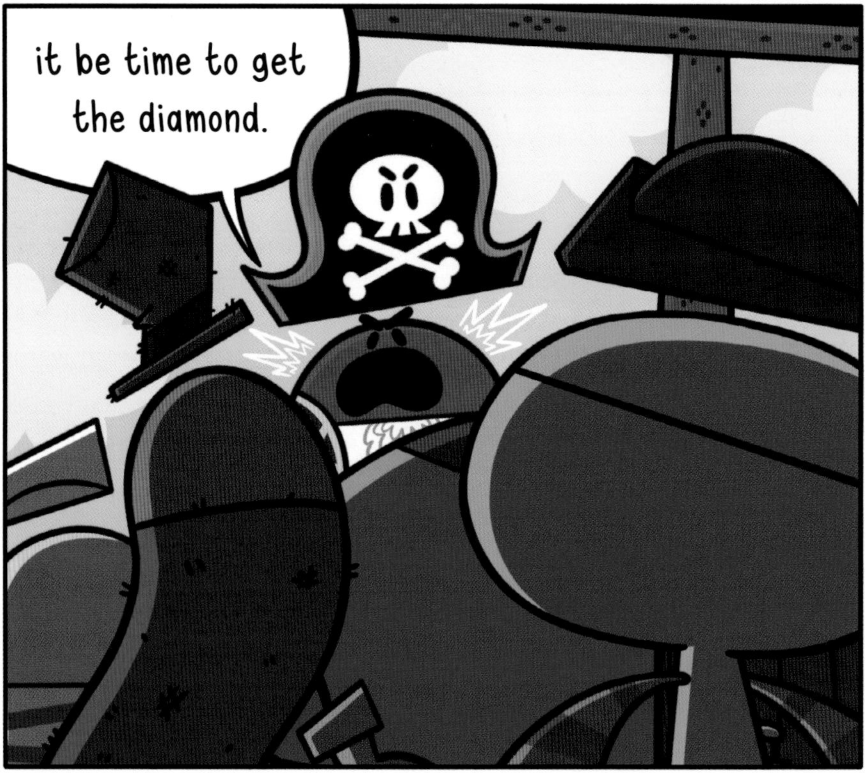
it be time to get the diamond.

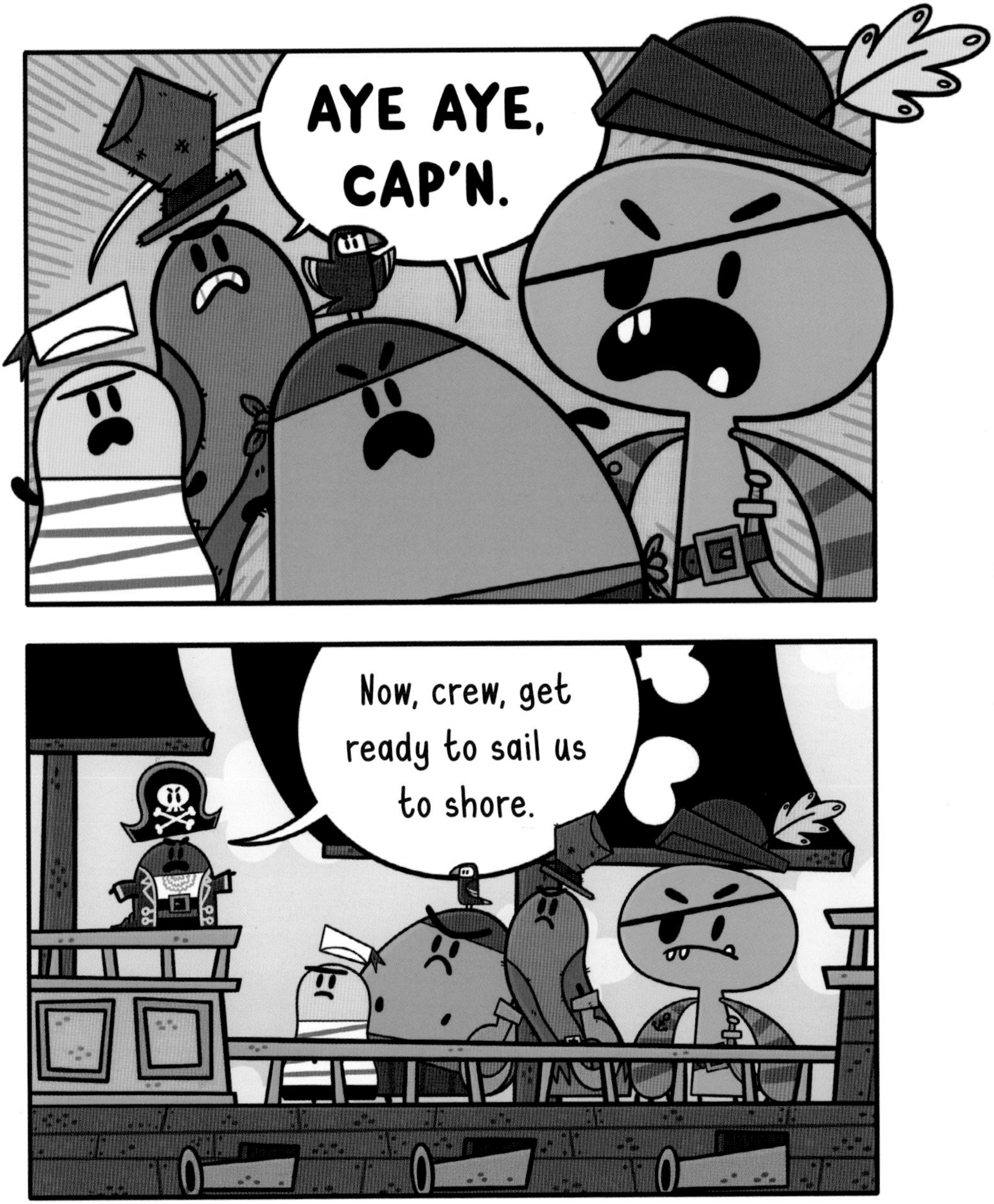
AYE AYE, CAP'N.
Now, crew, get ready to sail us to shore.

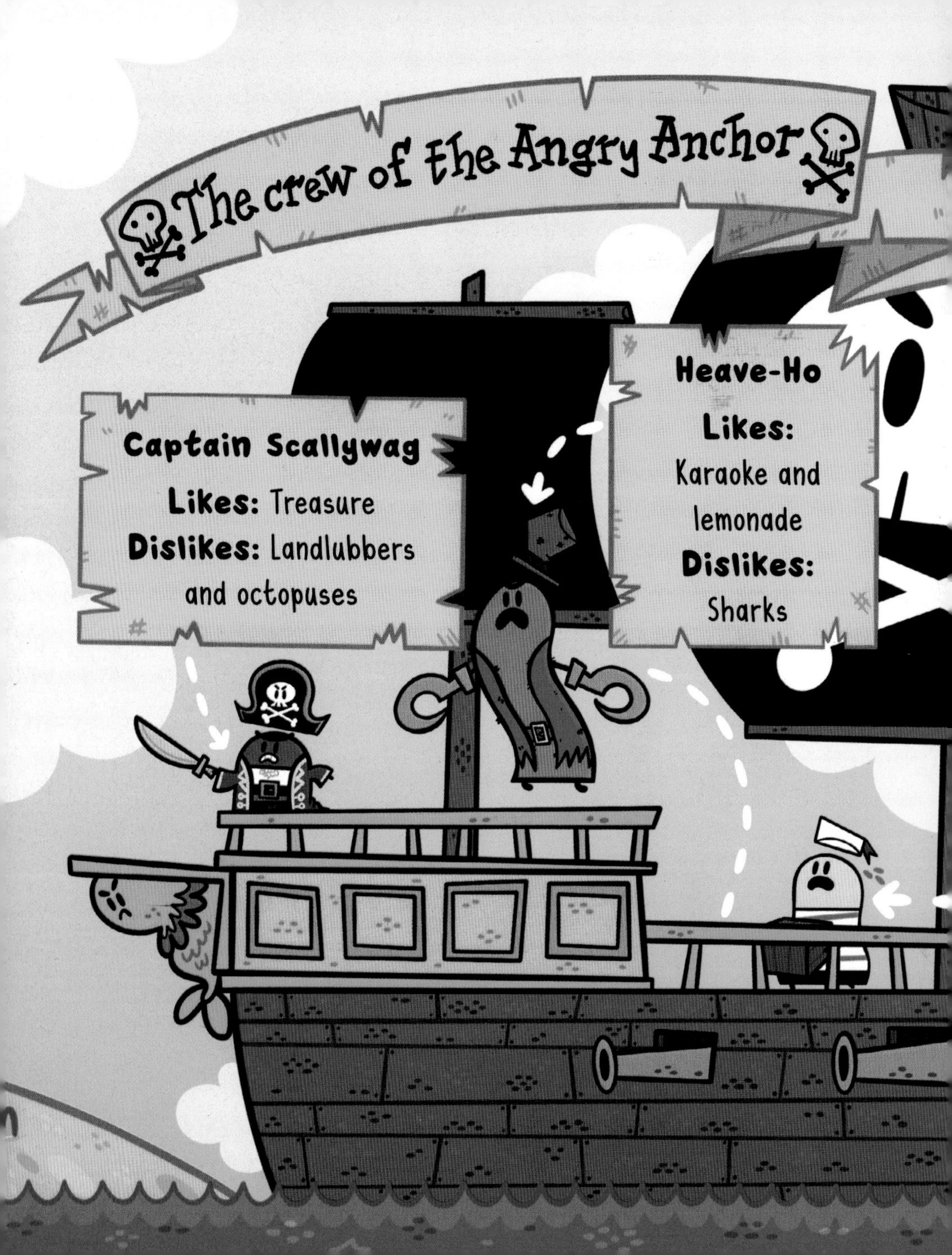

The crew of the Angry Anchor
Captain Scallywag
Likes: Treasure
Dislikes: Landlubbers and octopuses
Heave-Ho
Likes: Karaoke and lemonade
Dislikes: Sharks

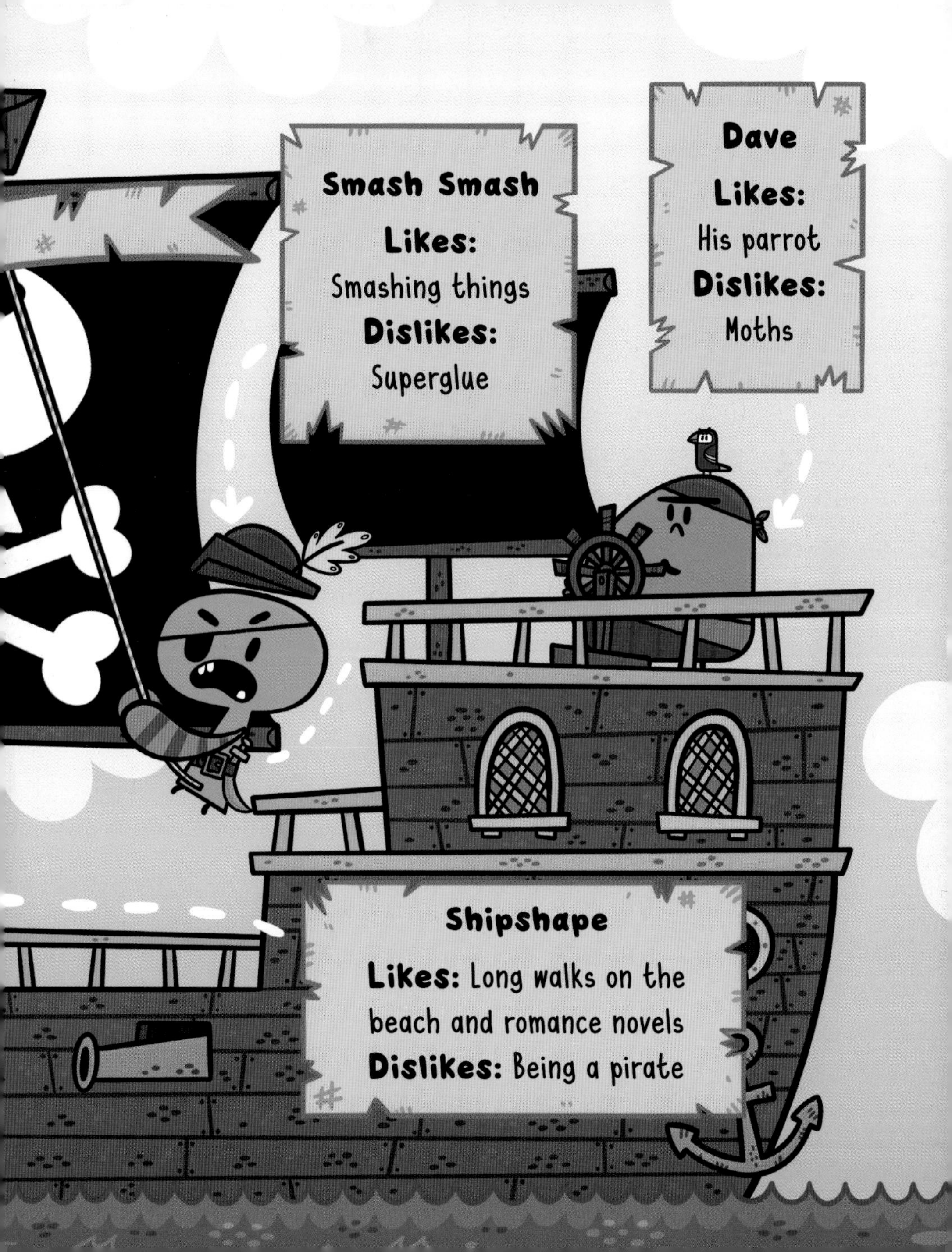
Smash Smash
Likes:
Smashing things
Dislikes:
Superglue
Dave
Likes:
His parrot
Dislikes:
Moths
Shipshape
Likes: Long walks on the beach and romance novels
Dislikes: Being a pirate

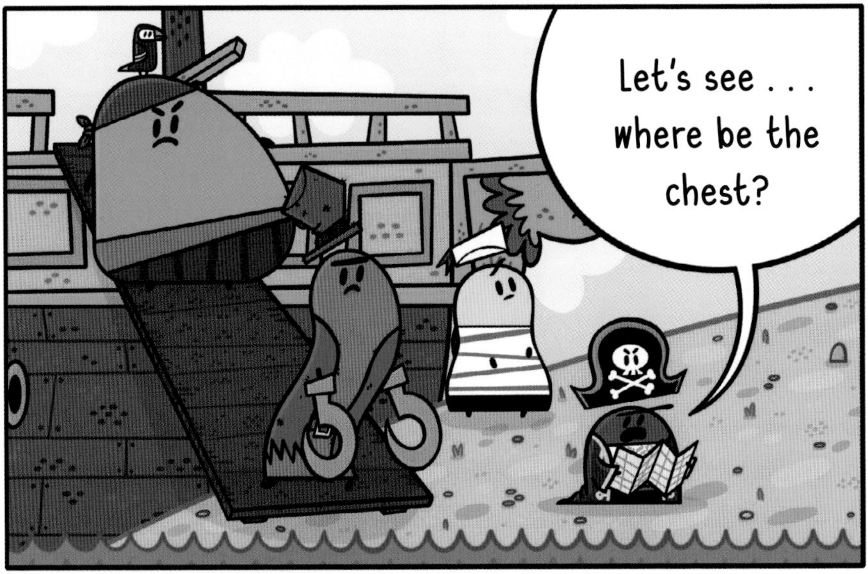
Let's see . . .
where be the
chest?

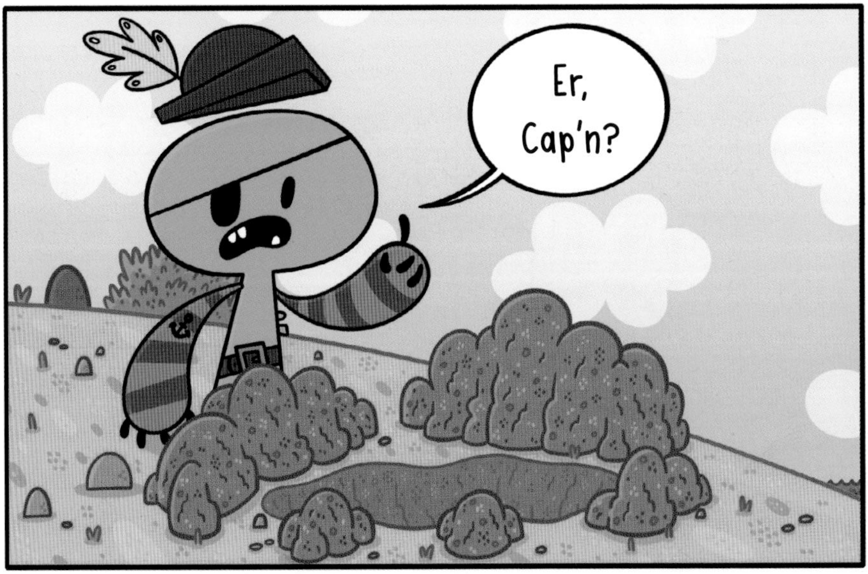
Er,
Cap'n?

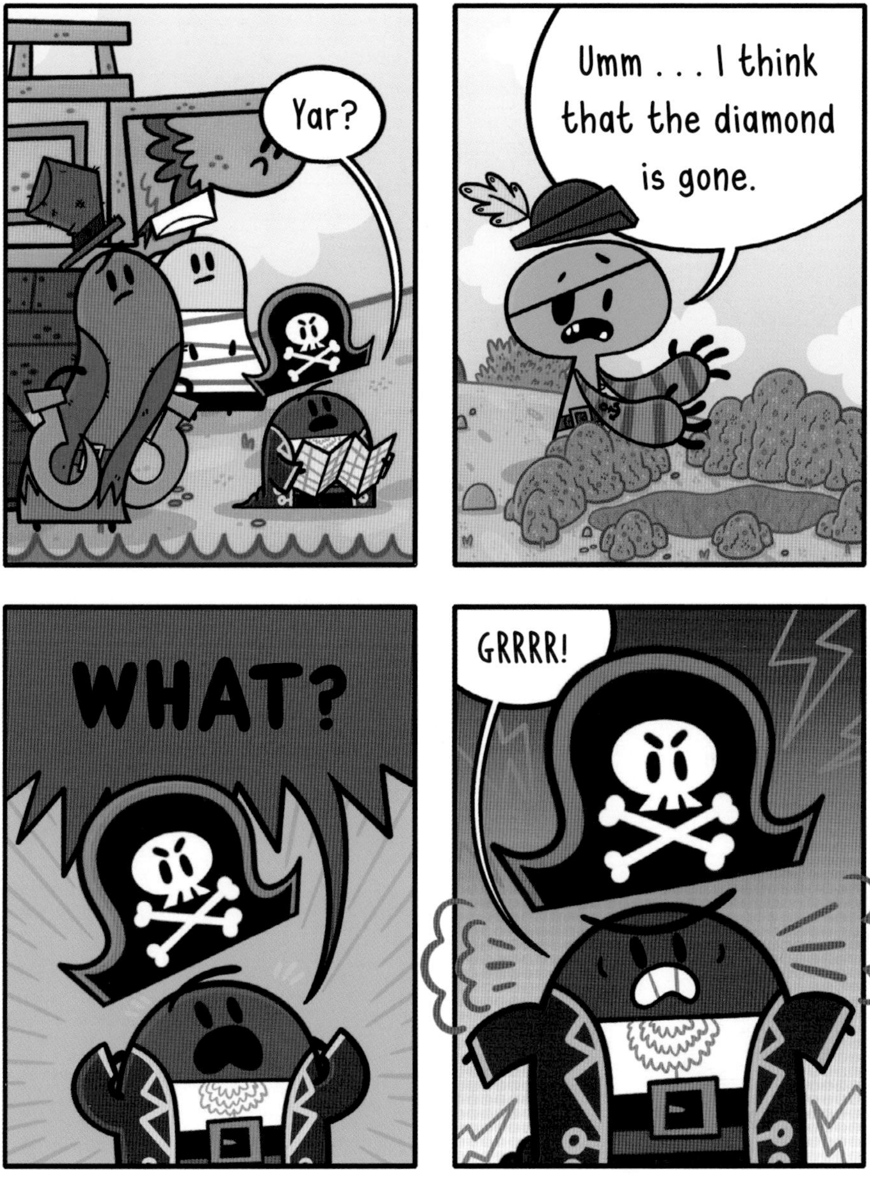
Yar?
Umm . . . I think that the diamond is gone.
WHAT?
GRRRR!

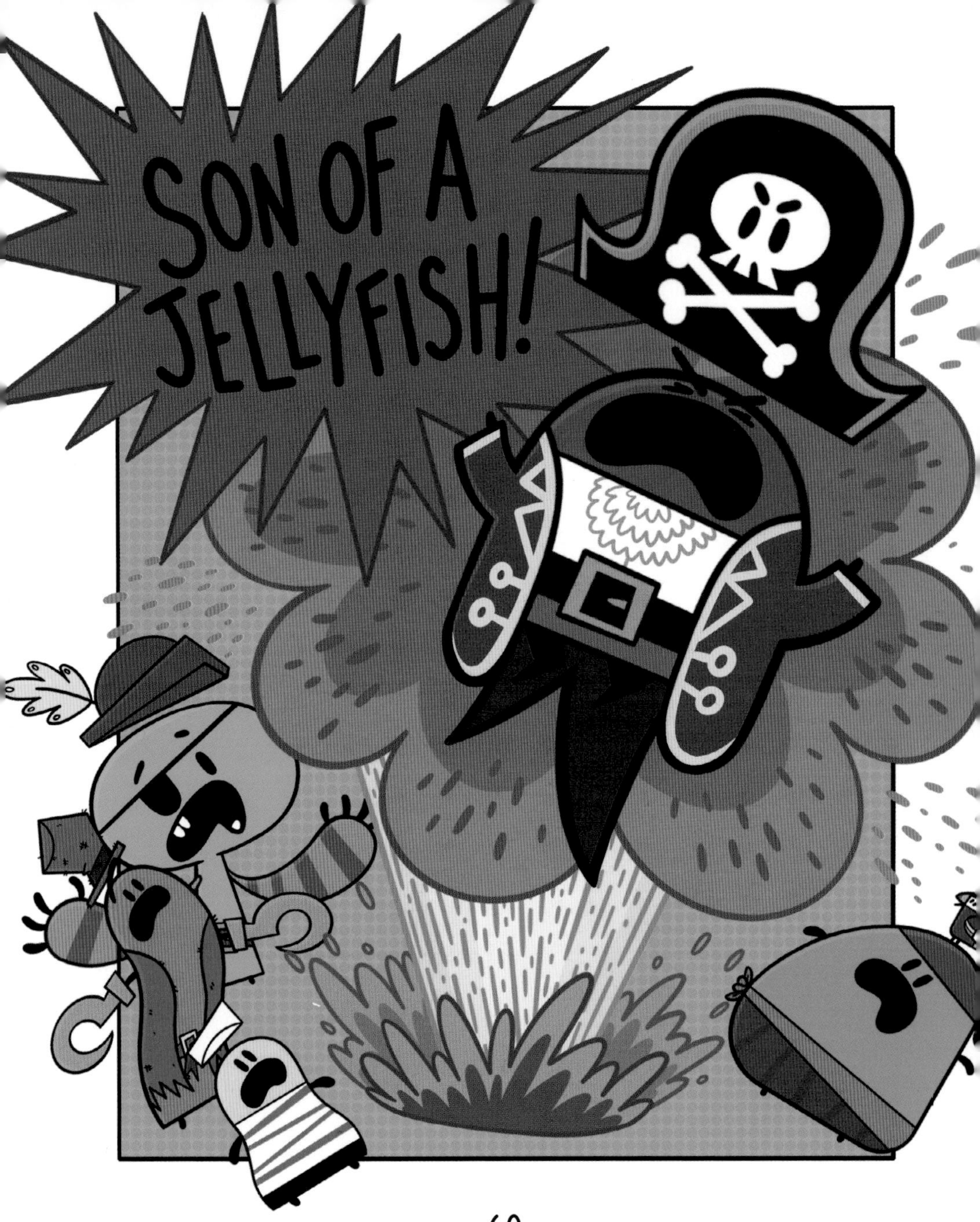
SON OF A JELLYFISH!

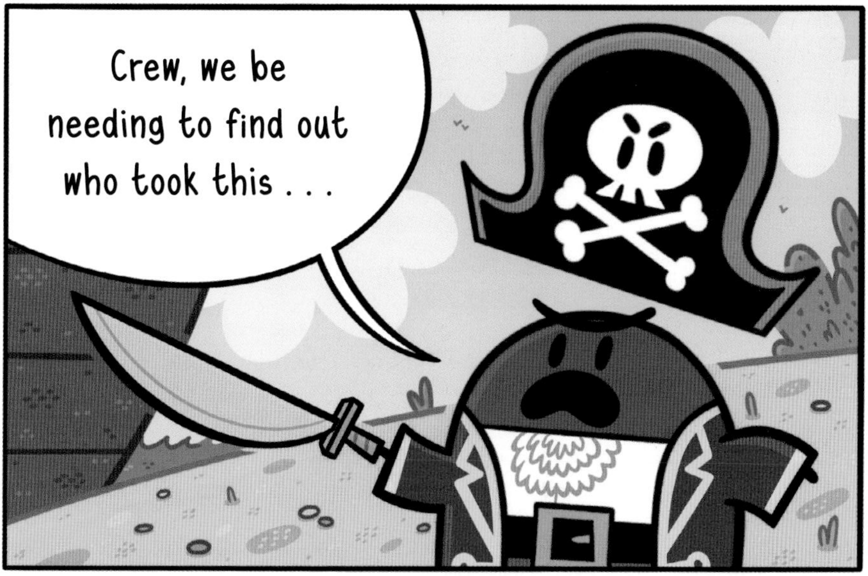
Crew, we be needing to find out who took this . . .

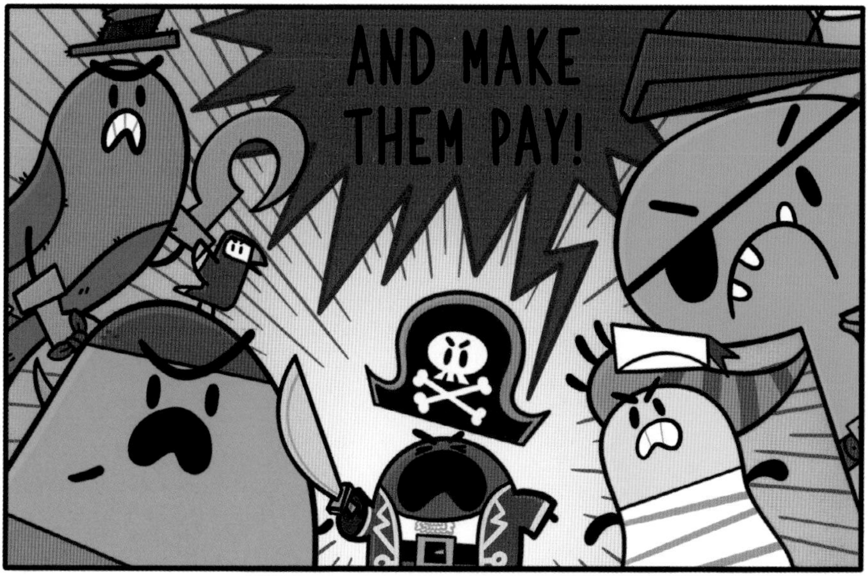
AND MAKE THEM PAY!

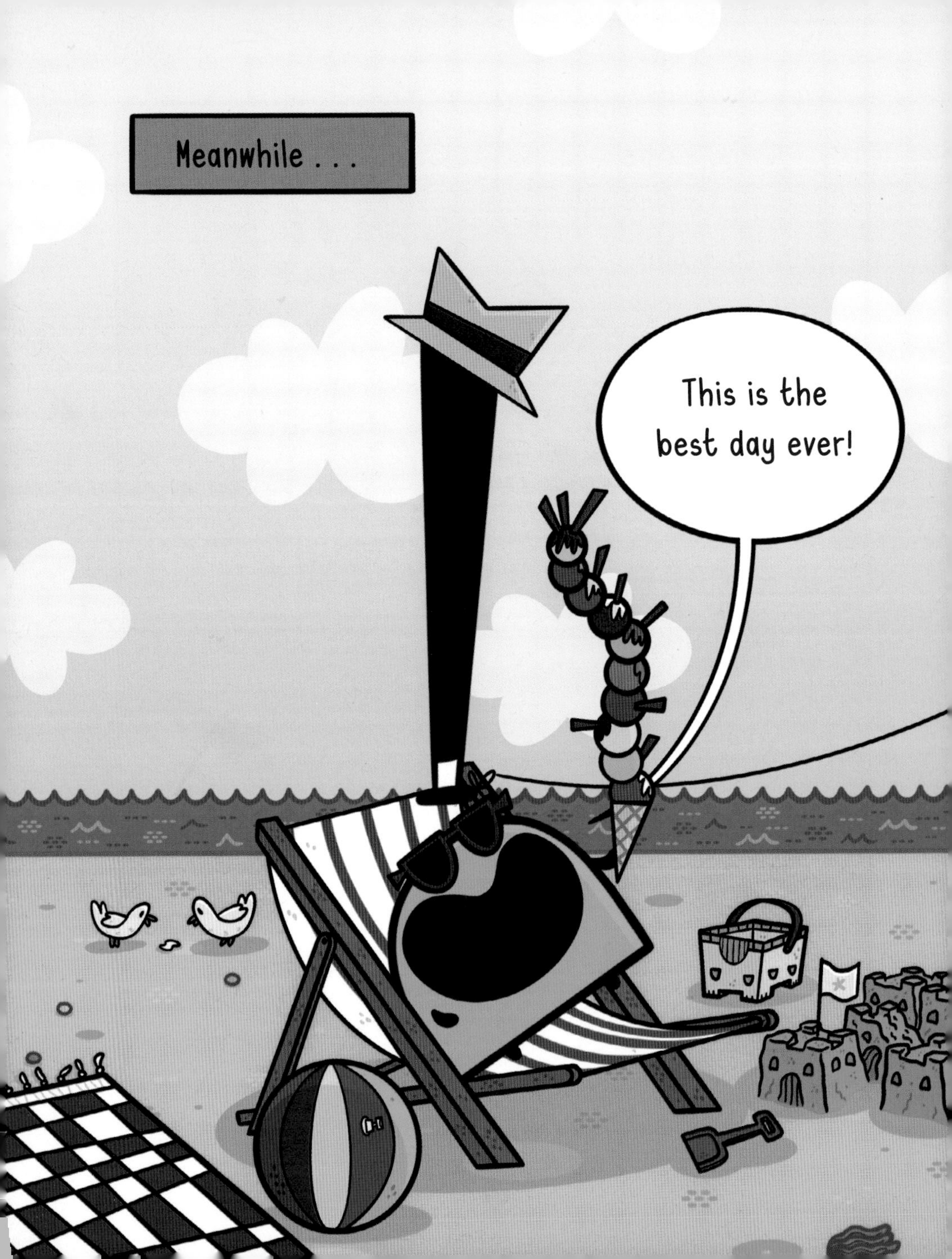
Meanwhile . . .
This is the best day ever!

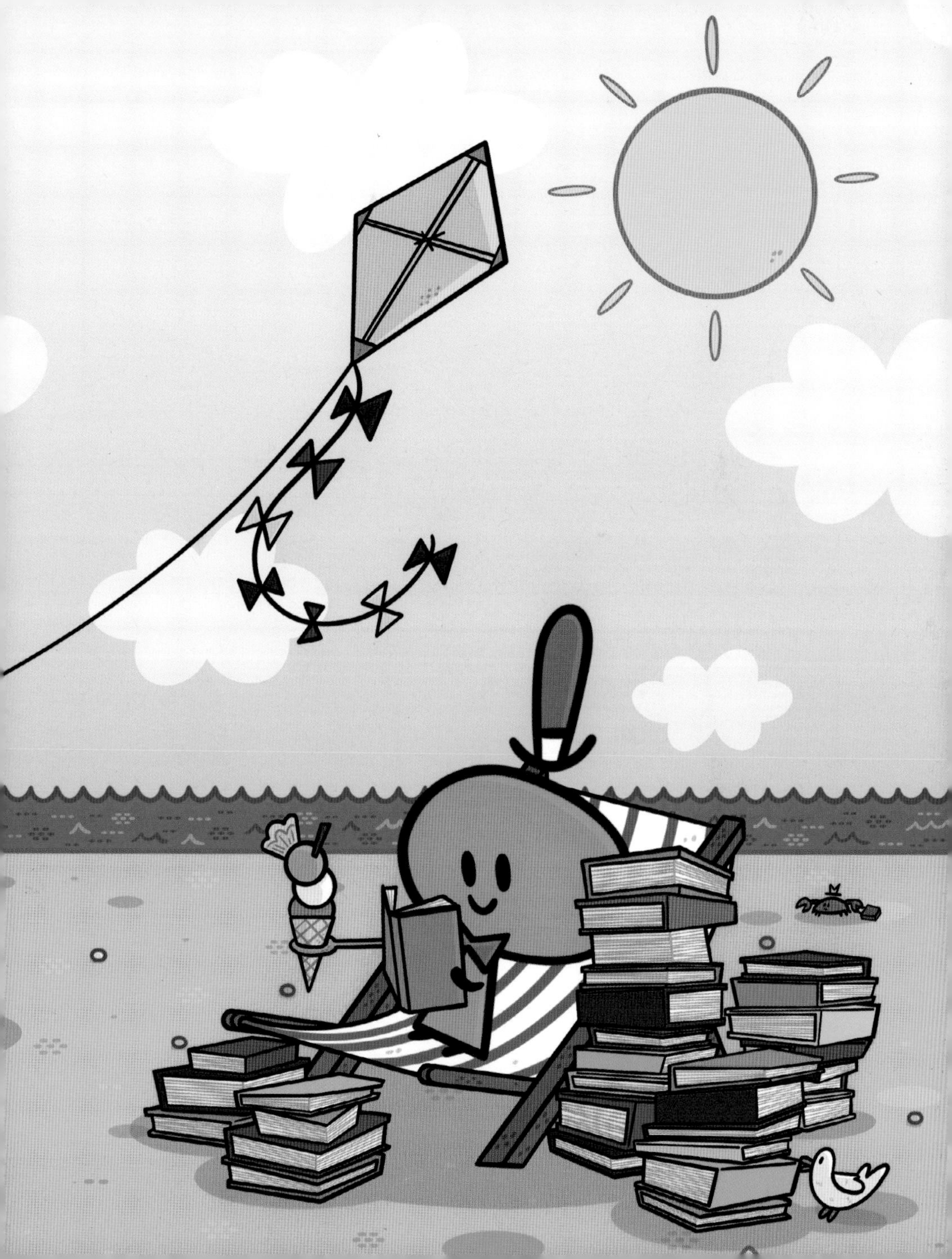

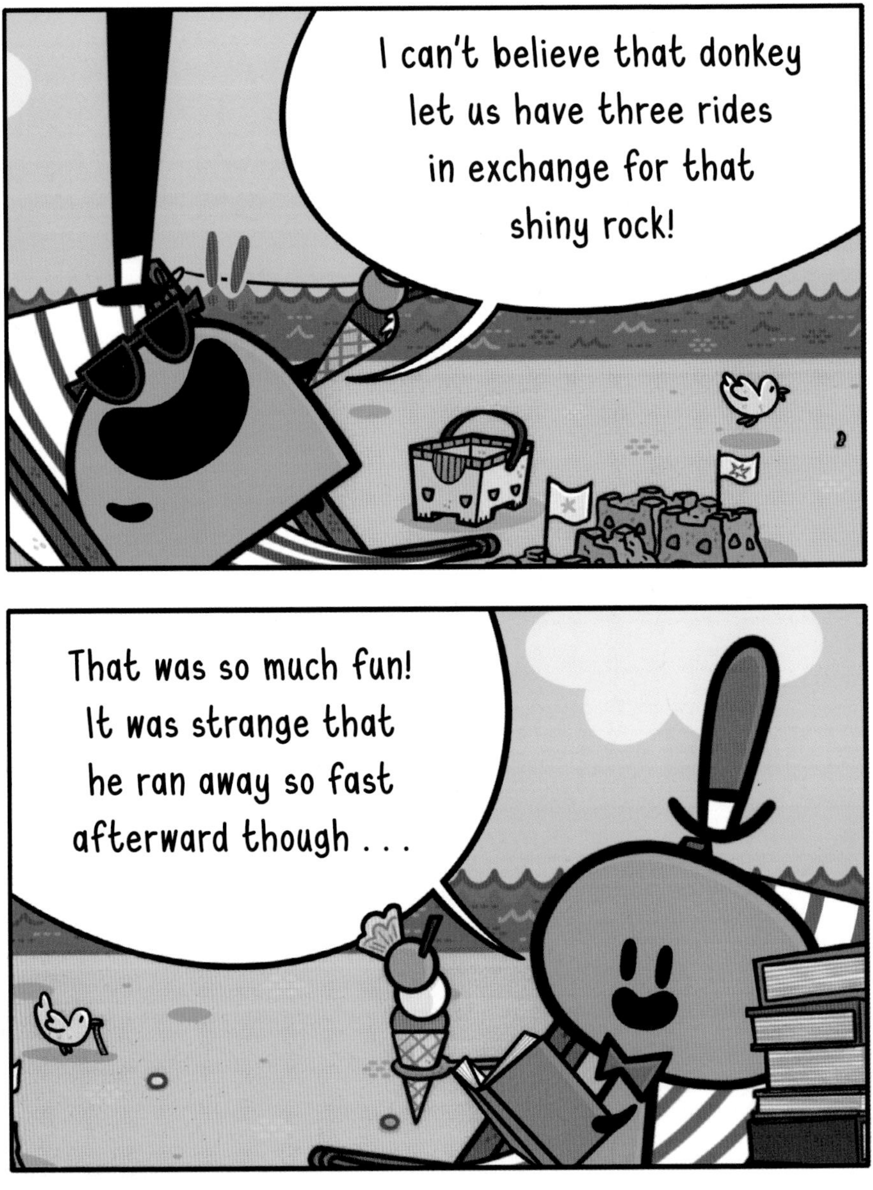
I can't believe that donkey let us have three rides in exchange for that shiny rock!
That was so much fun! It was strange that he ran away so fast afterward though . . .

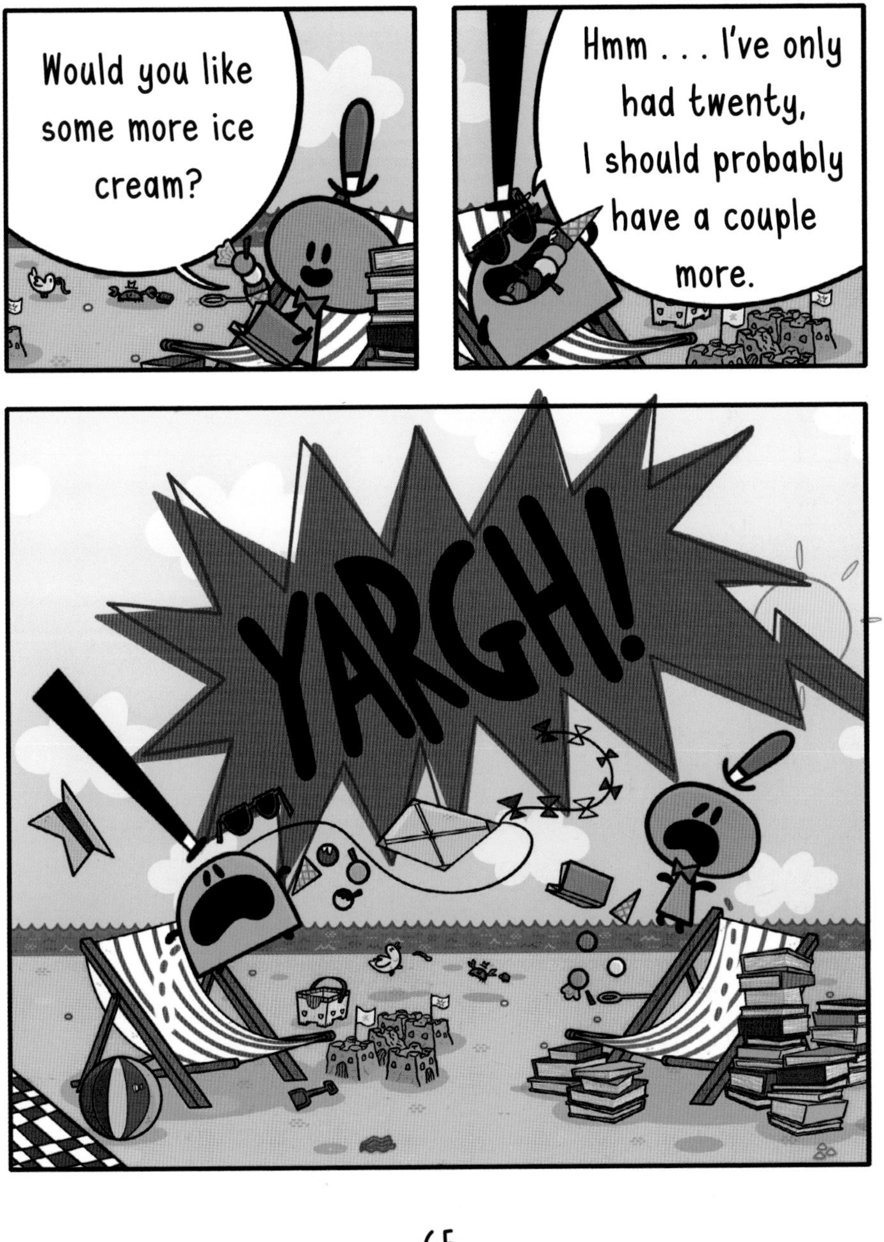
Would you like some more ice cream?
Hmm . . . I've only had twenty, I should probably have a couple more.
YARGH!

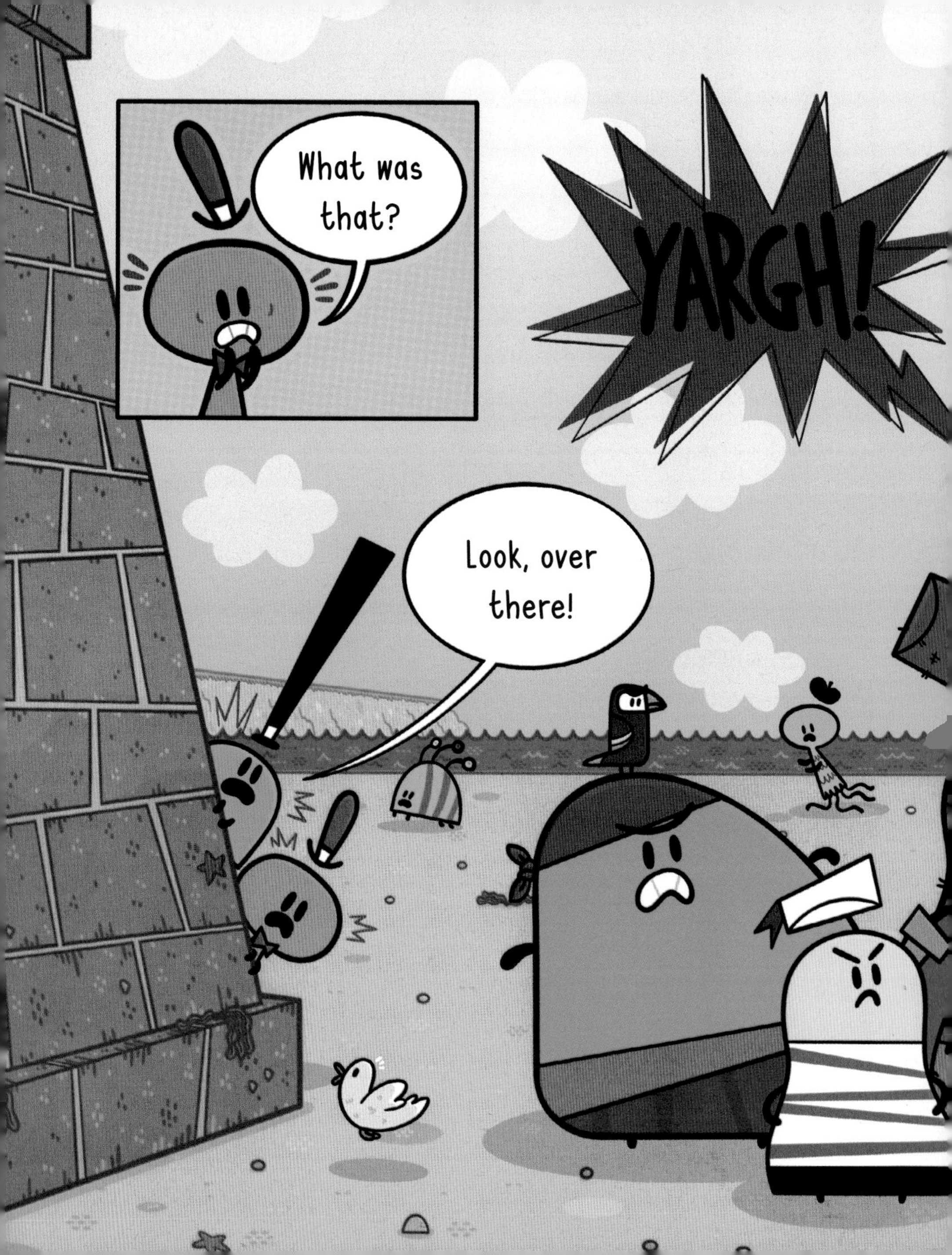
What was that?
YARGH!
Look, over there!

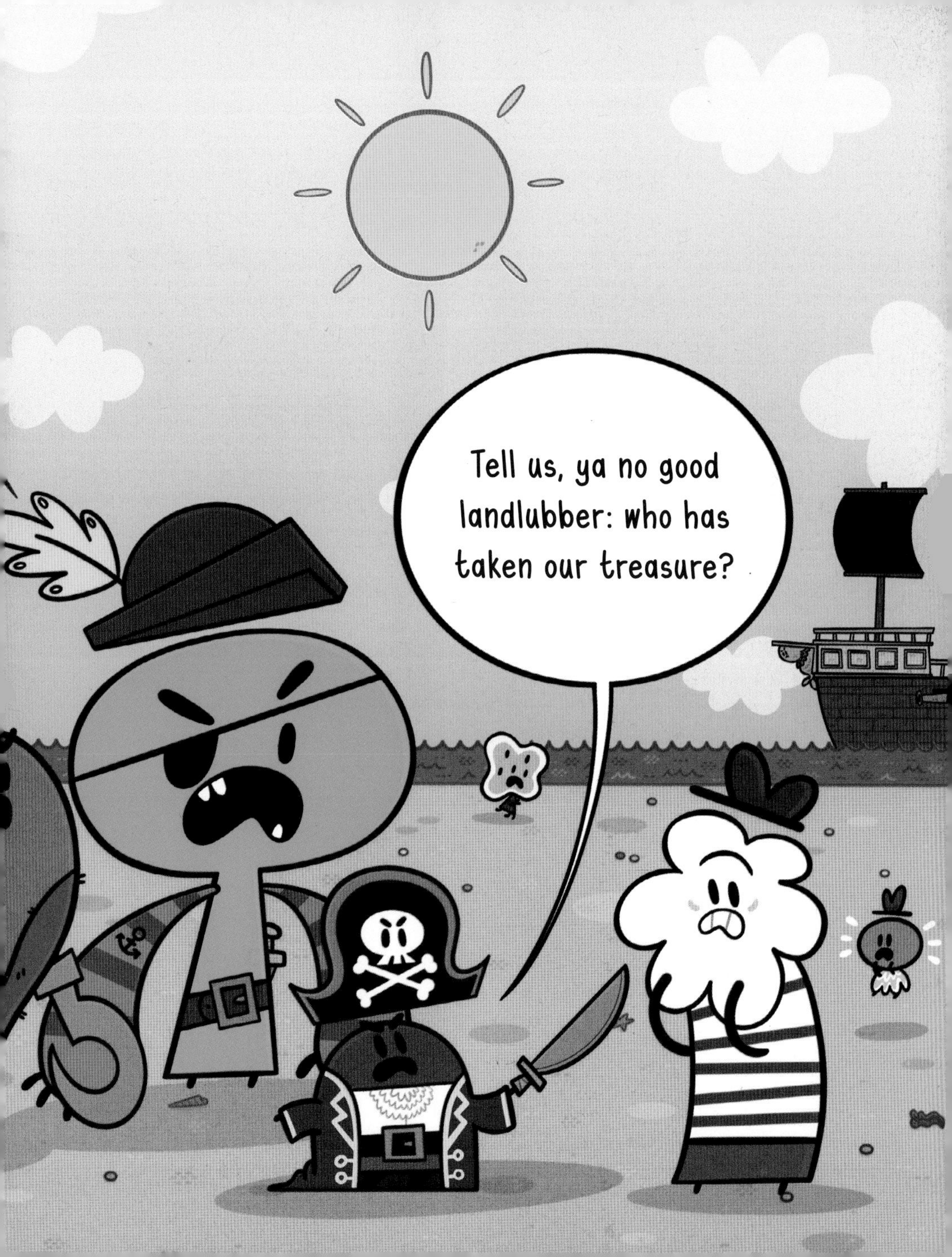
Tell us, ya no good landlubber: who has taken our treasure?

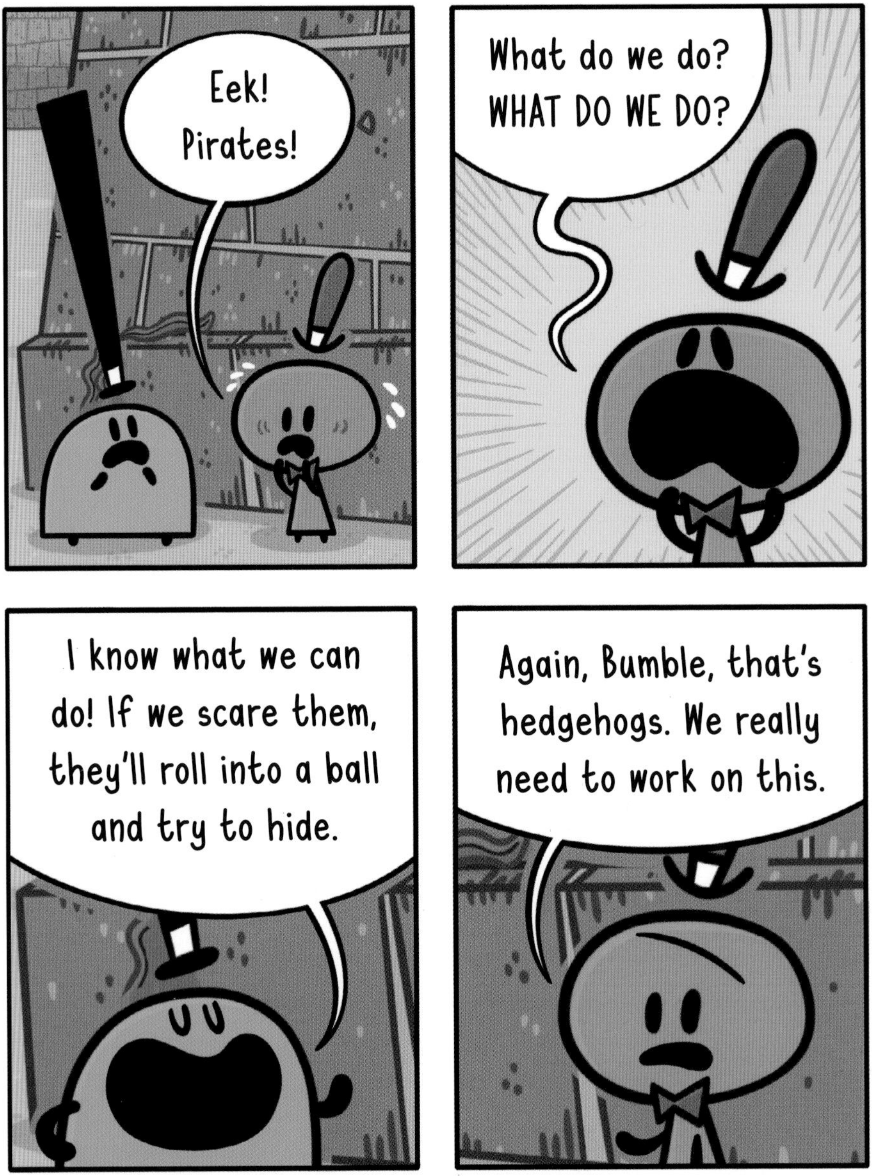
Eek! Pirates!
What do we do? WHAT DO WE DO?
I know what we can do! If we scare them, they'll roll into a ball and try to hide.
Again, Bumble, that's hedgehogs. We really need to work on this.

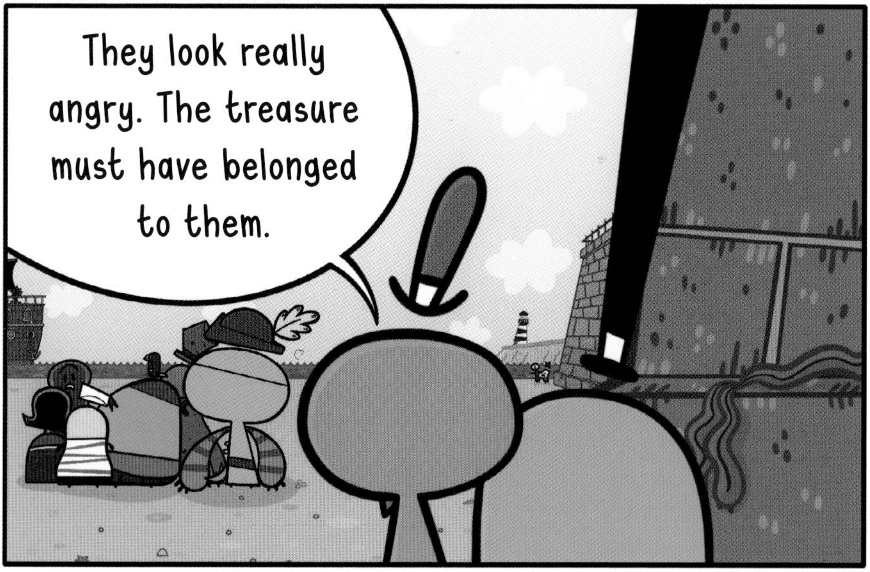
They look really angry. The treasure must have belonged to them.

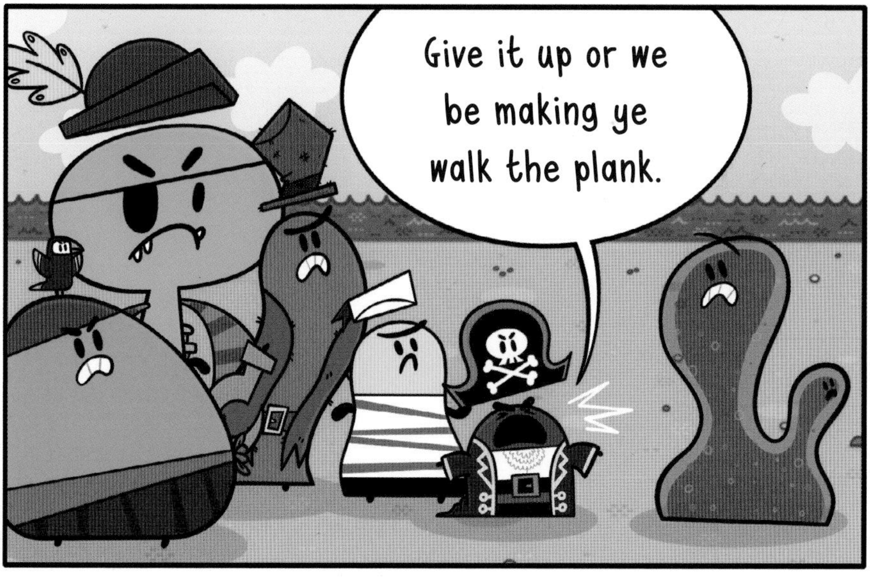
Give it up or we be making ye walk the plank.

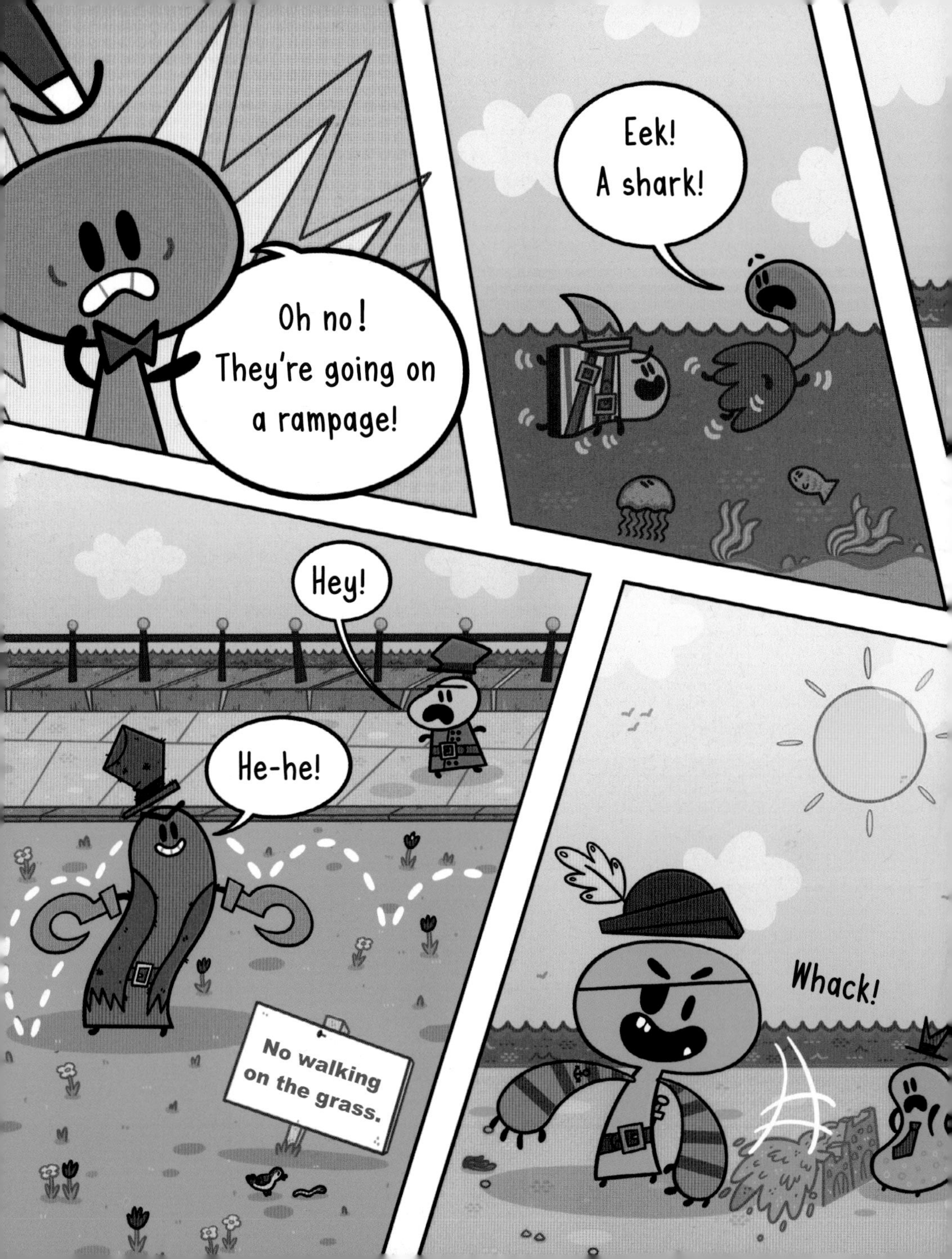
Oh no! They're going on a rampage!
Eek! A shark!
Hey!
He-he!
No walking on the grass.
Whack!

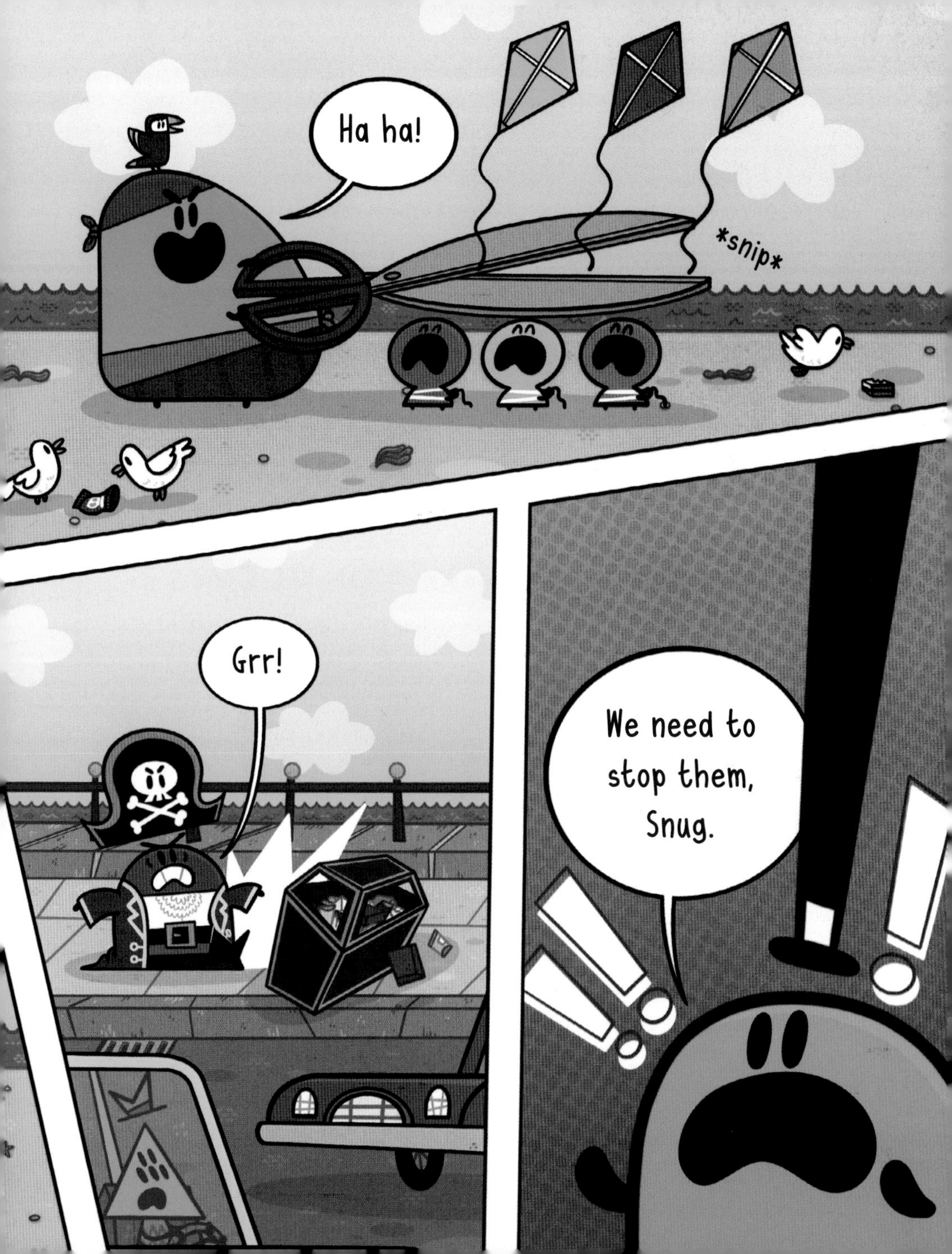
Ha ha!
snip
Grr!
We need to stop them, Snug.

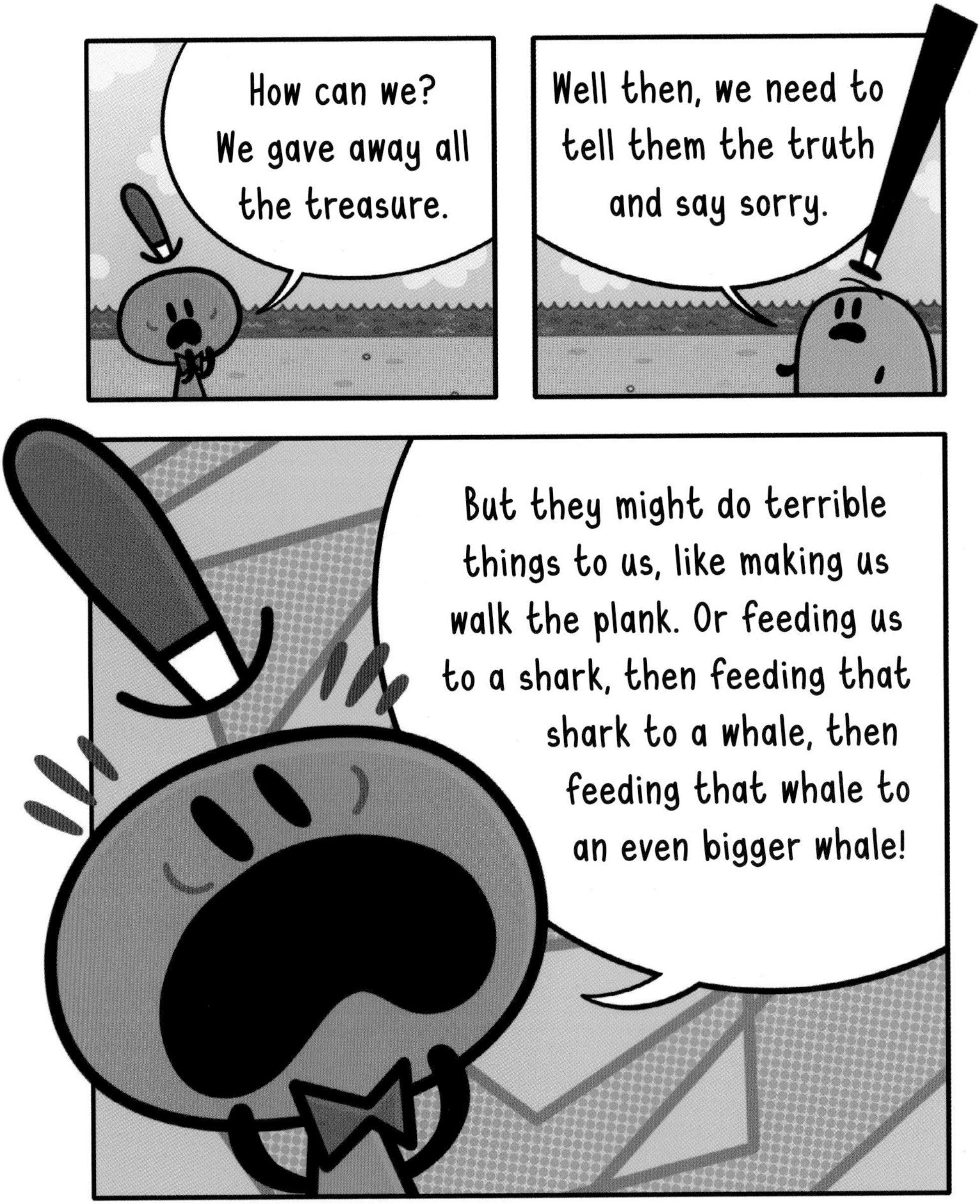
How can we? We gave away all the treasure.
Well then, we need to tell them the truth and say sorry.
But they might do terrible things to us, like making us walk the plank. Or feeding us to a shark, then feeding that shark to a whale, then feeding that whale to an even bigger whale!

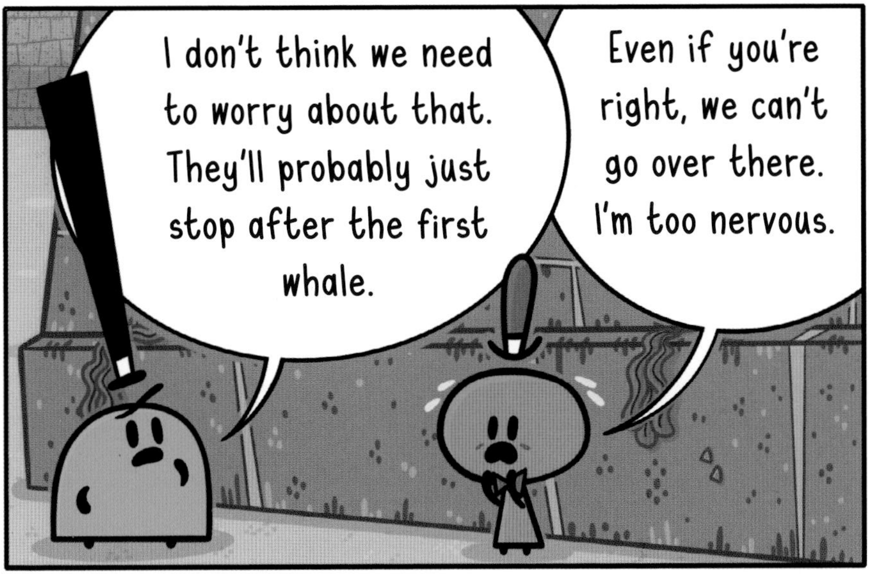
I don't think we need to worry about that. They'll probably just stop after the first whale.
Even if you're right, we can't go over there. I'm too nervous.

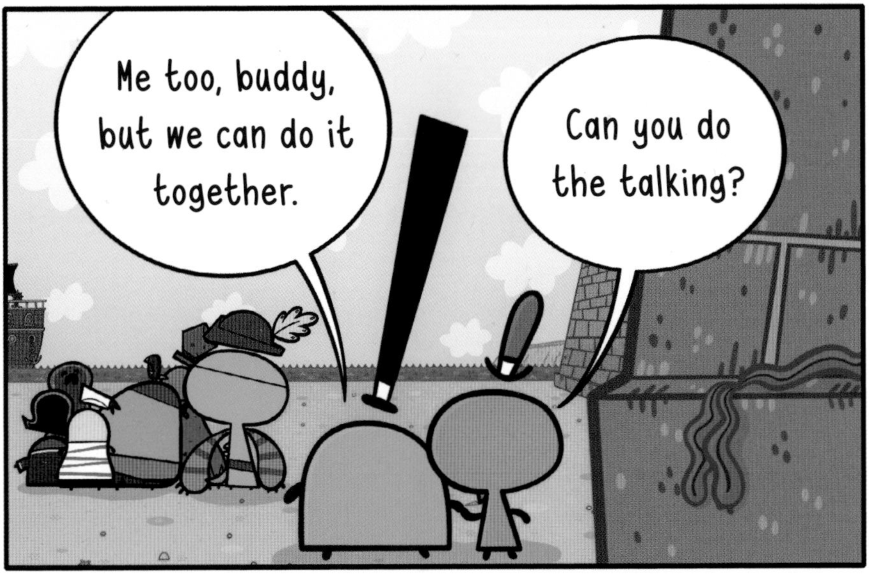
Me too, buddy, but we can do it together.
Can you do the talking?

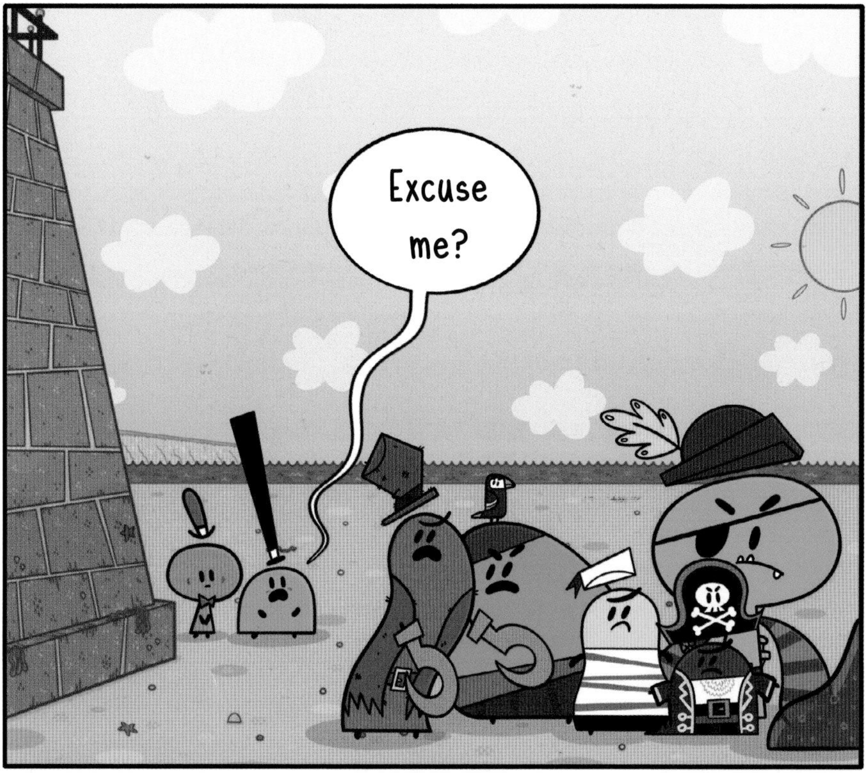
Excuse me?

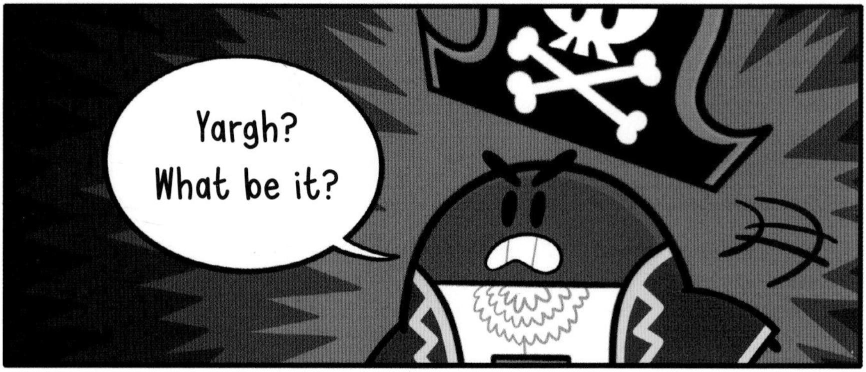
Yargh? What be it?

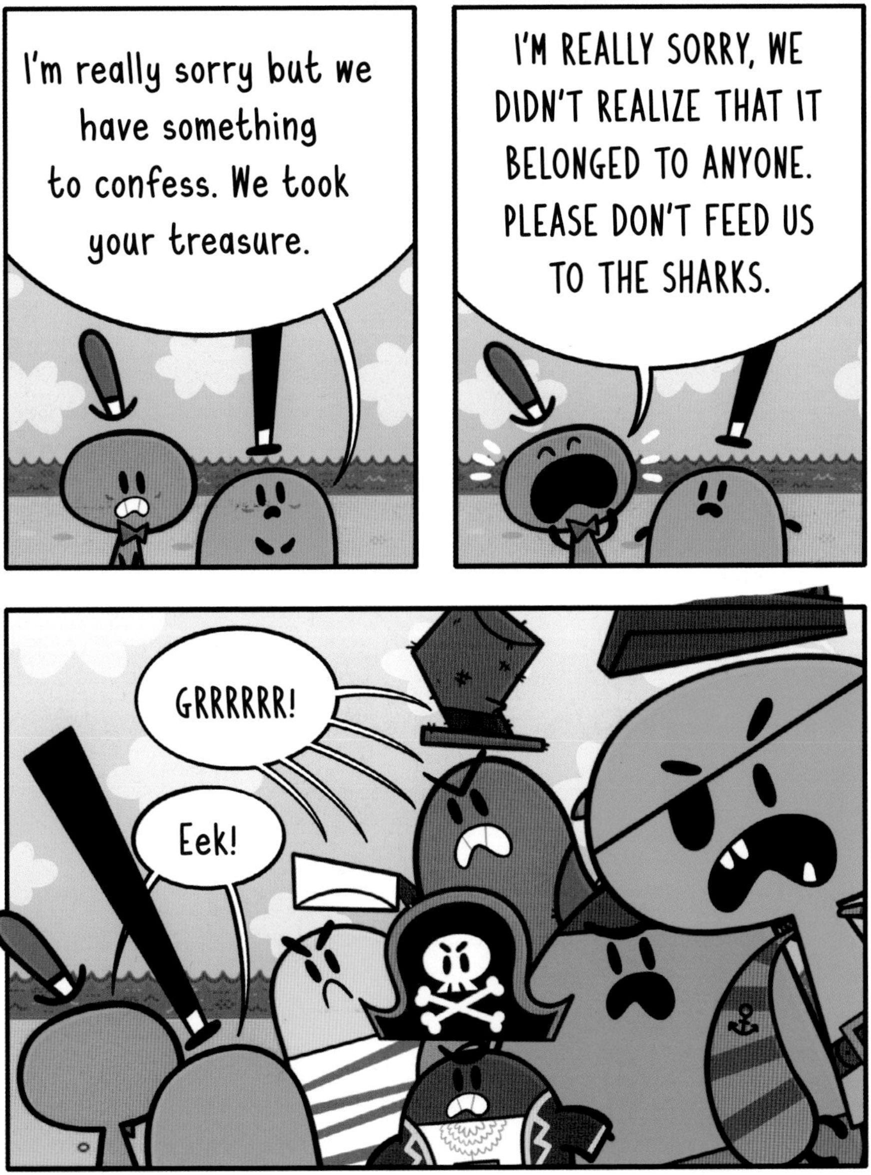
I'm really sorry but we have something to confess. We took your treasure.
I'M REALLY SORRY, WE DIDN'T REALIZE THAT IT BELONGED TO ANYONE. PLEASE DON'T FEED US TO THE SHARKS.
GRRRRRR!
Eek!

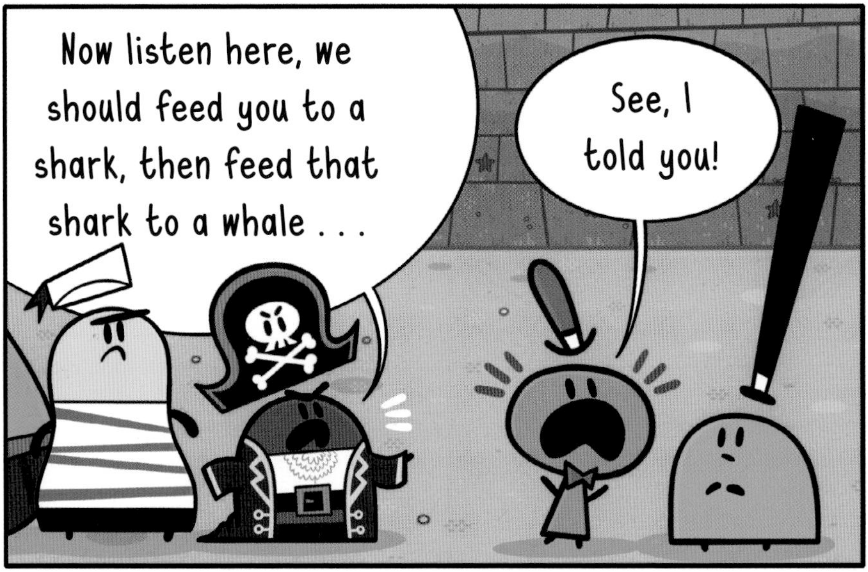
Now listen here, we should feed you to a shark, then feed that shark to a whale . . .
See, I told you!

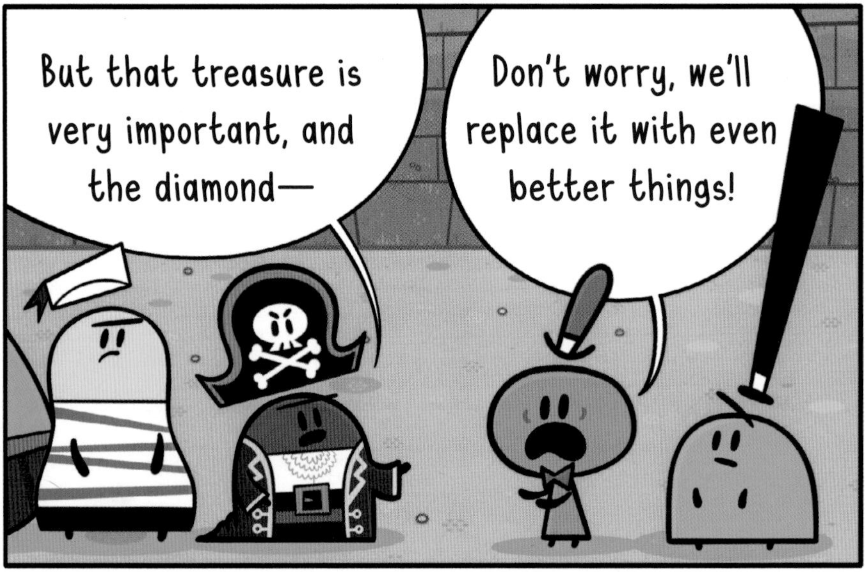
But that treasure is very important, and the diamond—
Don't worry, we'll replace it with even better things!

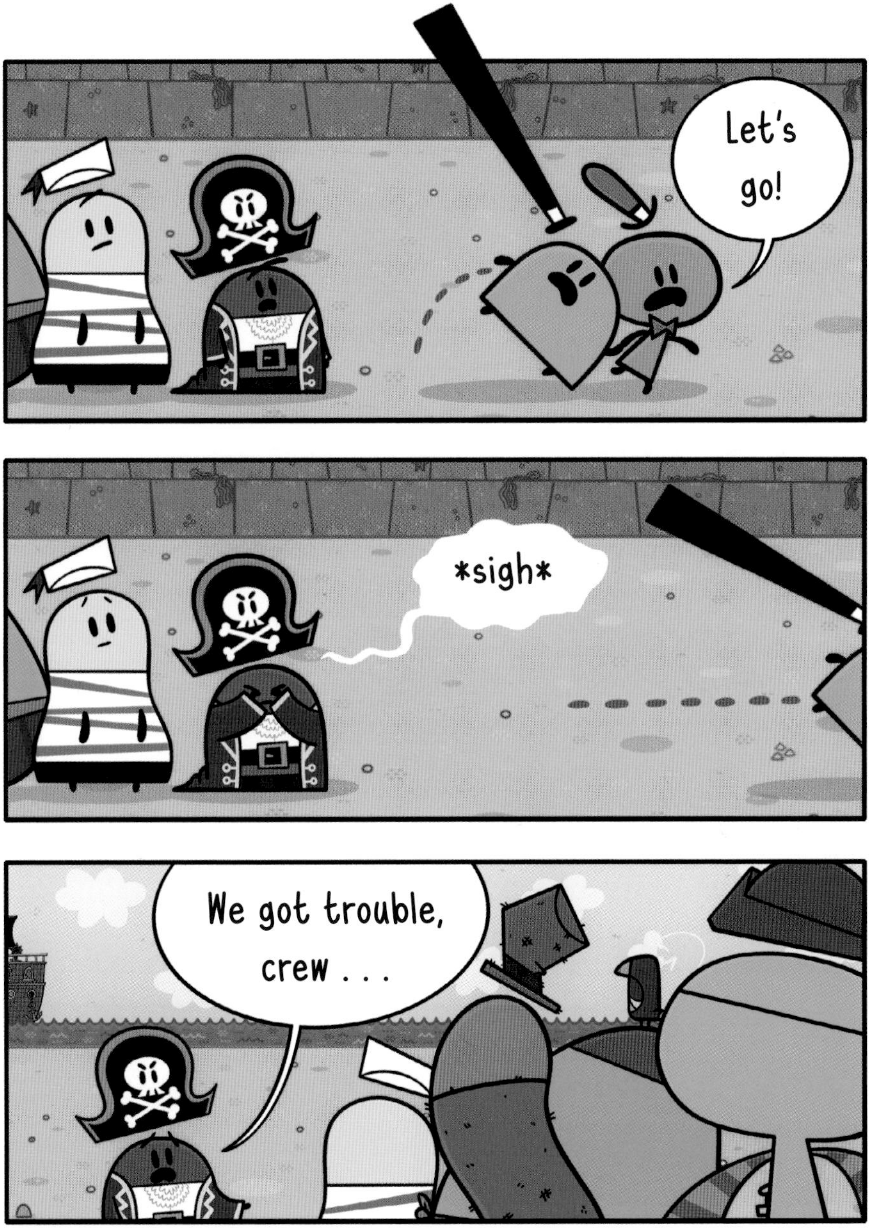
Let's go!
sigh
We got trouble, crew . . .

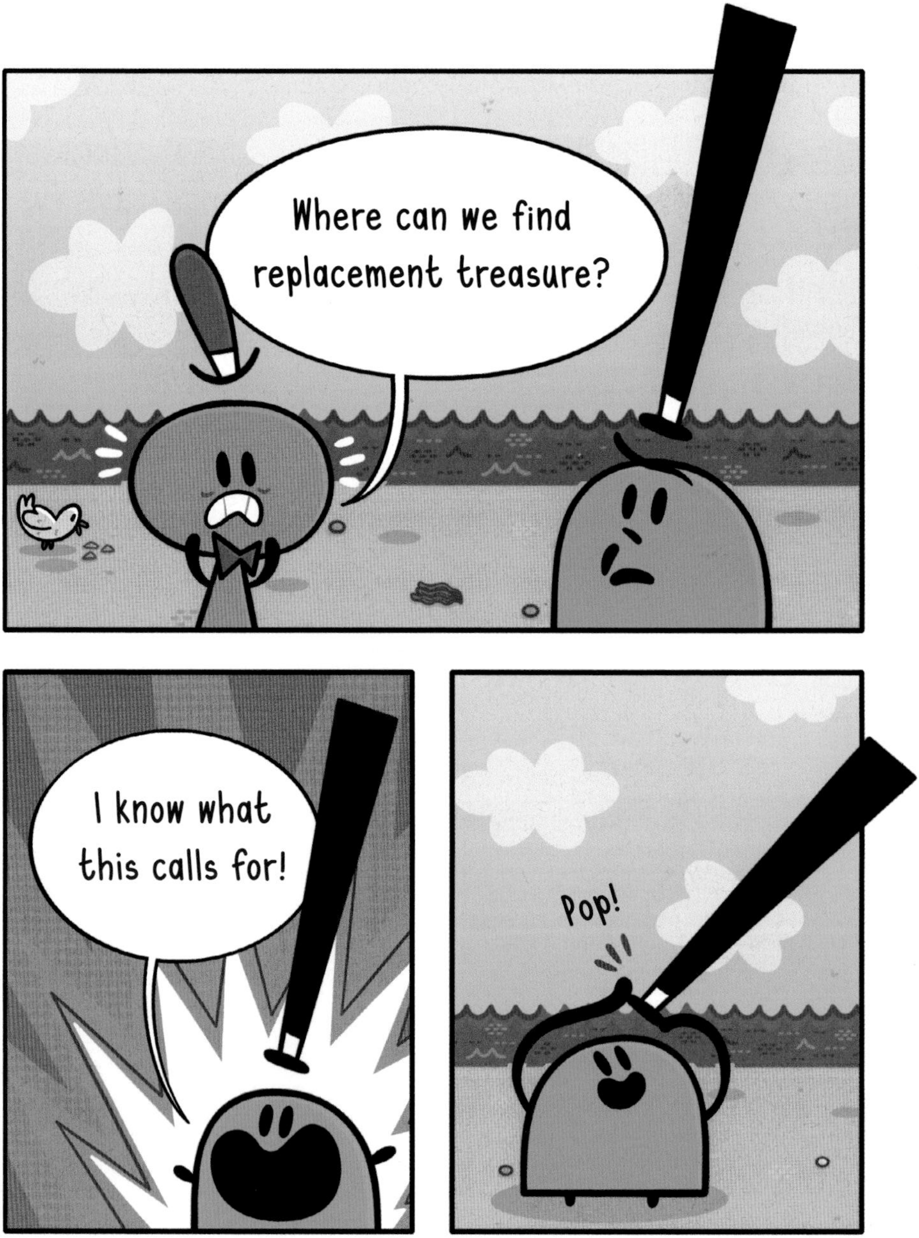
Where can we find replacement treasure?
I know what this calls for!
Pop!

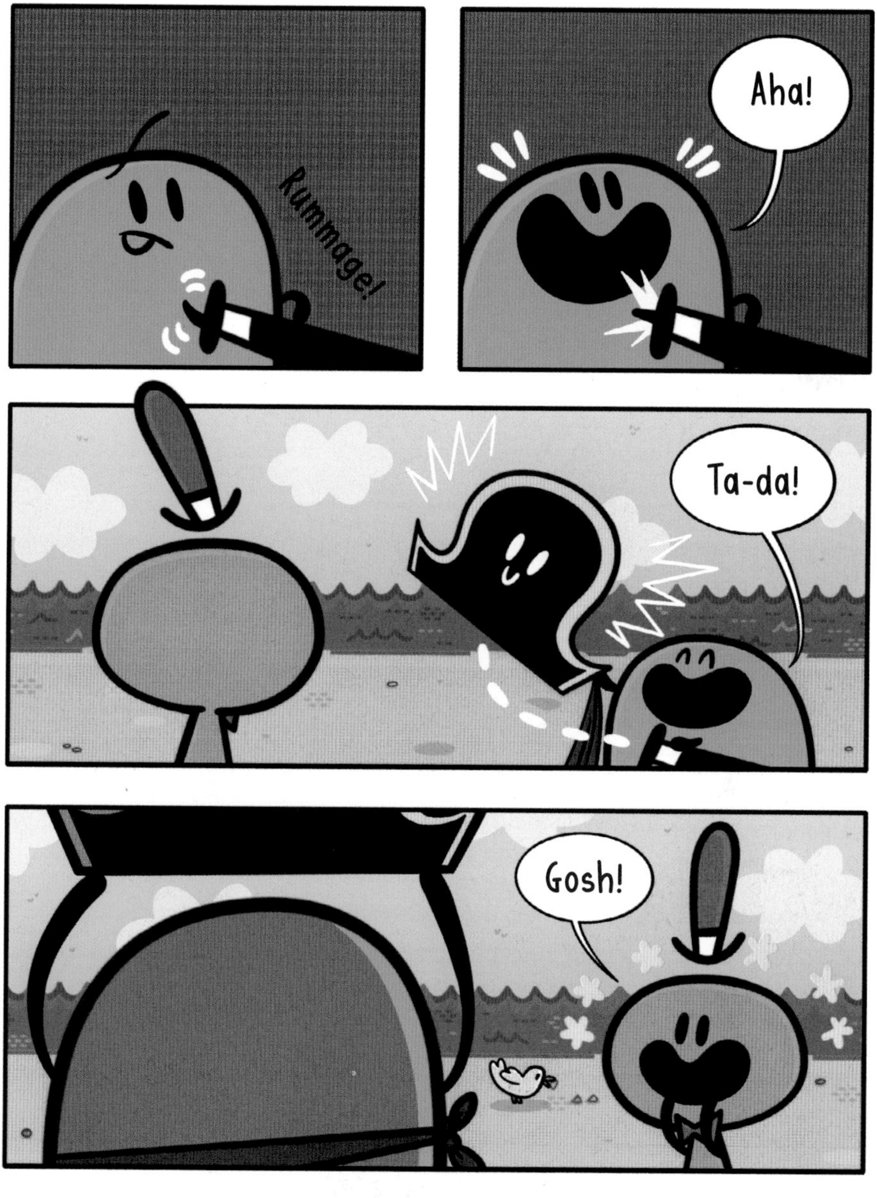
Rummage!
Aha!
Ta-da!
Gosh!

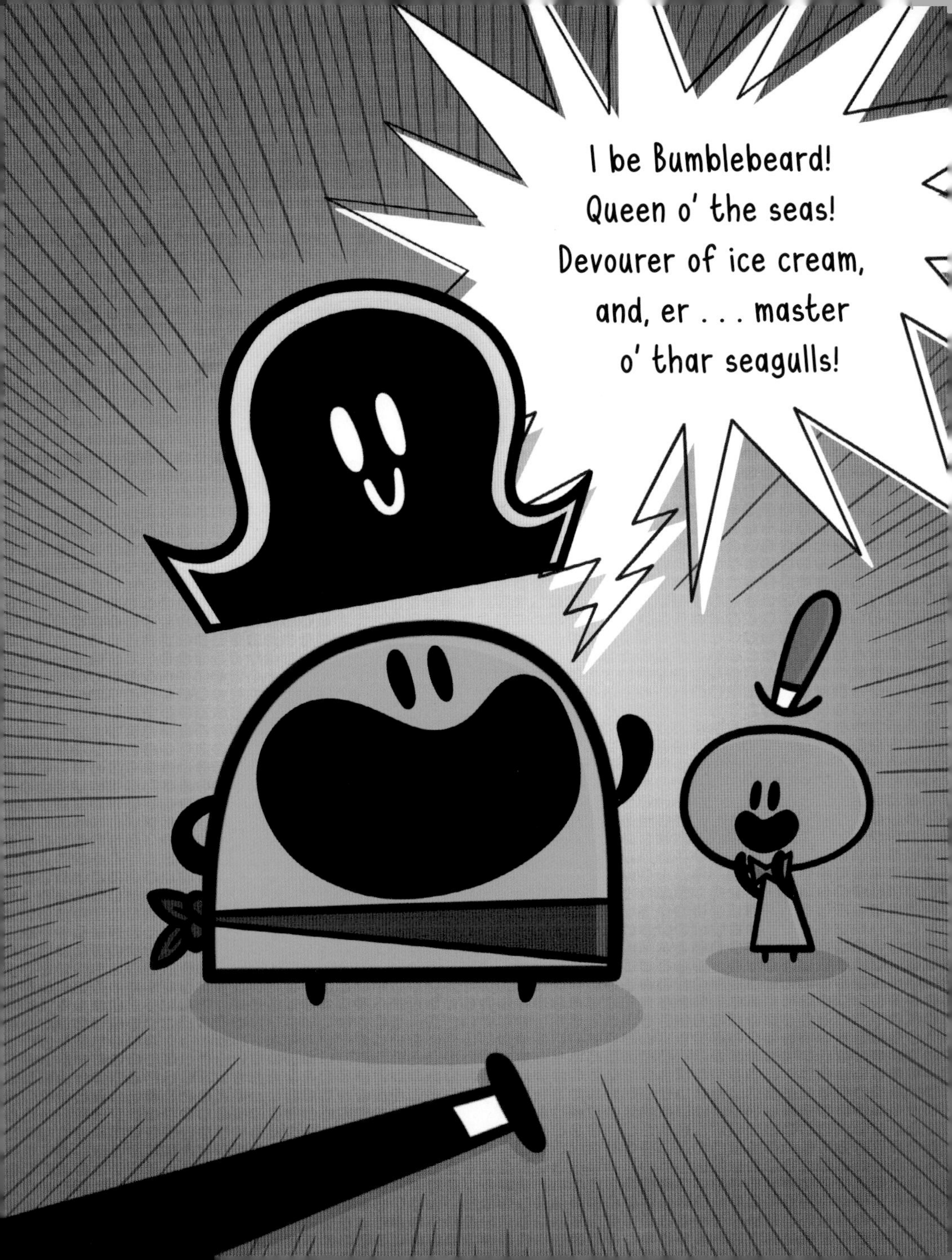
I be Bumblebeard! Queen o' the seas! Devourer of ice cream, and, er . . . master o' thar seagulls!

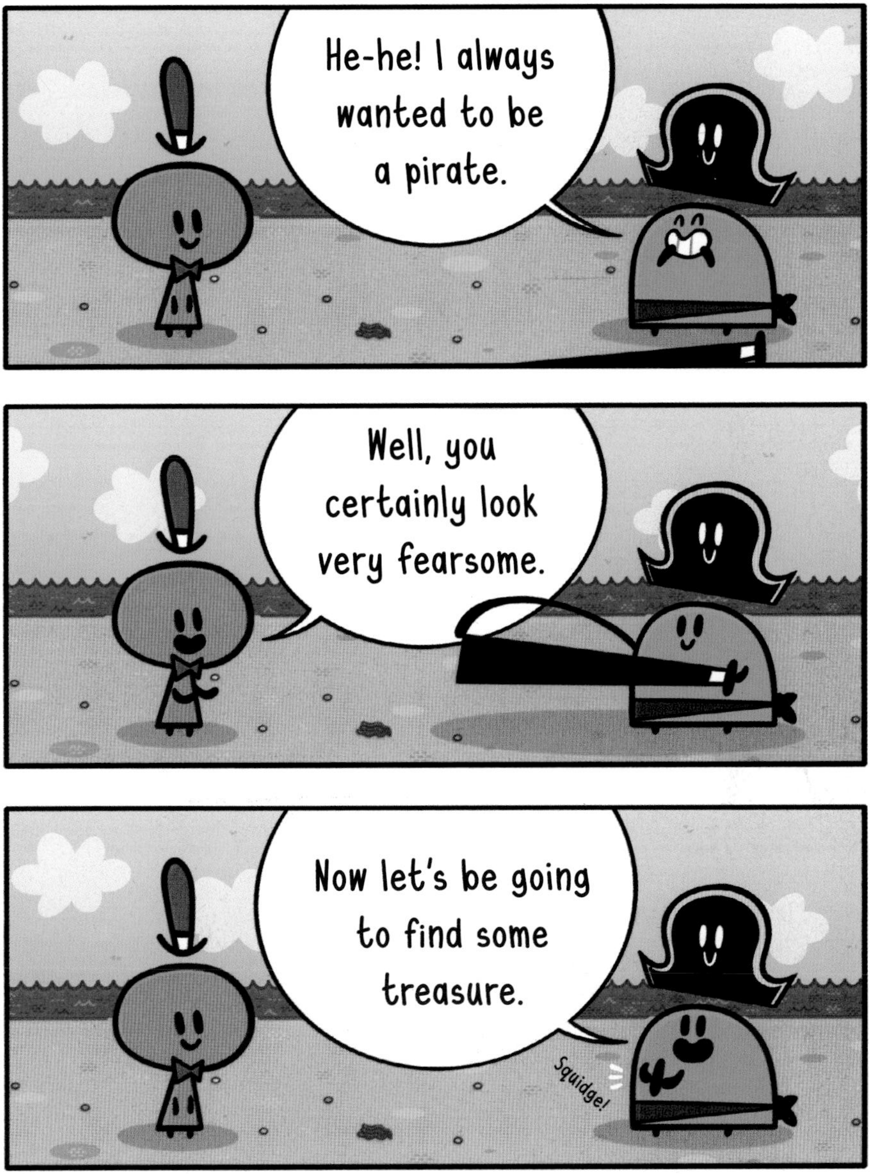
He-he! I always wanted to be a pirate.
Well, you certainly look very fearsome.
Now let's be going to find some treasure.
Squidge!

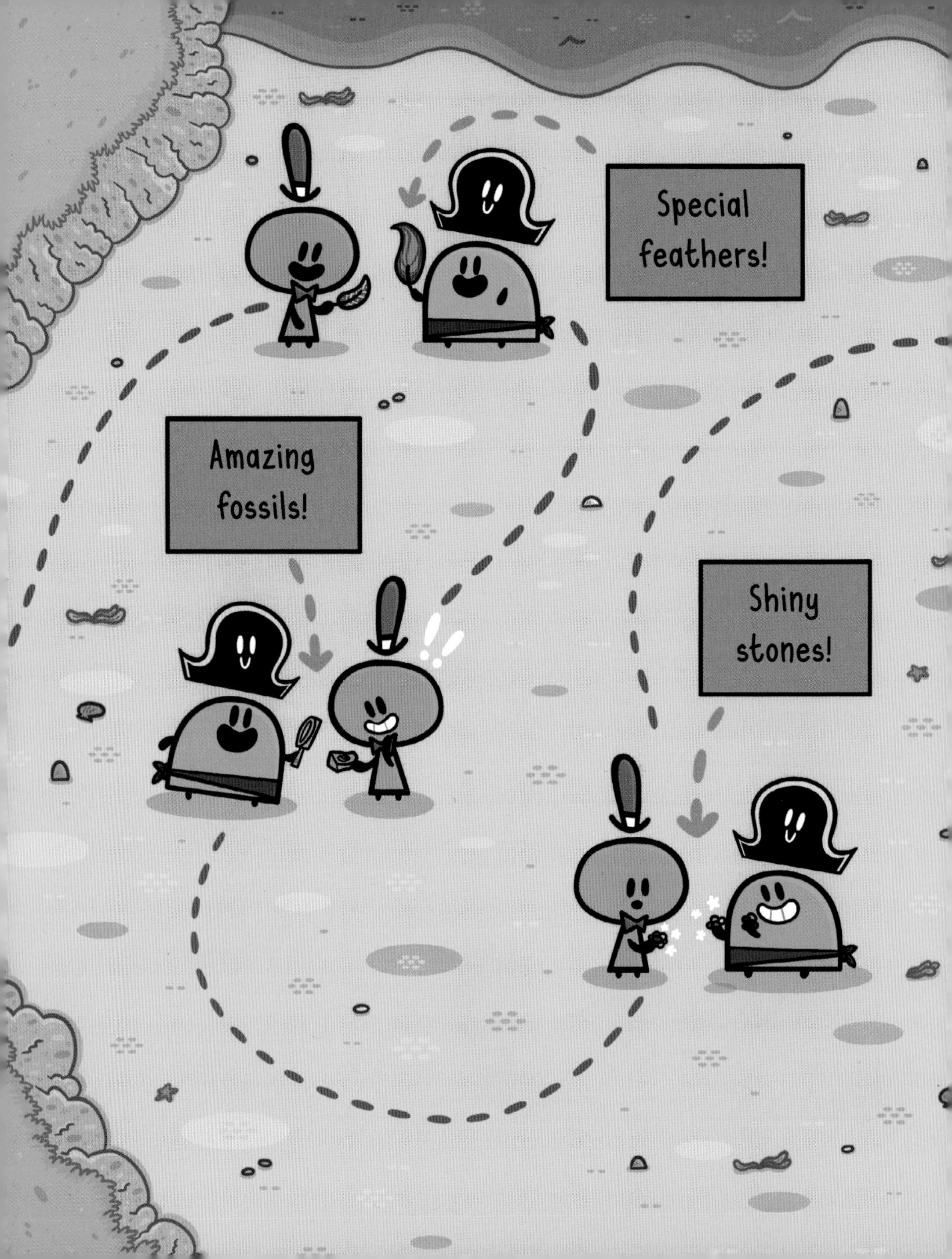
Special feathers!
Amazing fossils!
Shiny stones!

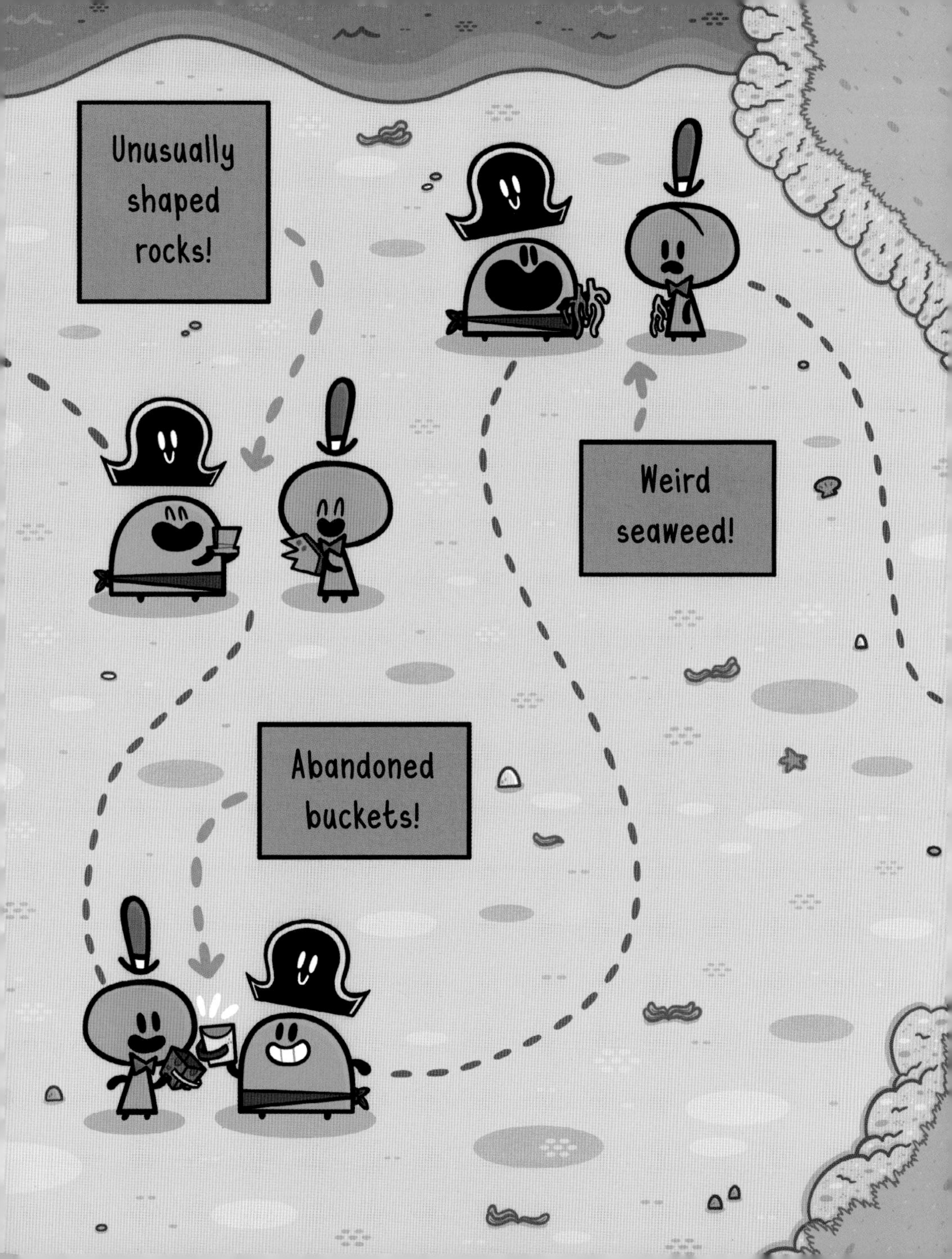
Unusually shaped rocks!
Weird seaweed!
Abandoned buckets!

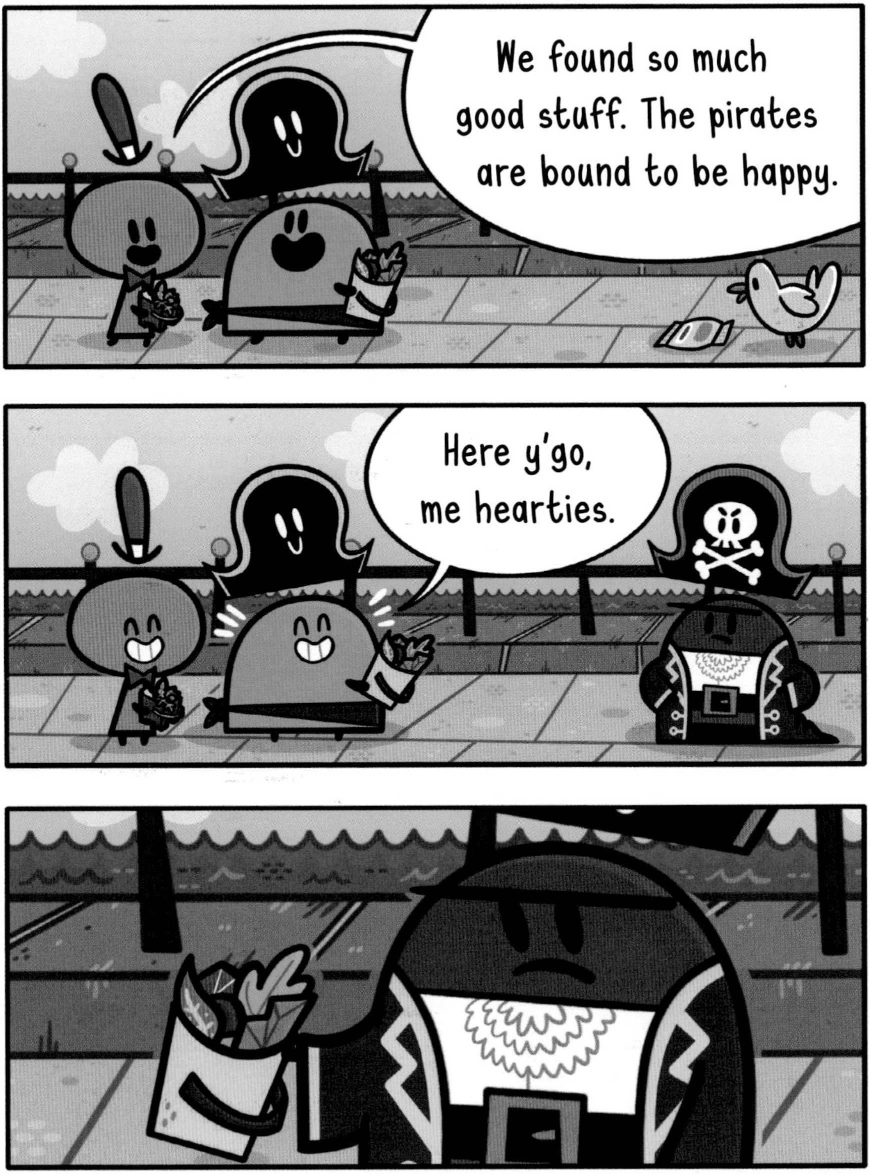
We found so much good stuff. The pirates are bound to be happy.
Here y'go, me hearties.

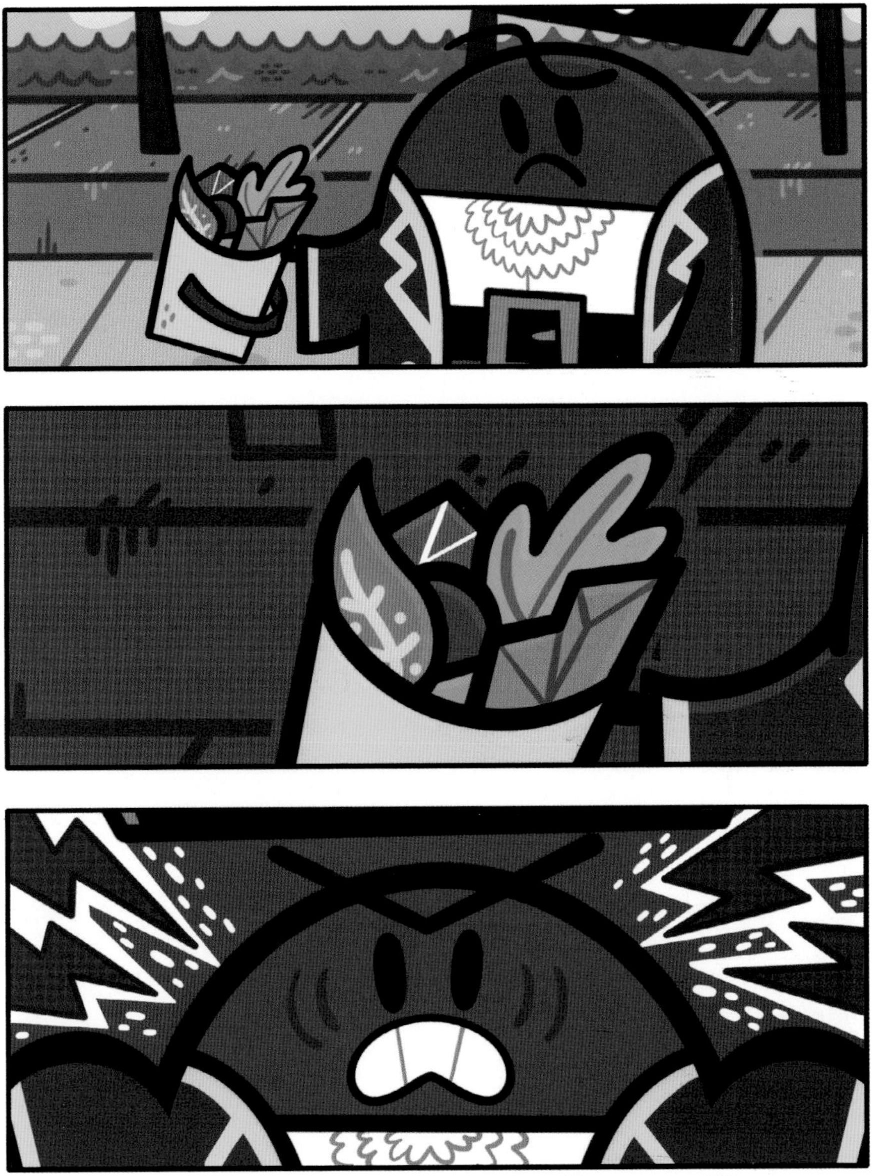

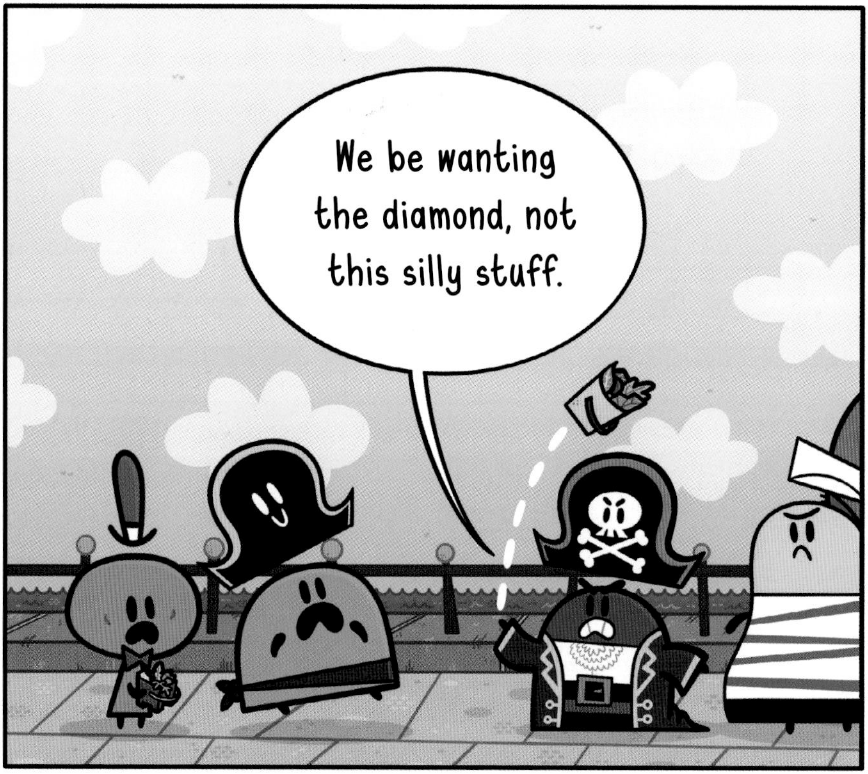
We be wanting the diamond, not this silly stuff.

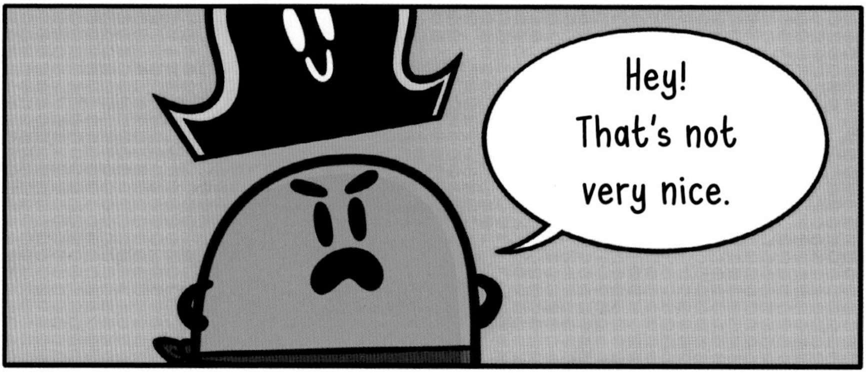
Hey! That's not very nice.

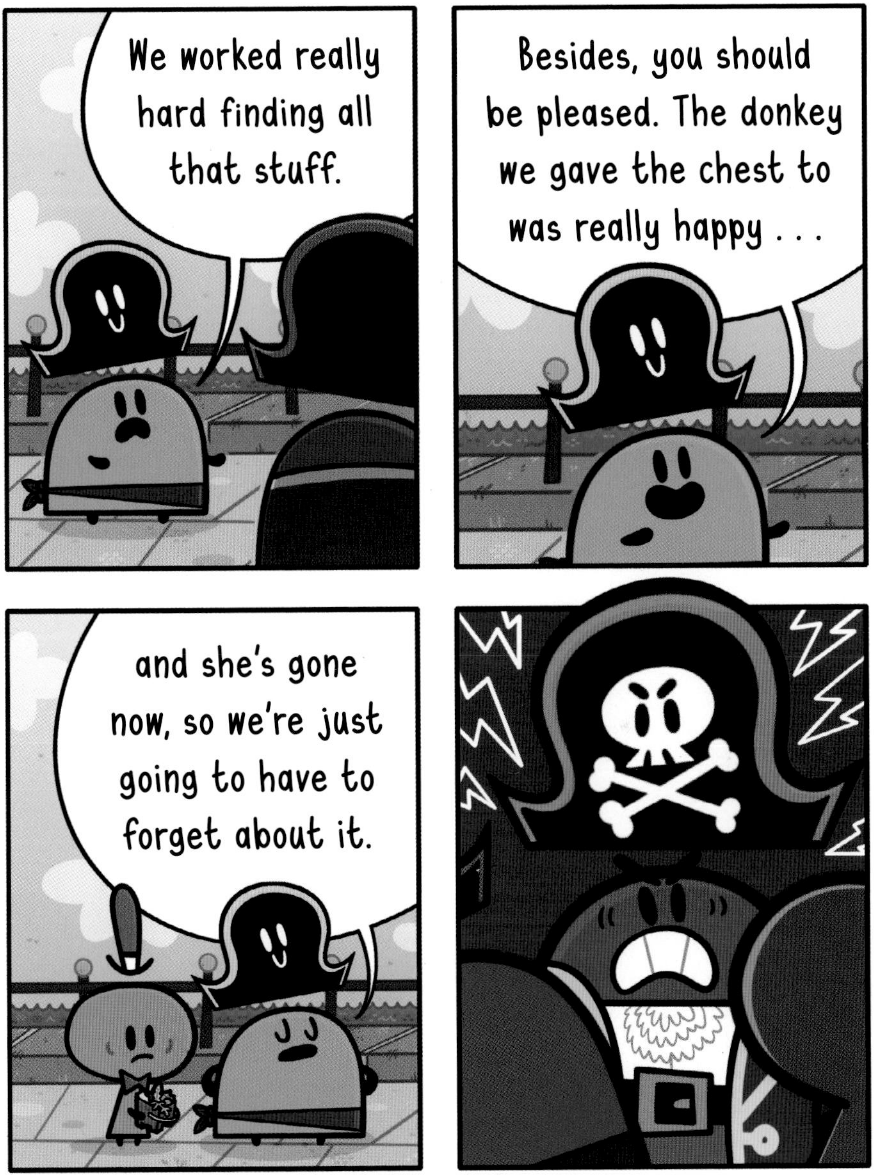
We worked really hard finding all that stuff.
Besides, you should be pleased. The donkey we gave the chest to was really happy . . .
and she's gone now, so we're just going to have to forget about it.

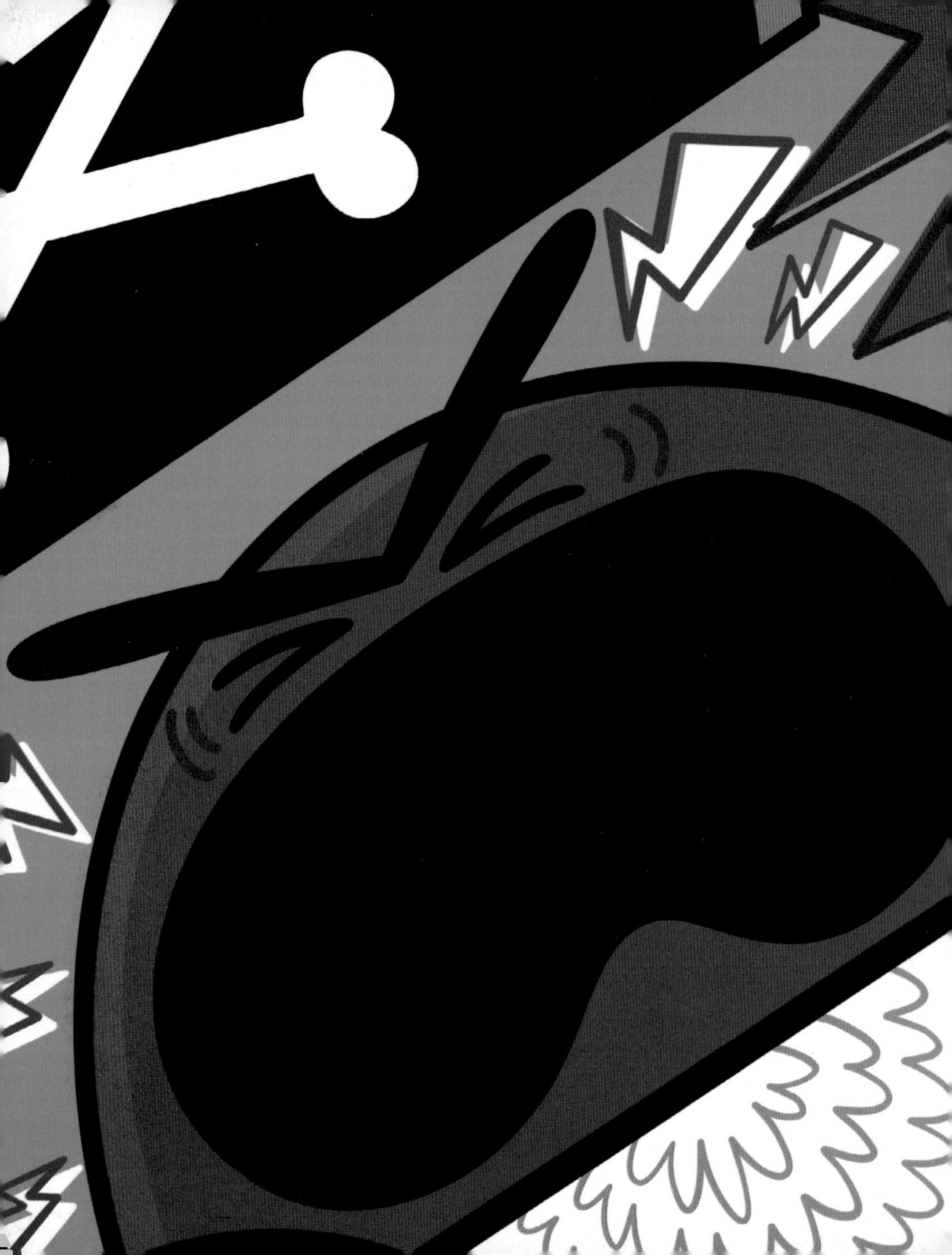

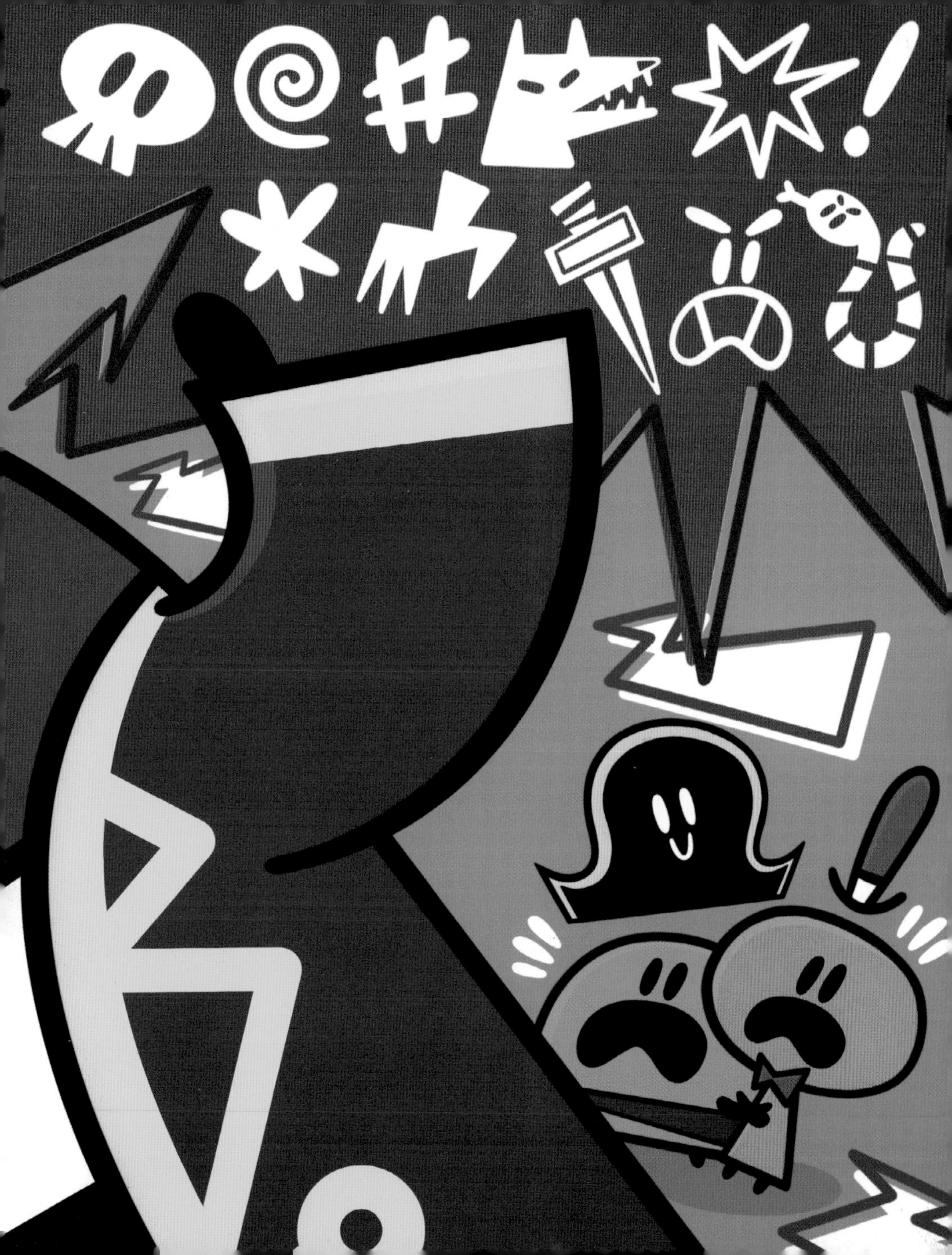

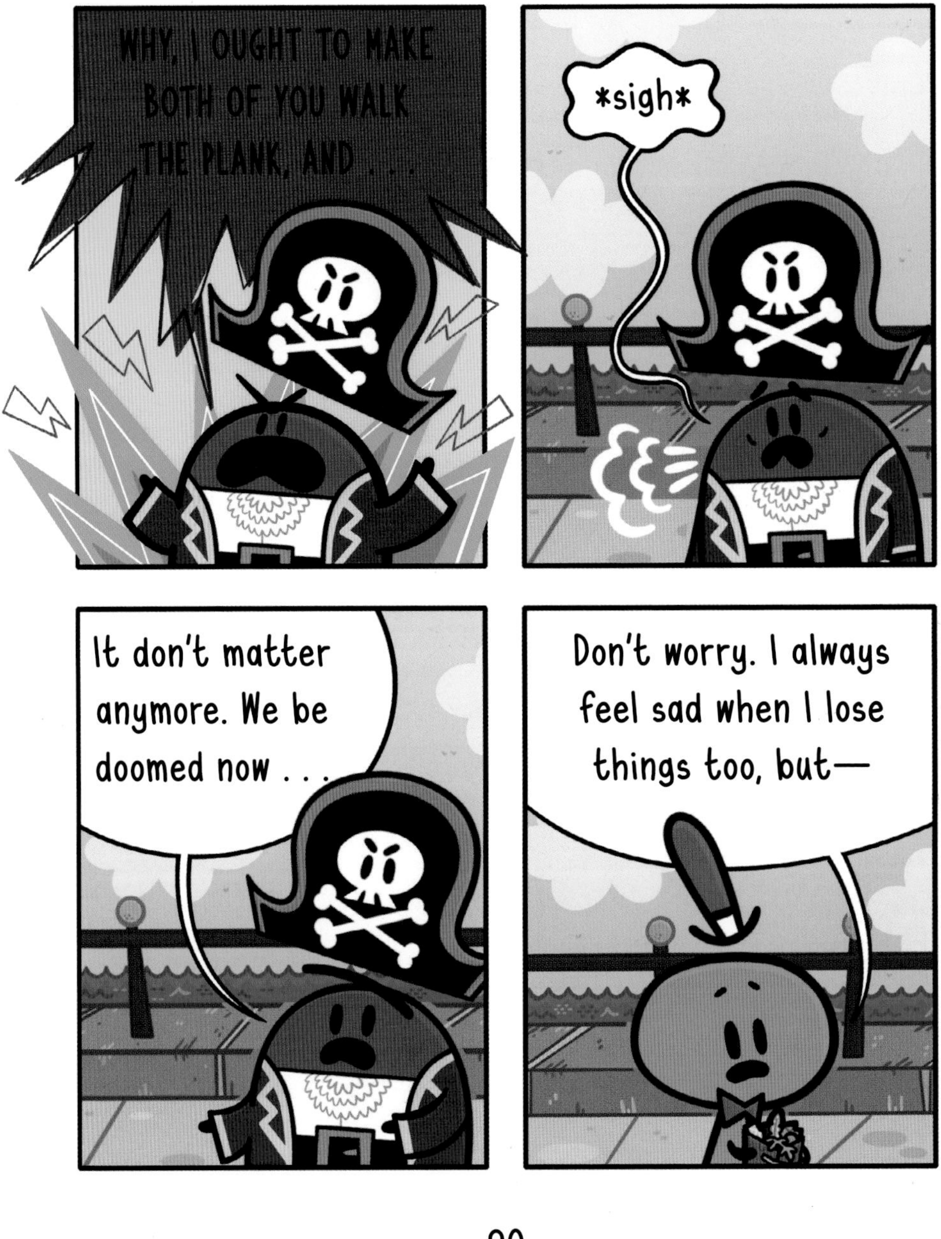
WHY, I OUGHT TO MAKE BOTH OF YOU WALK THE PLANK, AND . . .
sigh
It don't matter anymore. We be doomed now . . .
Don't worry. I always feel sad when I lose things too, but—

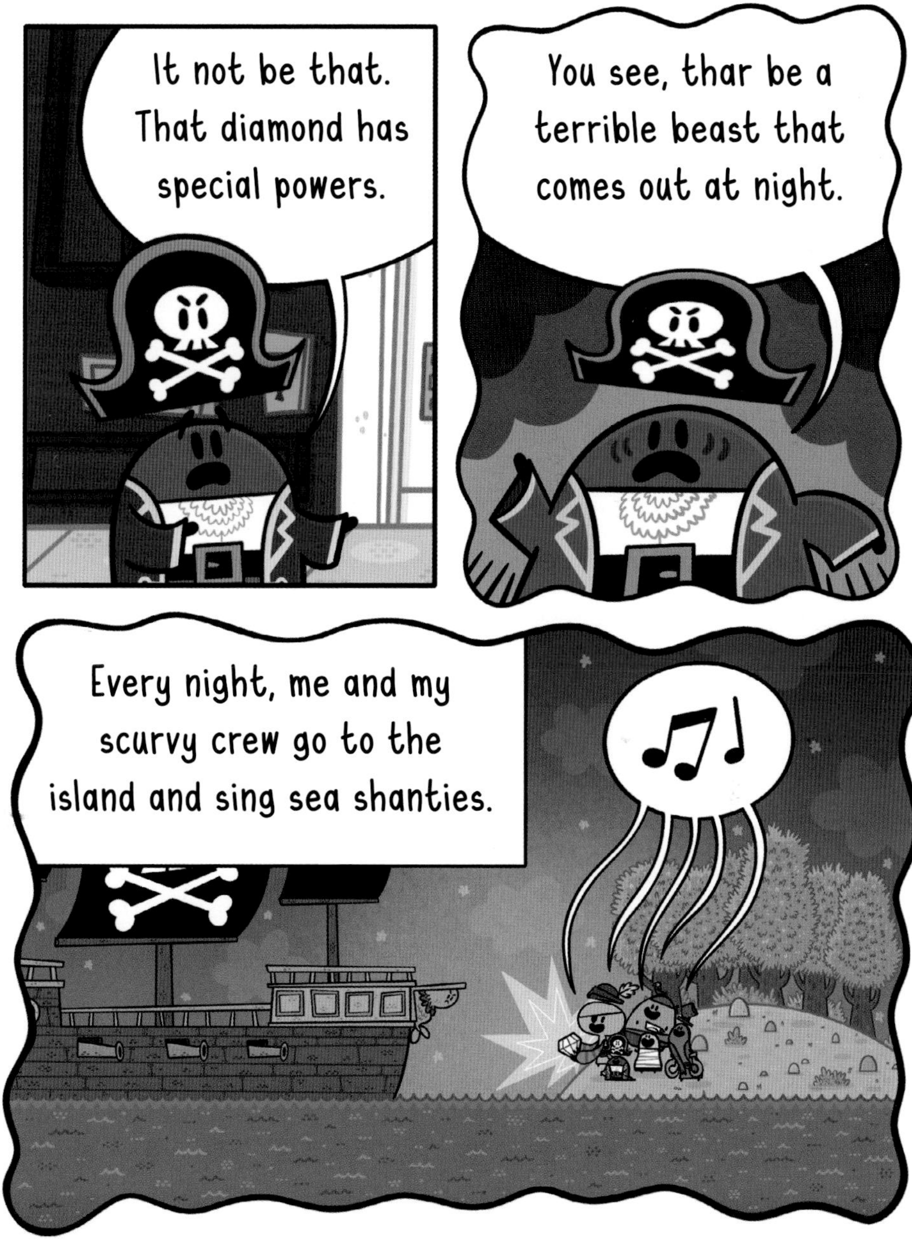
It not be that. That diamond has special powers.
You see, thar be a terrible beast that comes out at night.
Every night, me and my scurvy crew go to the island and sing sea shanties.

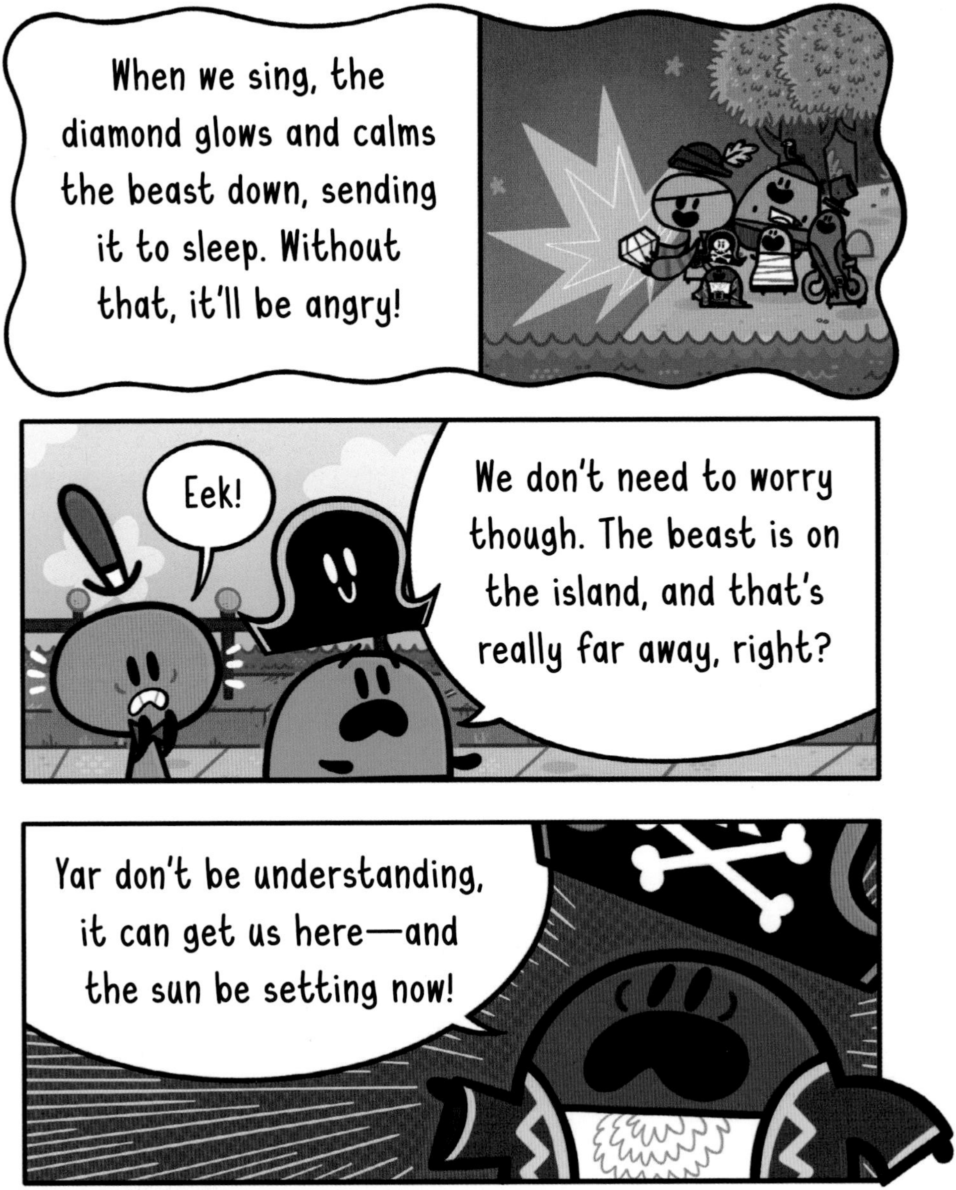
When we sing, the diamond glows and calms the beast down, sending it to sleep. Without that, it'll be angry!
Eek!
We don't need to worry though. The beast is on the island, and that's really far away, right?
Yar don't be understanding, it can get us here—and the sun be setting now!

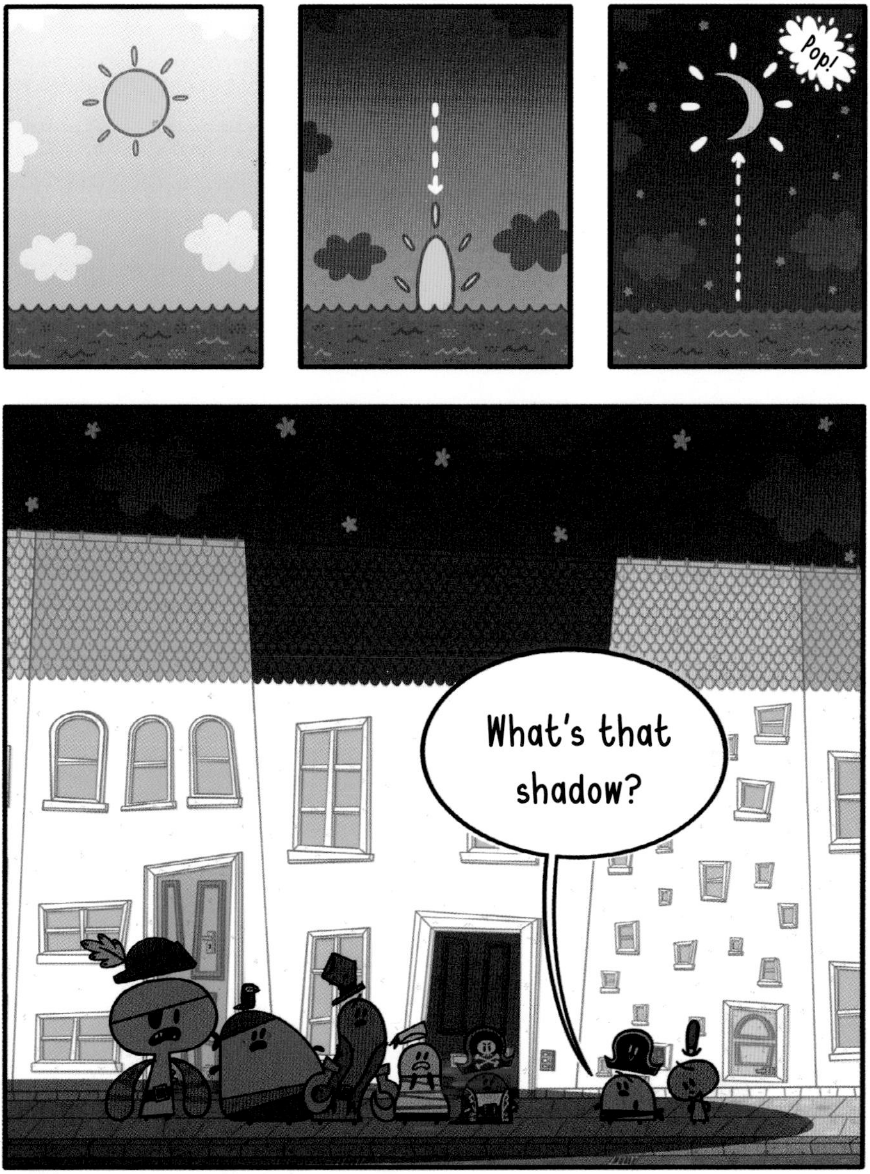
Pop!
What's that shadow?

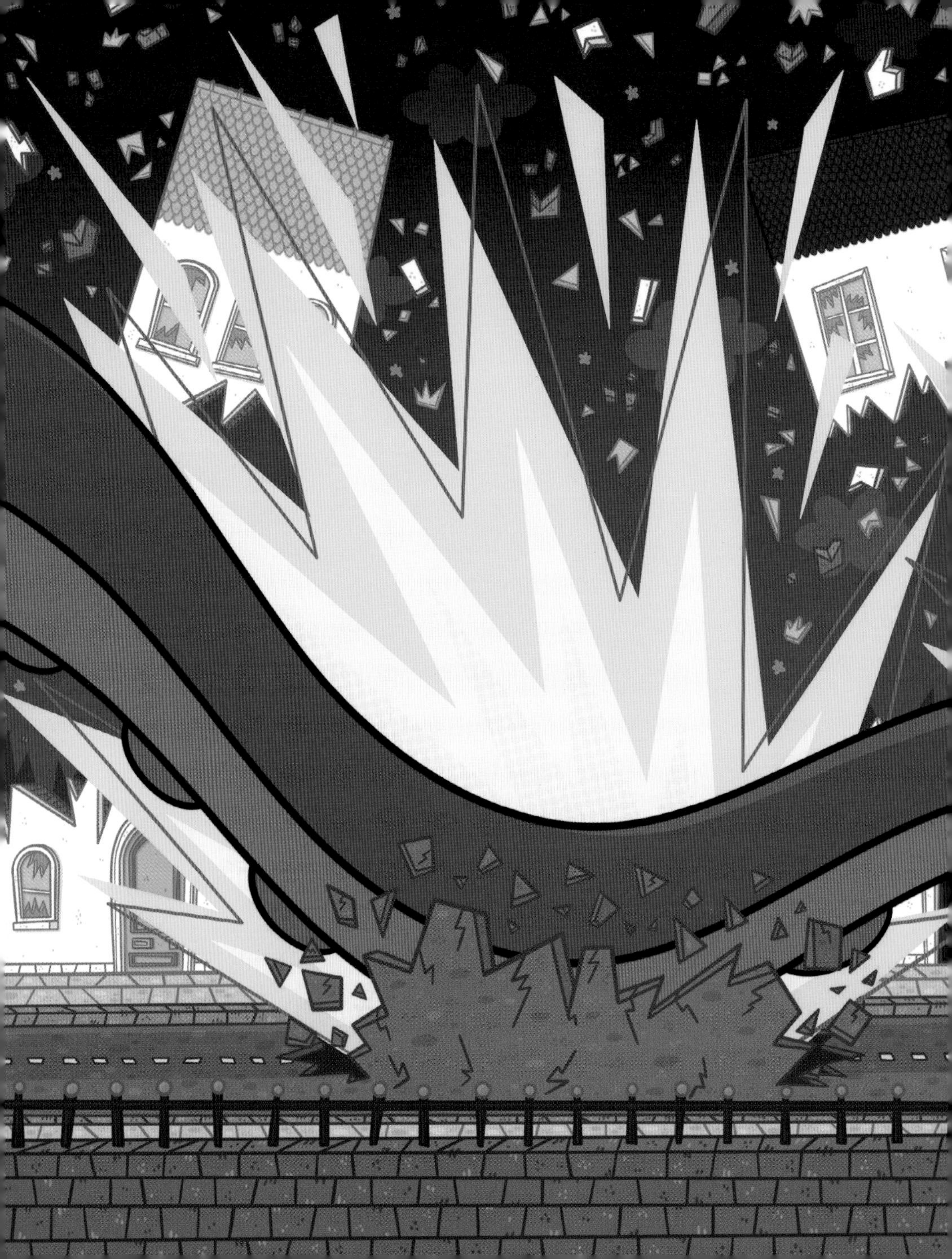

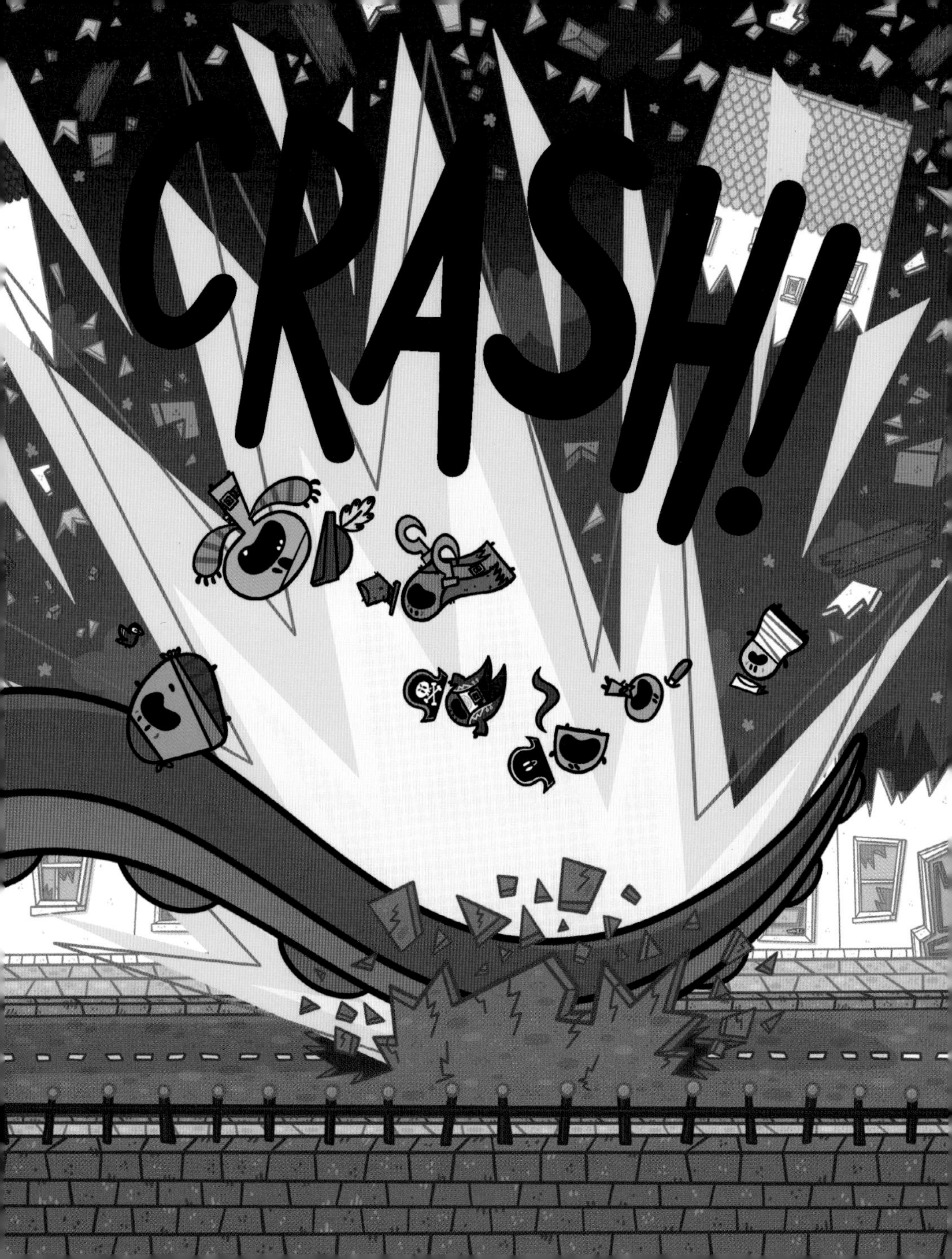
CRASH!!

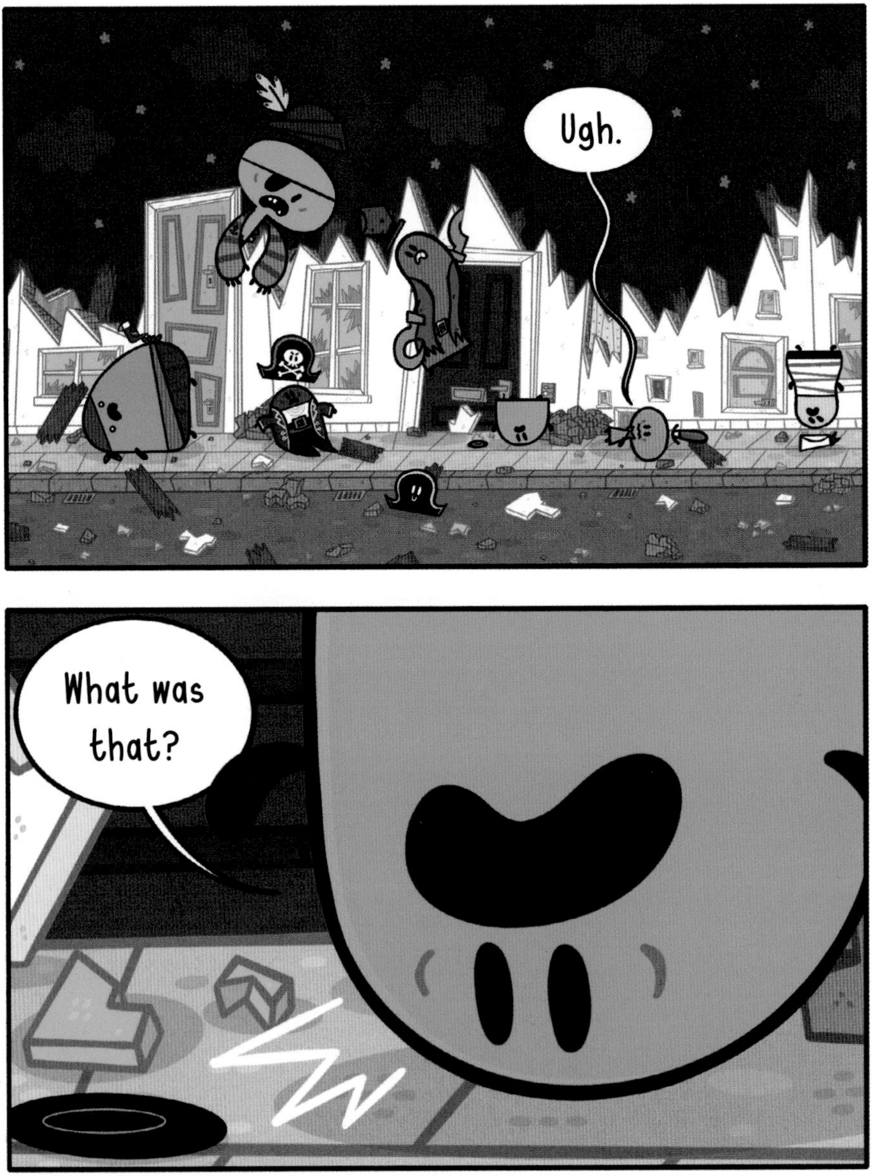
Ugh.
What was that?

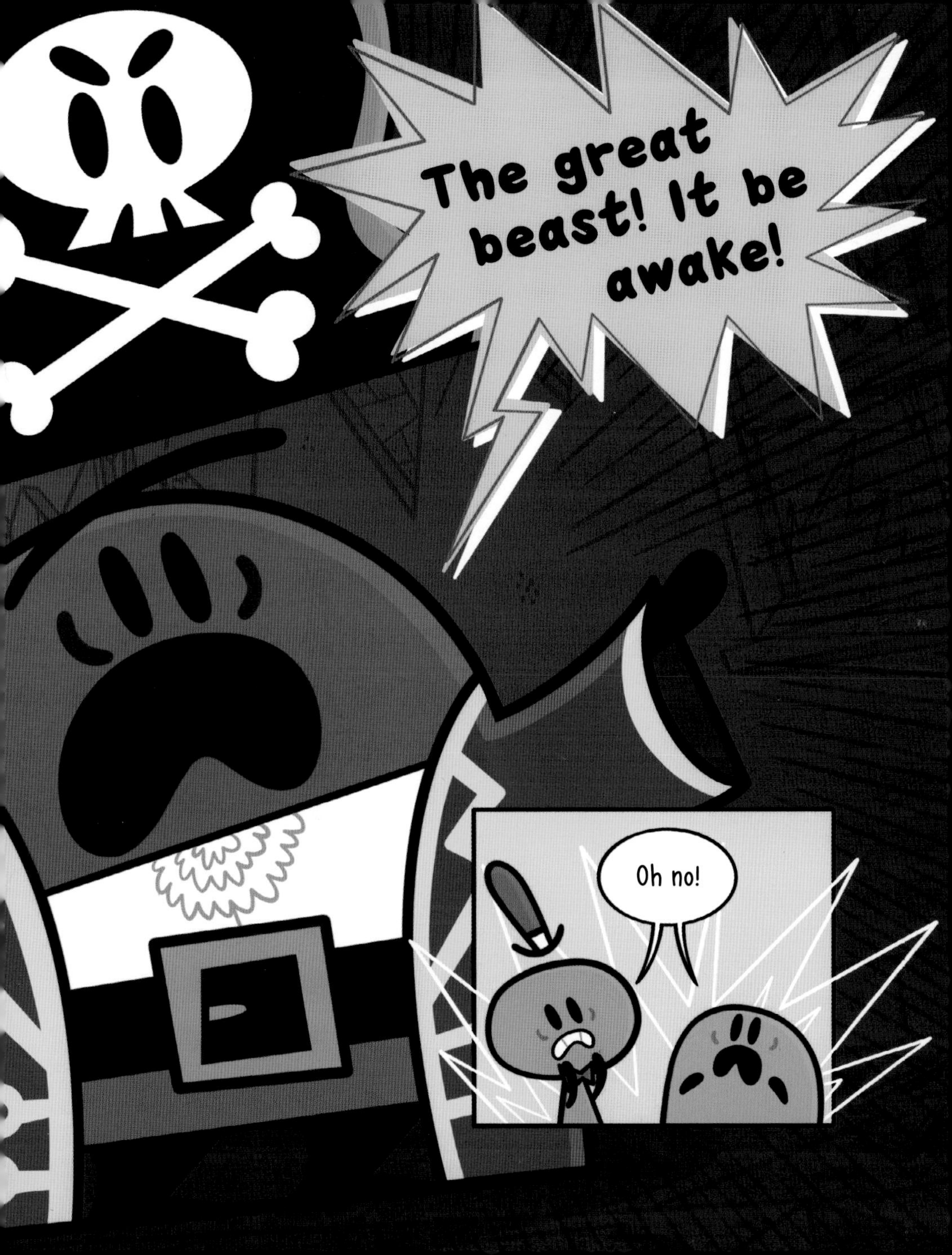
The great beast! It be awake!
Oh no!

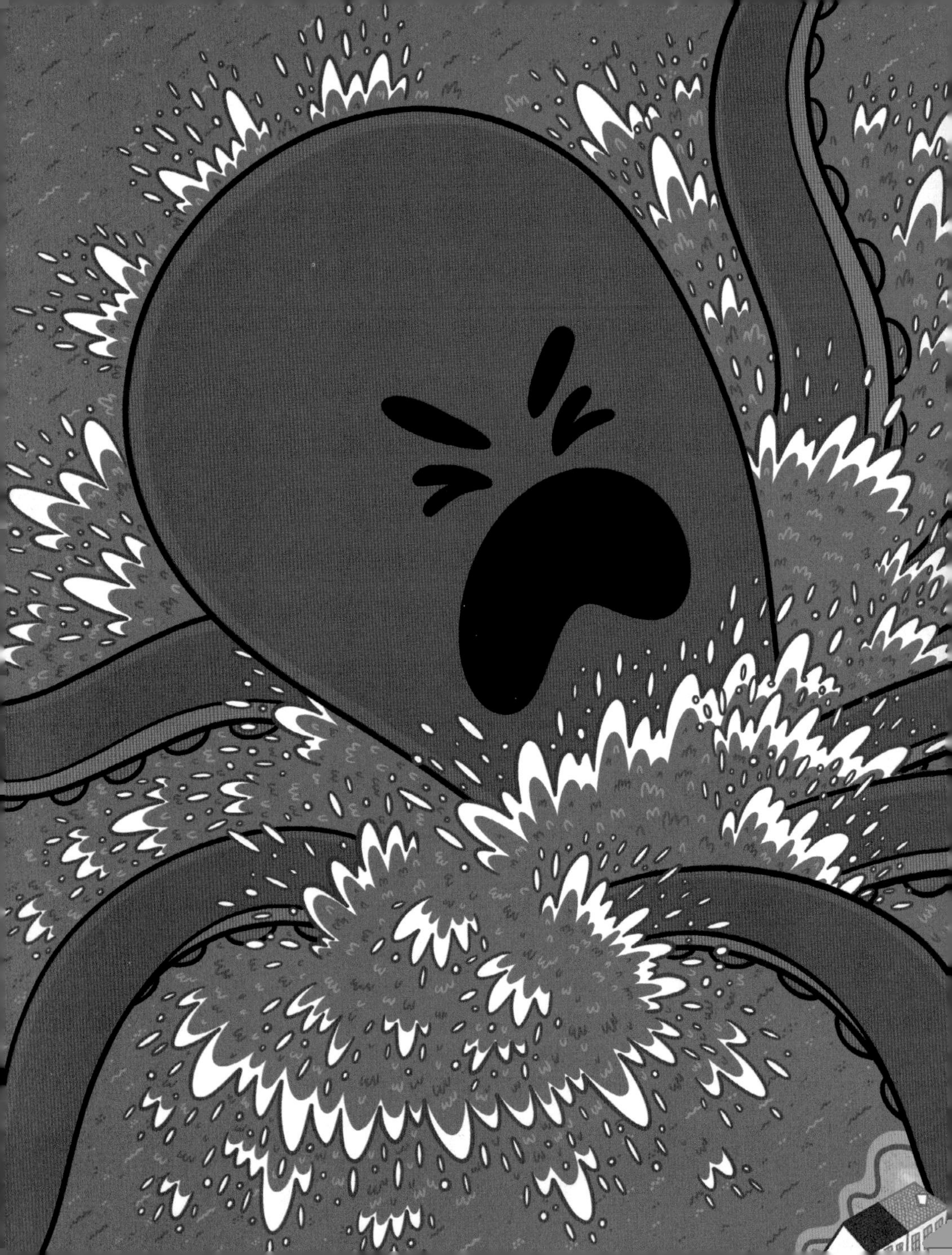

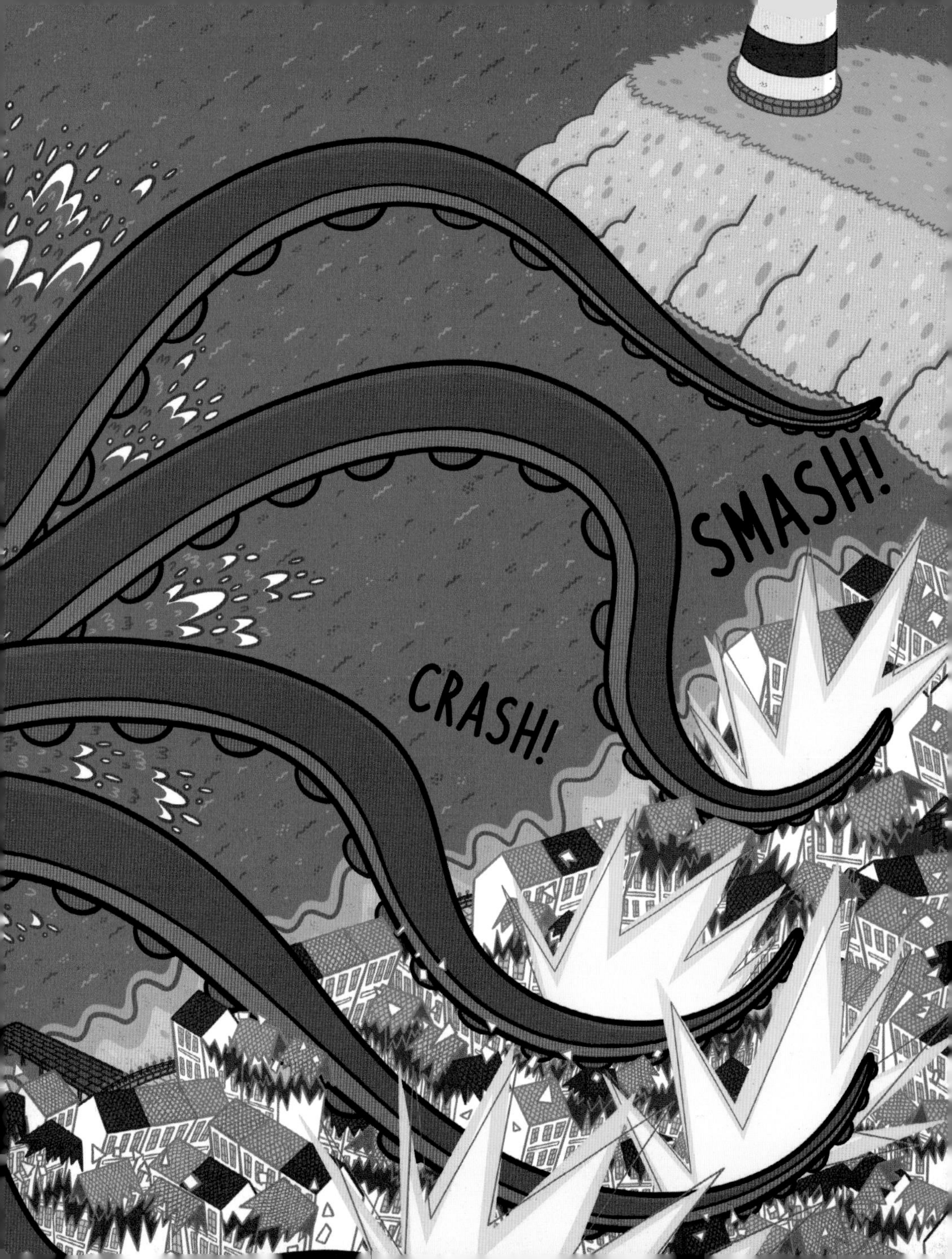
SMASH!
CRASH!

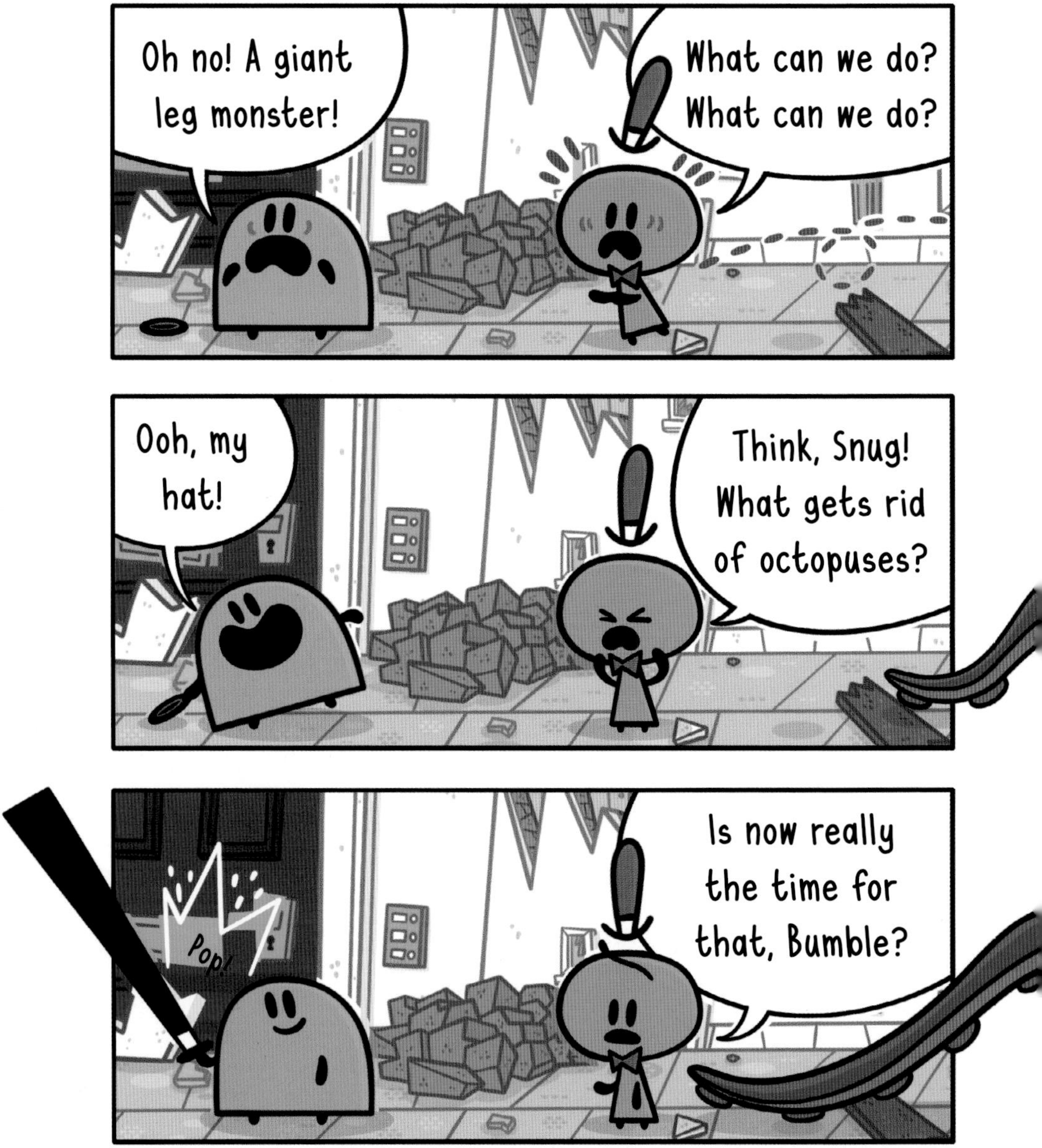
Oh no! A giant leg monster!
What can we do? What can we do?
Ooh, my hat!
Think, Snug! What gets rid of octopuses?
Pop!
Is now really the time for that, Bumble?

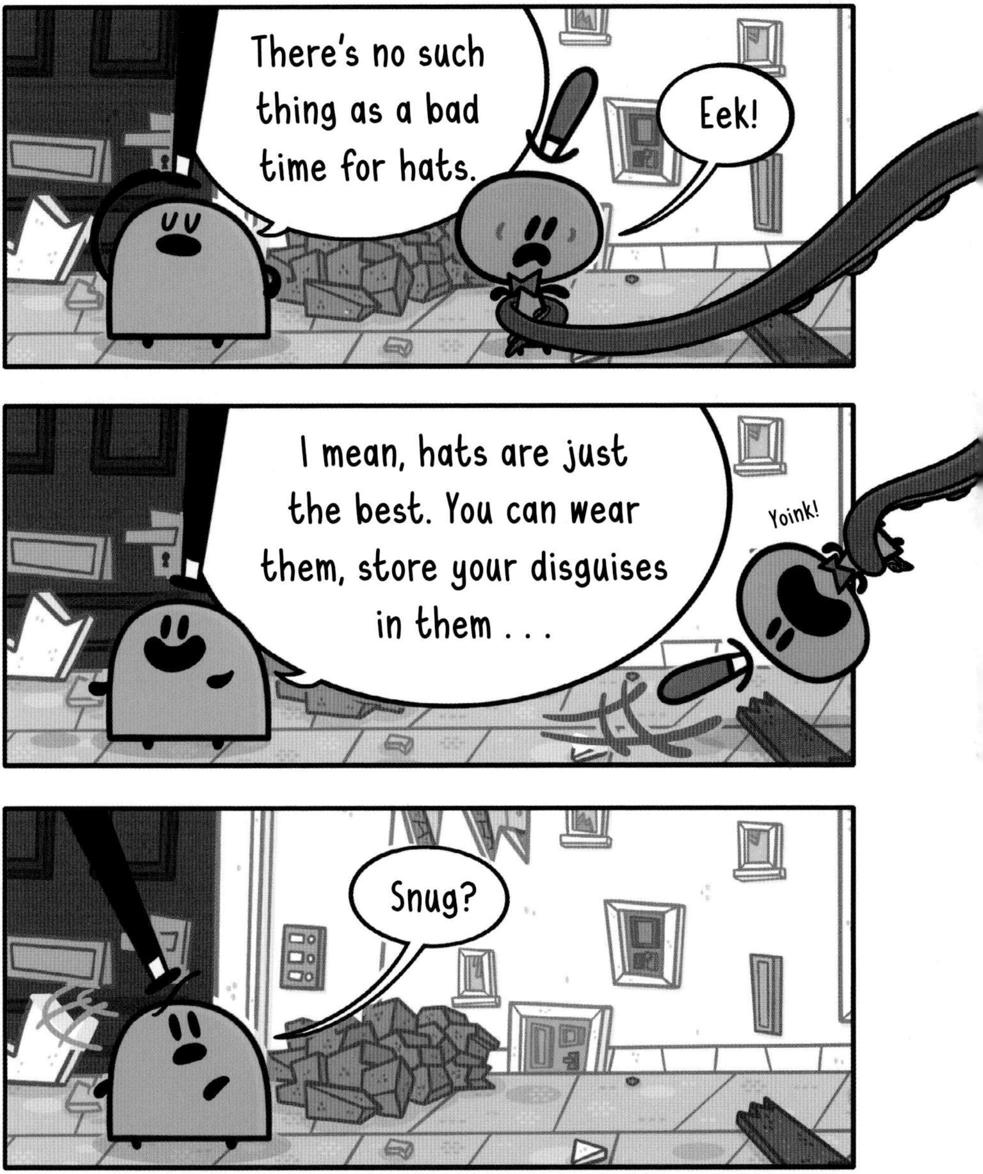
There's no such thing as a bad time for hats.
Eek!
I mean, hats are just the best. You can wear them, store your disguises in them . . .
Yoink!
Snug?

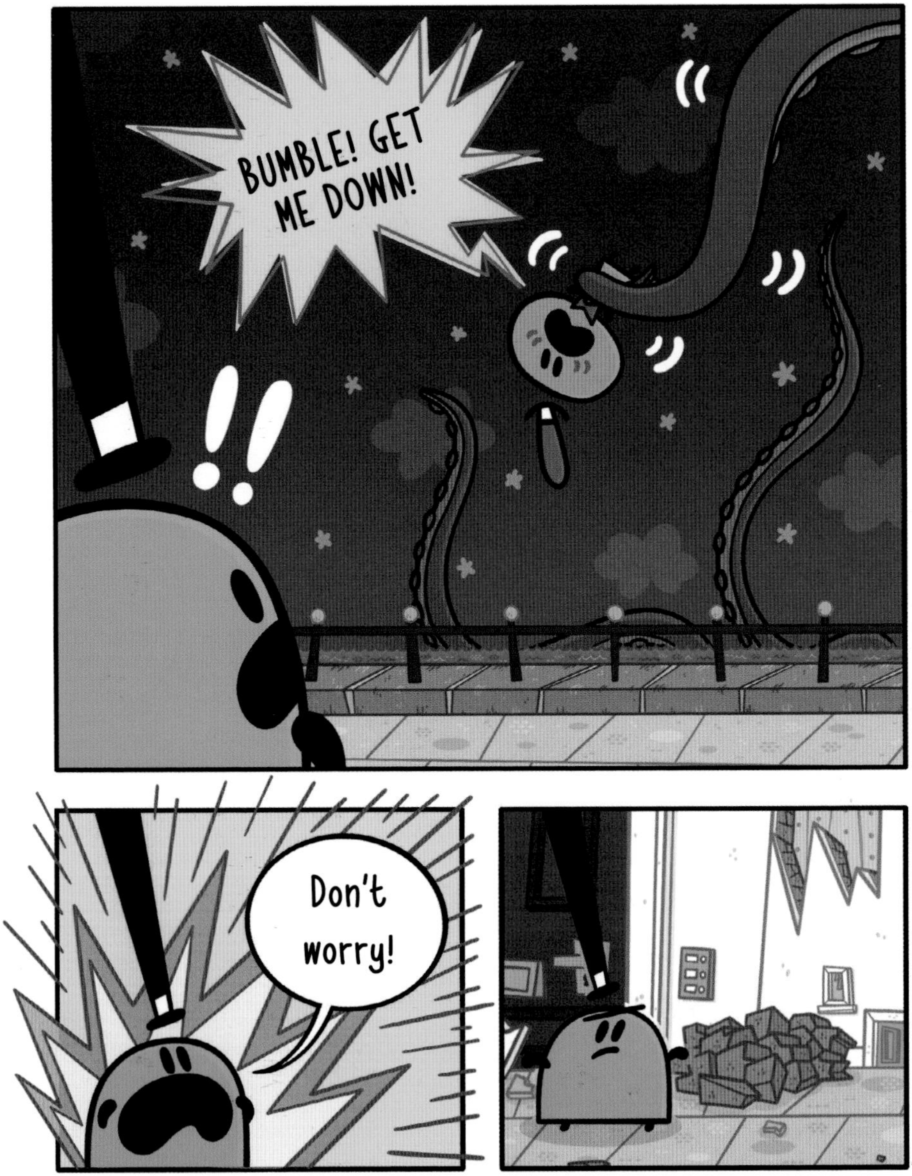
BUMBLE! GET ME DOWN!
!!
Don't worry!

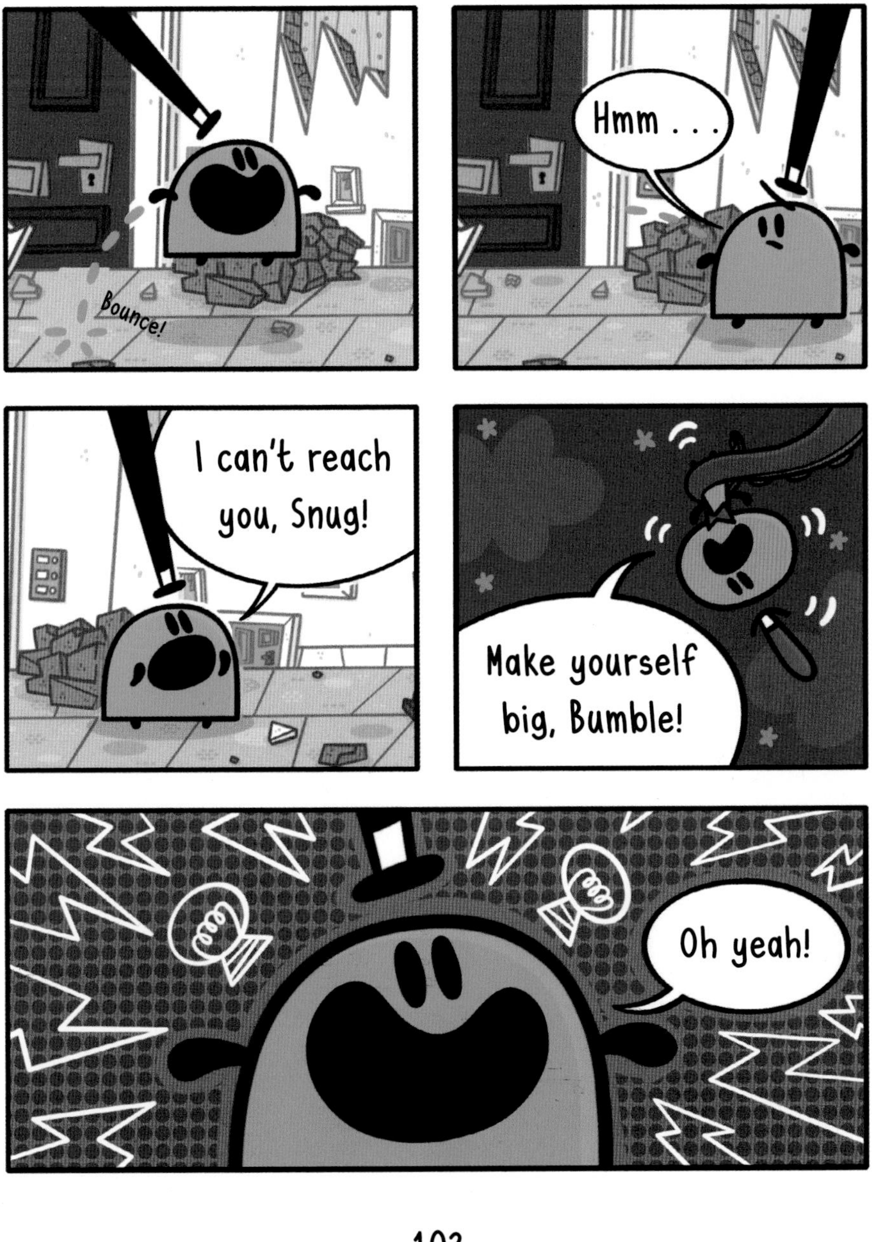
Bounce!
Hmm . . .
I can't reach you, Snug!
Make yourself big, Bumble!
Oh yeah!

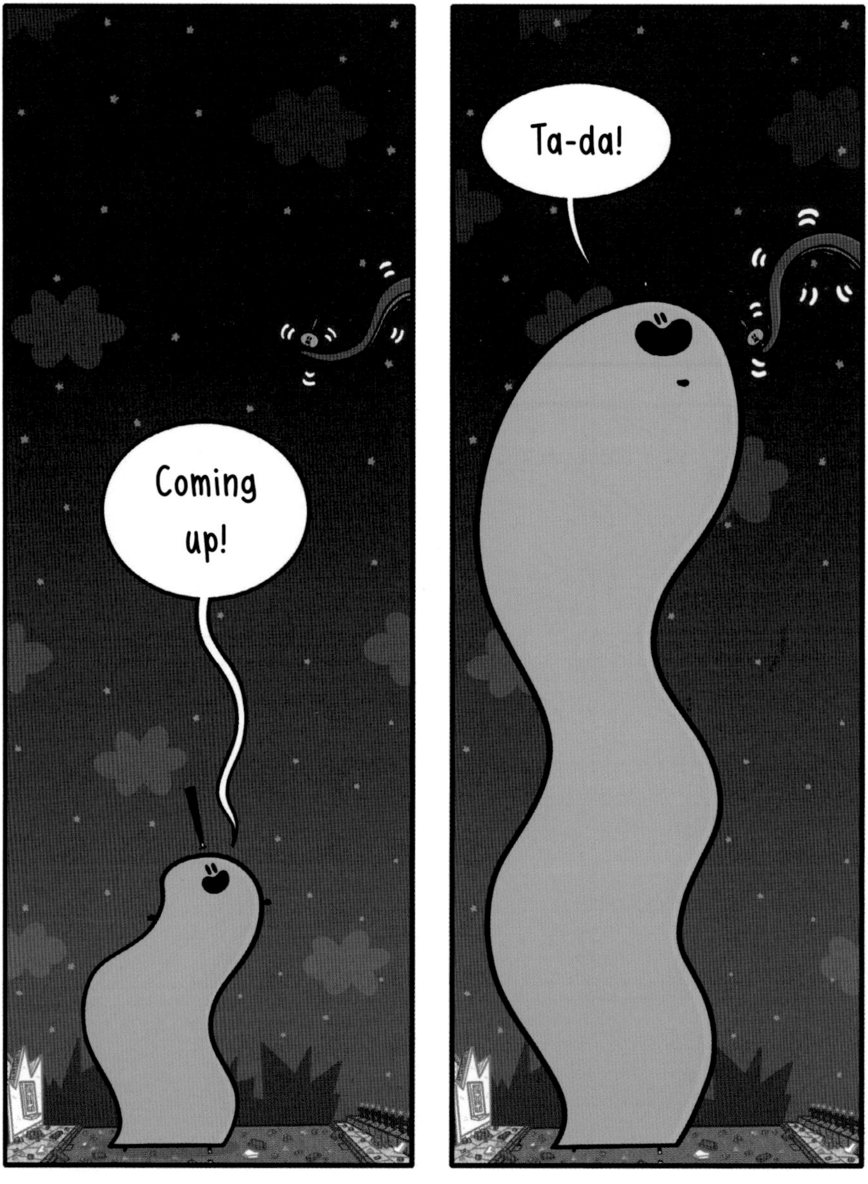
Coming up!
Ta-da!

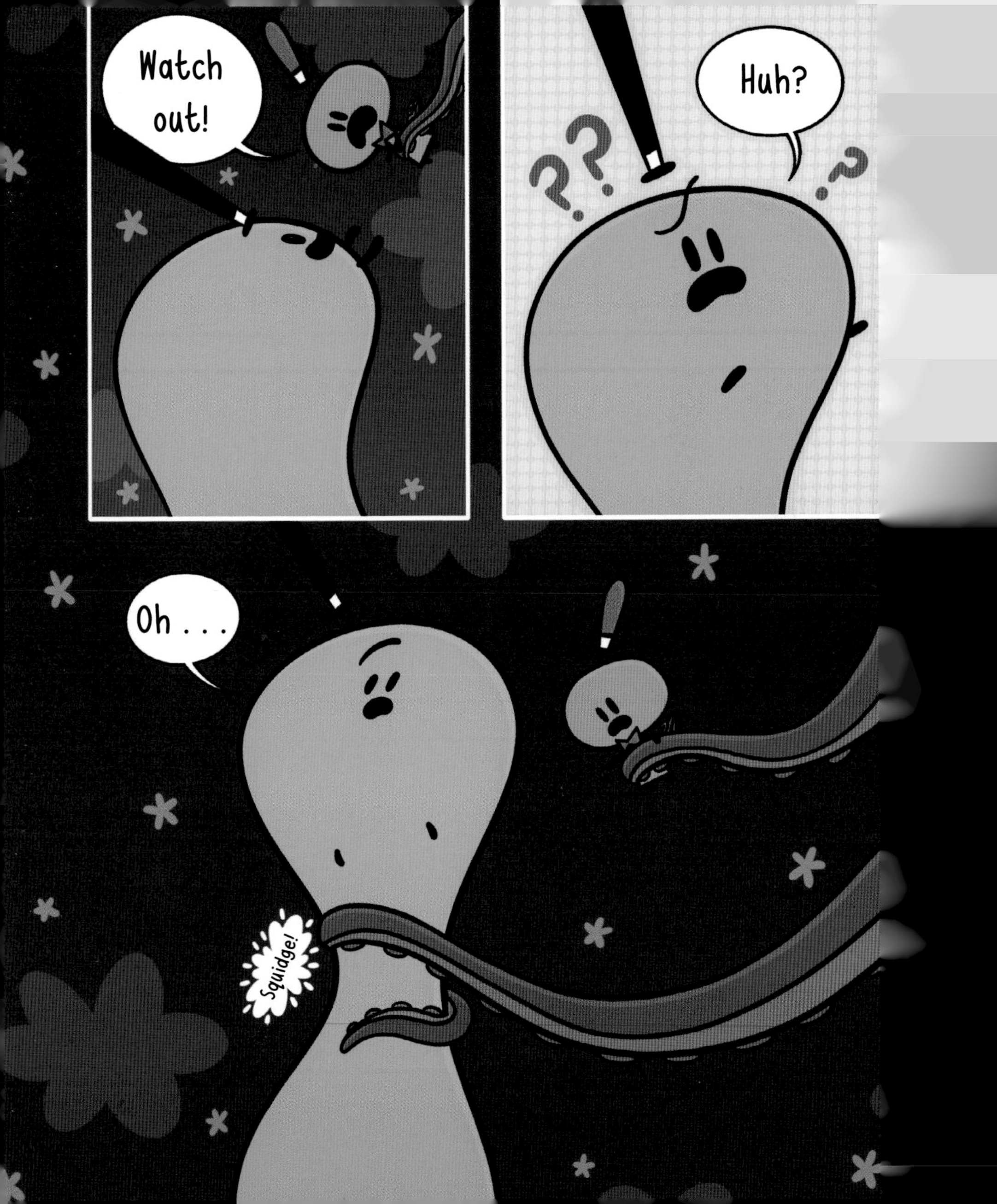
Watch out!
Huh?
Oh . . .
Squidge!

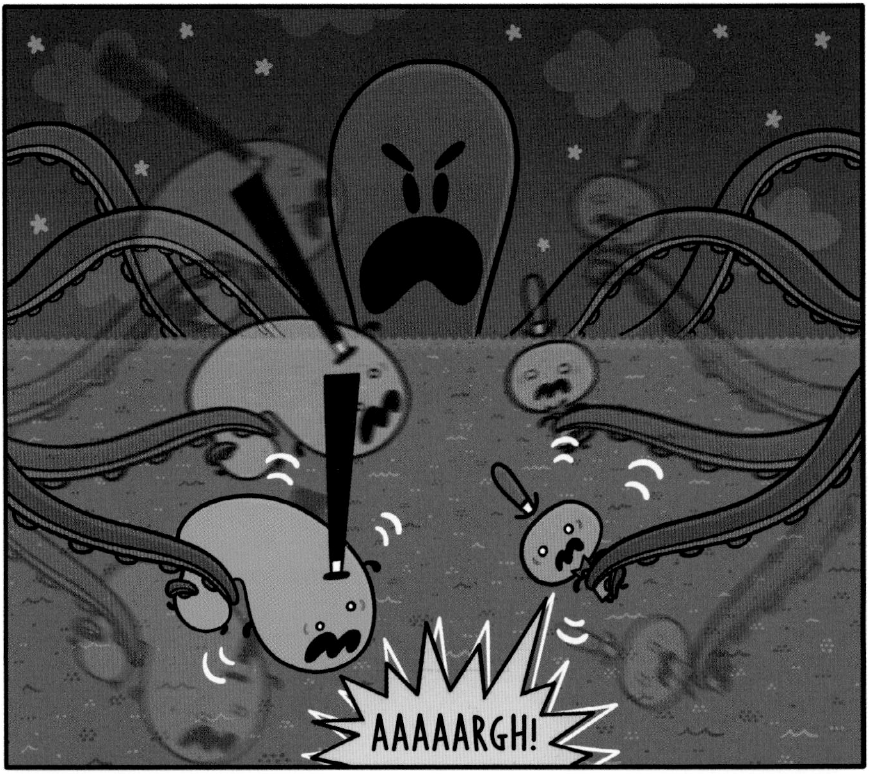
AAAAARGH!

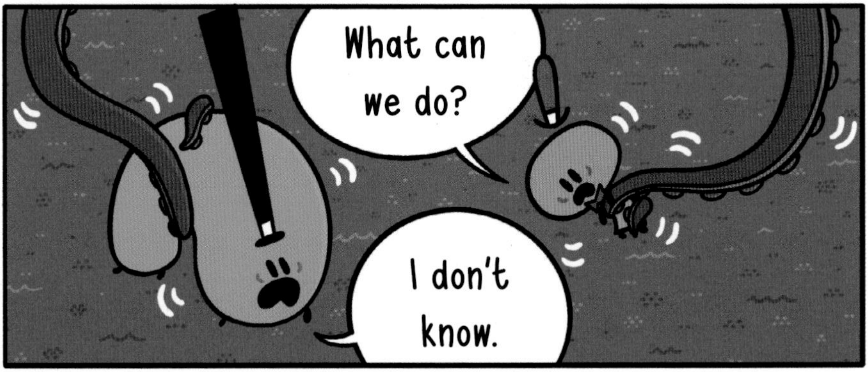
What can we do?
I don't know.

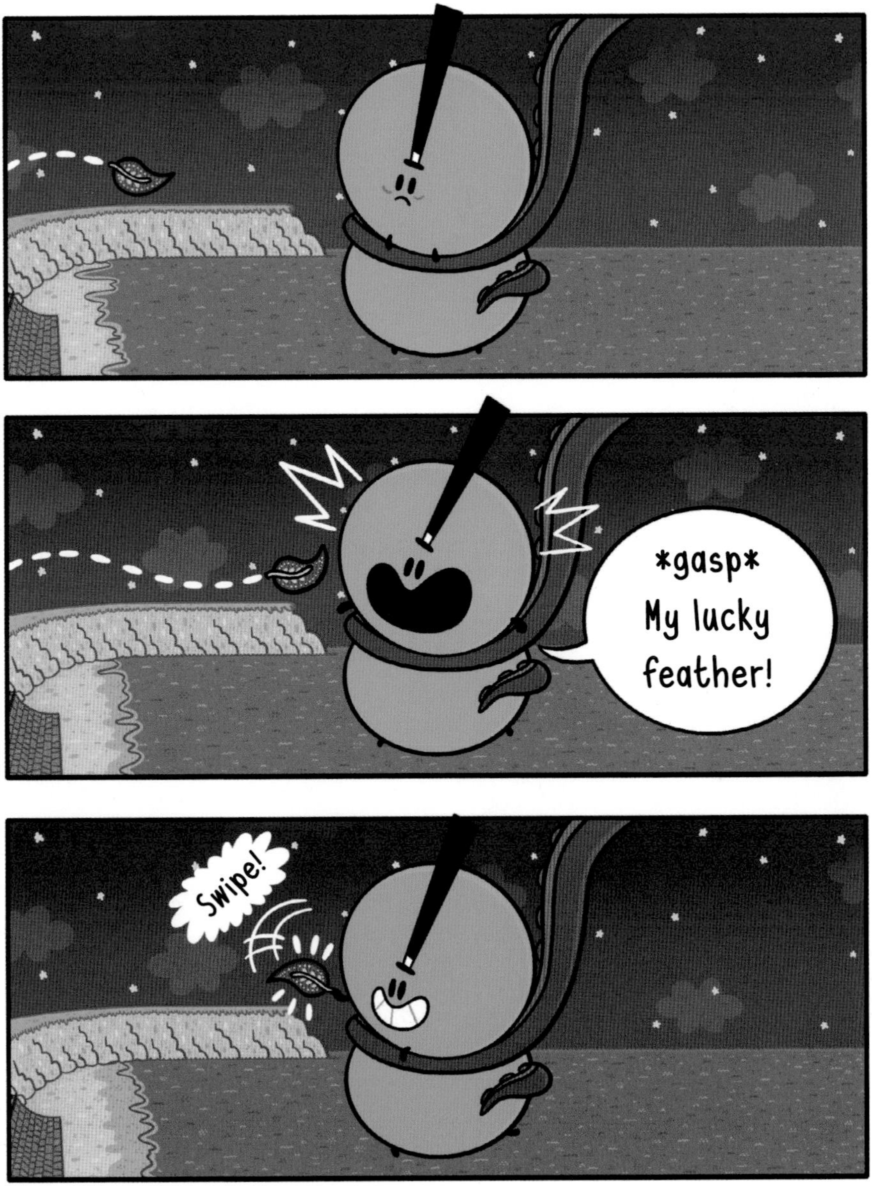
gasp
My lucky
feather!
Swipe!

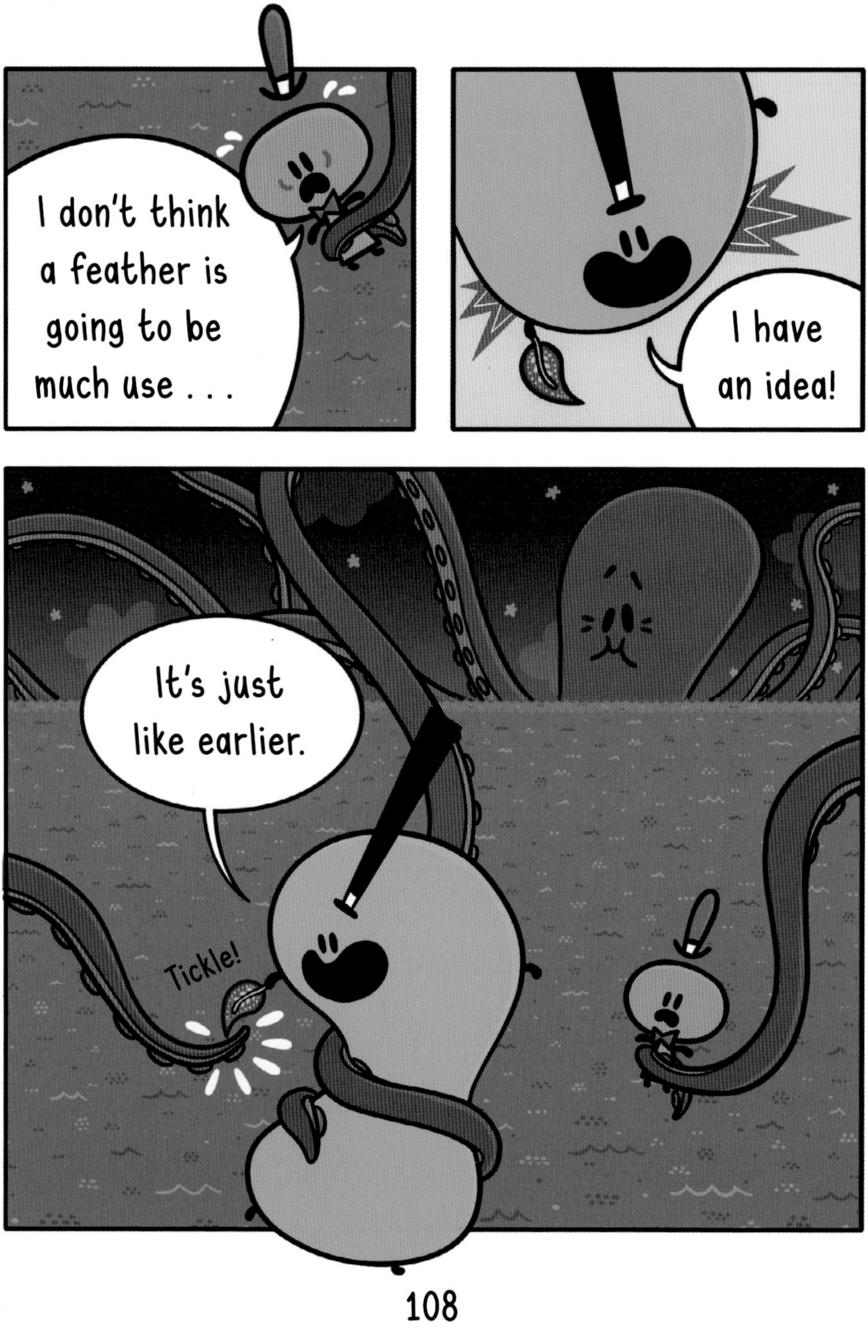
I don't think a feather is going to be much use . . .
I have an idea!
It's just like earlier.
Tickle!

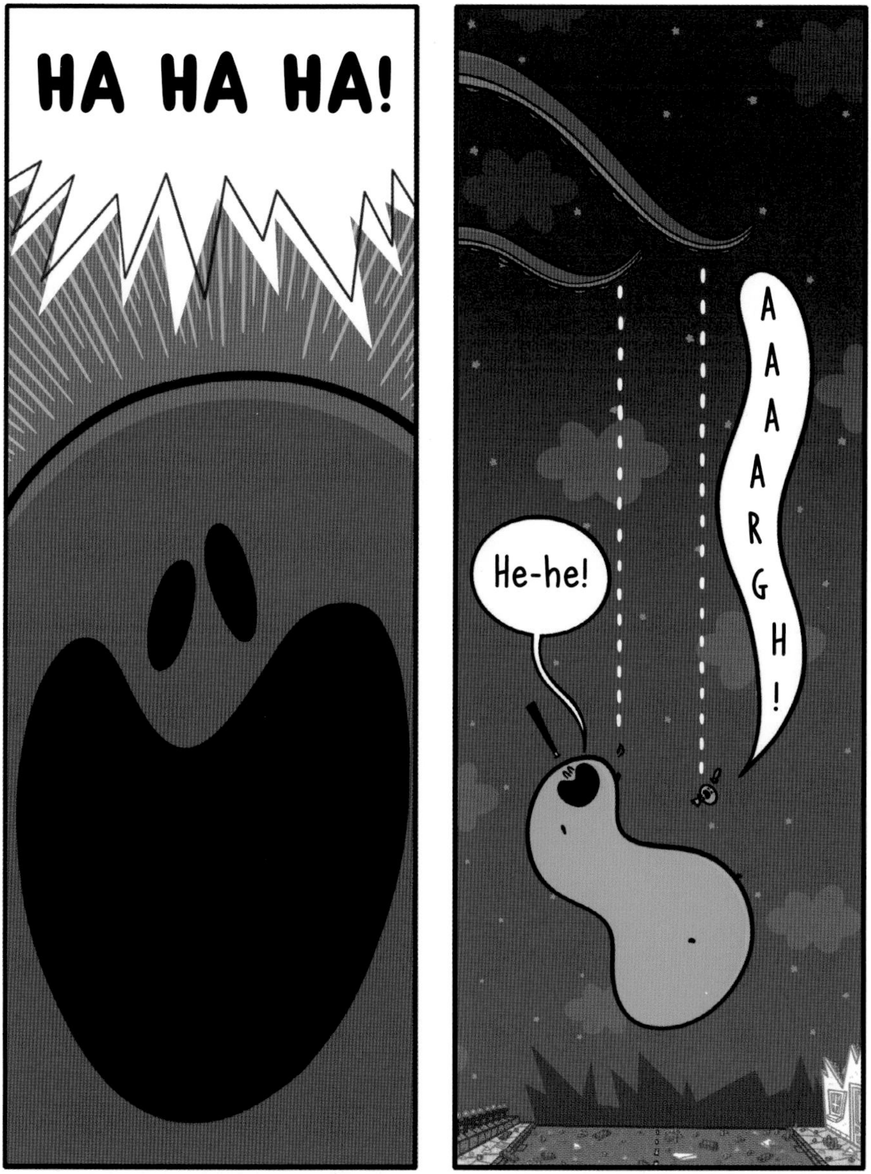
HA HA HA!
He-he!
AAAAARGH!

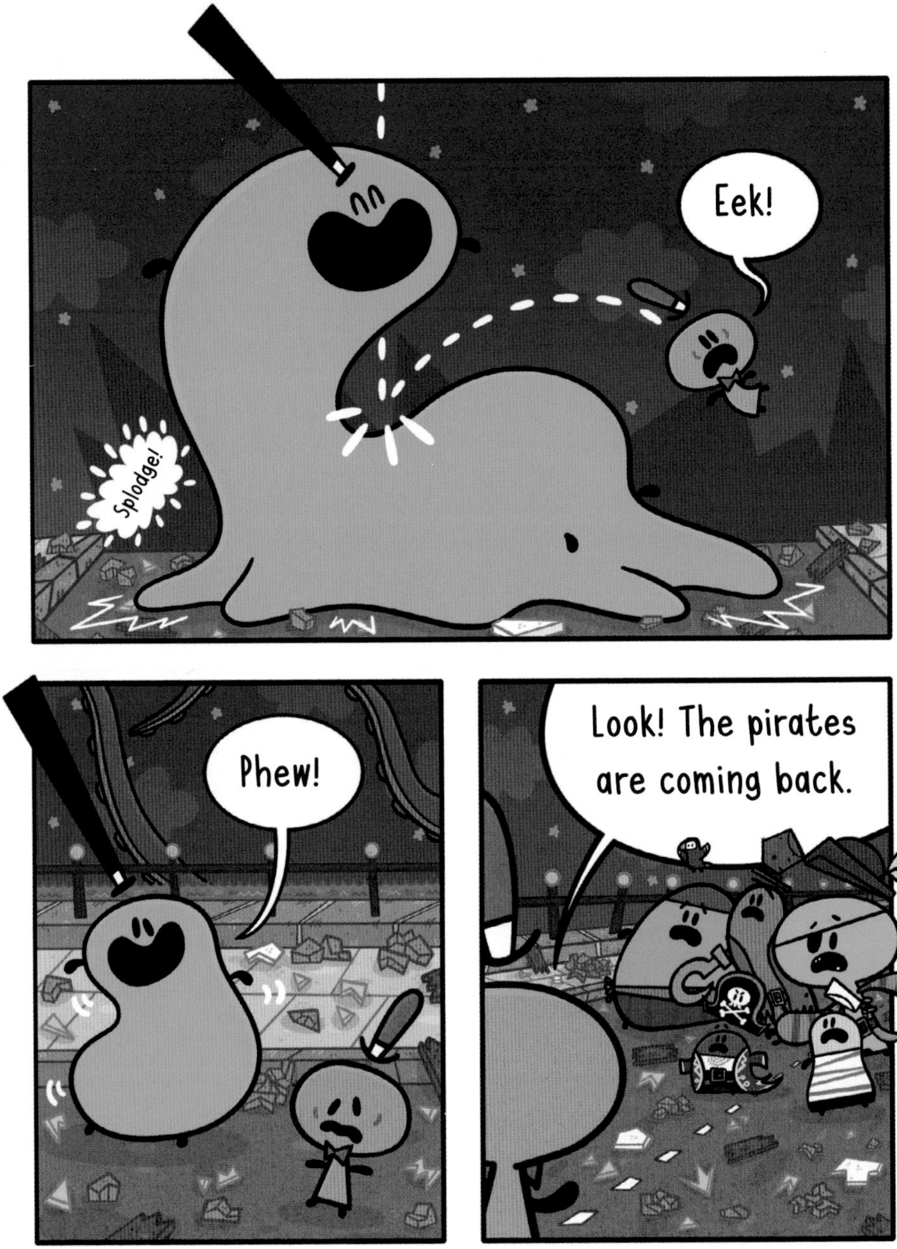
Eek!
Splodge!
Phew!
Look! The pirates are coming back.

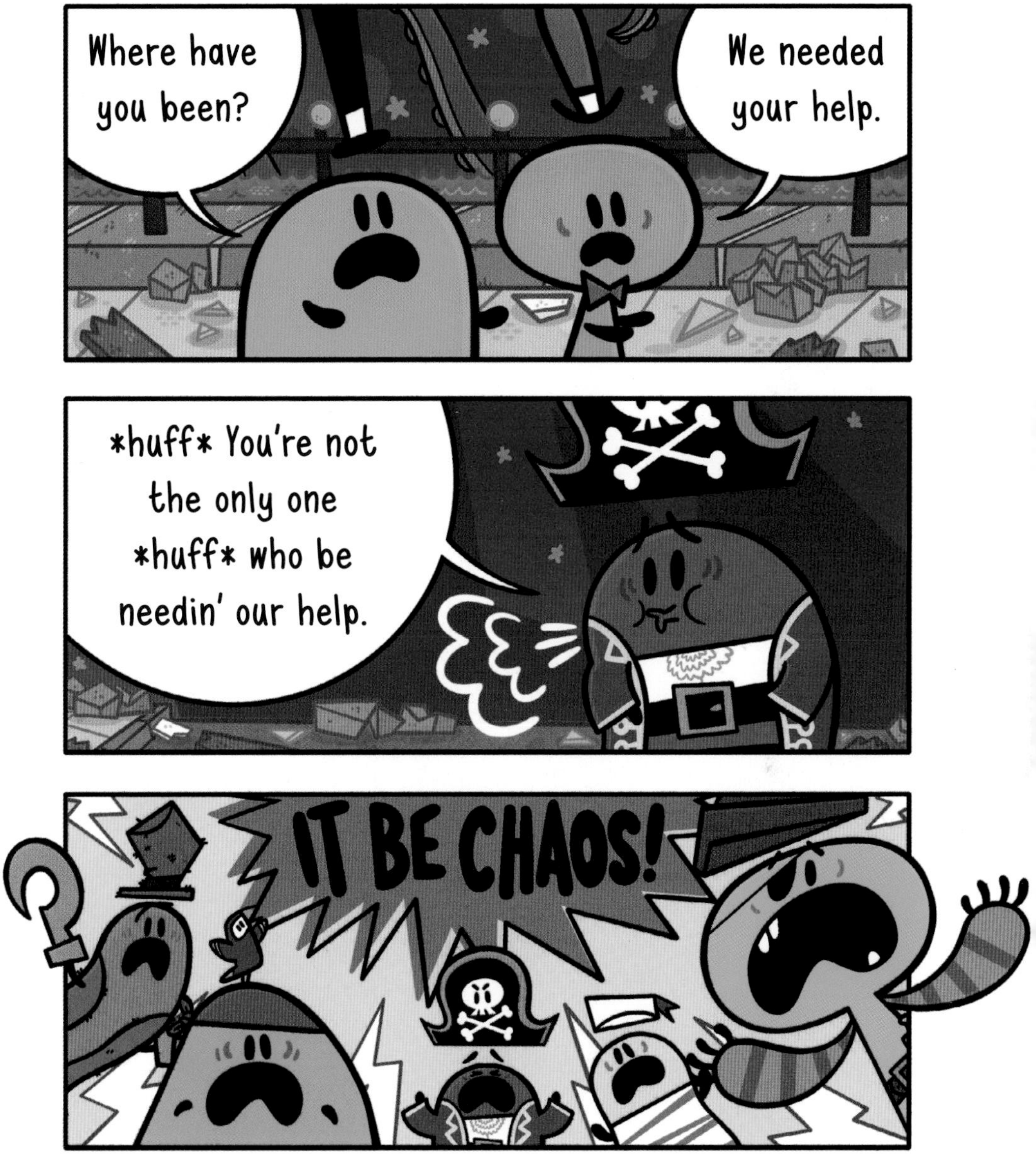

Where have you been?
We needed your help.
huff You're not the only one *huff* who be needin' our help.
IT BE CHAOS!

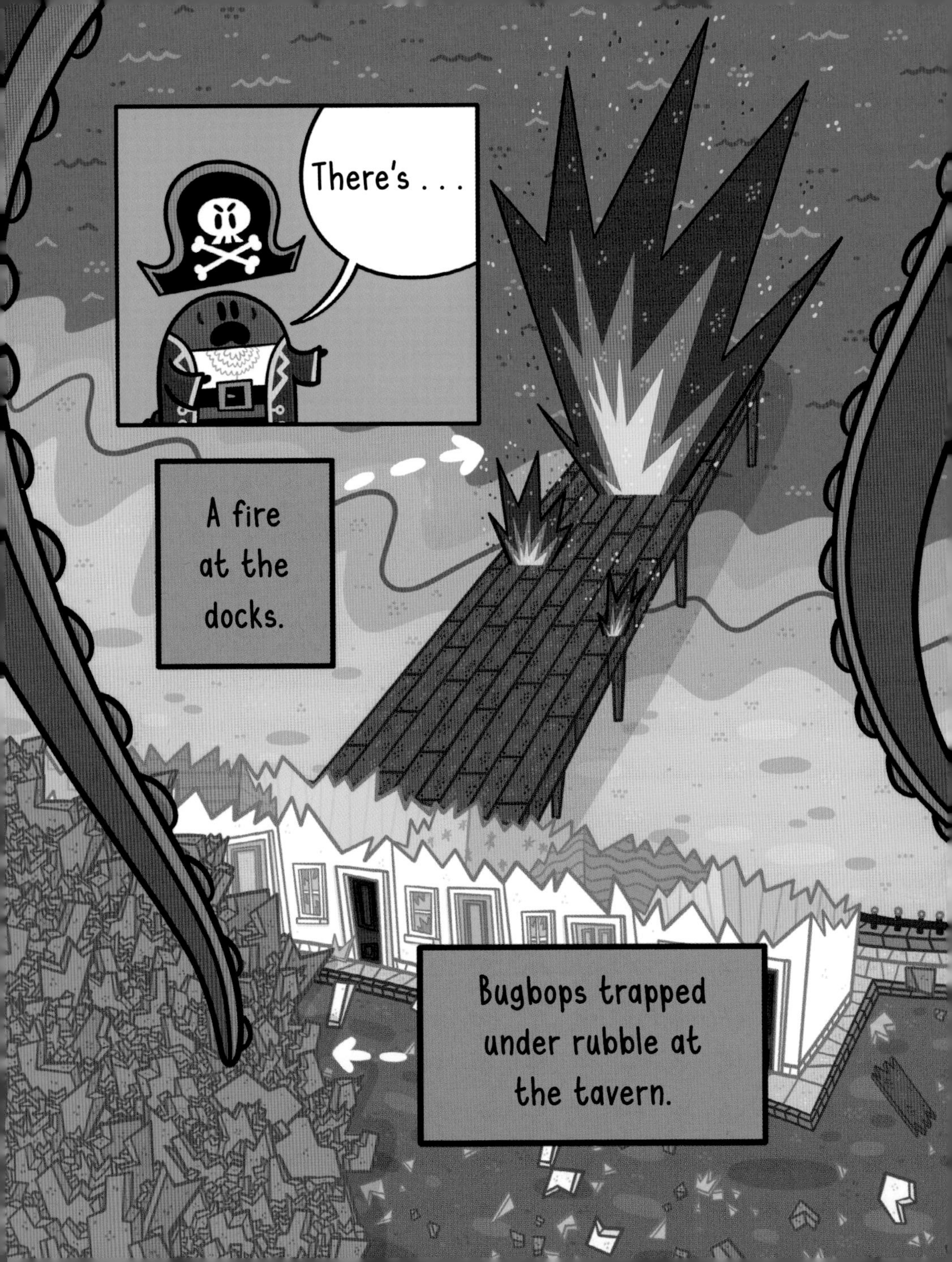
There's . . .
A fire at the docks.
Bugbops trapped under rubble at the tavern.

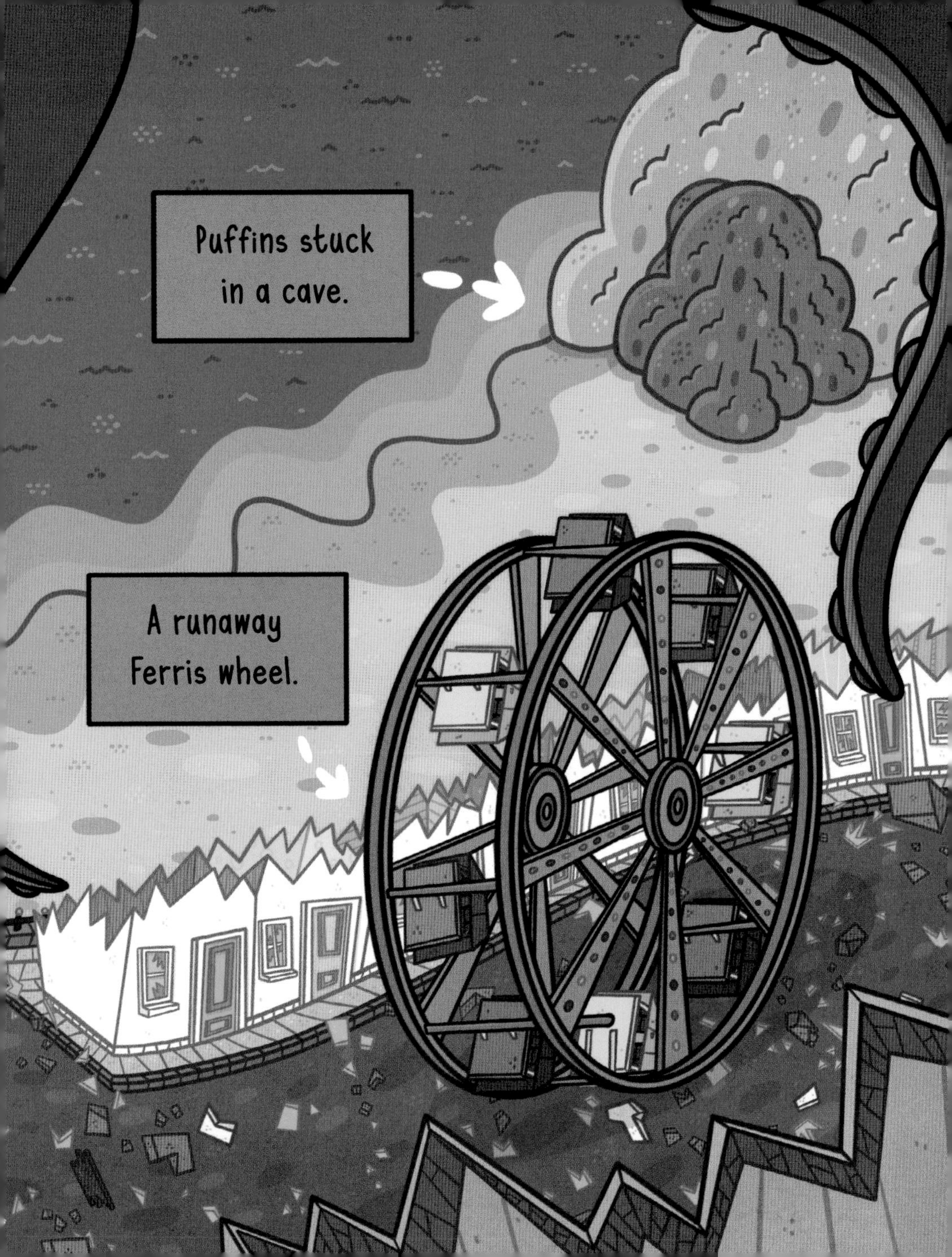
Puffins stuck in a cave.
A runaway Ferris wheel.

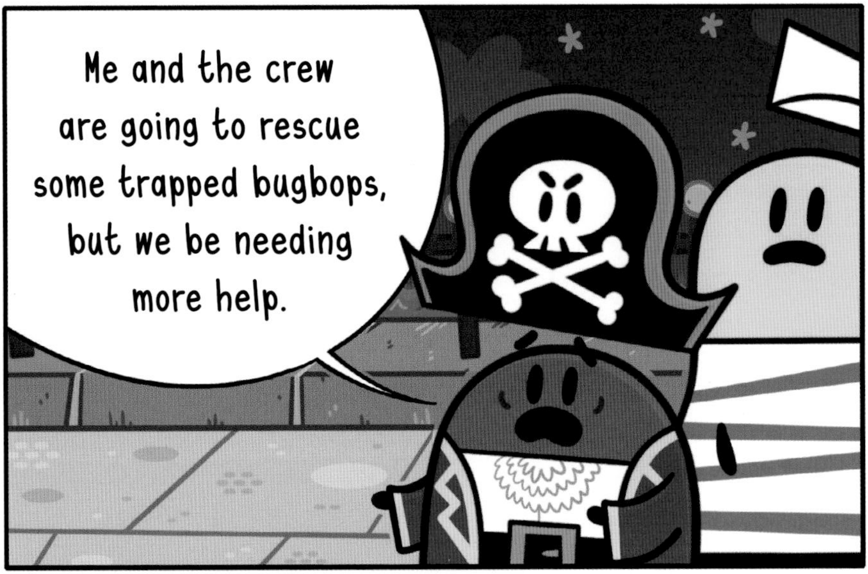
Me and the crew are going to rescue some trapped bugbops, but we be needing more help.

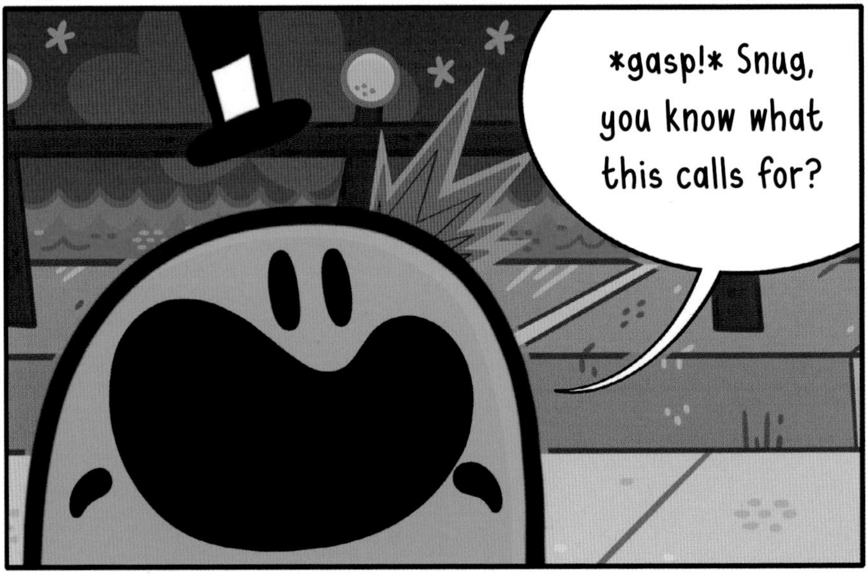
gasp! Snug, you know what this calls for?

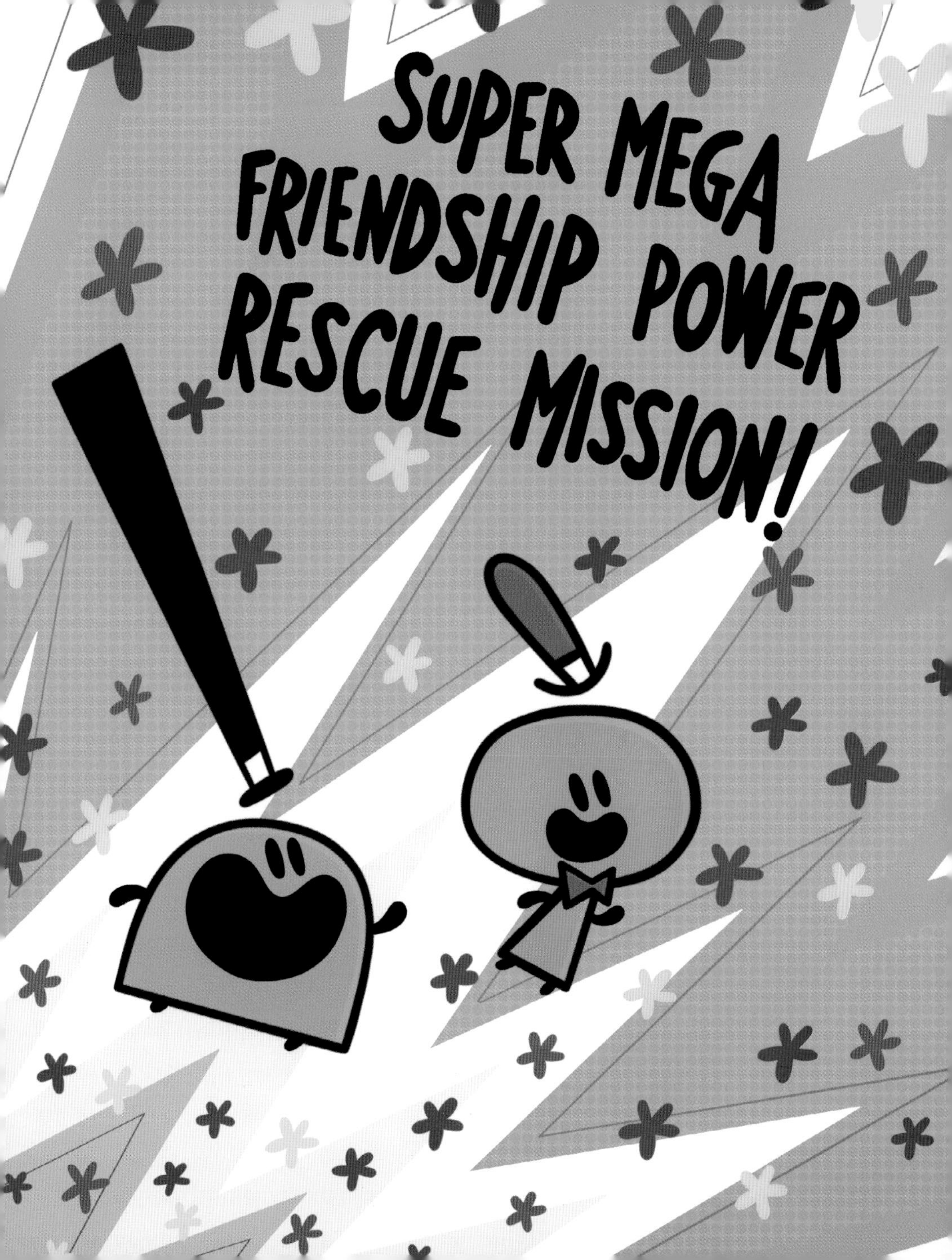
SUPER MEGA FRIENDSHIP POWER RESCUE MISSION!

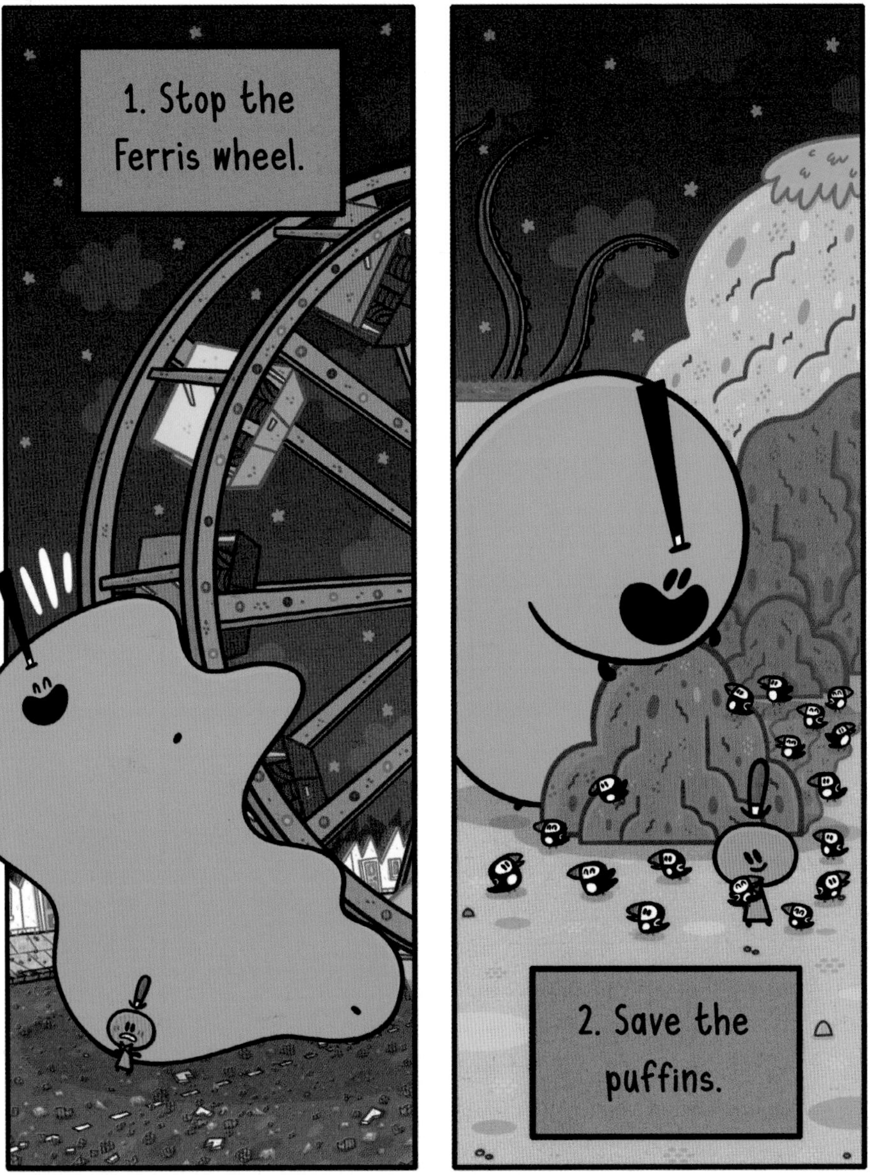
1. Stop the Ferris wheel.
Splat!
2. Save the puffins.

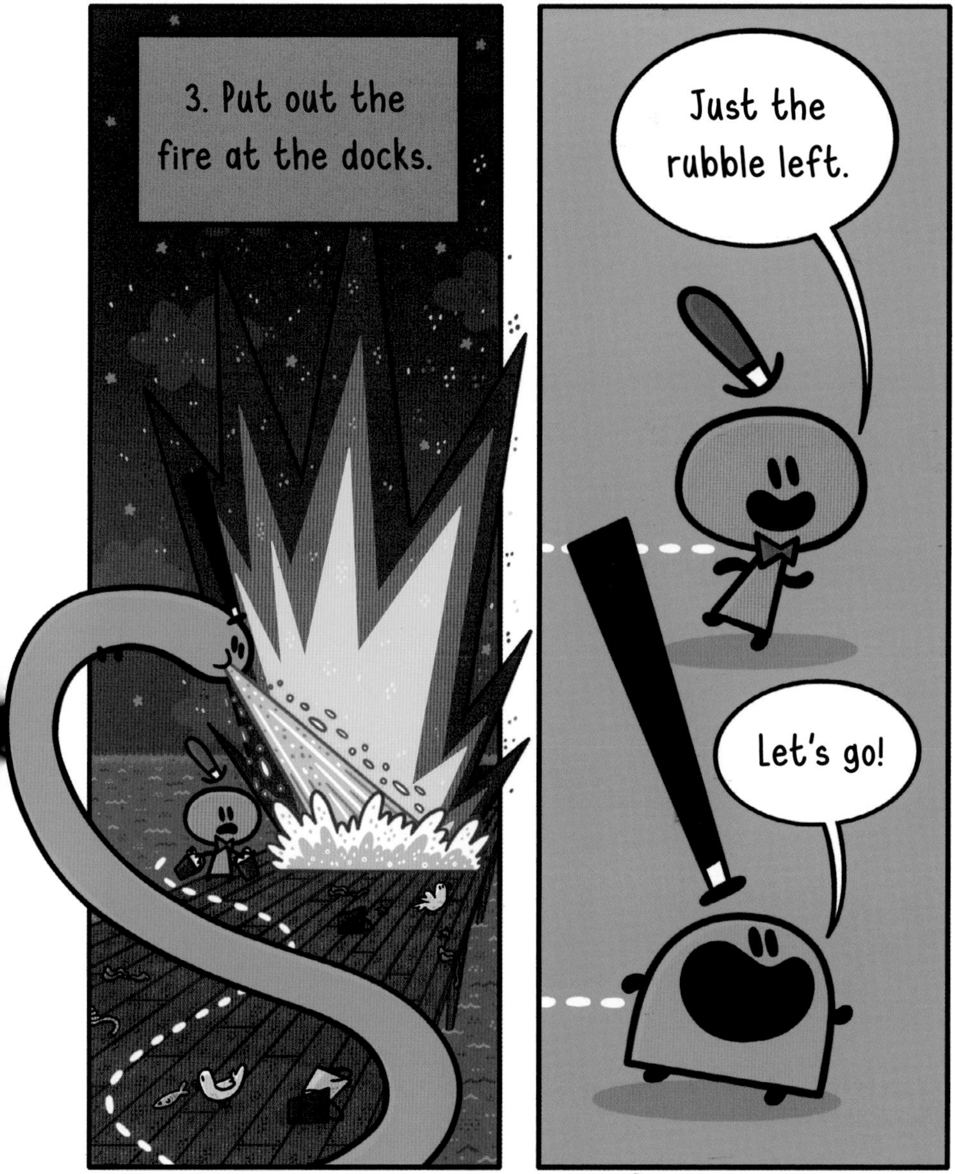
3. Put out the fire at the docks.
Just the rubble left.
Let's go!

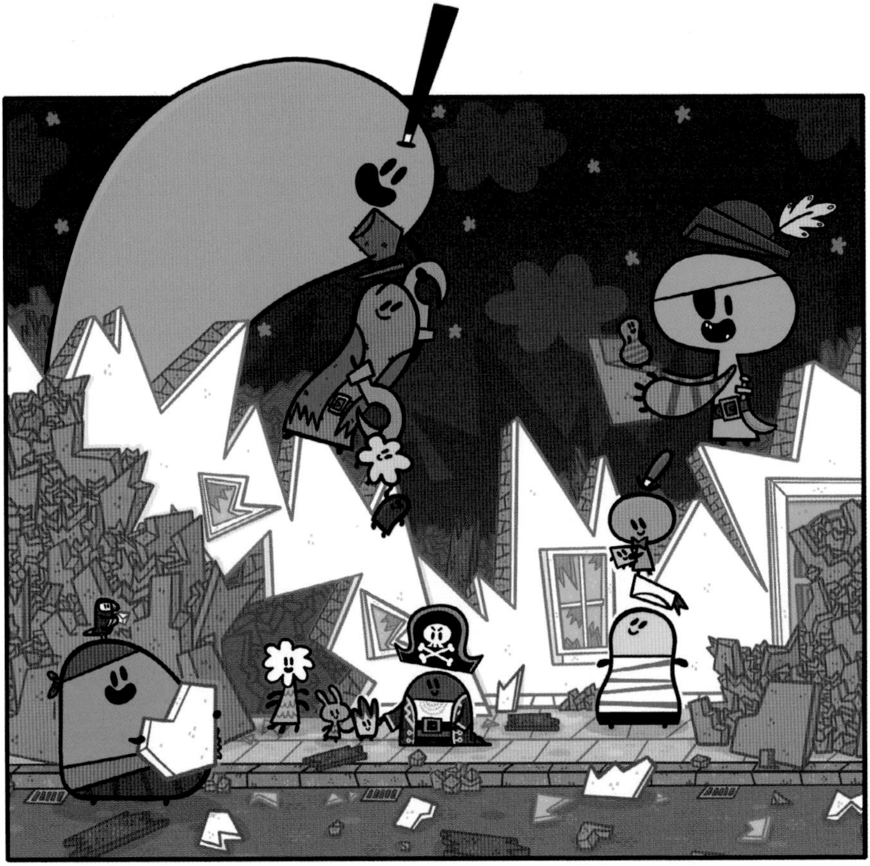

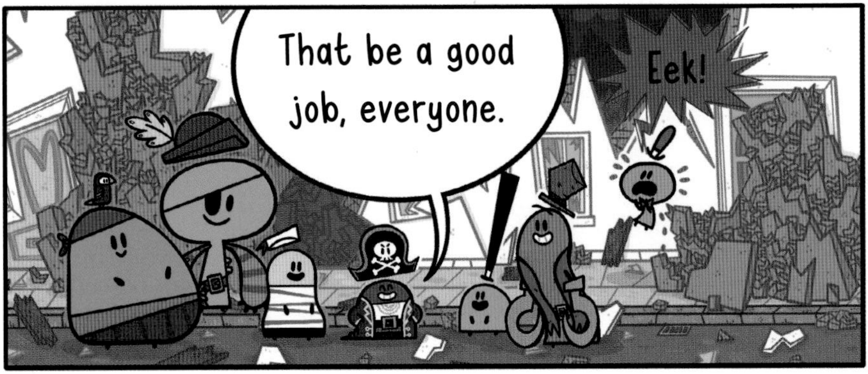
That be a good job, everyone.
Eek!

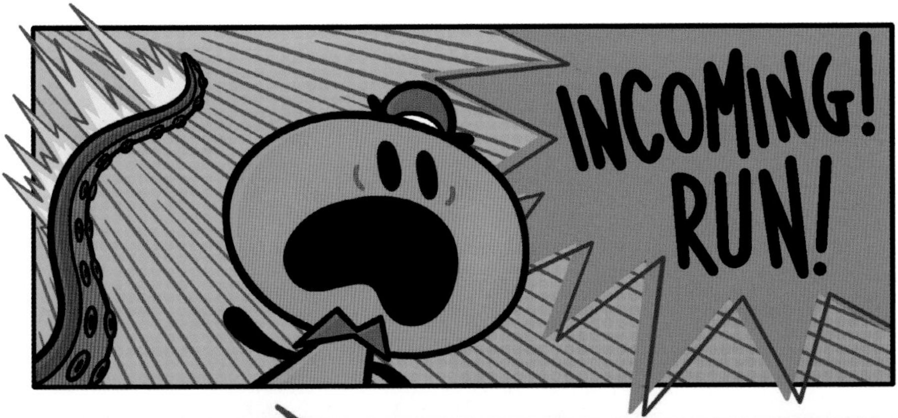
INCOMING!
RUN!

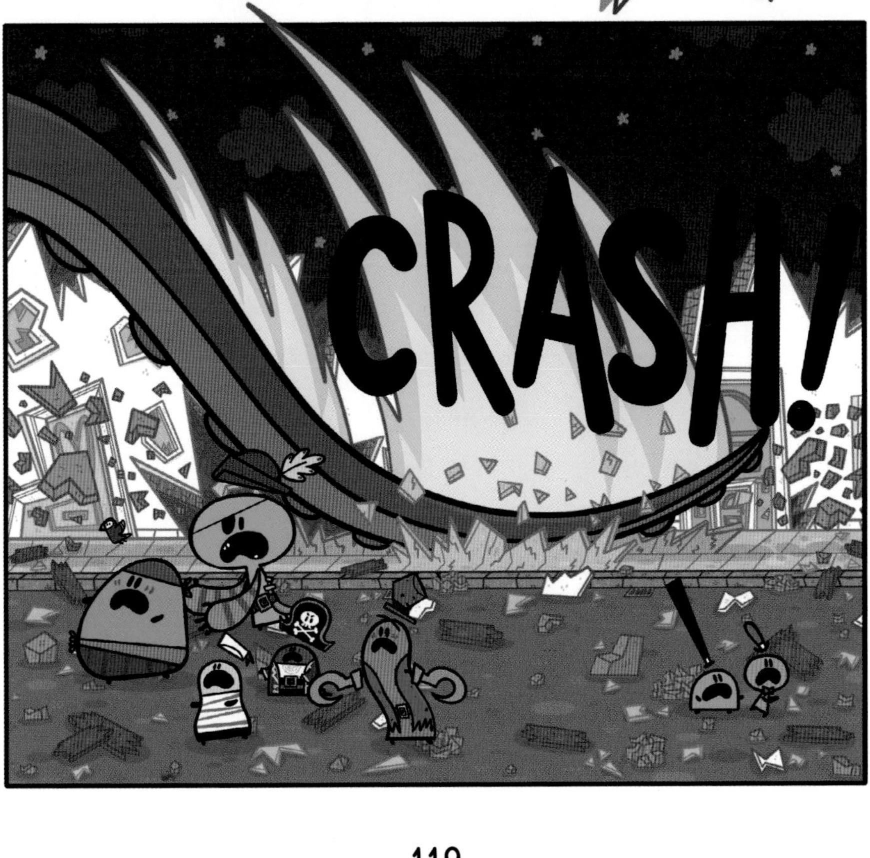
CRASH!

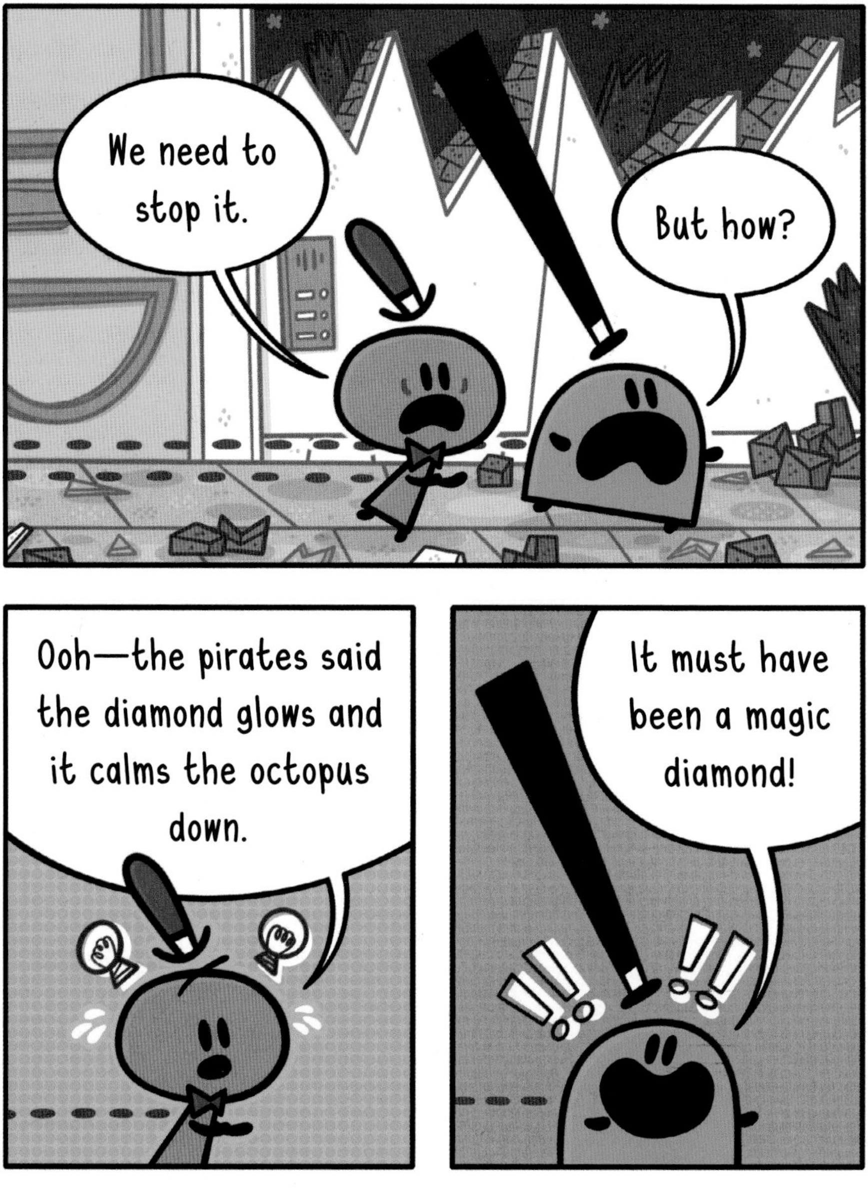
We need to stop it.
But how?
Ooh—the pirates said the diamond glows and it calms the octopus down.
It must have been a magic diamond!

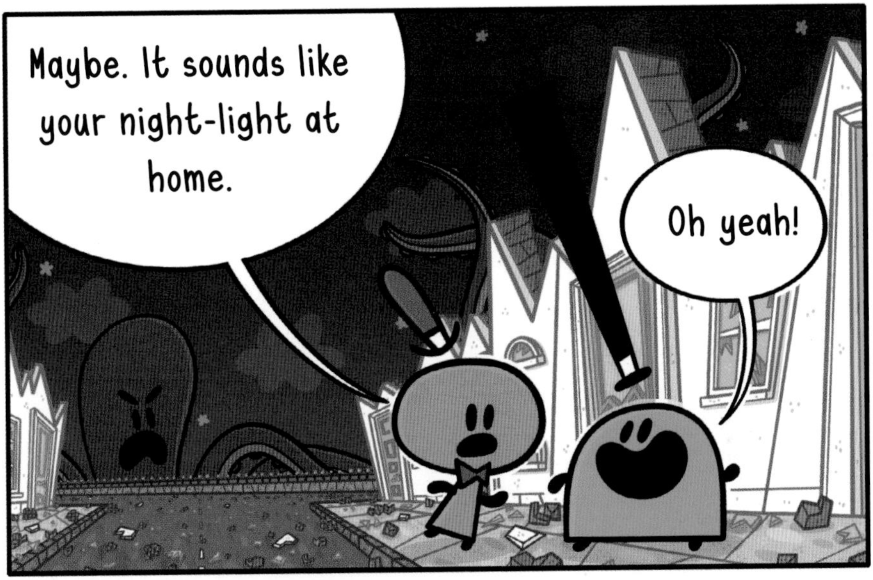
Maybe. It sounds like your night-light at home.
Oh yeah!

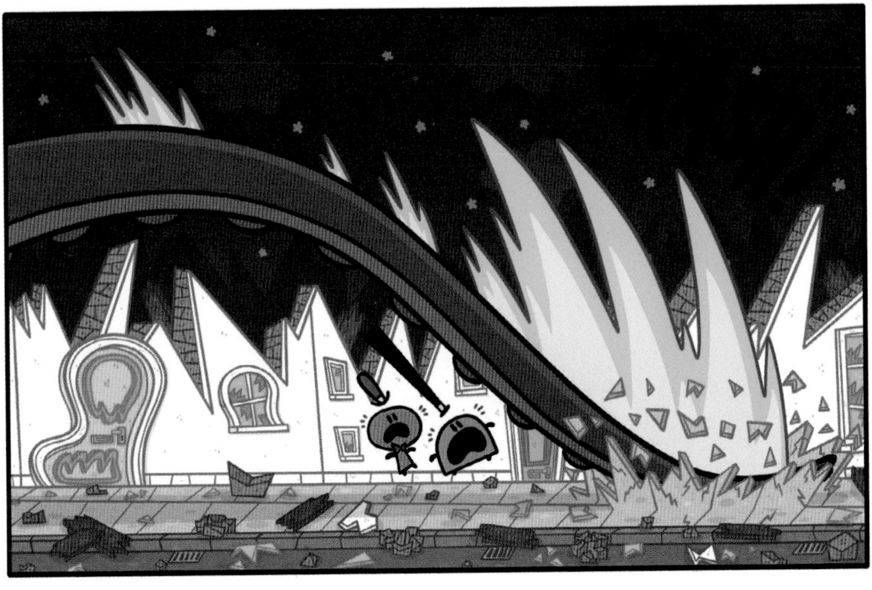

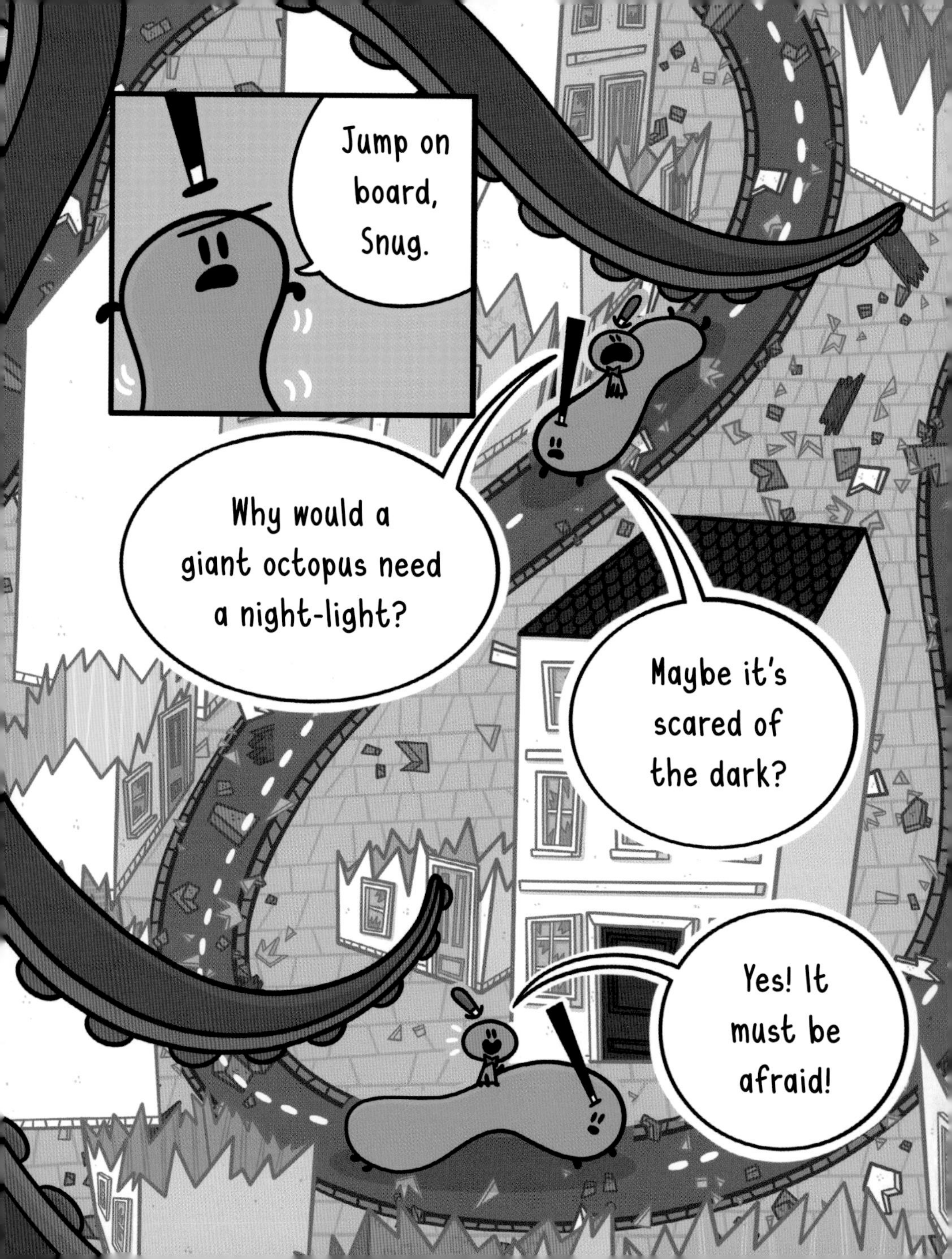
Jump on board, Snug.
Why would a giant octopus need a night-light?
Maybe it's scared of the dark?
Yes! It must be afraid!

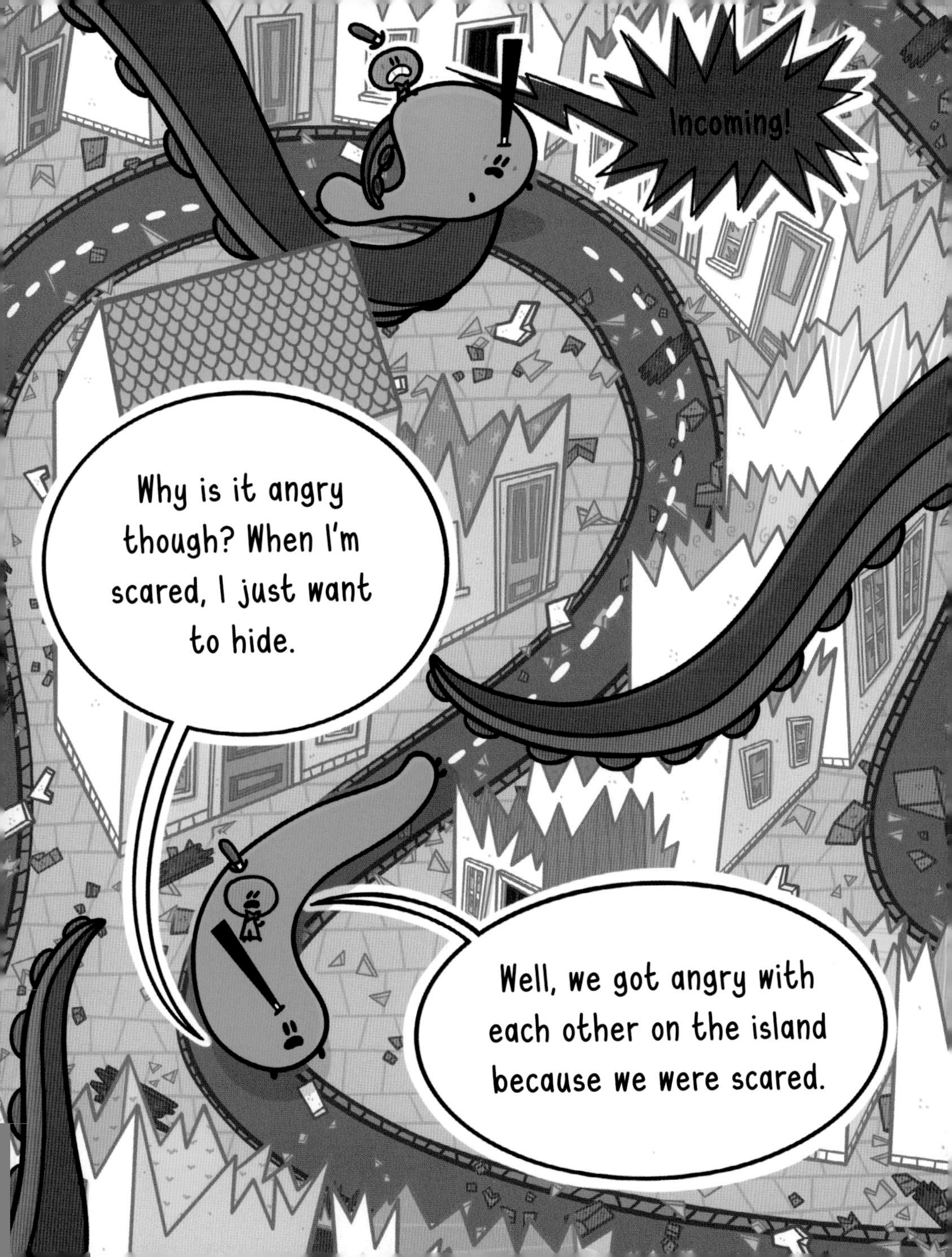
Incoming!
Why is it angry though? When I'm scared, I just want to hide.
Well, we got angry with each other on the island because we were scared.

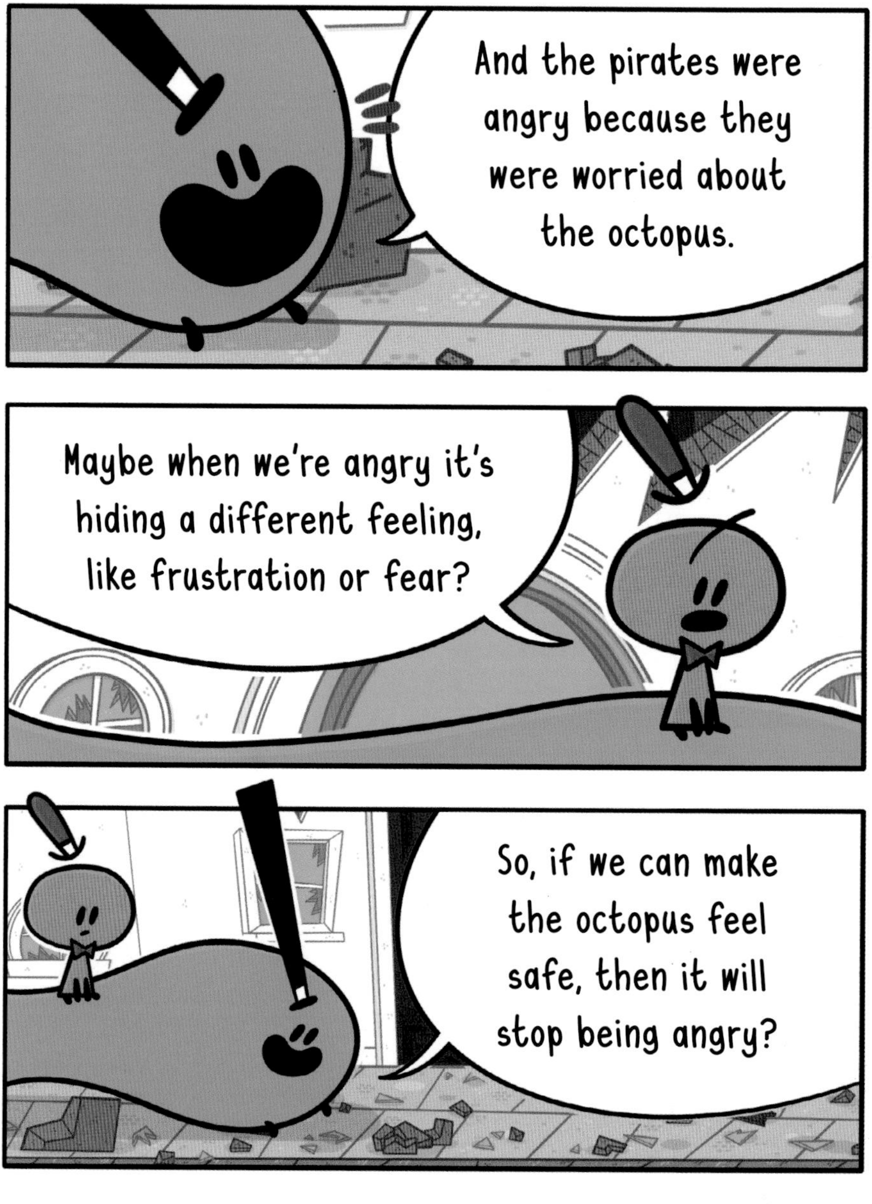
And the pirates were angry because they were worried about the octopus.
Maybe when we're angry it's hiding a different feeling, like frustration or fear?
So, if we can make the octopus feel safe, then it will stop being angry?

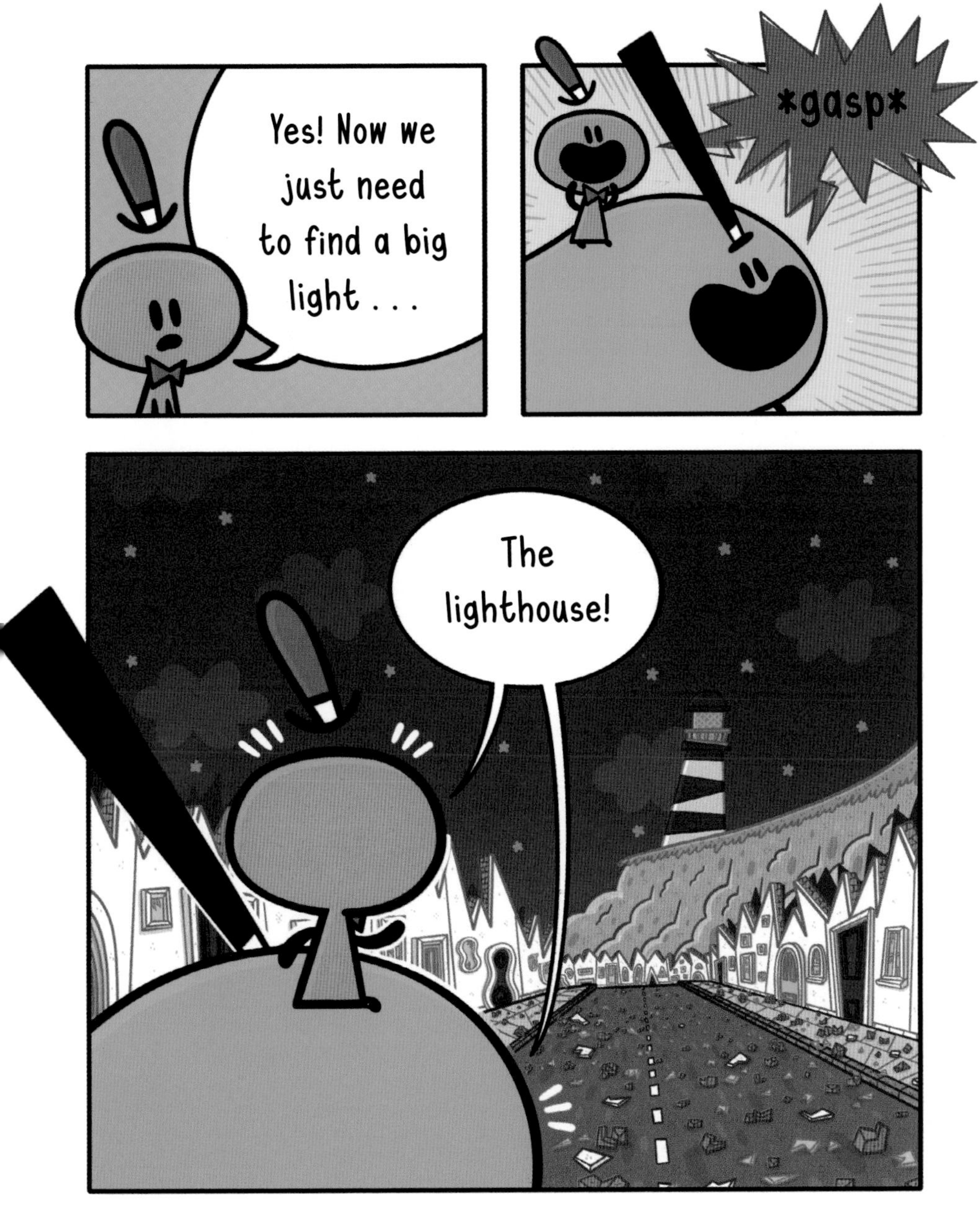
Yes! Now we just need to find a big light . . .
gasp
The lighthouse!

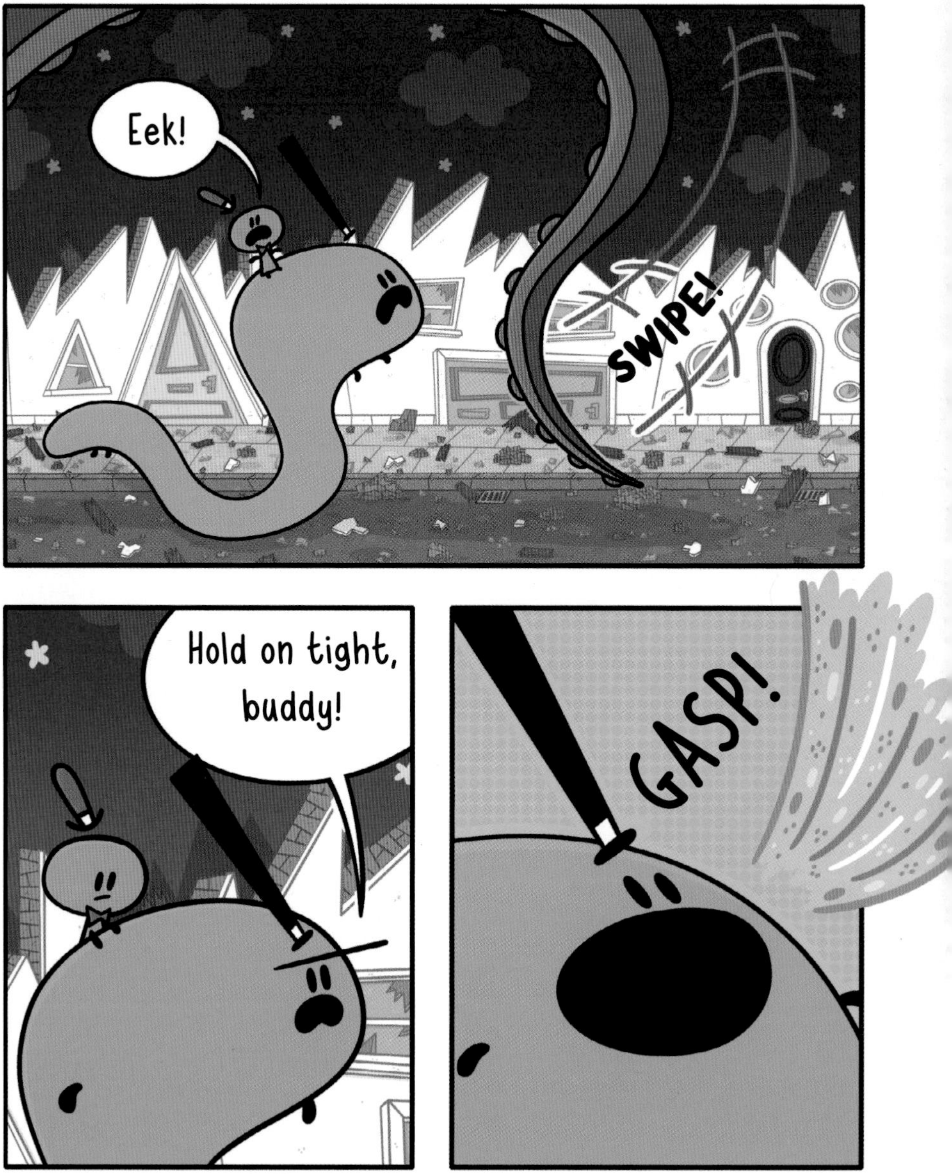
Eek!
SWIPE!
Hold on tight, buddy!
GASP!

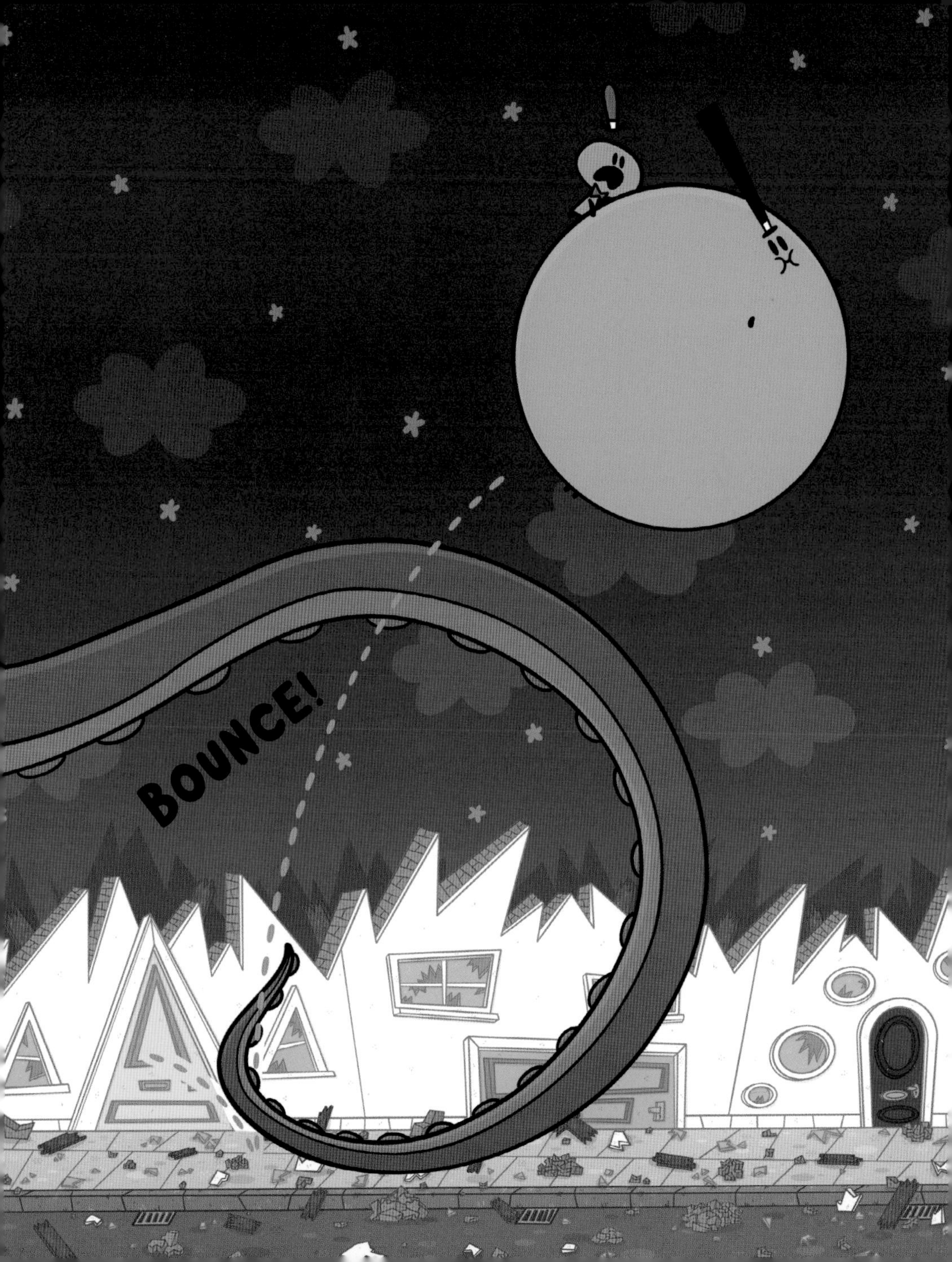
BOUNCE!

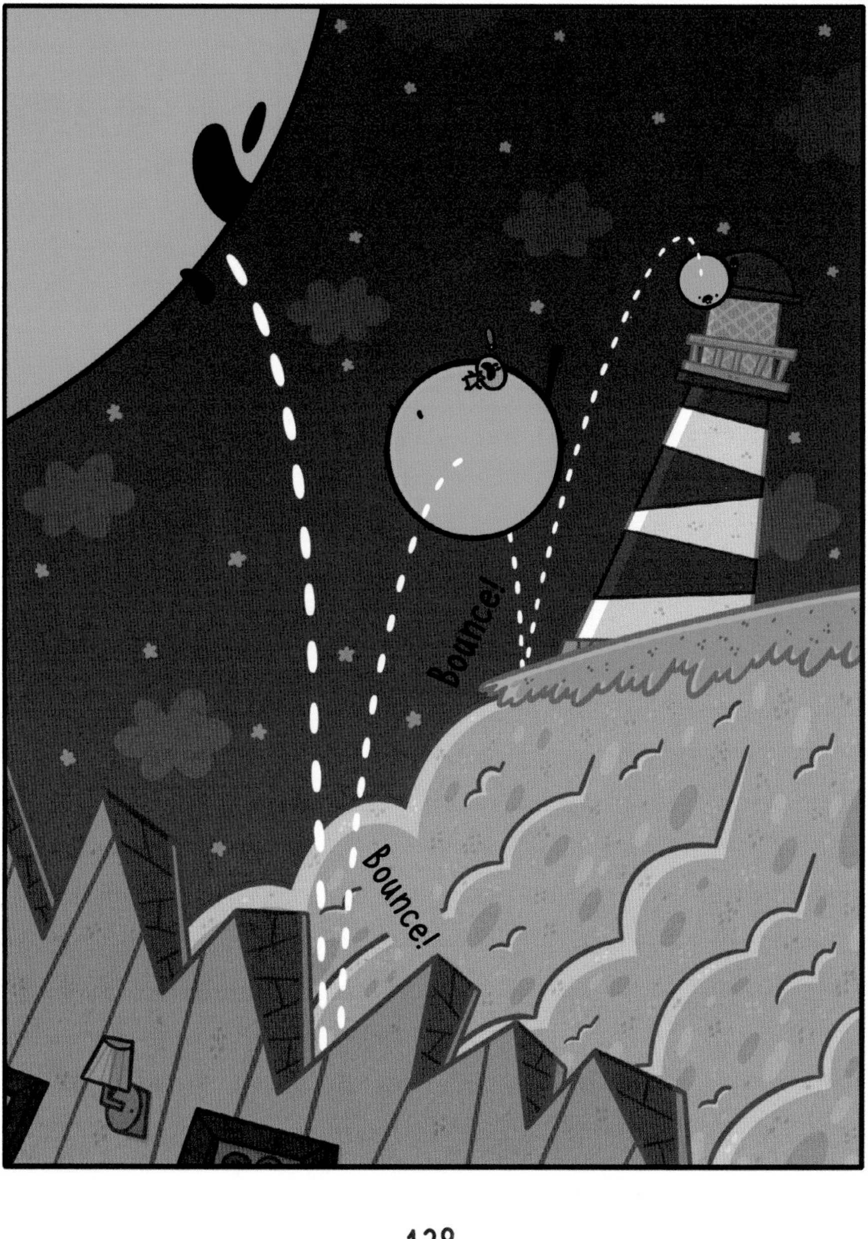
Bounce!
Bounce!

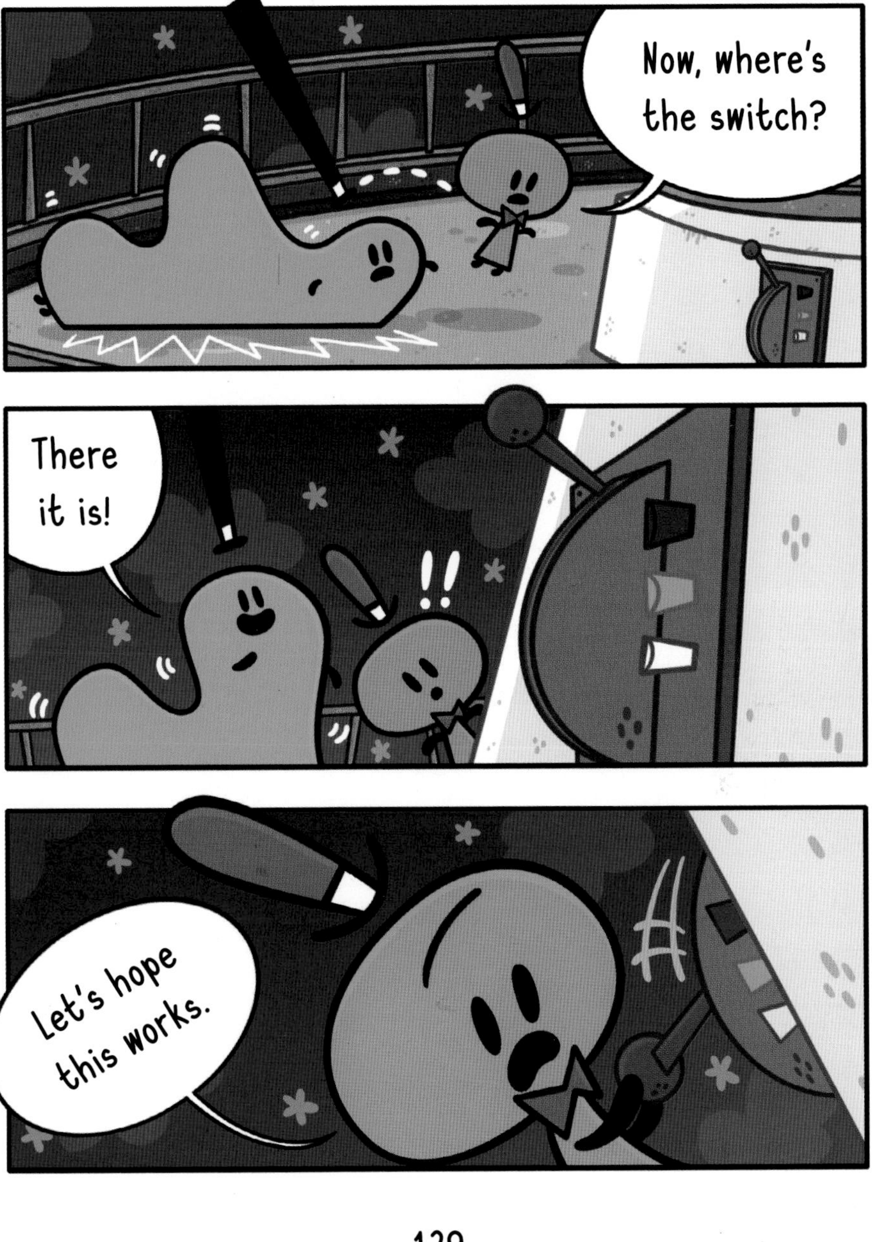
Now, where's the switch?
There it is!
Let's hope this works.

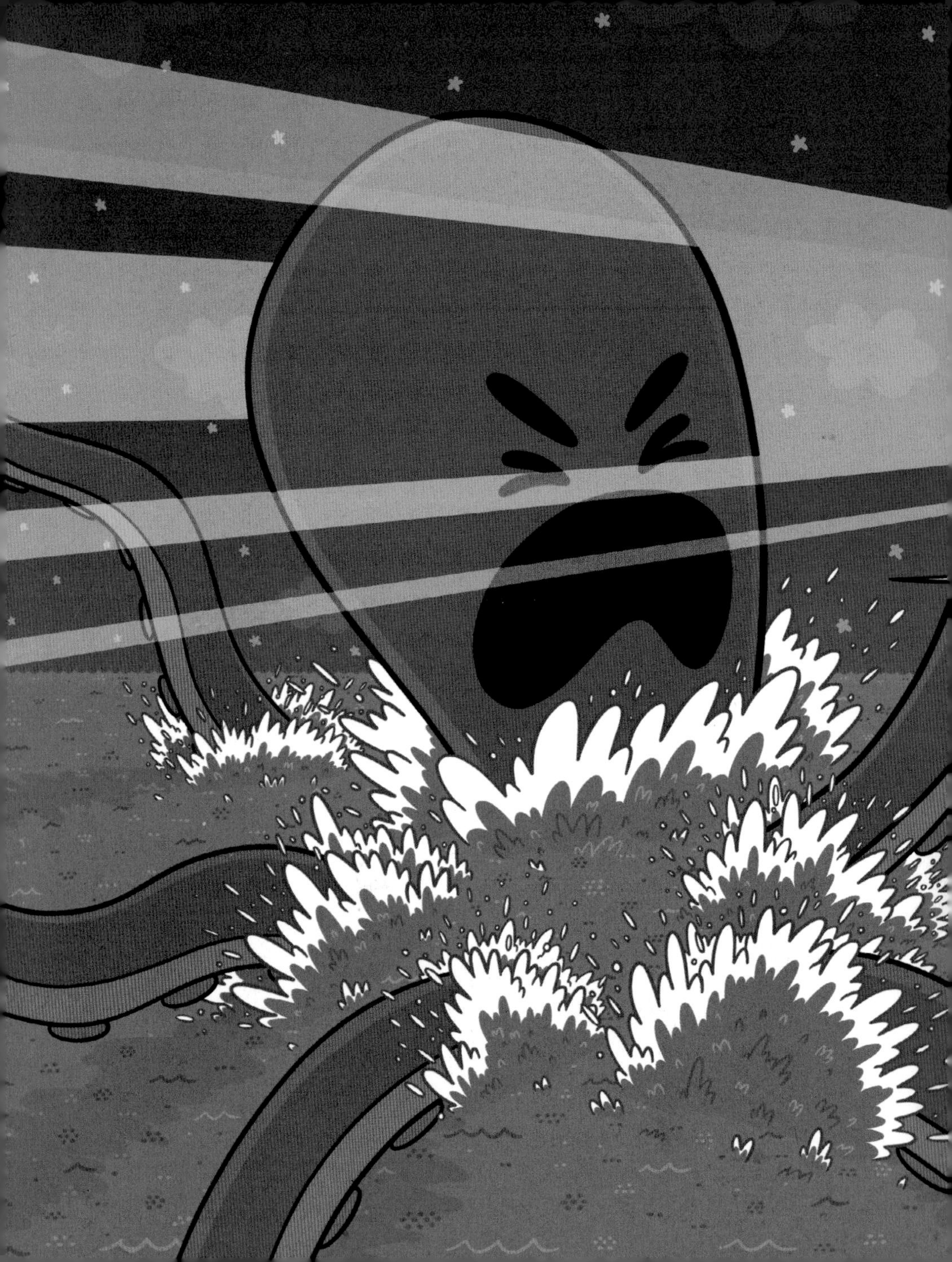

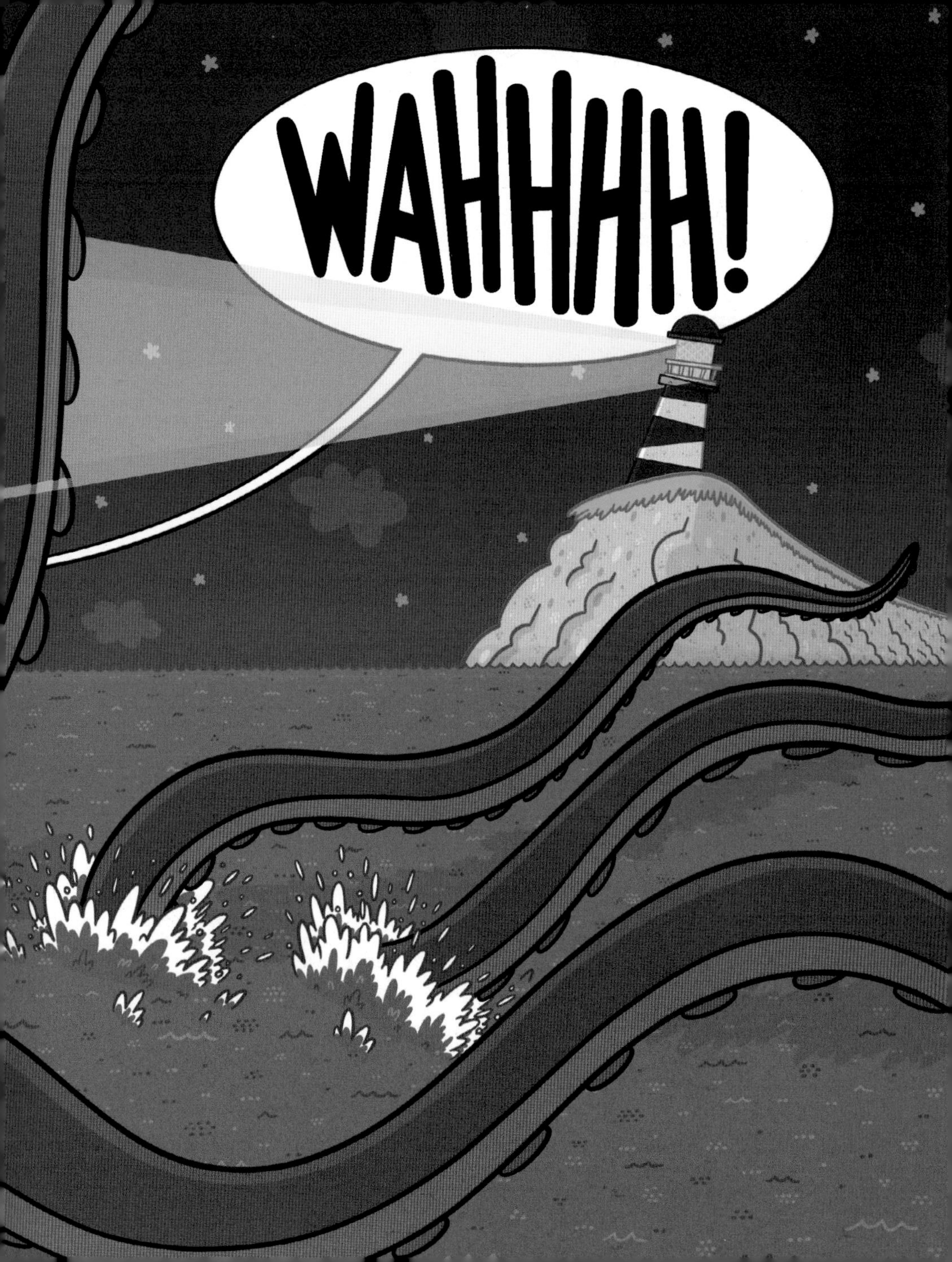
WAHHHH!

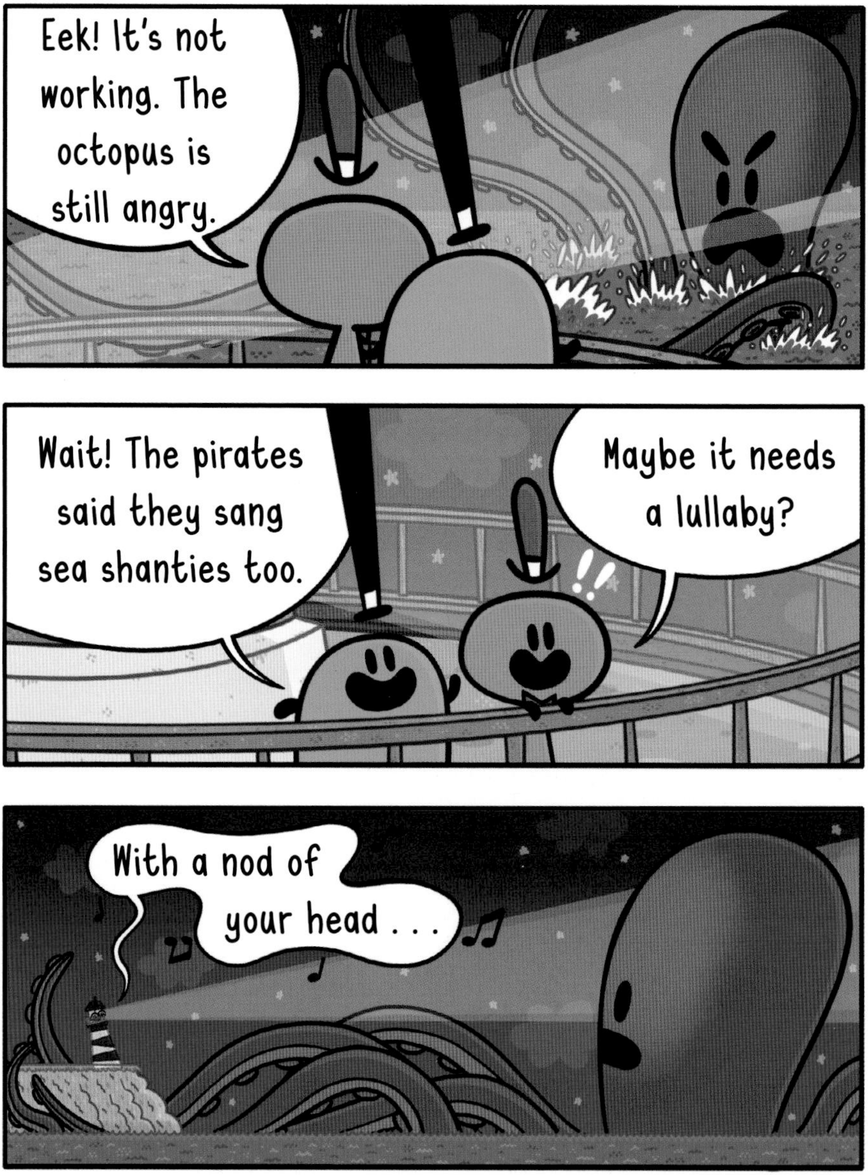
Eek! It's not working. The octopus is still angry.
Wait! The pirates said they sang sea shanties too.
Maybe it needs a lullaby?
!!
With a nod of your head . . .

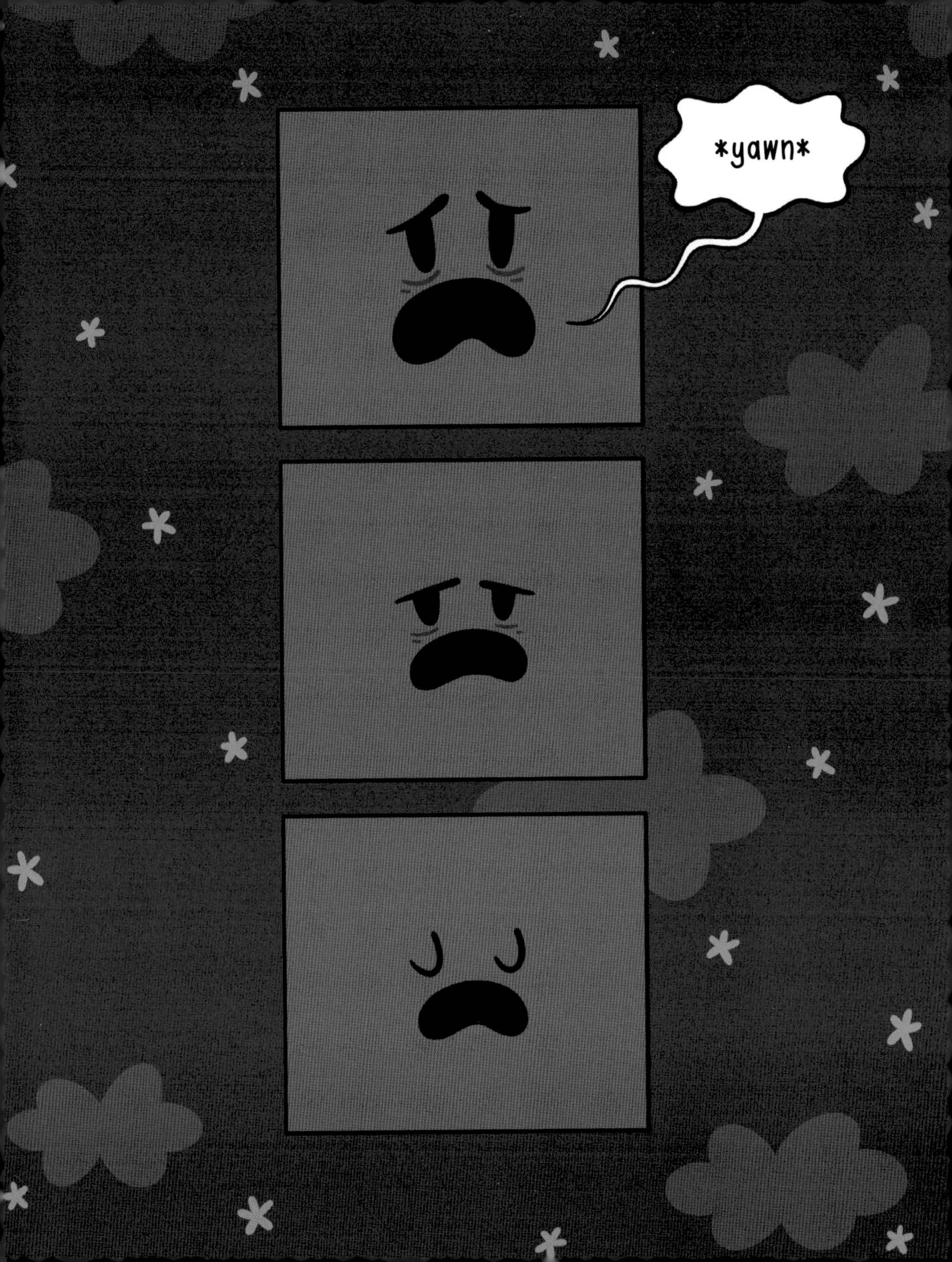
yawn

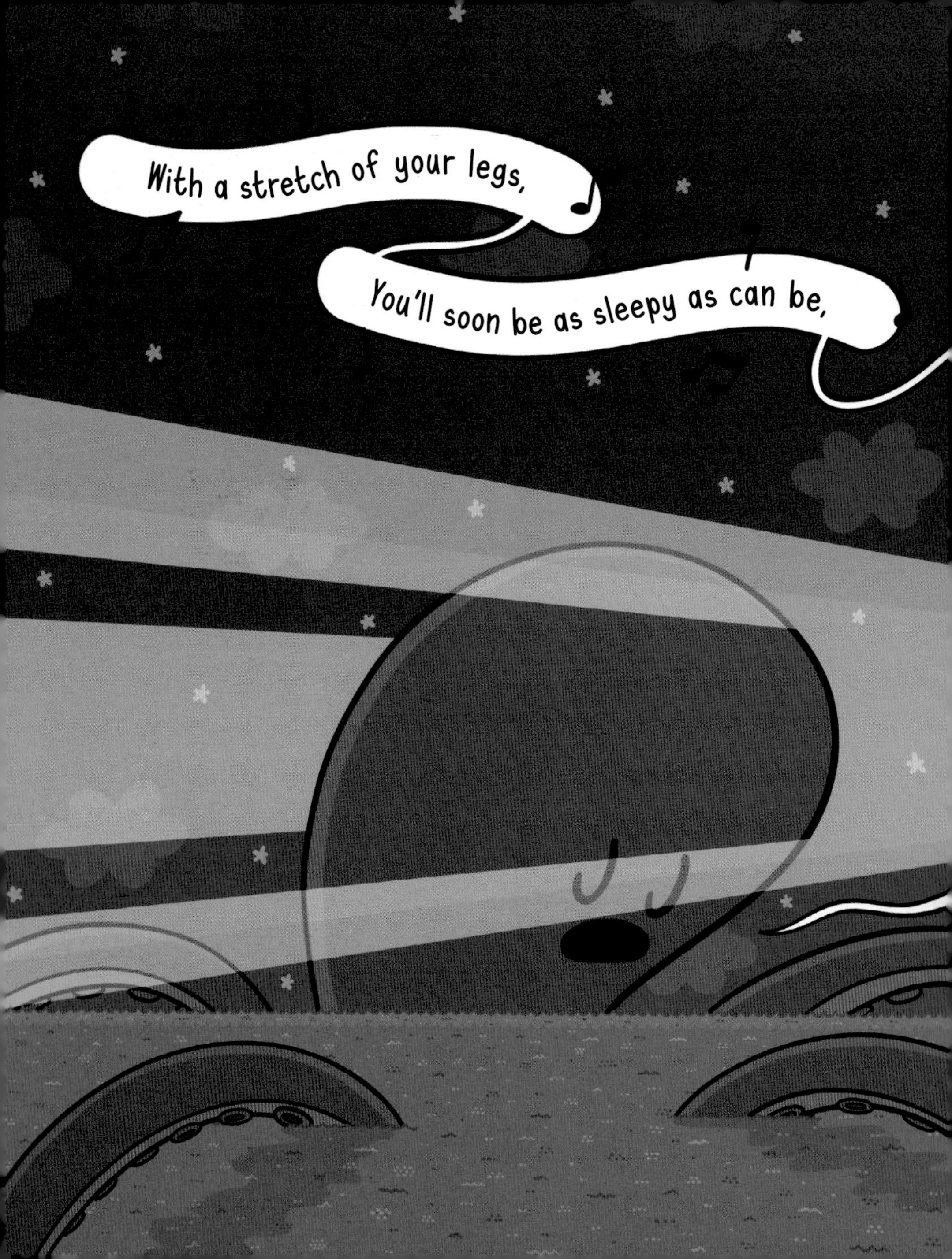
With a stretch of your legs,
You'll soon be as sleepy as can be,

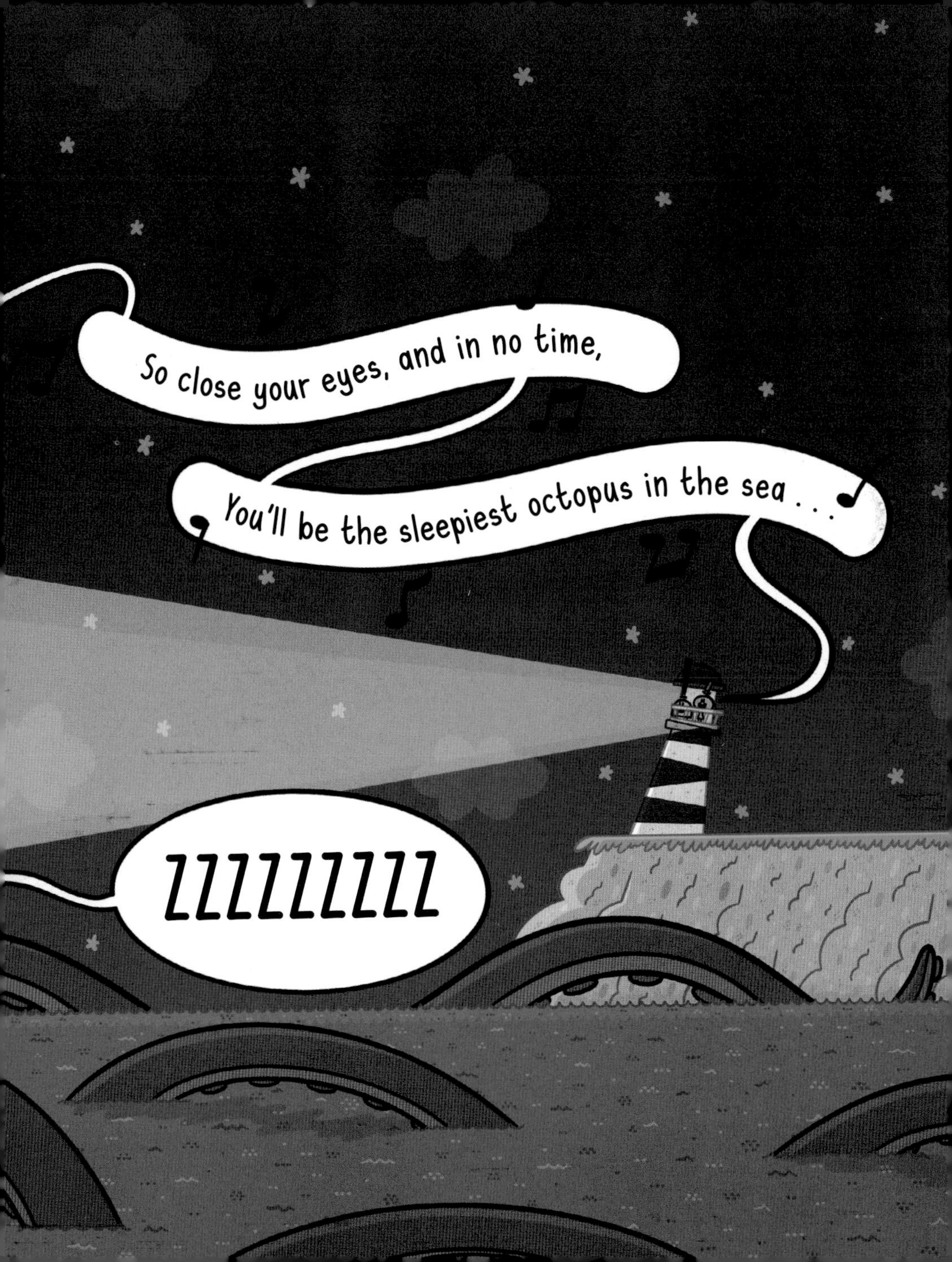
So close your eyes, and in no time,
You'll be the sleepiest octopus in the sea . . .
ZZZZZZZZZZ

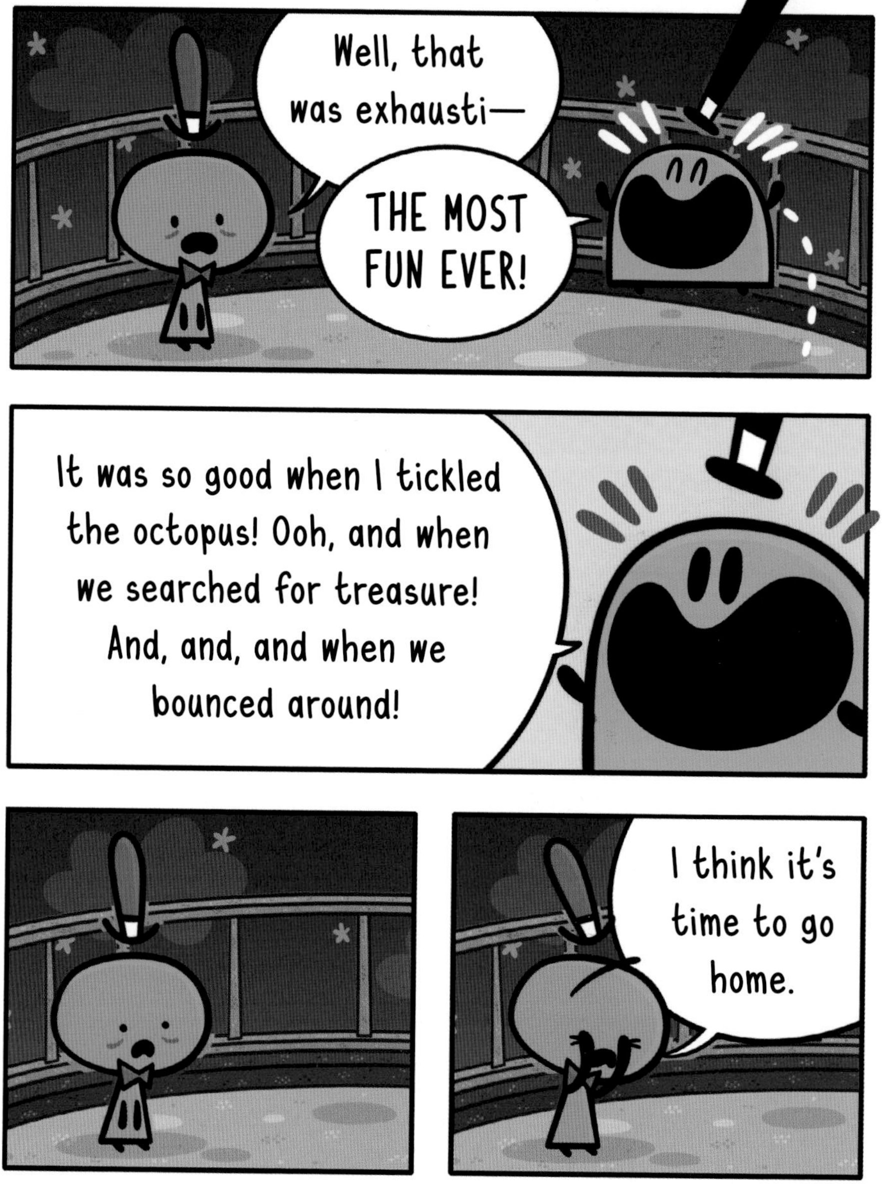
Well, that was exhausti—
THE MOST FUN EVER!
It was so good when I tickled the octopus! Ooh, and when we searched for treasure! And, and, and when we bounced around!
I think it's time to go home.

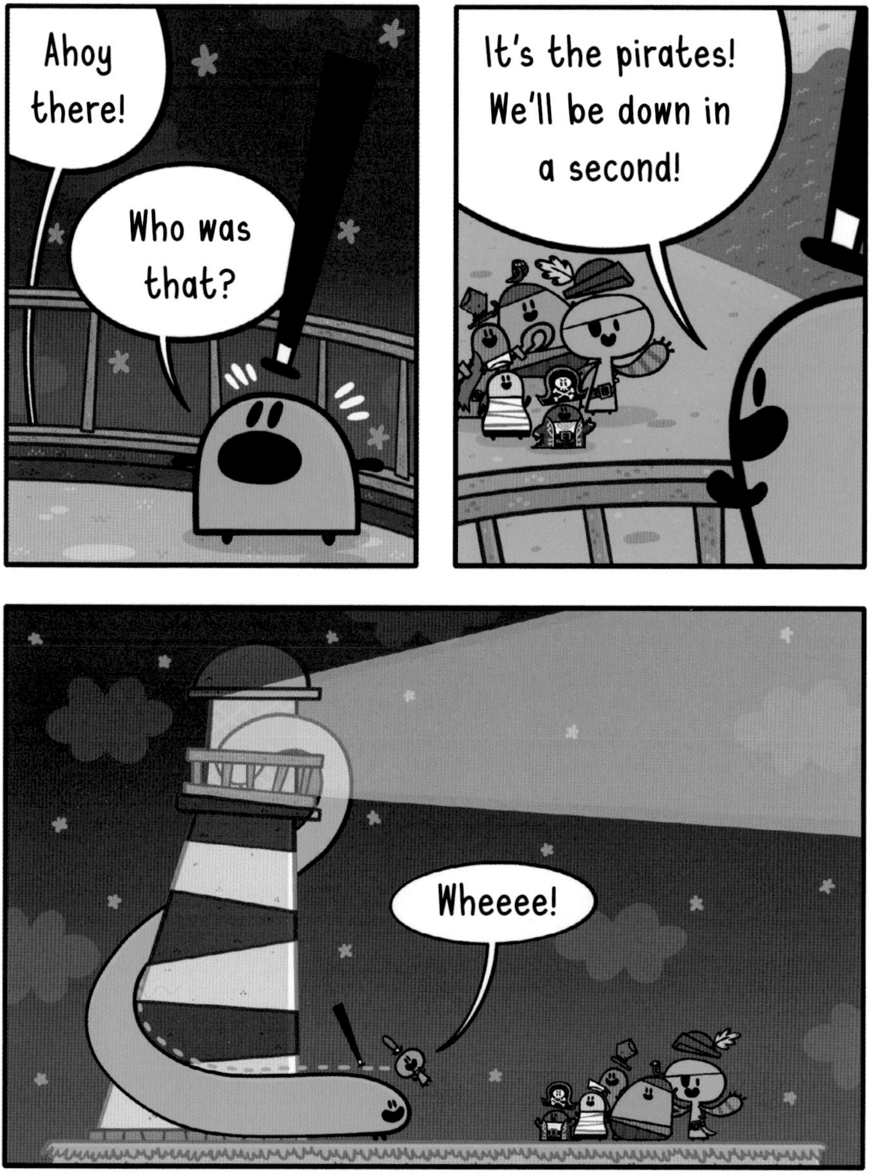
Ahoy there!
Who was that?
It's the pirates! We'll be down in a second!
Wheeee!

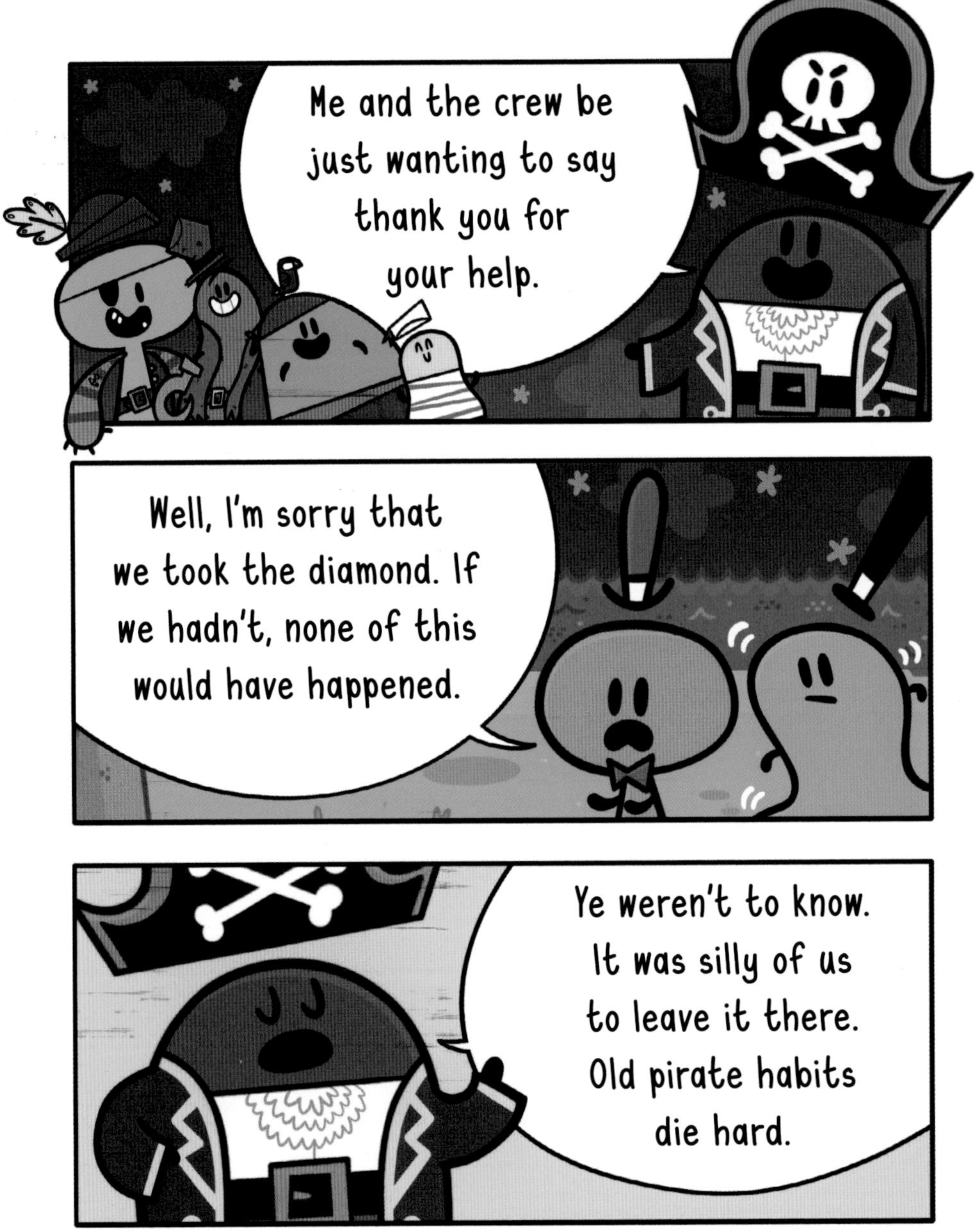
Me and the crew be just wanting to say thank you for your help.
Well, I'm sorry that we took the diamond. If we hadn't, none of this would have happened.
Ye weren't to know. It was silly of us to leave it there. Old pirate habits die hard.

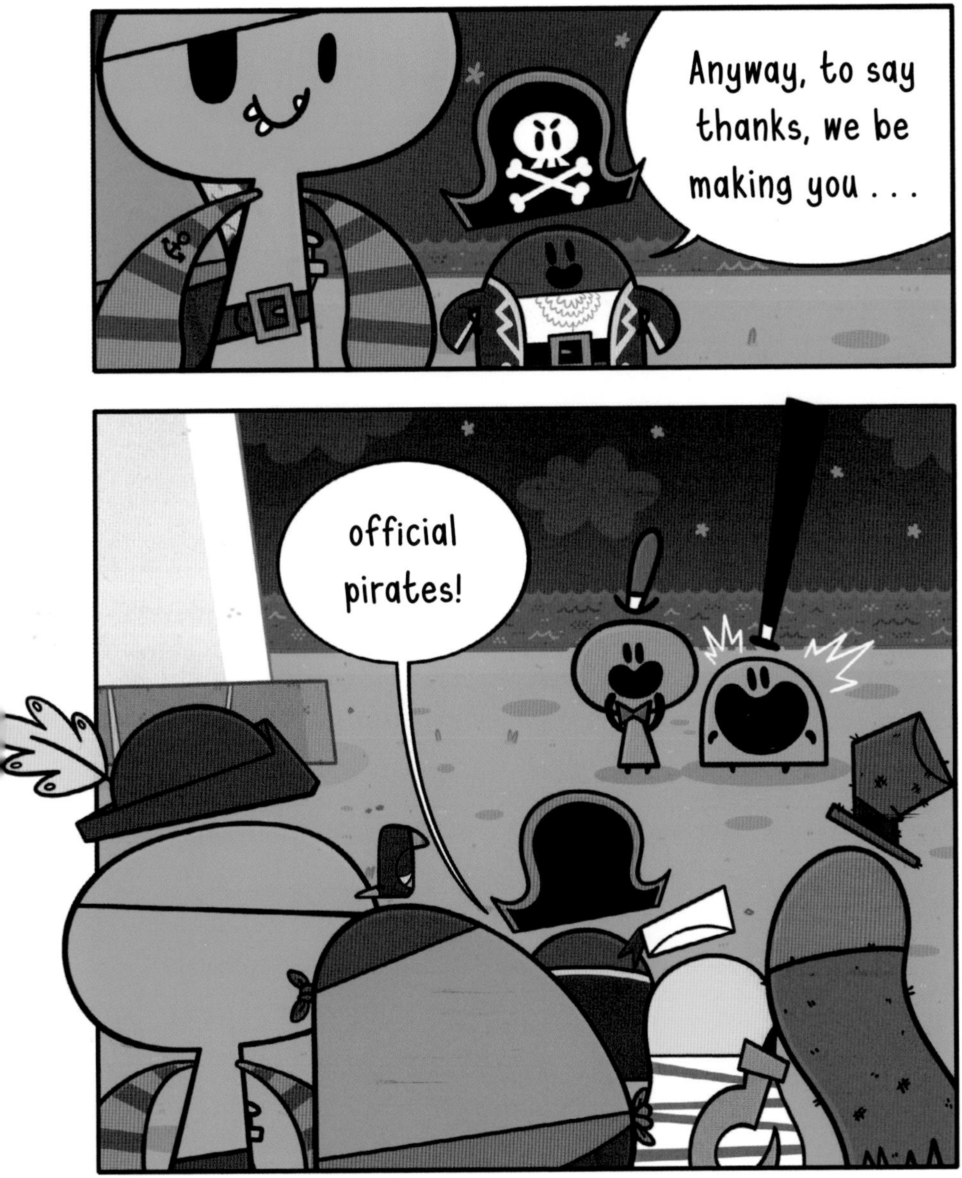
Anyway, to say thanks, we be making you . . .
official pirates!

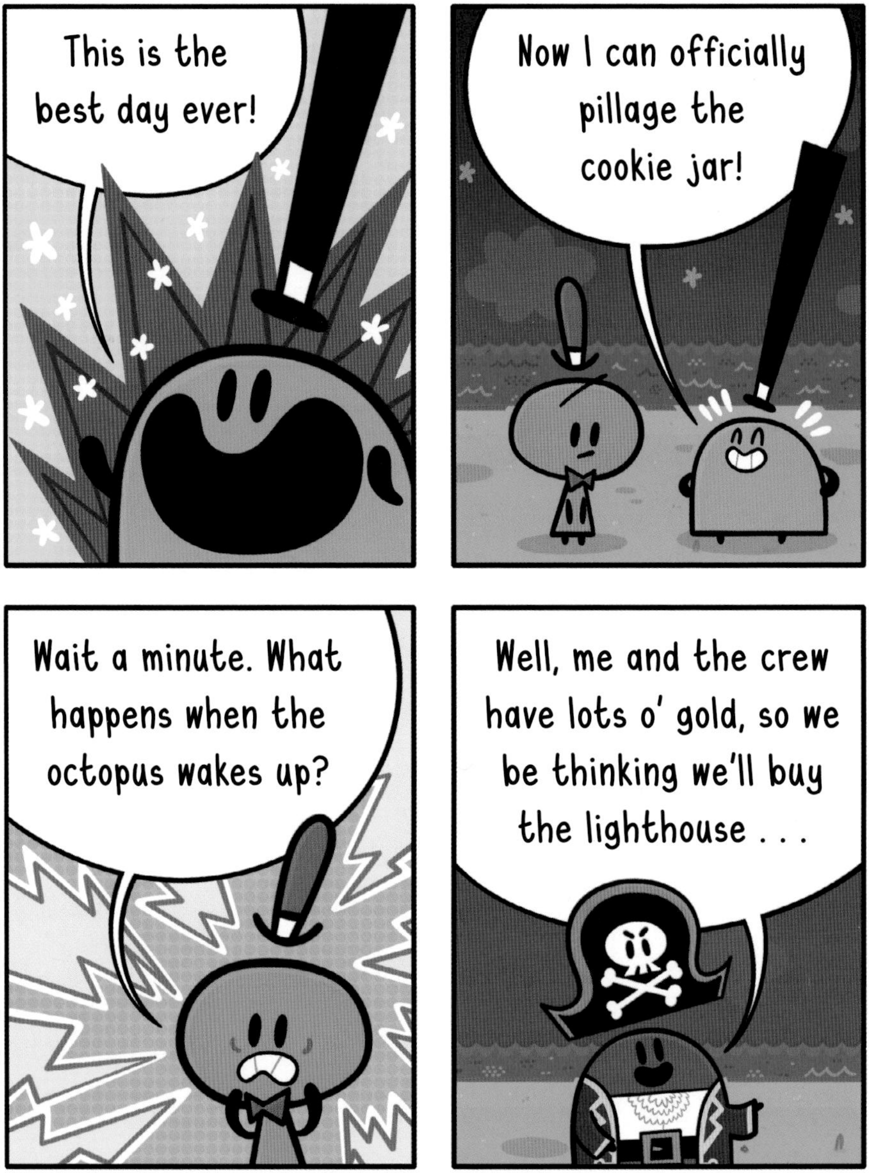
This is the best day ever!
Now I can officially pillage the cookie jar!
Wait a minute. What happens when the octopus wakes up?
Well, me and the crew have lots o' gold, so we be thinking we'll buy the lighthouse . . .

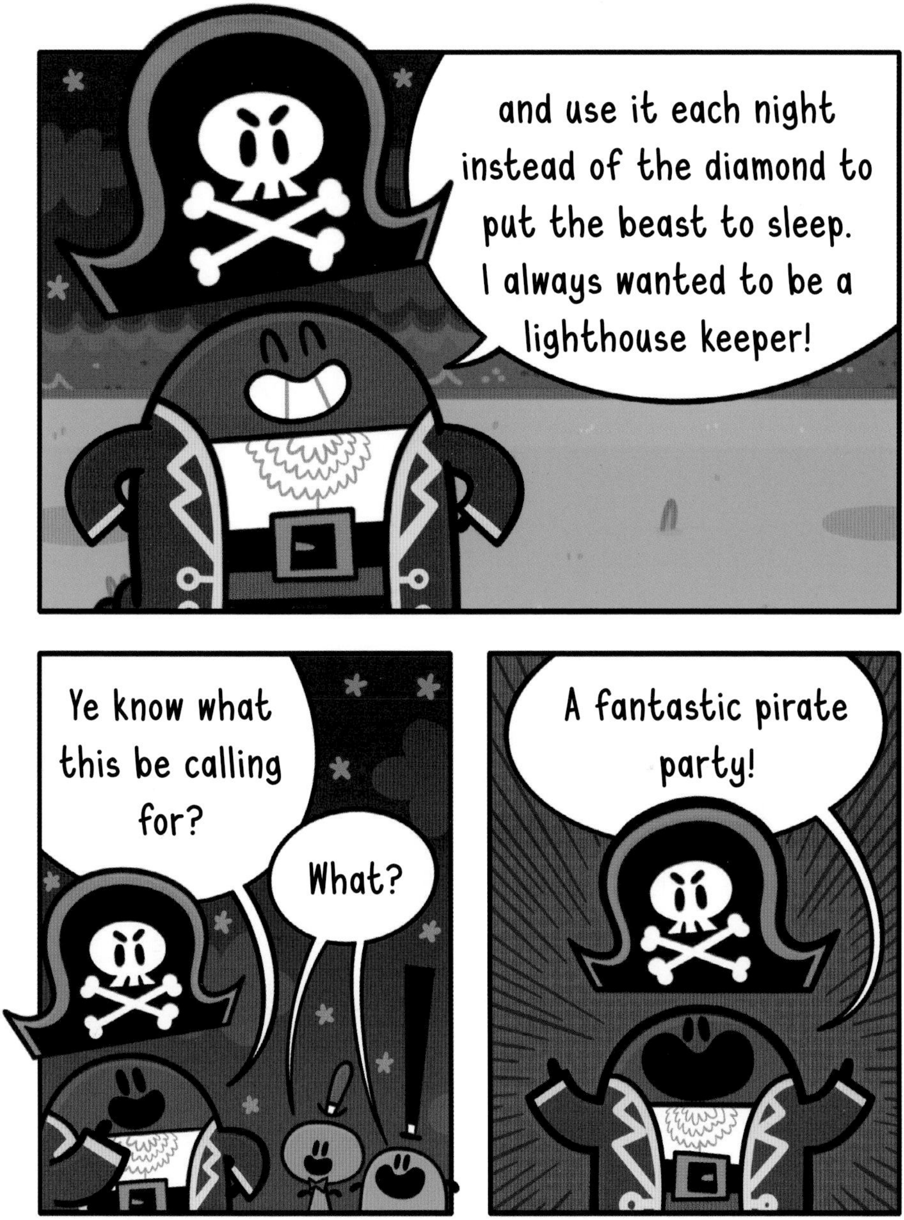
and use it each night instead of the diamond to put the beast to sleep. I always wanted to be a lighthouse keeper!
Ye know what this be calling for?
What?
A fantastic pirate party!

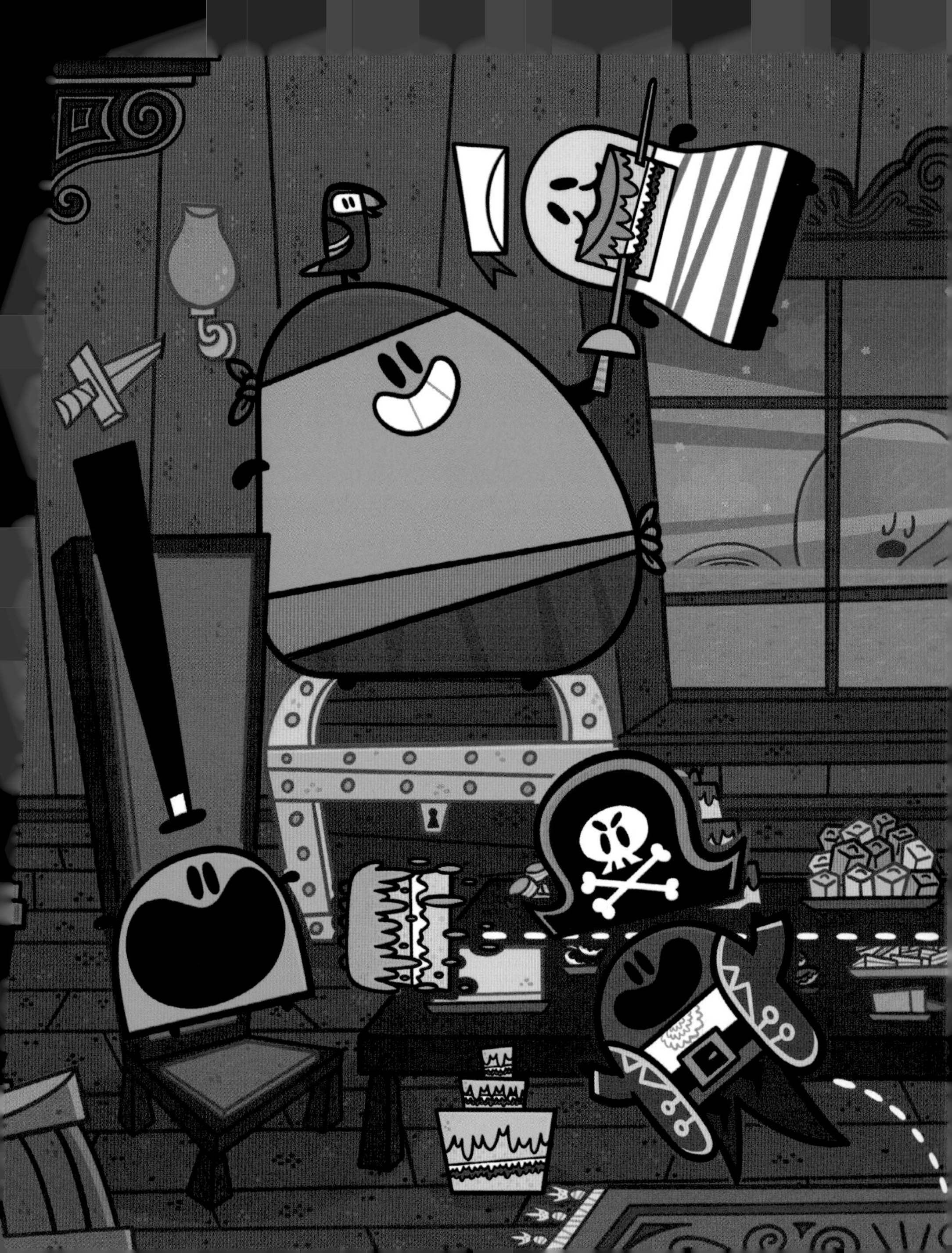

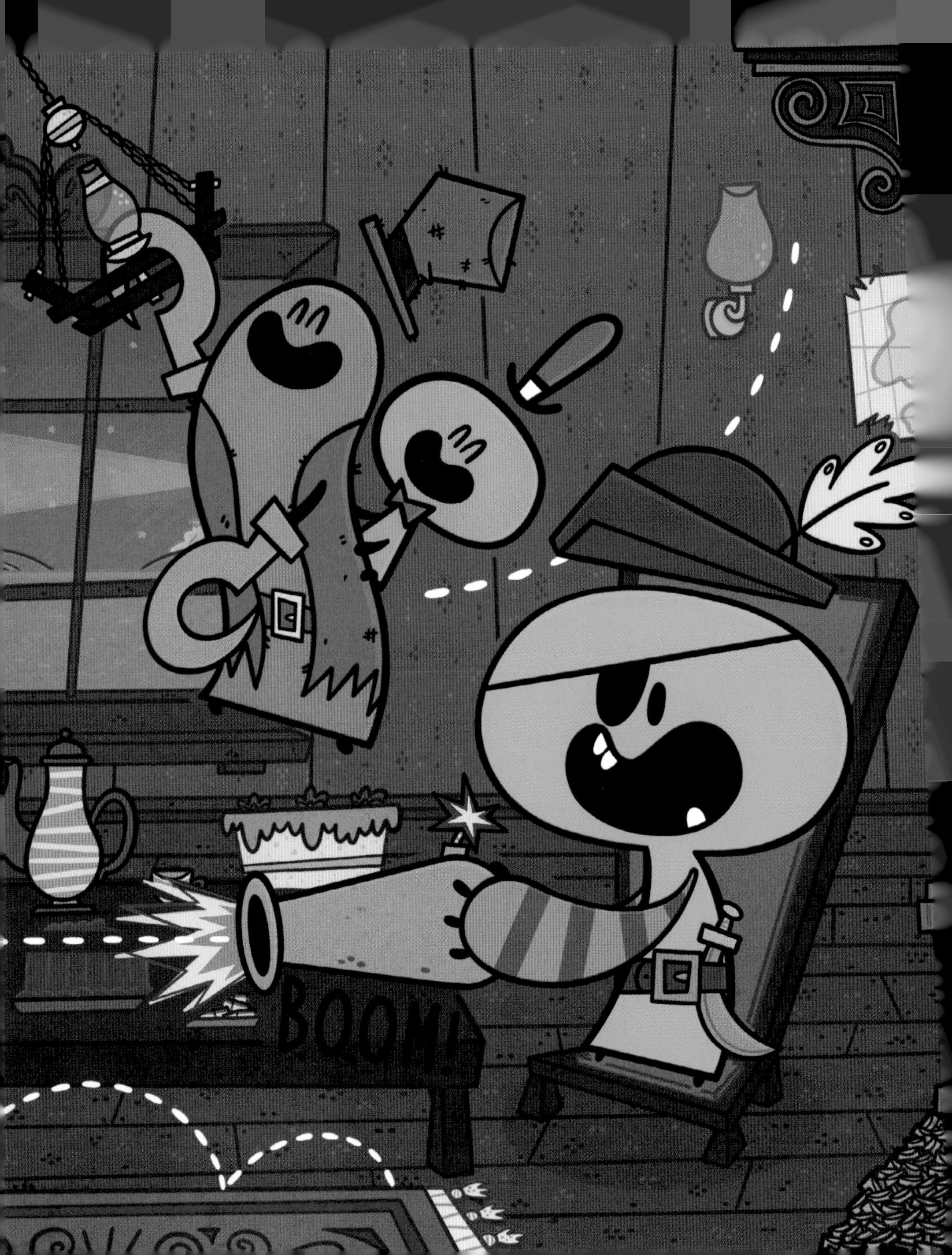
BOOM!

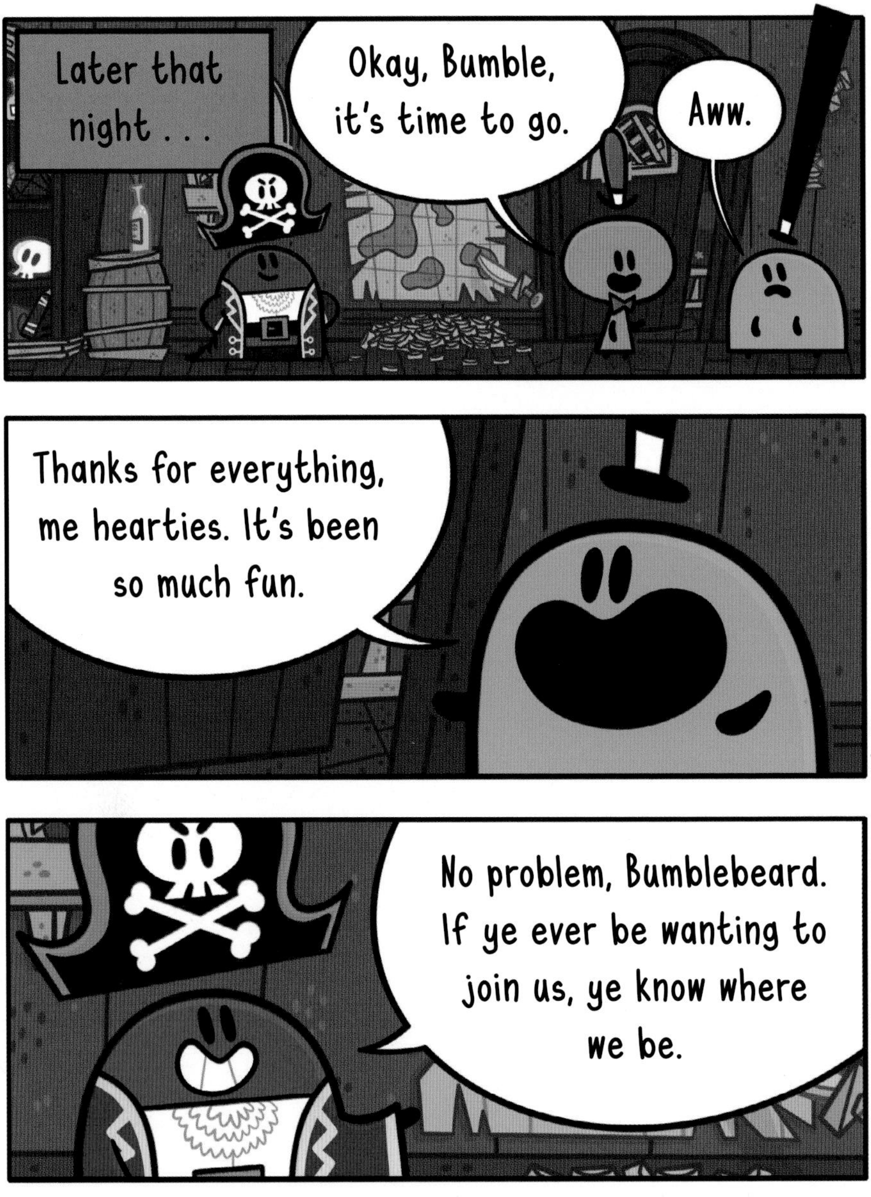
Later that night . . .
Okay, Bumble, it's time to go.
Aww.
Thanks for everything, me hearties. It's been so much fun.
No problem, Bumblebeard. If ye ever be wanting to join us, ye know where we be.

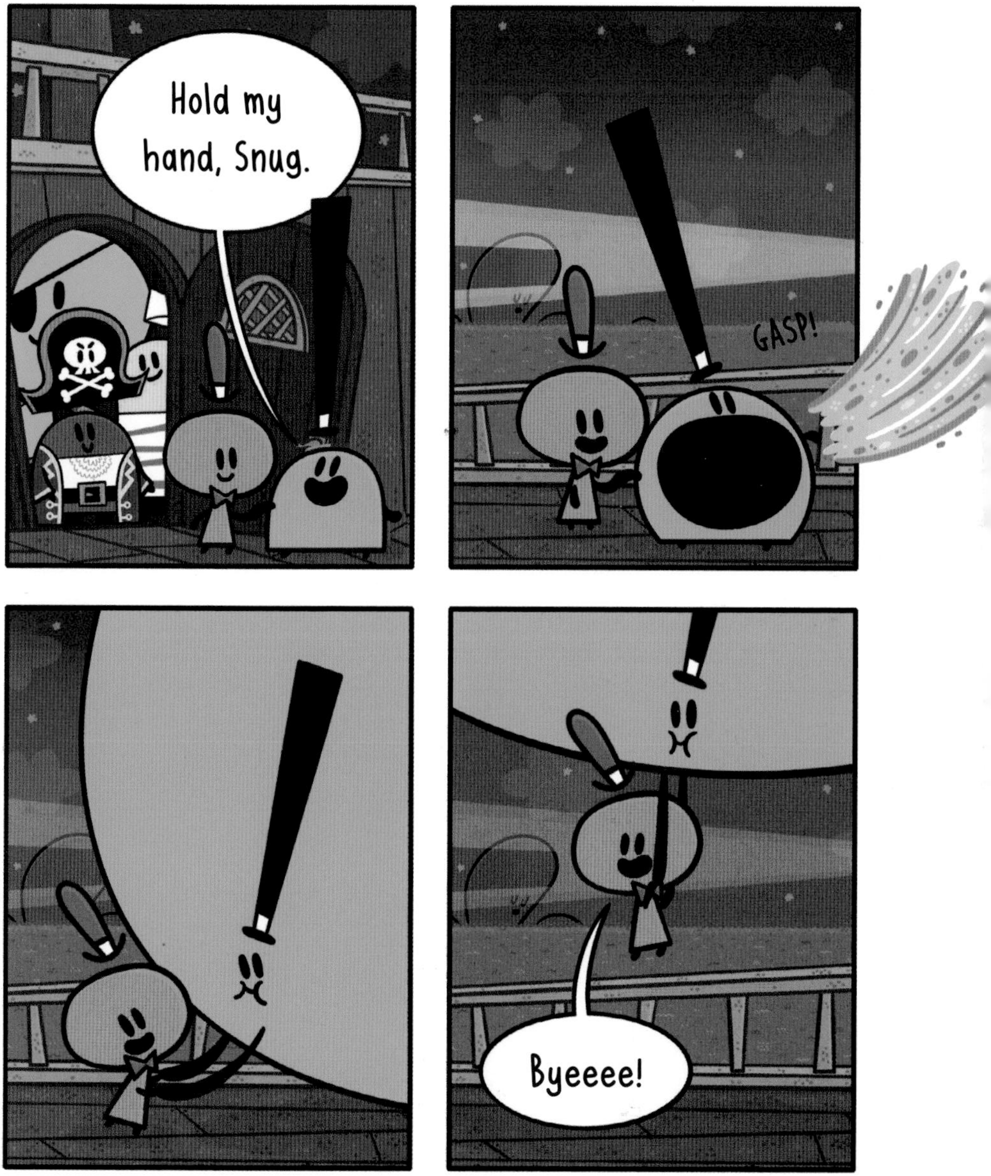

Hold my hand, Snug.
GASP!
Byeeee!

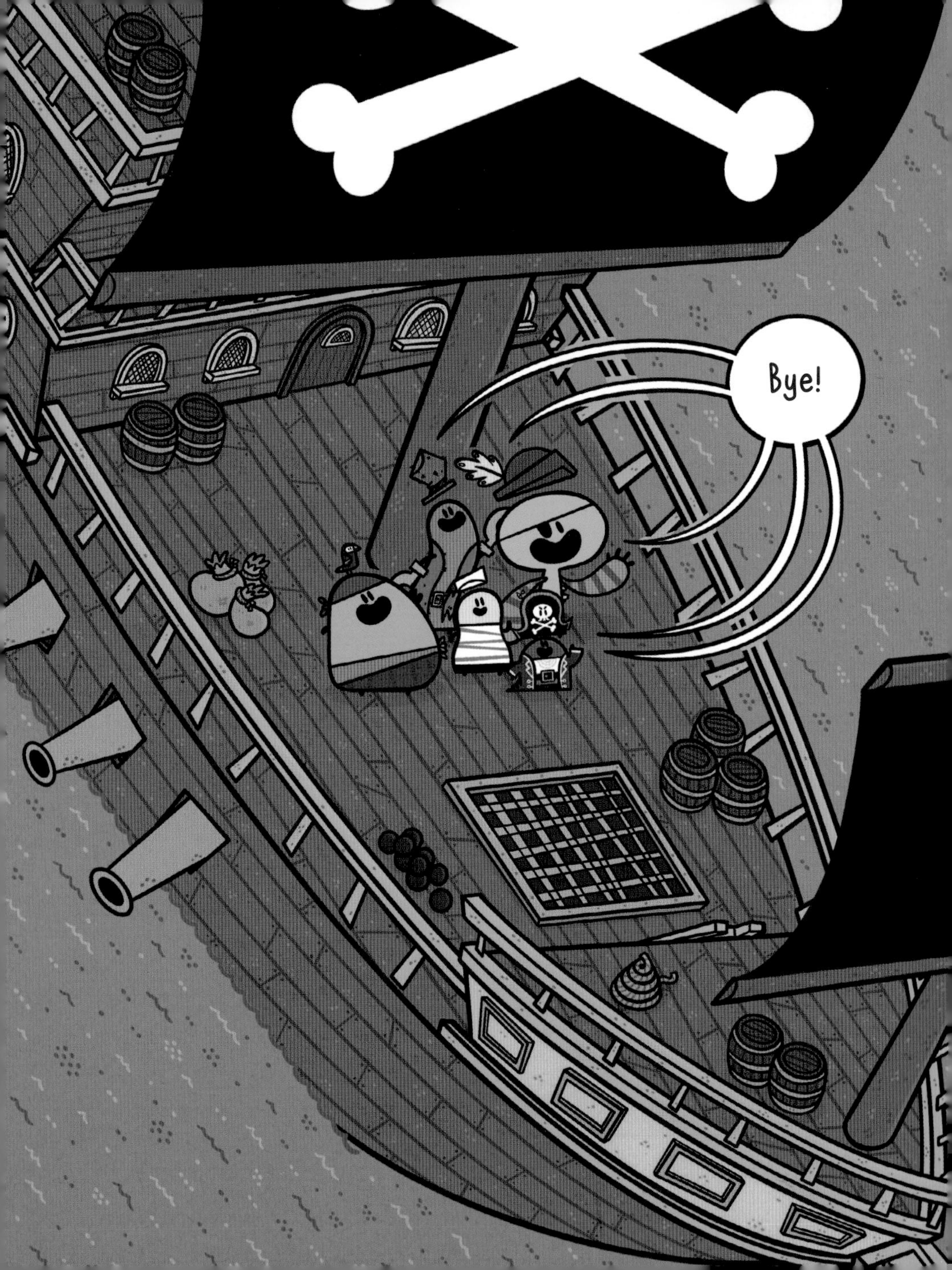
Bye!

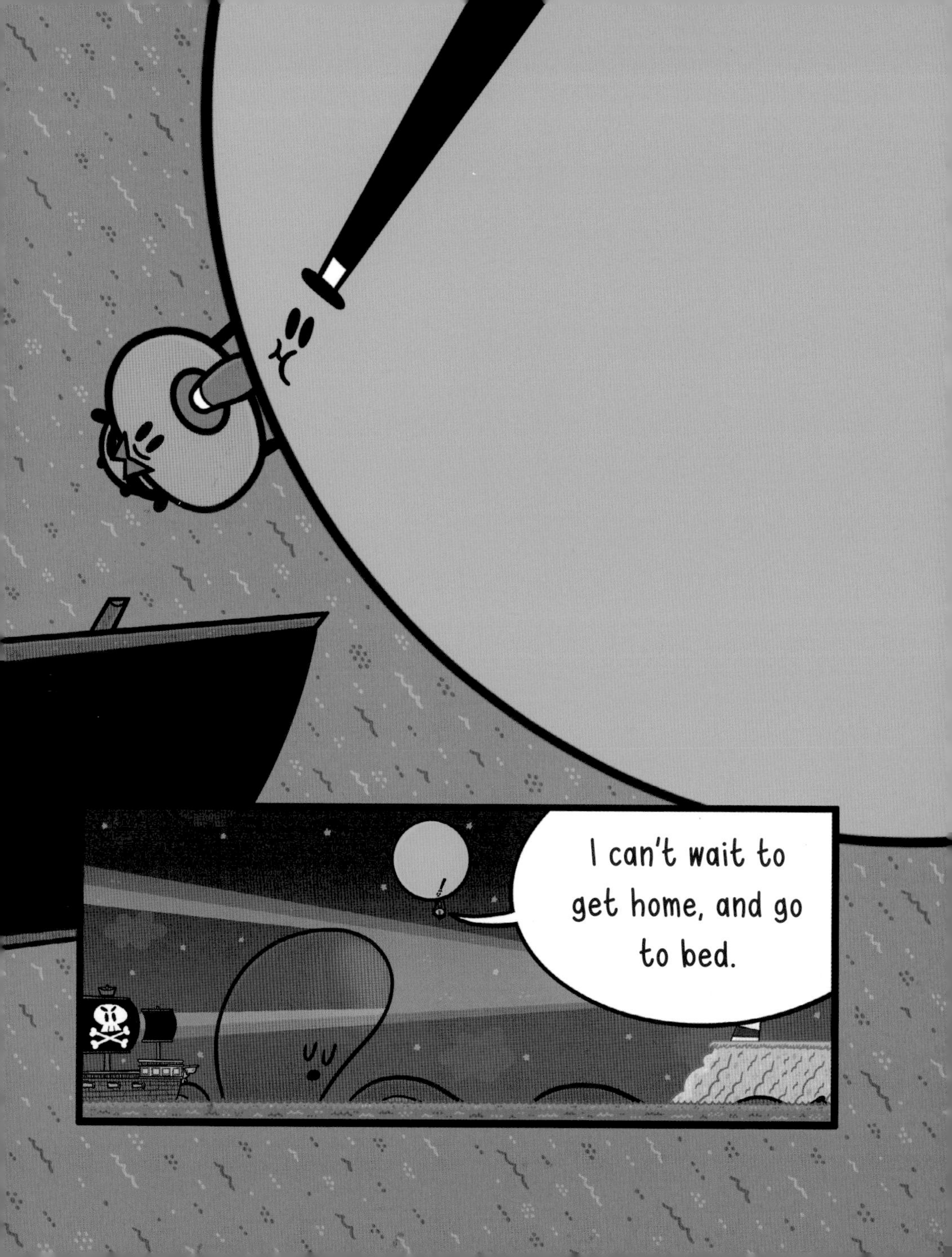
I can't wait to get home, and go to bed.

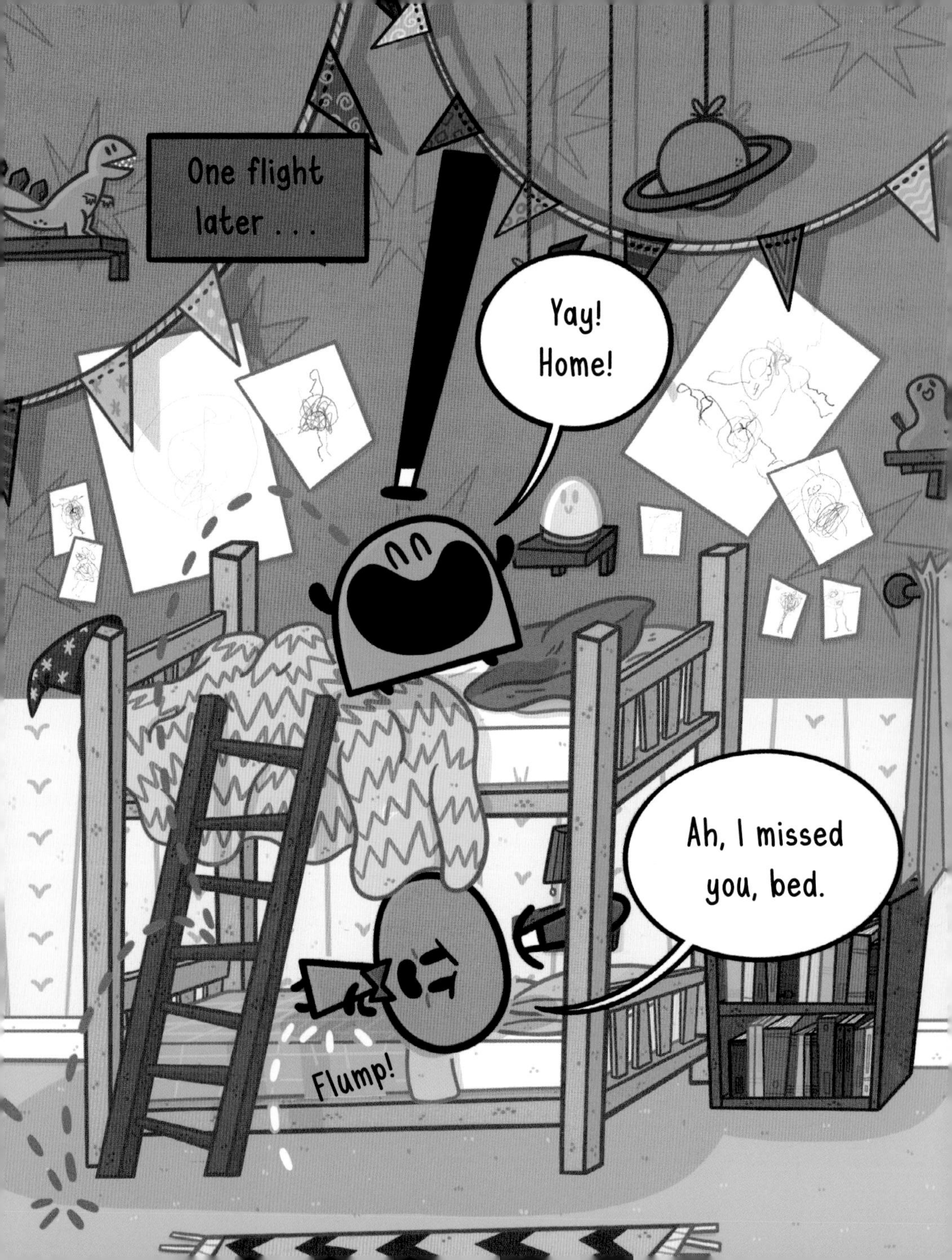
One flight later . . .
!
Yay! Home!
Ah, I missed you, bed.
Flump!

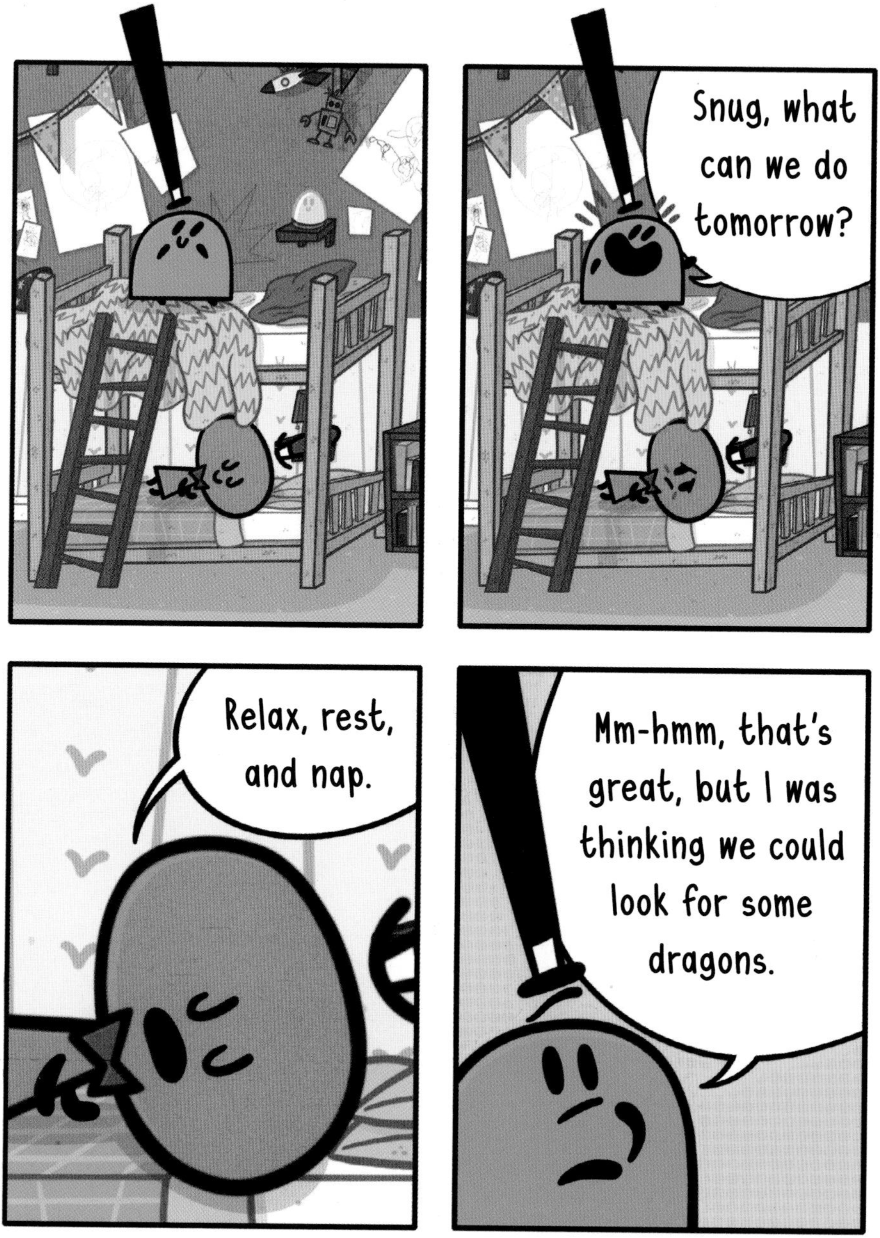
Snug, what can we do tomorrow?
Relax, rest, and nap.
Mm-hmm, that's great, but I was thinking we could look for some dragons.

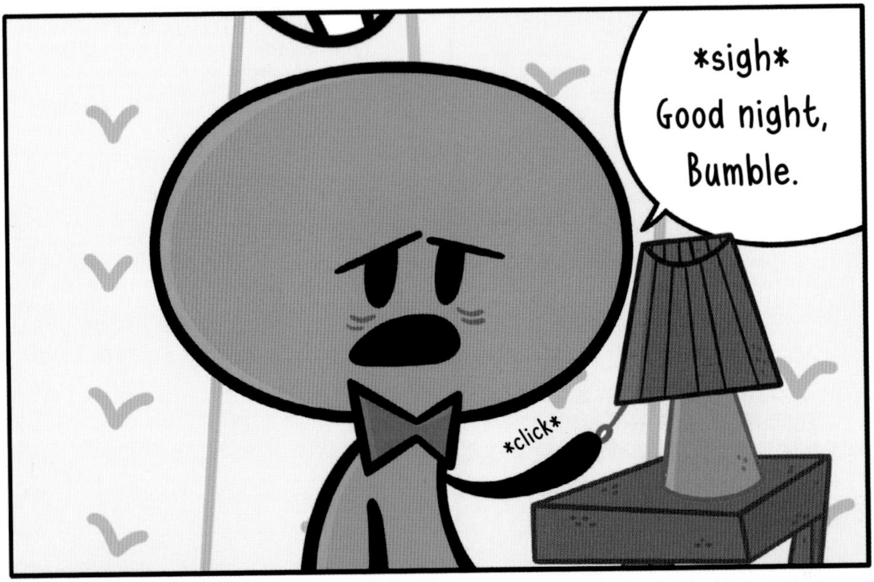
sigh
Good night,
Bumble.
click

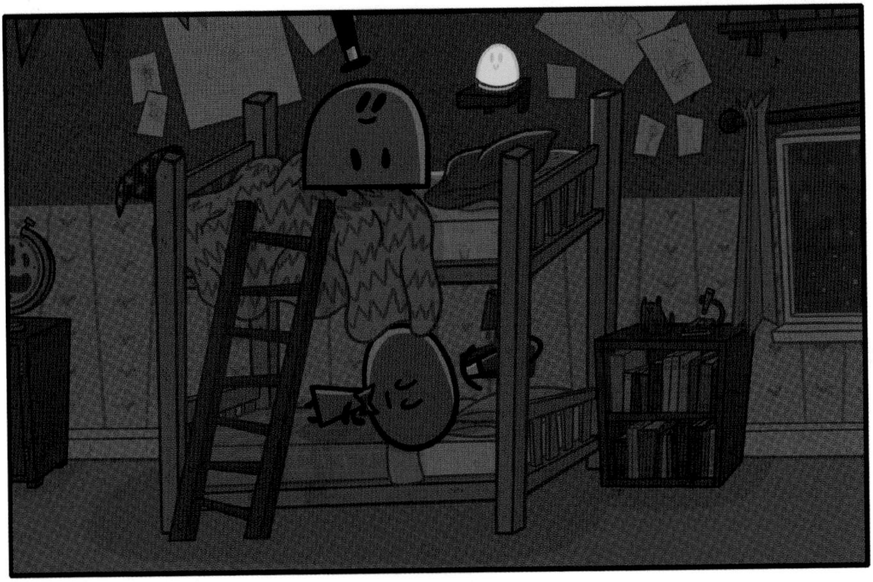

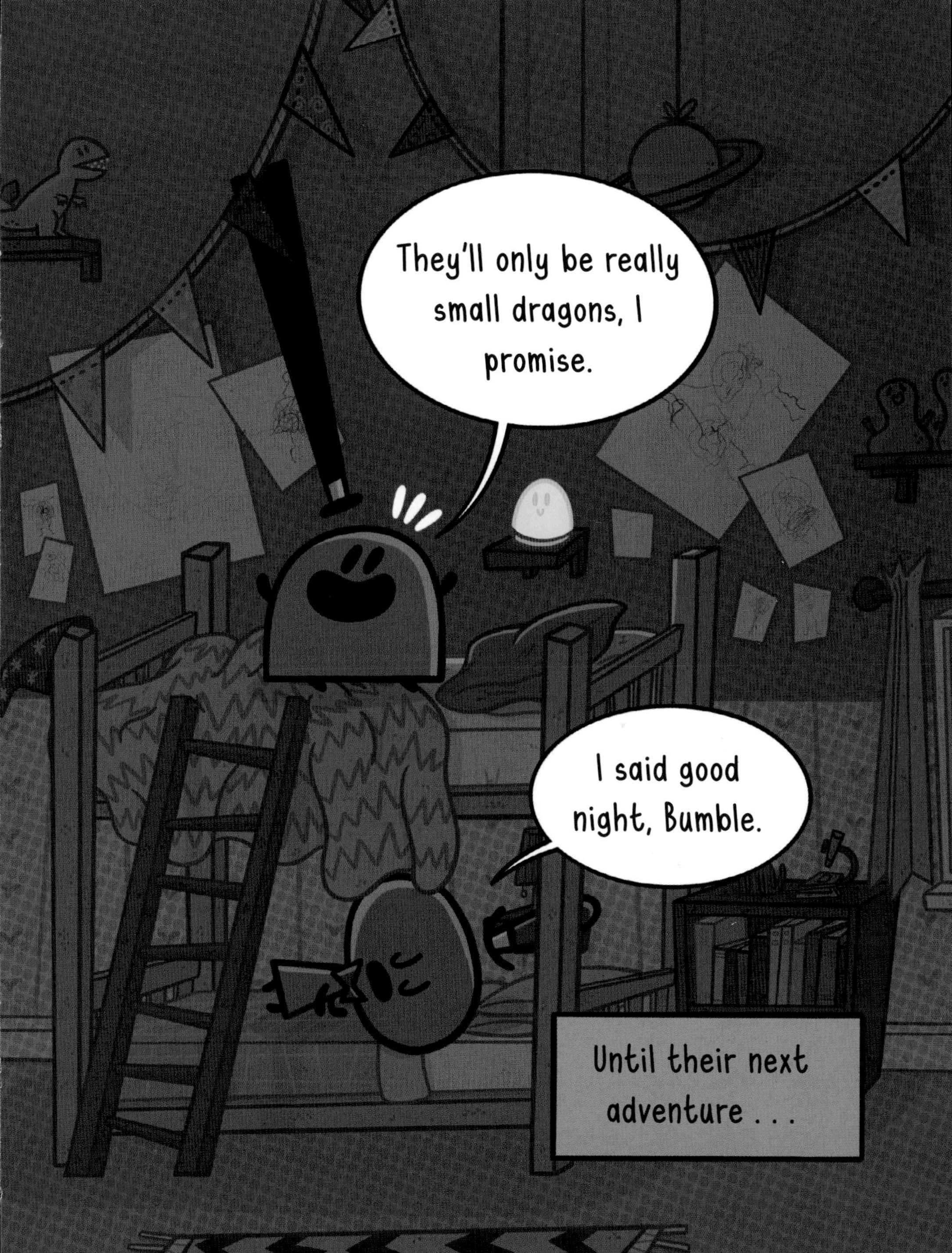
They'll only be really small dragons, I promise.
I said good night, Bumble.
Until their next adventure . . .

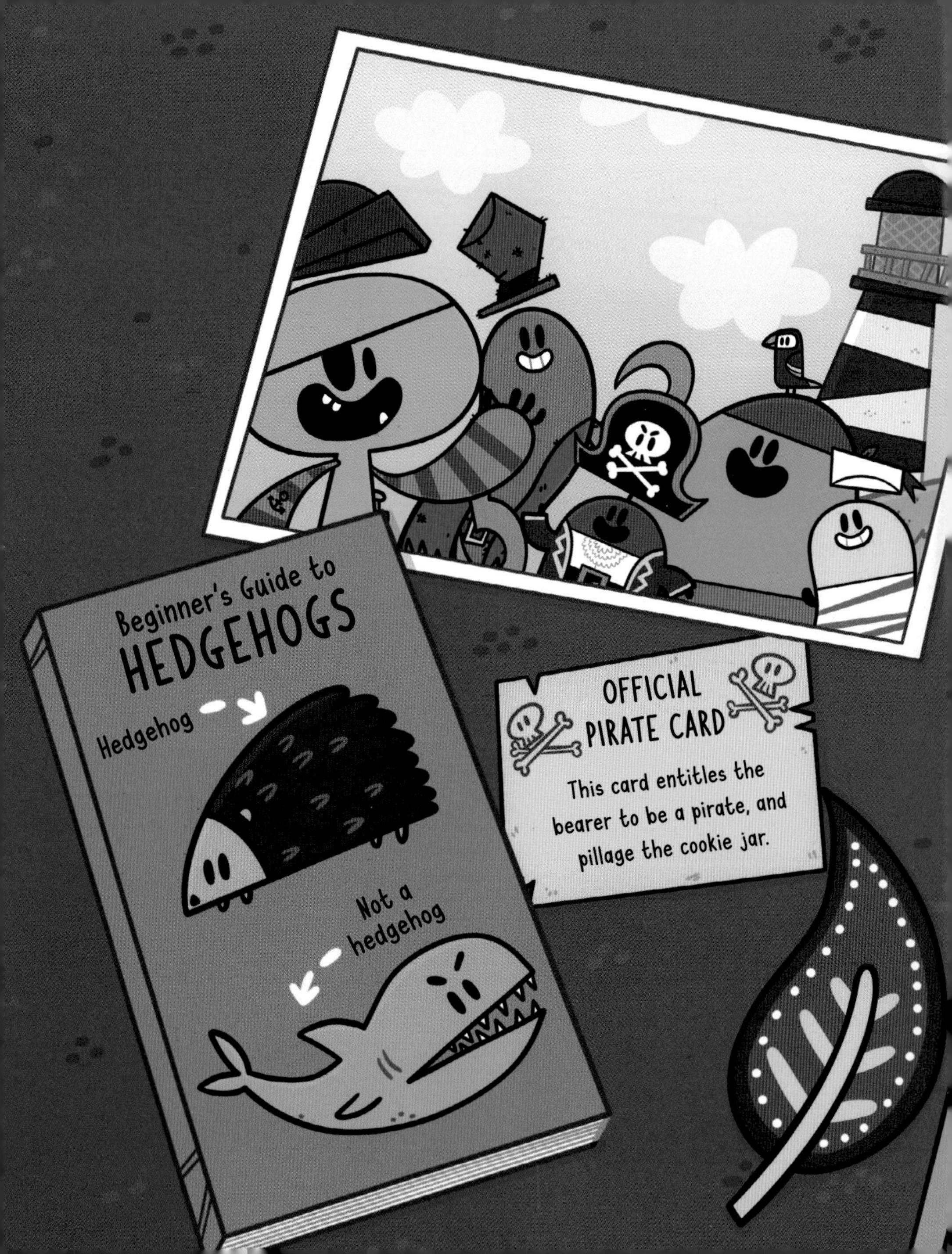
Beginner's Guide to
HEDGEHOGS
Hedgehog
Not a hedgehog
OFFICIAL PIRATE CARD
This card entitles the bearer to be a pirate, and pillage the cookie jar.

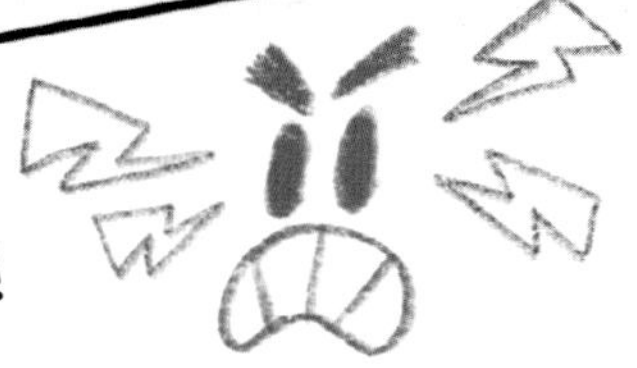

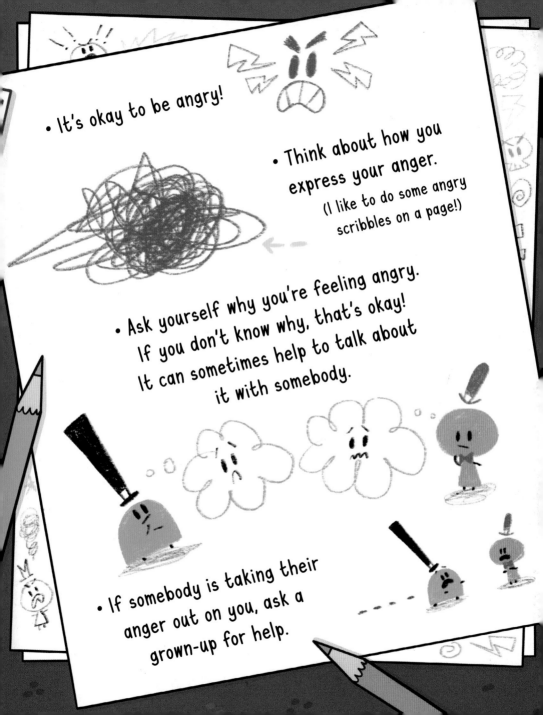

- It's okay to be angry!

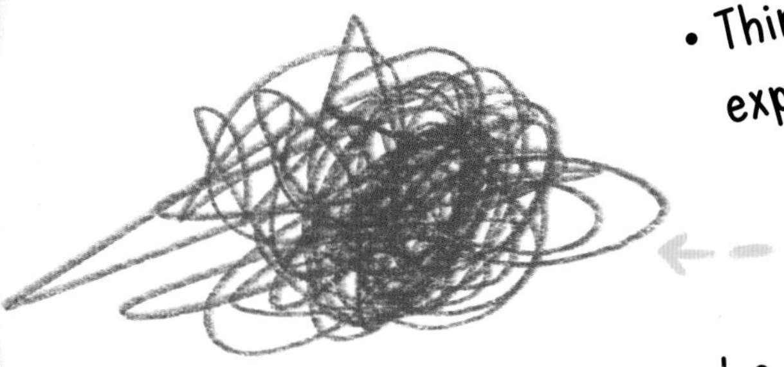

- Think about how you express your anger. (I like to do some angry scribbles on a page!)

- Ask yourself why you're feeling angry. If you don't know why, that's okay! It can sometimes help to talk about it with somebody.

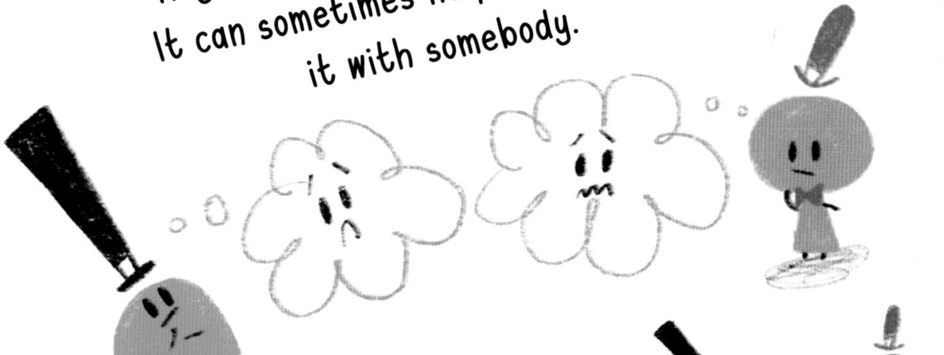

- If somebody is taking their anger out on you, ask a grown-up for help.

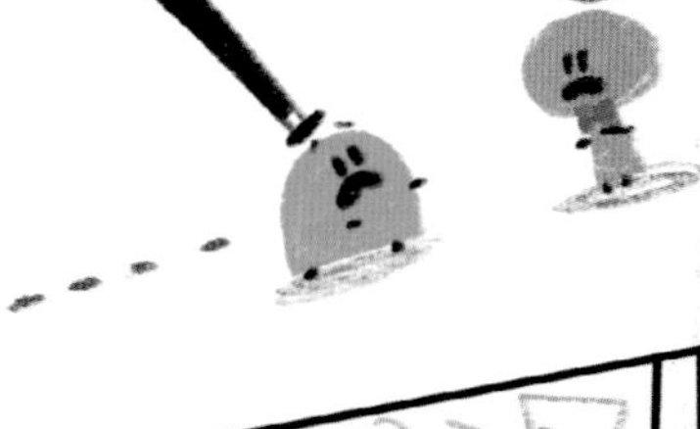

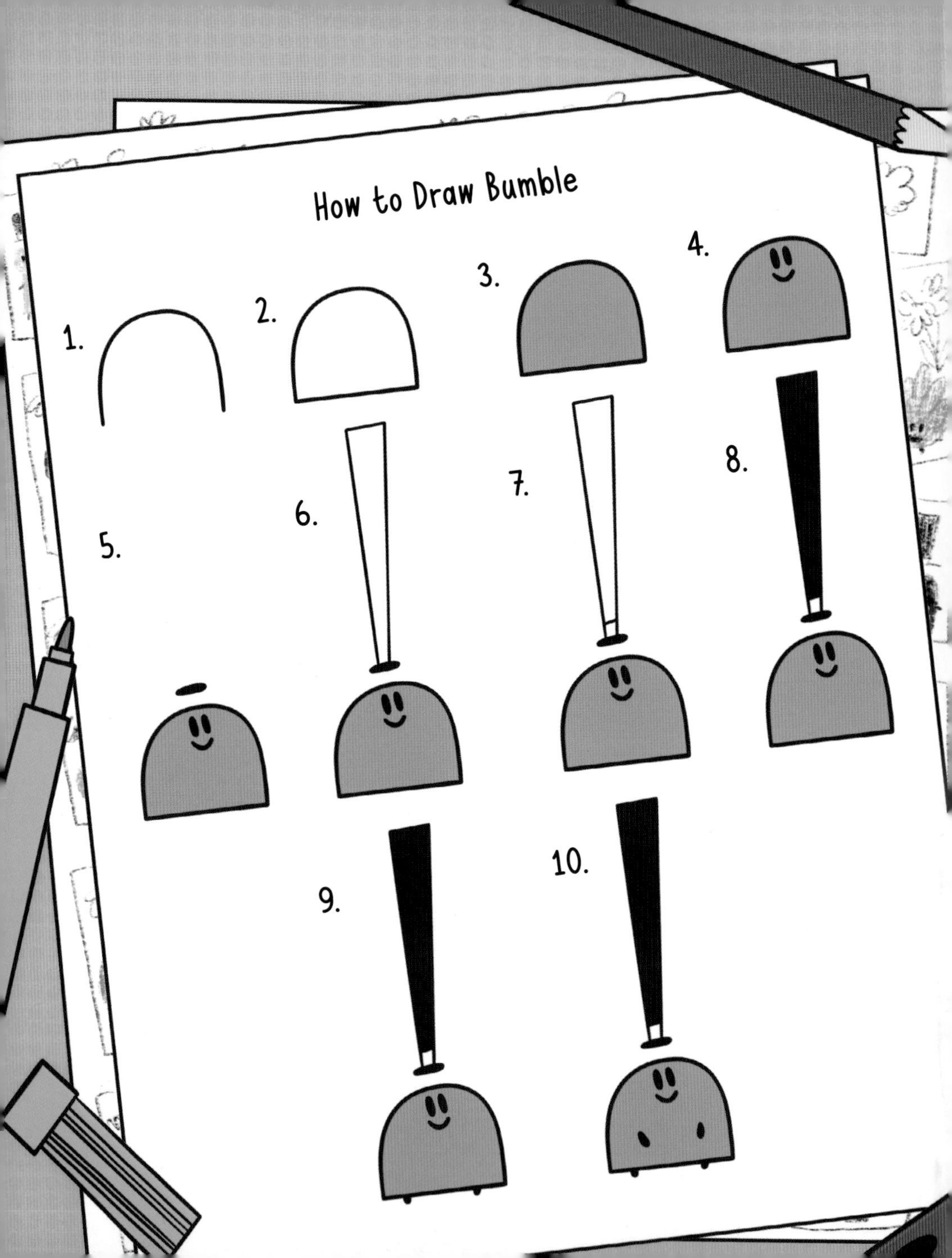
How to Draw Bumble
1.
2.
3.
4.
5.
6.
7.
8.
9.
10.

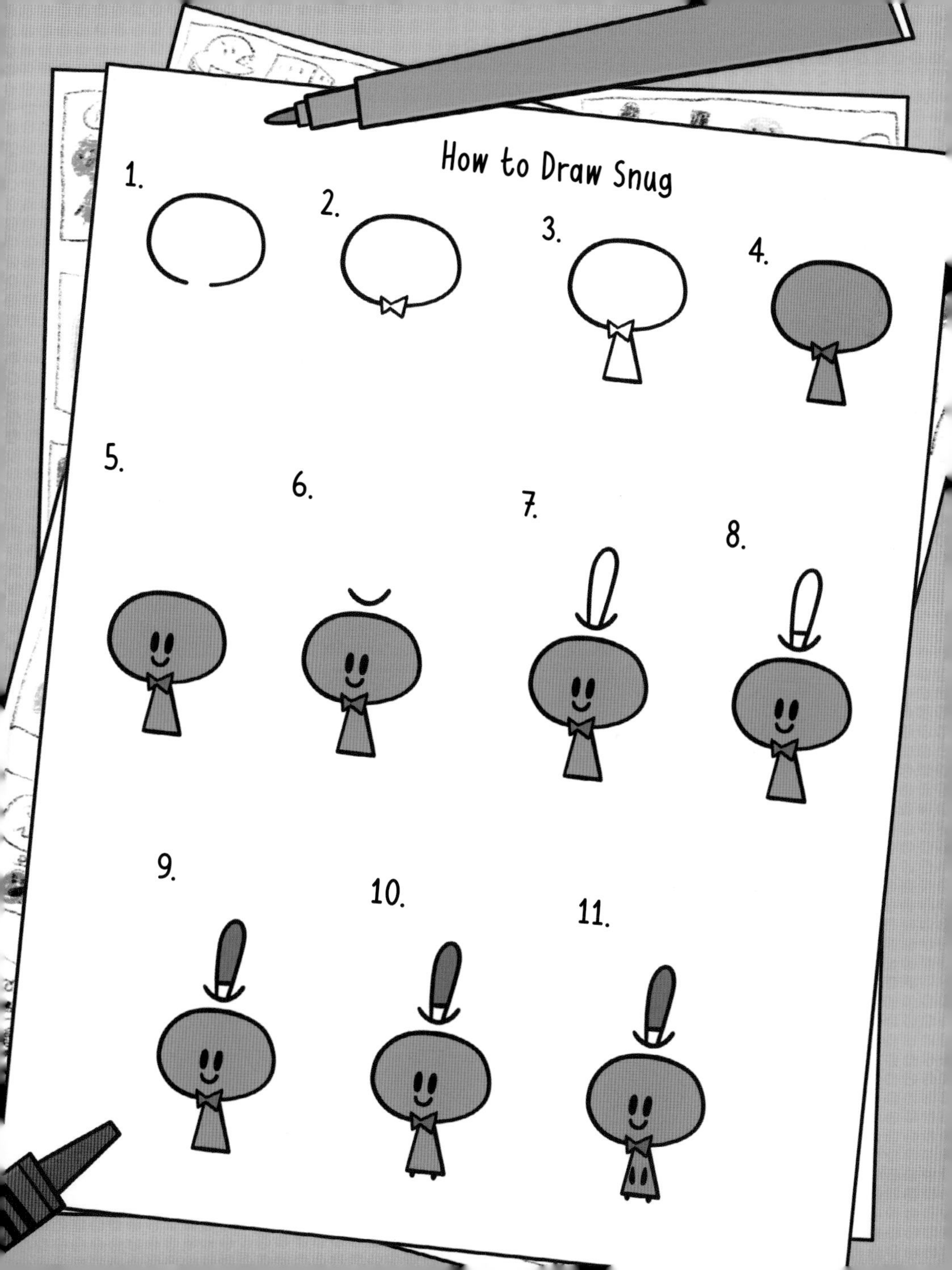
How to Draw Snug
1.
2.
3.
4.
5.
6.
7.
8.
9.
10.
11.

You can even draw your own bugbops!

Choose any color and make up your own shape.

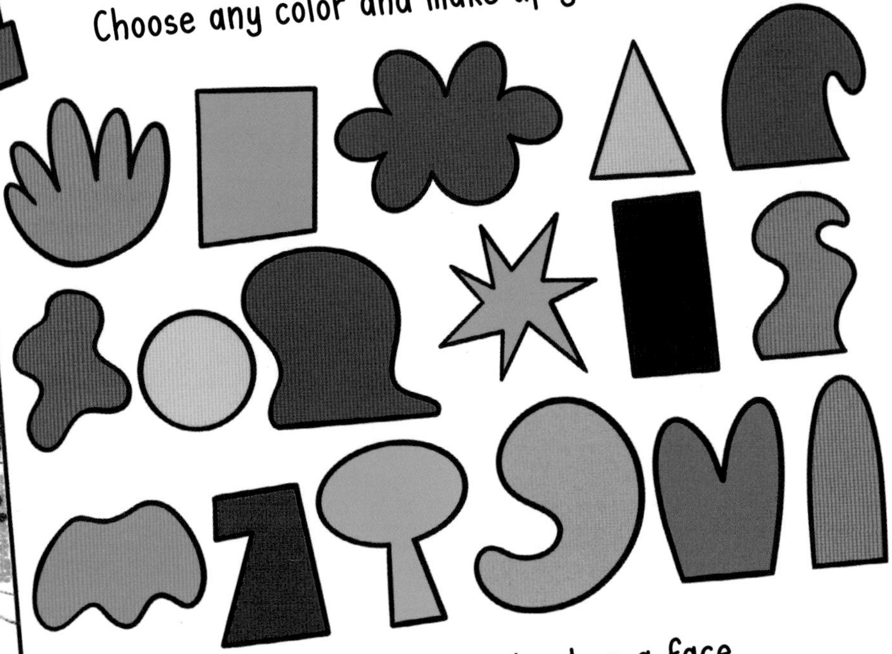

Then give your bugbop a face.

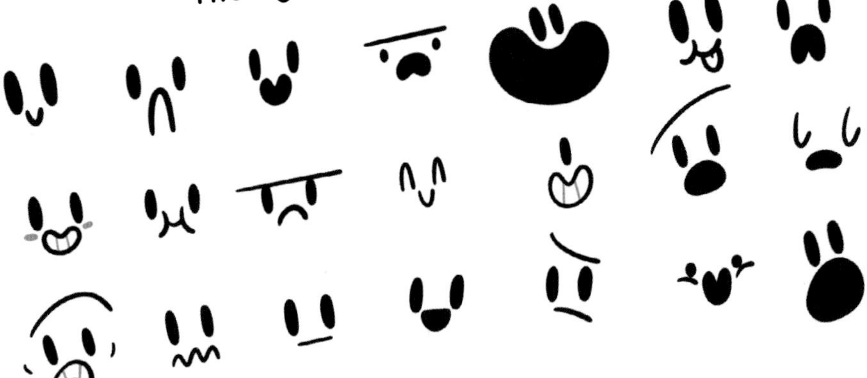

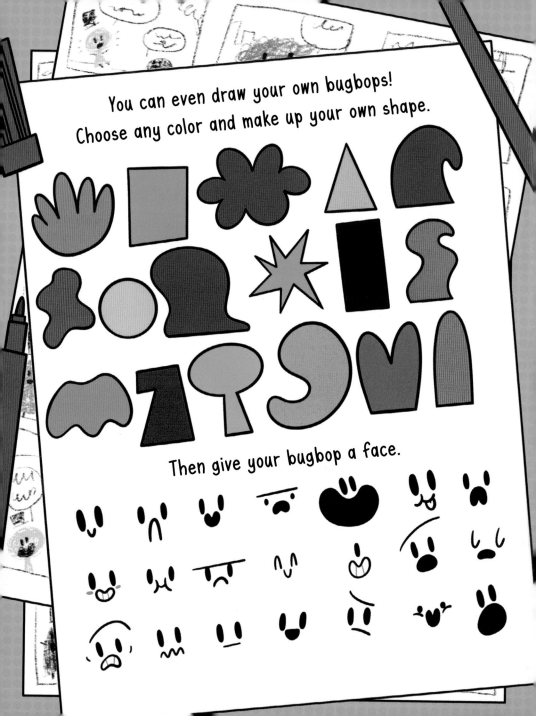

Now you can add some arms and legs.
Some bugbops have no legs or arms, some
have one or two of each, and some have lots!

Give your bugbops some accessories.
They especially love unusual hats!

Just remember that there's no wrong way
to make a bugbop.

Mark Bradley is a comic writer and artist, who lives in Yorkshire, UK, with his family. He grew up reading stories about ghosts and monsters, and promptly decided that he preferred them to humans. Having worked for the probation service for many years he saw firsthand how important a skill emotional literacy is and hopes his debut series will help young readers explore feelings in a fun setting. *Bumble & Snug* developed out of characters he kept drawing in the margins of other projects until he launched them on his Instagram account (@markbradleyillustration) and found himself with a book deal—something he never even dared to dream was possible.

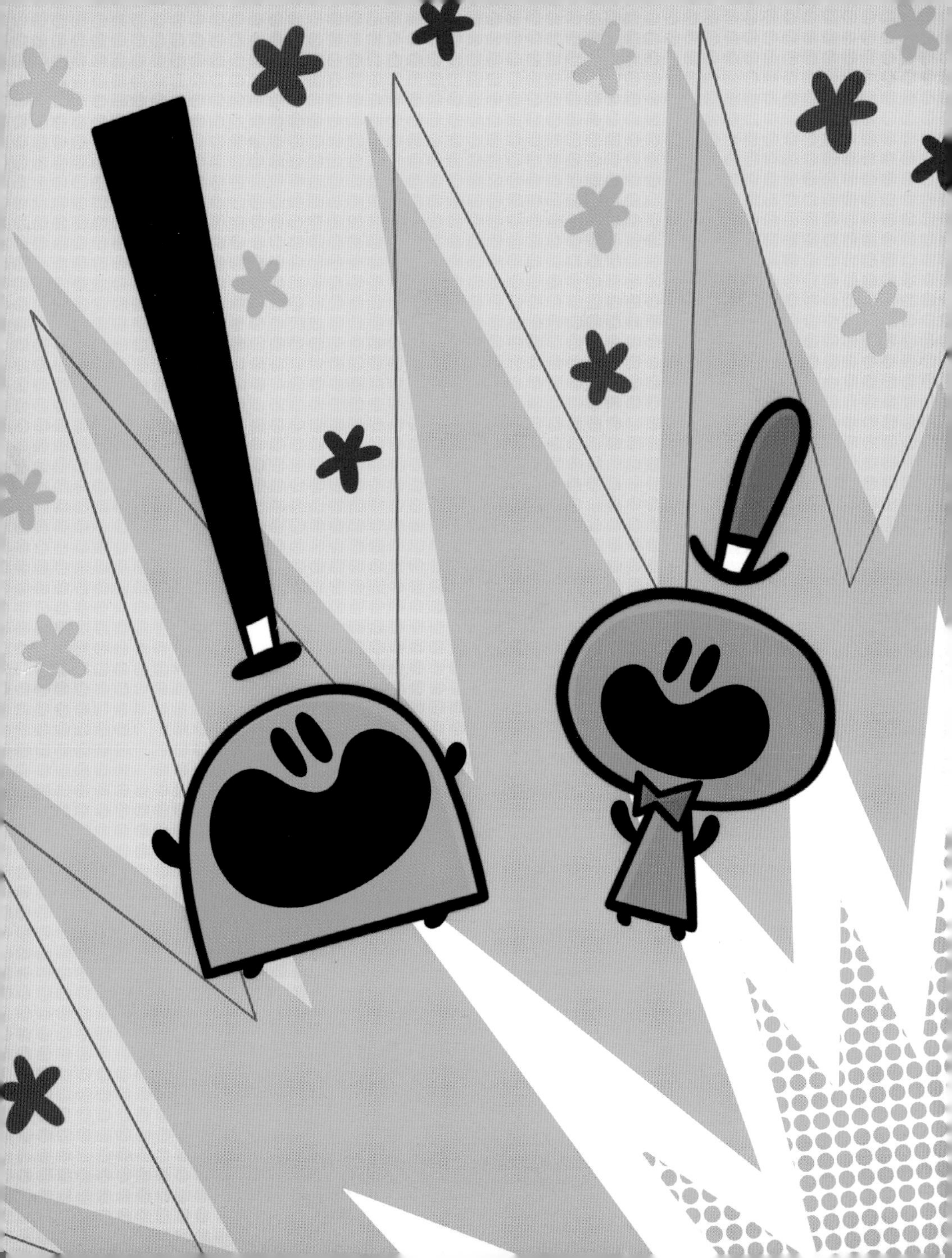

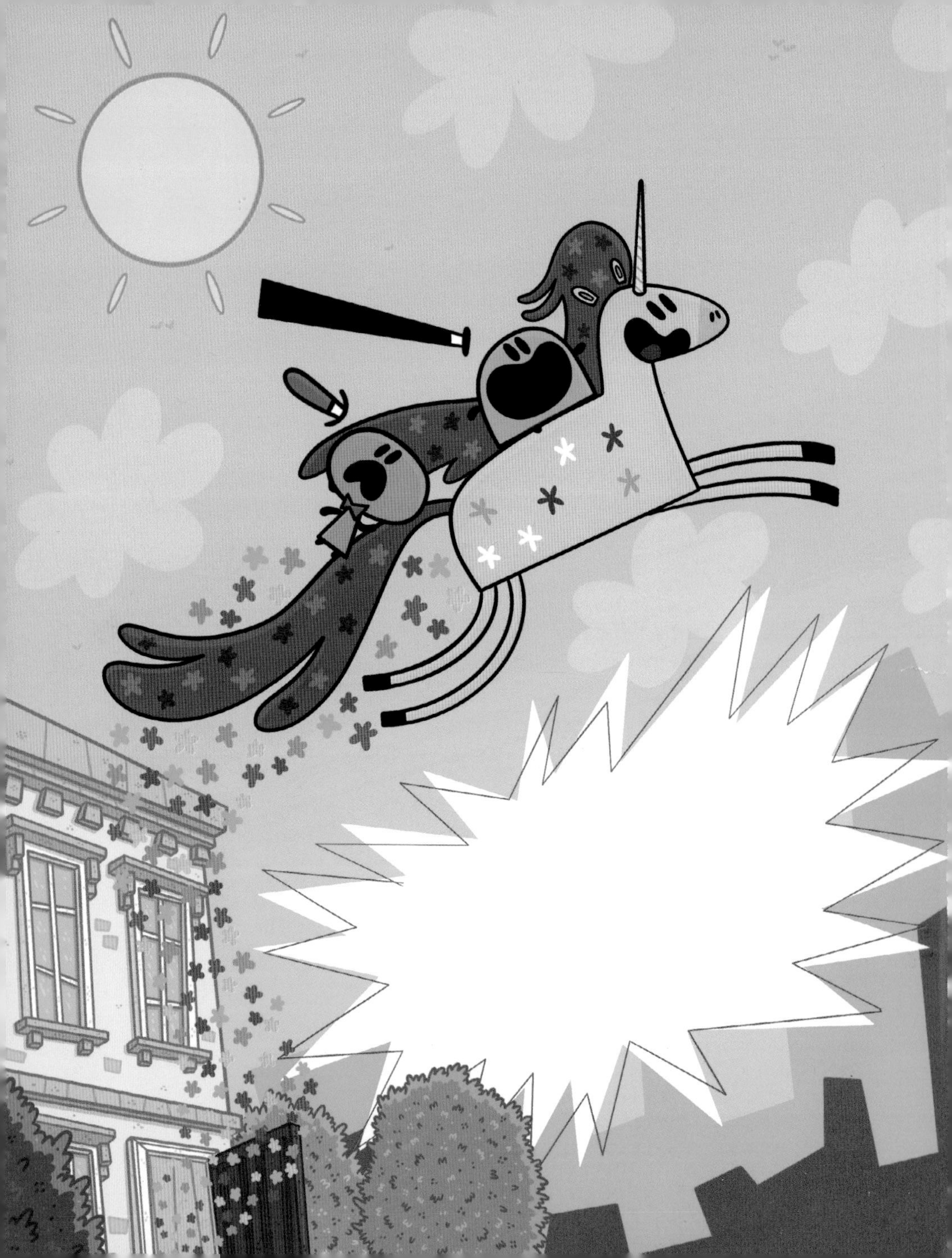